DYNAMIC OPTICS

A DEL SANDERSON ADVENTURE

DON JASPERS

ACKNOWLEDGEMENTS

For Marleen and Dave. I miss them.

For Coleen and Byran, my version of perfect children.

For Patsy, my soulmate. Her unwavering support allows me to write my stories. She is my treasure and then some.

For Sarah Vail, a friend and colleague. Without her help I would not be a published author.

For Suzanne who edited this fictional tale. She went the extra mile.

For Bitterroot Publishing who accepted putting my two books, *Deadly Optics* and *Dynamic Optics*, into print.

CHAPTER 1

Good or bad, change happens. I used to think of myself as an ordinary man—until loss and luck conspired to make me someone else entirely.

I often rode the bus from my new hometown of Bozeman, Montana. The bus stop was a six-block hike. Walking on a brisk spring day felt soft and easy. Maple trees were showing signs of new buds, and the lilacs already had small leaves. Arriving at my newly painted park bench, I laid my paper on it, and began picking up litter, as I always did.

I noticed a folded paper next to one of the scruffy spirea bushes framing a new big granite rock, and started to add it to my collection of trash. The folded paper revealed a corner of a hundred-dollar bill, paper-clipped to the note.

After throwing the rest of my collection into the trash barrel, I unfolded the note and put the hundred-dollar bill in my shirt pocket. I sat on the bench and read the note addressed to a person named *Michelle*.

I mumbled to myself, "My mathematical mind believes this is much more than just a note."

| Yours: numbers okay (47-94) | Slice of watermelon 88 |
| Open the Red Bottle (13-26) | Meet Jordan 15 225 |

"*Gibberish*" I mumbled to myself and stuffed the note in my shirt pocket with the money. Something fun to work on and maybe solve. My curiosity now aroused, I planned to work on the possible code after my trip to the library.

I heard my bus turn the corner, so started back to hop on board. I was glad I heard the bus, otherwise I would have stepped in a day-old dog deposit. My skip and hop deftly avoiding the catastrophe not noticed by anyone, I was sure.

"Good morning, Sanford, how are things today?" I asked the regular weekday driver, a middle-aged black man with an ever-ready smile.

"Morning, Del," a smiling Sanford offered. "Nice move. Guess you missed the dog stuff."

"Yes, I was not paying attention. You would have prevented my entry, right?"

"Oh yes. I have to clean up any and all messes when my shift is over."

I selected my usual faded mauve Naugahyde seat three behind the driver and secretly opened the note again. I did not have a clue, but knew I wanted to see if I could solve it. So far, I believe it was a coded system using twos. I felt excited to have a new project, wondering where it would lead.

There were two new passengers today, dark-skinned about five foot ten and slender, with no facial hair. They looked like twins.

I do not like surprises, so I processed all the scenarios I could think of and turned my worry meter on. They may just be new in America, but I could not shake my deep wonder and concern.

This bus makes six stops before it reaches the main library and the Daily Coffee, conveniently located across the street. I go to both, as the dark roast Sumatran coffee is my favorite, sometimes I add a blueberry scone.

The six-block walk to and from the bus stop to my house through a residential neighborhood was not enough exercise to wear off the extra calories, but one scone a week works for me.

I am happy to have something new to figure out. I absolutely wanted to be the person to solve what I have decided is a coded message.

Just a feeling I cannot shake.

CHAPTER 2

eturning home, I made three copies of the note and the one-hundred-dollar bill. I put both originals in my safe.

Two weeks later, I rode my regular bus to the library. The two dark-skinned young men were in the back two seats, again.

I chose to visit the Daily Coffee across the street first. Their bakery items are fresh every day, and I wished for a blueberry scone and a Sumatran dark roast coffee. The aromas draw many regulars. I added two brownies for later this evening, must spoil myself once in a while.

I was not the only regular, but most of the employees recognized me, had a smile and a word of greeting as they took my money. Since the day I found the note, I was one hundred percent positive the writer of the note and the person or persons it was intended for knew my identity, but not that I had the note. I am not sure why I felt they knew about me, but I trust my feelings, always.

I have ridden that route so often, I just feel like an old white-haired very fit man following a routine. I stand six-foot one weigh one hundred ninety pounds and have minimum body fat I pride myself being as fit as I am able. I know I can still run a mile under six minutes. Today, I had a copy of the note and bill. After my coffee and scone, I decided to sit in the library by the second story window and study the options presented by the words and numbers of the note. I wanted to see if I could figure out the code, and I could watch the traffic at the coffee shop.

Deciding to study the note while eating and enjoying my coffee, I sat at the back corner table so no one could see what I was doing. I felt an eagerness to solve the puzzle. The only thing I could decern after working on it for thirty minutes, was the use of multiples of two. The words could mean anything. I crossed the street entered the library and selected two newspapers, climbed the stairs to the second floor, sat in my favorite chair and started reading. Three *adventures* could happen soon. Time to start planning.

I put the papers down and dug out my copies of the note and bill again. I realized the puzzle solving process gave me a strong sense of purpose. I knew the bill was real and not counterfeit, because I asked a teller at my bank to check. I started over, using every math skill I could think of. Some even numbers and some odd. Most divisibility rules would not apply. Two was a link, but not the main code I decided; it was too obvious. The code had to relate to a place or city. I asked the librarian for a cross-reference book for the city of Bozeman. I did not find any location using the red bottle, nor a Watermelon Street.

The note was dropped by someone riding the bus on an earlier run on this past Tuesday, because the note felt new to me. I decided to ride the earlier bus tomorrow, Tuesday. I am sure who ever lost the note and money, retraced their steps and did not find it. Maybe someone was in serious trouble.

In Bozeman, I am known as Del Sanderson, and only him. I have three alternate identities that no one knows about, except my close friend, Cliff. He does not have the facts about them, but could obtain those facts, if he ever chose to.

Cliff Rawlings, the new Special Agent in charge of the Salt Lake City FBI Field Office, is very fit and does not look his age. At about five-eleven and two hundred fifteen chiseled pounds, he has close cropped brown hair with graying temples and piercing brown eyes. His walk is smooth, hinting of his martial arts training. He has a noticeable scar above his left eye, and the broken nose look. He is always tanned.

I sent him a copy of the note and the hundred-dollar bill, relating the entire story and what I had done so far. He texted he would ask one of his agents that specializes in code work to look it over.

The following morning, I rode the earlier bus throughout much of the route. A new passenger today. My quick glance did not allow me to see her well as she sat on the back seat and was reading something in her lap. At the first stop (after my regular one) an elderly woman with a big tote bag, a cup of coffee and the daily paper, joined the commuter group.

She said, "Good morning," and sat next to me. A small, neat woman, who took pride in her appearance, with white permed hair and just enough makeup to look fresh, opened her paper, looked at me and added. "You're new."

"Yes, I am. I usually take the next bus, but wanted to get to the library early. The new book releases come today, and I want to get a chance at them before everyone else paws through them." I felt positive the new passenger heard our conversation.

Smiling, "You go to the library or to the Daily Coffee across the street."

"Both. I like my coffee and treat myself to those low-calorie pastries. I have tried them all in the past, but like the blueberry scones the best."

"Cinnamon rolls for me," she answered, shifting in her seat to look at me. Offering a small fragile hand she added, "I'm Mable Simpson."

I took her hand, "I am Del Sanderson. How often do you ride this bus, Mable?"

"Almost every day. I have a pass so can ride any bus. It costs two hundred twenty-five dollars per year to ride all you want. You just need to be older than sixty-five."

We both exited at the library. The new petite woman passenger walked past my seat with her face covered, so I would not recognize her. "Let's go have some coffee and a scone, or do you need to go to the library first?"

"I should, but coffee wins today, only if you will let me buy."

"Of-course," she answered, smiling.

Mable waited for me to open the door, then proceeded to the only empty table by a window with a reserved sign on it. A small vase with two yellow roses perched on the windowsill. You could smell the fragrance of the roses. I watched as she sniffed the flowers.

"I always sit here, then smell the flowers," she said, letting me help her with her chair.

As I sat across from her. A twenty-something young girl materialized, sporting purple hair, a little wire nose clip and many ear-studs. She patted Mable on the shoulder. "I have your cinnamon roll warming. Here's your tea."

"My friend will have dark roast Sumatra coffee and a blueberry scone, Zella. New hair color today. I like it."

"Thank you. I was tired of the red and needed a change." She sped off to get the pastries.

We chatted about the coffee shop, the weather, and her grandchildren. Zella brought the coffee and the treats. "I'll bet you are wondering how I knew about the Sumatran Coffee, you told me about the scone."

Taking a sip of the coffee, "Yes," I answered

She didn't answer right away. "I don't stand in line like the rest. This is my table. I know most of the regulars and what they prefer. You get to enjoy free today. No sense in paying myself. I own the Daily Coffee. Most of my employees have been with me for years. I don't meddle much. I am eighty-seven and don't need the money. This place keeps me young. All the pastries are my own creation. I can make all of them and once did. My husband and I operated a bakery for forty plus years."

She looked at her phone, "I have a meeting in a few minutes. I do hope you will join me again, if you see me here."

"I will, Mable. A very pleasant morning. Thank you for the coffee." I excused myself, put the chair in its place, and started for the door.

Zella interrupted me, "A refill sir?"

"Yes, thank you. In a to-go cup please," I answered, handing her a tip.

"You got it." As she filled my cup, she added, "She likes you."

As I started to push through the door, a small dark-skinned woman wearing her traditional dress, opened it for me. She looked like the woman who was on the bus earlier, but I was not sure. She smelled different, but I could not place the new smell, nor did I catch a whiff of her scent while on the bus.

"Thank you," I smiled softly, receiving only a muted nod.

But I heard Zella say, "Hi Michelle. How's things?"

"The same, Zella, always the same." Michelle's English sounded nearly perfect.

Walking across the street, I said to myself, *Not a coincidence: the name Michelle and the bus and the note. She is the person the note addressed.* I needed to finish my coffee before going into the library, so I selected a USA Today from the kiosk and sat in the outdoor reading area facing the coffee shop.

I was in the middle of the crossword, when I noticed the two dark-skinned young men exit the bus I usually rode. They joined the woman, that had opened the door for me, at an outdoor seating area in front of the coffee shop.

I whispered to myself, "Arab, or Pakistani, or India." I continued working on the crossword and occasionally watched. I could not hear a word, so went into the library and looked at the new releases. Libraries have their own smell. Too often smelling like the last person to arrive.

There was still one copy of John Sanford's new book, just for me. I checked it out then went up to the second floor reading room, selected the Journal and watched the trio. Only the woman purchased anything, she looked often at her phone.

My *I wonder what is going on senses kicked in.* The two young men saw a bus coming, so, they left the table and boarded the bus. The woman also left, but only walked to an apartment building across the side street and third from the corner. She did not appear to use a key to enter a four-story rectangular brick structure that showed its age. Then I left for home on the next bus.

I decided to rent a truck and drive by Michelle's building, front and back.

CHAPTER 3

Tuesday morning, I was at the bust stop close to my house at my regular time. Two pieces of litter and no notes. The two young men who sat with Michelle were sitting in the back two rows in separate seats. They did not say a word all the way to the library.

I skipped my coffee, and went directly to the library. Selecting a newspaper, I sat in a recliner by the window.

The two men went to the coffee shop and sat at the same outside table. They were in a waiting posture, both looked fidgety, but did not speak to each other. Both sat silently with their elbows on the table in front of them. One occasionally doodled in a notebook.

After my usual stops in the library, I went across the street to the coffee shop. The many smells greeted me. I needed to learn how to make cinnamon rolls.

Zella greeted me, "Dark roast Sumatran, and a double blueberry scone?"

"Perfect."

"Mrs. Astineau is not here today, but I am supposed to ask if you could come about the same time next Tuesday," said Zella.

"I will write that on my phone calendar." Mable had said *Simpson,* when I met her. My secret. I did not ask Zella about the different last name, as I did not know her well enough.

I found a seat that allowed me to watch the two men. Three buses came and went. They did not move. *Too long for those two to wait,* I thought. Watching the third bus go up the street. I glanced at the apartment building Michelle went into. I saw her standing in the front corner apartment so I knew she could see the coffee shop and the two men sitting at the outside table.

Zella brought my coffee and scone. "Why do you like the library?"

"Just for the many newspapers especially the Wall Street Journal, and the new book releases. Why?"

She offered a mildly flustered response. "Cause younger people don't use it much. I was thinking I should check it out." Somehow, I did not feel comfortable with the question or the response. Did Mable ask her to probe? I doubted that, but my alert meter buzzed. I trust that feeling.

CHAPTER 4

Saturday morning, I strolled into the EGGE, my favorite place for breakfast. "Morning Madeline," I said loud enough for all to hear. "The omelet today."

"Sure thing," floated out from the kitchen. Madeline owns the EGGE, and looks as she did in High School; she has lost many pounds. The everyday cinnamon roll tray was down to two. I resisted. Shelly came by and poured my coffee. "Cindy was by yesterday, and said to ask you to call next time you came in."

"Thanks, Shelly."

Cindy used to work at the EGGE, but I am helping her finish her teaching degree at the university. It will be neat to talk to her, but she has my number, so could call me anytime. Hmm.

Sunday morning's yellow sun beamed a beautiful Montana day. I drove a black rental truck with tinted windows through the alley behind the apartment building Michelle called home. I noticed the fire escape was an old iron grate type with a weight induced last set of steps—very rusty and did not look usable. A noise maker when in use if it worked. The building looked tired and it's faded light tan bricks were very dirty. No maintenance in a long time.

Driving by the front of the apartment building, I saw Michelle again watching the coffee shop from her front corner window. I wondered why, as her watching made little sense to me. Then made a second pass through the alley, I needed to be sure I did not miss anything.

Rounding the block after leaving the alley, I passed the Daily Coffee. I saw a line out the door and at least twenty people waiting their turn. All the tables were full, and some people sat on the lawn. Mable does very well. I could not tell for sure, but I could not see any dark-skinned patrons. Maybe they were just people enjoying America. I knew I would keep watching.

Time to call Cindy and see what she is up to.

CHAPTER 5

"Good morning, Cindy."

"Del, wow it's great to hear from you. I've been so busy. Shelly said she saw you. Can we meet for lunch?" Cindy was smiling. I could tell.

"Name the place."

"Applebee's, say one-thirty."

"Perfect, see you then." I arrived early and took the same table we used many months ago.

Cindy came sashing in like she always did when she is happy. Cindy was tall and slender and made clothes look wonderful. Her blonde-colored hair was cut shorter than usual. "Same table, I like that," she said as she sat across from me.

"Same pretty dress," I said as I stood to greet her.

"Only one I own. I will shop some when I graduate, so I can look extra fine for the interviews.

"Today is an unexpected pleasure.

"I'm going to finish my classes this fall semester and get to start student teaching in the spring at Williams Elementary, like I hoped. My counselor suggested I line up some people to write a letter of recommendation for me. You and Madeline are all I have."

I interrupted her immediately, "I would consider that special for me, to write a recommendation letter for you."

"I knew you would, but I had to ask. Madeline is going to write one, but I am supposed to have four. One of my teachers will write one, but I need one more.

"What about Sylvia? She eats at the EGGE as much as I do."

"Don't think so, Del. She once told me I flirt too much with the men and don't talk as nice to the women," Cindy answered.

I just looked at her and smiled.

She frowned at me, "Did I really do that?"

"Oh, yes. But you knew the flirting increased your tips from men. Everyone could see that. Is the teacher you plan to ask for a recommendation male or female?"

"Mrs. Brockman. I've had her for three classes. She's a taskmaster but fair. I am sure she liked me."

"Then who else is a regular that might be worth asking."

"Buzz Soloman, but he don't talk so good—I'm being bad. He's nice, but I don't want to sort of owe him anything."

"You are bad, but you have him pegged right. Did you talk to Carl Djorek enough to know about him?"

"Carl was always nice, but rarely said much. Someone said he's a retired IRS accountant."

I tried one more. "How about the rancher guy that comes to eat almost every day?"

"Hardly said three words to him except, 'You want more coffee?'"

"You know what? I will bet we could get a quality letter from Jack."

Cindy grinned mischievously from ear to ear. "Madeline is falling for him. They've had a few dates."

"I will talk to him. No, let us go see him after you are done with classes Monday, and set it up."

"Ya think?" Cindy smiled again. "Listen to me. I need to talk better when I'm a teacher. Can't have those little kids using poor grammar. Sounds super, Del. You're always helping me. I can count on you to come up with the right stuff."

"Okay. Just walk to school Monday, and I will pick you up there at three thirty."

"I get done at three, so that works. I'm excited to see Jack again!"

"Did your counselor give you some examples of quality letters?" I asked.

"Yes, I have some, and I'll bring them."

"Date."

"Why of course, Mr. Sanderson. That will be two this week."

"I enjoy watching you when you are happy." Strolling to our cars, we touched hands like always and went our separate ways.

It will be good to see Jack, one of my four special friends. He is not a tall man, but might be the strongest man I know.

I picked up Cindy at 3:20pm. She wore school clothes, jeans with the necessary holes and a MSU sweatshirt. She looked like a million dollars to me.

"Hi, Del. Got the samples. You think Jack'll remember me?"

"Jack, not remember you? Only if he is dead. Jack remembers every beautiful woman he has ever seen. I called him to make sure he would be there. He does not know you are coming."

Jack and his twin sons operate a five bay big rig repair business near Manhattan, Montana, 23 miles west of Bozeman. They are always busy.

We parked right in front. Cindy was out of the car before I could open the door for her.

"Ah, Del. I screwed that up, didn't I. I am not used to nice stuff." She was smiling as she let me open the office door for her.

Jack was on the phone. When he saw Cindy, ignored me, and said into the phone. "Got to go—a special customer just walked in." He put down the phone, stood up and took Cindy's offered hand. "Why am I so lucky today, Cindy?"

"Del says you do things for free."

"Oh, he does, does he? Hi Del, what are you two up to this time? You got me good last Thanksgiving."

"Just a small favor," Cindy cooed as she batted her eyes and cocked her head.

Jack sat back in his chair, but couldn't erase the softness in his face.

Sitting down in one of the old oak chairs, I answered. "Cindy needs some letters of recommendation for her teaching resumé, so when she finishes her classes next June, she can start looking for a position."

Jack shifted in his chair then ran his fingers through his hair and said, "I would be glad to, Cindy, but I don't know how to make those so they read right."

"I have some samples, and Del will help us."

"Tell you what, Jack, I will write it, you can sign it, and we will give you a copy. Then if anyone askes, you will have that to refer to."

"That's a deal." Jack looked back at Cindy, and continued, "Can I buy your dinner? We can let him come along." His sly smile proved he was playing with us.

"Why sure Jack, Del and I will gladly join you for dinner, but then I have to hustle home and do some homework."

"Let's meet at the Century. They have great seafood."

Jacob and Jason were already at the table when we arrived. Jack came out of the kitchen sporting a big smile after talking to the chef, a-long-time friend. A whole new set of restaurant smells of fish greeted us. The Century is a long time locally owned premier restaurant specializing in seafood. "All set, I hope you like seafood, Cindy. I know Del does."

"Yes, I do," she replied, "especially shrimp."

While Jack and I ate and listened, Jacob, Jason, and Cindy talked about school, football, and trucks. Cindy surprised us all talking very knowledgeable about trucks and cars.

Jacob said, "How do you know so much about trucks?"

Cindy paused a while then answered. "My dad was a long-haul trucker. He owned his own rig and worked on it when he was home. He didn't have a son, just me, so he explained to me everything he did and why. He could have gotten a job fixing rigs, but he preferred the freedom of the road. He was gone a lot." Something in Cindy's tone and the changes in her mannerisms suggested much more than she offered.

Jacob said, "Jack, maybe she should work here and make more money than teaching." The twins always called their dad Jack.

Cindy changed back quickly and answered, "It wouldn't be good for my nails, Jacob. I don't want grease and car stuff on my hands every day."

The food came, and we dined on a super meal.

"Wow," Cindy said with a beaming smile as she pushed herself away from the table. "I'm stuffed, thank you so much, Jack. You're a dear."

Jacob and Jason said together, "Thanks Jack, you're a dear."

Even Jack laughed.

Cindy was silent most of the twenty minutes back to her apartment. She finally asked, "You going to write Jack's letter really?"

"Sure, I will have both ready in a week or so."

"Del, I have something I need you to know. I lied to you last fall about not knowing why my car quit. I just didn't want to explain stuff. I lived in Miles City, Montana for most of my growing up years. My dad was gone a lot driving his rig. He was not a nice man. He treated my mother horribly. She died from cancer when I was fourteen. My real last name is Cantelay. You and Madeline are the only people I have told that last name to. It's on record at college, so some kids have heard it, but I rarely use it. I am very nervous tonight, but here goes.

"My dad tried to rape me one night in our garage. He was too drunk, and I got away.

"I took everything I owned that fit in the car, faked his signature on the car title and six checks, and cashed them for a bit over twelve hundred dollars. I used my new driver's license and drove straight through to my grandmother in Havre, started school there and tried to fit in. Never happened. I quit school the day I turned eighteen, and started working at the truck stop restaurant. I could have had a thousand dates, but I let on that I was gay. Word got around. I had few problems. I know my dad never tried to find me.

"I took the test to get my GED and left for Billings. I worked at a truck stop off I-90. I made very good money. An older man, Tyler Spivey, charmed me out of my virginity. When he found out I was pregnant, he first called me every name in the book, then beat me up bad. I spent two weeks in the hospital, lost the baby, and may never be a mother. That's how I got this scar."

"She unbuttoned her blouse enough to show me an ugly scar from her sternum to just short of her shoulder, on the right side of her chest. "Three surgeries and hundreds of stitches." She continued, "I hope someday to have that fixed. I left the hospital owing thousands of dollars. The surgeon gave me 300 dollars and told me go somewhere. 'We won't try to find you.' I hope I can pay the doctor back someday. I lived in my car two weeks or so, trying to make the money last.

"I happened to stop at the EGGE to eat one morning, as I hadn't eaten at all the day before. Madeline was trying to do everything. The waitress was a no show, so I started pouring coffee and busing the tables, then found an order pad and started acting like I worked there. She gave me the job, no questions asked.

"When she found out I was living I my car, she took me into her house and gave me a room in her basement. I lived there a year before finding my own place. I owe her a lot. I hope she and Jack make it. She deserves some good times."

We had been parked at her apartment fifteen minutes before she finished her story.

"You are the first person I have ever told, and the only one to see the scar. Somehow you are just special. I am lucky to have met you. I know my secret is safe. I can feel the release getting the story out. I love Del Sanderson."

"I love you too, Cindy, and that is okay. May I take a picture of the scar? Will you be okay tonight and at school tomorrow? You certainly may use some of the money I gave you to pay the doctor back and to go shopping for new clothes now. You should not wait until you graduate."

"Even better. A sense of freedom. Thank you for listening. I will send the doctor the $300 dollars tomorrow, thank you for letting me spend your money. My two school friends and I can go shopping this weekend, so I will have clothes for student teaching that make me look like a teacher. Why do you need a picture?"

"I want to do some research on how to fix your scar," I answered.

She looked at me a long time, then said, "Okay." She touched my hand like always, 'Let me take the picture,' but added a peck on the cheek, opened the door and started up the walkway.

I watched her walk away. I knew she was crying. She opened the door, switched on the light, turned back to look at me, and smiled. A finger flutter wave, and she closed the door. Amy, the mother of my children would approve.

I researched Montana and Salt Lake City about Cindy's scar. A Salt Lake surgeon offered to change the scar to a pencil line and sent examples of his work. I called his office and arranged a consultation next June. Cindy would be finished with school, so I hoped she will go with me to the appointment.

CHAPTER 6

efore going to Casa Grande, Arizona, I wanted to practice some long-distance shots at a thousand yards. I belong to a long-distance shooting range in a huge gulley near Manhattan, Montana. Rick Sherman, retired from military special ops, owns and manages it.

He and I have become very good friends, and share two secrets we will take to our graves. He still helps train others wishing to be special ops with the Army. He was spotting for two teams of military shooters when I drove in. He offered a quick wave, and I went to his office to wait. Twenty minutes later, after finishing with his military shooters, he came to greet me.

"Good to see you. Del. Done traveling and ready to shoot?"

"Yes. I hope to work at one thousand yards. It is windy today, so I can polish the effects of wind on those longer shots. Then I need to do a session with my nine mm."

"I'll get your rifle." Returning with my rifle, he continued. "Cliff stopped by last week. He had someone with him, and you wouldn't have recognized him. Jim has survived a lot of surgery, his voice is raspy and lower, and he weighs thirty pounds more than the skinny guy we knew. He actually looked fit, although, he is not totally healed mentally, He asked about you and Tony.

"I told him I didn't know where Tony is, because I don't. I told him you come by from time to time, but not in a while.

"Art came by and mentioned to me he did the security on your Lincoln cabin. You asked years ago, if I would hunt with you. I will buy a general elk tag and both deer tags. No promises that I'll shoot. That, okay?"

"Super. We will bunk out at the Lincoln cabin." My two hundred plus acre cabin site includes several huge ponderosa pine trees and most of the rest is covered with a thick stand of Douglas fir, some very large. I continued, "I have not seen a lot of activity up to now, but will look harder to select good hunting spots. It will be special having a new hunting partner. I always hoped my son, Curt, would hunt with me, but a senseless crime prevented that." I told Rick the whole story about how he died, including talking to the judge.

"Interesting story. I didn't know about your loss. I can't imagine what you went through. Rick reached out and held my hand at least a minute. "You could have told me earlier, but I feel privileged that you told me now." Let's go shoot. I'll set up your thousand-yard targets." When he returned, he parked the quad next to the shooting station. "Ready when you are."

"Do you think I should refit my rifles with the new state of the art optics? I read in one of your magazines that they do almost everything."

"I've studied up on those as well. I bought two very new rifles while in Arizona a month ago. One of them has those-newer type of optics. I suspected the guns were stolen, but he only wanted three thousand, and I carried enough cash in my truck, so I took the chance. No papers, not even a bill of sale," said Rick.

"Did you ask Cliff to check about the guns?"

"Yes. He didn't find anything, so we think the owner didn't report them stolen, because he wasn't supposed to have them, either. I'll go get them. You watch the shop."

Rick had been gone less than ten minutes when a dark blue Lexus parked next to the office. The driver exited his car, but waited for me to return with my target.

My company, a Caucasian male, stood at a least six foot three, slim, with neatly trimmed white hair, and wearing navy silky slacks and a light blue polo shirt. He watched me intensely.

I stopped, so when I got off the quad, it would be between me and him. I am certain he noticed.

"Are you Mr. Sherman the owner?" knowing I was not Rick.

"No Rick is gone on a short errand. I am covering for him. If you want to wait a half hour, he should be back soon."

"I'll wait, if you don't mind."

"I have one more shot to try."

"May I watch?"

"Sure." I was setup to shoot and had my ear protection in my hand, when he walked up to my shooting station. I gave him a spare one to wear.

"How many yards will you shoot?" he asked, as he fitted the ear protector in place.

"One thousand to the target. Are you a shooter?"

"Never tried."

I made the shot, and put my gear and rifle away, then took the quad to retrieve my target. My phone was in my shirt pocket. On my way to retrieve the target, I passed through a small drainage ditch. Five seconds at the most. I risked using the phone on the downslope, barely moving my hands and touched Ricks number. I did not know if my watcher was using my binoculars from the shooting station. I never looked.

"Yes?" answered Rick.

"Company, and he is real."

"Got it."

When I returned with my target, he was back in his SUV. The binoculars had not moved, I felt sure. He stepped out and walked over to see my target.

"Very nice shot."

"I am Del. I did not catch your name."

"Rocklin Scanlon. You always shoot that well?"

"Usually, though I am still learning to trust the equipment. The settings are important. You want me to call Rick?"

"No, I'll just wait," I never saw Rocklin smile. I believe he does not know how to smile.

I took my targets to Rick's single desk office, and Rocklin followed me inside and busied himself looking at the targets pinned to the corkboard. I laid my targets on Rick's desk, and could feel Rocklin watching me. As soon as Rick returned, I was going to retrieve a pistol from his office desk drawer.

When Rick drove through the gate, he continued past the office and another a half mile to his house.

Rocklin stood up from his chair, "Nice to meet you, Del," and walked to his SUV.

He did not wait for my answer, yet did not hurry. He followed Rick's path. I knew he knew I would call Rick.

I did. "He is right behind you." I told Rick as I retrieved a 9MM pistol and extra clip, from a desk drawer.

"Thanks." He hung up.

What seemed like an eternity, making me very nervous and very scared. Ten minutes after sitting down on the bench under the huge cottonwood tree, at the south end of the shooters' stations, I heard four shots. Another eternity—twenty more minutes, then Rick drove down the road in his truck.

"You need my help?"

"Yes." He acted powerfully intense. I had seen him like this once before. He was machine-like, but extremely athletic in his actions. His words were crisp, and he seemed to have a sixth, seventh and eighth sense, absorbing everything.

"The SUV is an airport rental. We need to return it without being seen. You drive me back to my house. I'll drive the Lexus to the airport. I know where to park it where cameras aren't around. You park in the short-term metered area, and wait for me there."

I did as I was asked. After thirty minutes, Rick entered my truck.

"Ready, let's go back to my house." He did not say a word the entire forty minutes.

I knew to wait, as I could tell he worked at his way of destressing.

When we reached his house, he looked much calmer, but still tightly wired. Finally, after we parked, he spoke. "I was ready for him. He acted too confident. When he stepped out of his car, he had a suppressed pistol. My hands were hanging in my truck bed so he couldn't see them. I asked who sent him."

"He answered, 'Bully's attorney gave me ten and promised ten more when I presented a picture of you dead.' I shot him three times. He didn't get a second shot. His first is in the side of my house. I shot three because he still twitched after two."

"Getting to be a cemetery here."

Rick tried to smile, but still too tightly wound, yet very much in control.

"I didn't bury the two Bully boys here at the range. Rocklin will join them in an old gravel pit thirty miles from here, now filled with contaminated water. It's about two hundred feet deep, and is posted and listed as too deep for swimming. The edges are steep with no real way to get in or out."

I argued, "Bully will try again. He knows you can take care of yourself, but he thinks he is better. My guess, he will send two or three to catch you off guard next time."

"I'm always watching. I found where the Russians watched us, while they planned their attempted killing of Jim. I now monitor that sight and the only other shooting location within fifteen hundred yards of here."

"Rick, we should go to Texas Roadhouse and enjoy some ribs."

"I need to take care of Rocklin and transfer him now. I'll meet you there at six-thirty."

"Deal," I answered.

I could smell yams and steak as I entered the venue. I think the restaurant intentionally allows those smells to escape into the restaurant.

When I arrived, Rick was already there. As soon as I slid into my side of the booth, he made a short-whispered statement. "His nude body with the bullets removed is in a sealed rubber bag (with extra weight) when I slide it into the water. All other stuff makes it to the landfill after a fashion. That's all I will tell you."

We both chose a half rack of ribs with sides for our dinner. Ribs have their own unique smell. Rick commented, "Sure smells good in this place. I enjoy the barbeque smell. Del you asked about new optics earlier. You are very good with the ones you use now. Let me see if I can get a company or two to let me test their equipment at my range. Maybe I can find one I can rep for. Could save us both some money. I have done a lot of thinking since the Bully boy caper. I think it is time I rejoined society. I'm going to find a sales rep job related to long distance shooting. I'm going to hunt with you. I'm going to take up bowling again. I used to throw a pretty good ball."

I did not answer right away. When Rick was extra intense, he did not like to be interrupted.

"Del, I know about my intensity, but have learned to manage it. You saw the only time I have been locked in the last ten years during the Bully Boy caper. I am as comfortable as I know how to get."

"Well, going hunting together will be special. I have always hunted alone. But we will be a good team," I answered.

"What kind of rifle will I need?"

"A 308 will be perfect."

"I have one," Rick answered.

We talked about growing up, sports and school. We laughed a lot, Rick and I.

"Del, would you cover the range for me, if I find a rep job?"

"I am gone so much, Rick. But I would like that."

26

"I know, but you are the only one I would trust. I wanted to ask you first."

"You can give me a set of keys and combinations, whatever you are comfortable with," I suggested.

"I will give you everything you need. I knew what your answer would be. I respect that deeply. The range has never made money. I will give the leader of the pistol club a key to the gate, so his group can shoot, but no access to the buildings." Rick looked up as our waiter passed by.

He said, "Traveling will let me take care of this Bully business. I think we should call Cliff about Bully." Rick took out his phone.

He did not elaborate, and I did not ask. I think Bully will soon be history.

"Cliff, what can we do about Bully?" Rick asked after Cliff picked up his phone.

"Not much we can do, Rick. He has money and contacts. We believe his attorney is the go between. But if he is, we can't figure out their code. That attorney lists many clients in that prison. We will never put an agent in a prison undercover. He wouldn't last a week." Rick listened intently.

"Cliff, Del and I need to know if he is ever released. We will both need time to prepare."

"Rick, I guarantee it. Someone from my office will call you both if he is ever released," answered Cliff as he hung up his phone. Our dinners arrived smelling great as expected.

"I am going to Casa Grande and will be gone a couple of weeks. Rick, we need to mail a letter to all LD shooters telling them I will place an ad in the Bozeman Daily Chronicle when the range will be open. Are you still going to help the Army with their shooters?"

"Yes, and I'll text you the dates, as they are quite flexible. I am going to start my search for a rep job. I'll make a call, and the letter will go out today, Del."

Outside, as we left the restaurant, we shared a solid handshake, and went our separate ways.

Rick made twenty-three calls. He called the newspaper and his attorney to type the letter about the range, and process the mailing. The most important call netted him a 'rep' position with Sig Sauer. He would travel to gun shows and man their kiosk, wearing their line of clothing and demonstrate their rifles and pistols. An expense paid commission arrangement suited him. He felt somewhat nervous, joining society again, but he knew he could do it. All the other calls were needed to call friends to help locate which prison housed one Selmer Varnel.

CHAPTER 7

I called Cliff the next morning, "For Cliff."

An hour later, the special phone Cliff had given me, announced his return call.

"Hi, Del. What's up?"

"Hi, yourself. Did you get the copies of the note and the hundred-dollar bill?"

"Yes, we are fitting it in. We didn't see anything right away," Cliff answered.

"I have been playing with it some, mostly the numbers, I think it is a message for more than one person."

"Because of the number two?" asked Cliff.

"Can you come by next Wednesday morning, if you are in the area?"

"Why?"

"Will tell you when I see you."

"I'll let you know. Godspeed."

"Always." Our closing words to each other for over fifty years.

CHAPTER 8

I took my coffee, the paper, and two cassettes of fifties music out to my veranda. It was five a.m. Wednesday morning.

I hadn't heard from Cliff about his showing up this morning, so I was surprised to see him sitting quietly in the shadows in his favorite double cushion-corner chair. We sat in silence as we often do. He watched intently, while I swept the patio and back yard.

My patio, twenty feet by sixteen feet, is completely covered by a shingled roof. A small glass-topped table and four wicker chairs complete the arrangement. The table and chairs are left over from the previous renter.

Cliff allowed me to complete three alternate IDs. Sven Hansen owns a small house in Mitchell, South Dakota; Spencer Morgan has a hide away in Cheyenne, Wyoming; and James Colbert owns a small condo in Billings, Montana. Sven, once and Spencer four times have completed my *adventures*.

I put in a cassette and the Brothers Four started our day. I went back into the kitchen and filled Cliff's coffee cup. Then detoured through my garage to see if my neighbor, Ben Degler was outside. He usually goes to a coffee group gathering at a nearby McDonalds. He was gone.

"Before we talk about the note, Cliff, do you have someone who can get me information on long haulers living in Montana? I have a lead I need to check. I do not want the FBI involved yet.

After taking a sip of coffee, "I will call Billy Crocker and have him send you the info. Anything I need to know now?" Cliff asked.

"Not yet. I do not know enough as of this moment."

"Okay, Del, I trust you. Nothing on your note yet. We are checking if the bill's serial number is on any of our lists, but we need the actual bill to see if it is counterfeit. I did pass on what you had done with the numbers. We have a techie who loves that stuff, so we'll see.

"Cliff, I think the numbers and the short sets of words have only one meaning and the rest are diversions. There is a meaning there, we just have to find out for sure who Michelle really is. I think she rides the bus often, and is the key person. She is the leader, but I do not think Michelle is her real name. But, Zella, at the coffee shop called her Michelle, and Michelle's English is near perfect.

"I went online and checked traditional clothing from the Arab countries. My best guess is she is from Jordan. I am positive she does not know I found the note. She meets with two dark-skinned young men at the Daily Coffee. They look like twins to me. I asked a bank teller to check the bill, and it is real." I paused and went to get both of us another coffee.

"Really, three in the group?" Cliff asked when I returned with more coffee. "You make good coffee."

We always visited by speaking just above a whisper when on my veranda, even though I swept it for bugs every day. His voice became extra soft after I mentioned the two men.

"Yes, but the twins only seem to listen. None of the three pay any attention to me or what I do. Whoever lost the note, must have covered their back trail and when they knew it was lost, they just got another note from the source. They are operating as though nothing has happened. I believe it is significant and worth our time.

"Your techie needs to work the numbers using the starting point as the day I found the note. Then try every-which-way imaginable. I think the *red bottle* is the name of an establishment in whatever town they are planning to use. *Watermelon* is a code word related to an event or the next note pickup spot. The *forty-seven* is a street or road number, because I do not see another way it fits, the 225 number must be an address. I could be wrong about everything, but I would like to be proven wrong first."

"Cliff, if you are going to get agents involved, they need to be the best. No rookies. I must remain sterile and unknown to the trio and the agents. I do not want to see new people start appearing. Zella could be part of things, but that is a weak guess. I think trying for a picture would be a dead give-away."

"The woman is the most interesting. Zella called her 'Michelle' you said. They know each other then," interjected Cliff.

"I agree. She seems to be the mover, and the twins do not like it. That is my observation. She can watch the coffee shop from her building, as she rents the front corner room. She usually wears the traditional loose-fit flowing dress and could hide a lot of stuff. It may be three people enjoying America, but I feel a buzz. And, as you know, I trust that feeling," I answered.

"Let me make two calls," said Cliff. He used a small flip phone he was carrying. After five rings he hung up. Less than three minutes passed before it rang for Cliff to answer.

"Good morning, Marty. Would you send me pictures of Pakistani, Afghan, and Indian nationals? We are looking for groups that could be off the grid now. Age near thirty, possibly twin males and a small woman who has an English name of Michelle. She may be from Jordan."

After closing the phone, Cliff said, "Let's go have some breakfast and wait for Marty to sort and send. I will call a retired female agent and see if she is available to check at the apartment building Michelle is using."

He hid in the back seat of my Ram to protect our relationship, while I drove to the Home Depot parking lot. I watched the lot as he exited and surfaced at the end of the row of trucks and walked into the store. I drove to the contractor-loading door and picked him up. He had a new look. We went across the street and into Betty's breakfast Bar. "Have you been here before?"

"Never. I usually go the Perkins," answered Cliff.

"Well, you are in for a treat. This is one of my two favorites."

"How's Dutch these days?"

"Not sure, Cliff. He has his metal fabrication business up for sale. He sold me his airplane, terminated his hangar lease, and put his house up for sale. 'Time to move on', is all he said."

"Let's go see him tomorrow. You can drive."

"Are we going to tell him we are coming?"

"No. I have an undercover agent in Great Falls I need to check on, so we could be two days."

"I have the plane here now. We should fly up to see him."

"Good idea. You have wheels up there? Let's leave early enough to fly over the cities on highway 2."

"No wheels. I either rent or ride with Dutch."

Cliff's phone beeped. Thirty-one pictures flowed onto the small screen, they were quite small, but the twins were there. I was ninety-nine percent positive. Cliff called Marty.

"Thanks, can you send all you have on the *twins,* we'll call them? We have been looking for those two. They are Saudis. Expand your research to see if we can match the young woman. I'll get the stuff at the Bozeman field office. Good work." Cliff paid for our meal.

"I have a lot to do to work on this lead, so I'll walk to the field office. I'll be at the airport around nine-thirty tomorrow."

"Perfect, but I will have to tell Dutch. He would not expect a surprise drop in visit from me."

"Whatever you think is okay with me."

Cliff called, retired FBI Agent Marla Gentry. After she retired, Marla enrolled in college to work on a Special Education Teaching Credential. "Marla are you available to come to Bozeman and complete a one-day surveillance job for me?"

"Yes, Cliff, that would be fun."

"Travel to Bozeman and go to our local office. Let me know when you are in town."

Marla, disguised as a seventy-plus elderly woman, adding an overdose of extra smells, she went to Michelle's apartment building, on the pretense of renting an apartment. She walked with a fake limp.

The landlady who used a first-floor apartment, wrinkled her nose after getting a whiff of Marla, making Marla smile, then showed her two apartments, both on the second floor.

Marla asked, "Is this a noisy place?"

"Not really. We have two sets of newlyweds, an older gentleman who walks all over town lost in his own world, two very quiet college students, and a woman from Jordan who says she is a graduate student, though she doesn't act like it."

"I would rent here if I could get a place on the first floor. I have a bad leg, and the stairs would be too much for me," Marla told the landlady.

Marla called Cliff and mentioned the woman in question did indeed come from Jordan, and rented two apartments on the second floor, the front corner one and the adjoining one next to the fire escape.

"Thank you, Cliff, I enjoyed myself." Marla was unable to confirm from the landlady that Michelle used the rear apartment as her command center. The landlady didn't know why Michelle rented two apartments. She possessed sophisticated equipment to maintain contact with her handler in Jordan, but only Michelle knew about her equipment. The twins did not know. Marla felt she didn't learn enough to be of much help.

"Thank you, Marla, I will be in touch."

Cliff stayed with me for the night and told me, as we ate breakfast the following morning, "You were right. Michelle is from Jordan." Cliff also learned from his sources that Michelle's Jordan name was Besan Haddad.

"I made my first batch of cinnamon rolls yesterday, so you get to sample them tomorrow morning, Cliff."

CHAPTER 9

We left Bozeman at nine-thirty the next morning to go see Dutch in Great Falls, enjoying a beautiful Montana big sky day. We flew into a low-pressure counterclockwise wind of near thirty knots. It took a full extra hour to complete our journey. Many diversions, including Cliff's request to see some of the towns along the northern tier of the state, covering at least Havre, Shelby, and Cutbank.

"You want to fly for a while? You did not say if the cinnamon rolls were okay."

"The rolls were fine, maybe too much cinnamon, but they sure hit the spot. Flying is your job. I have a few notes to read and review my options when we get there. Not going to be a fun night or an easy day tomorrow."

I knew better than to ask.

"When do you hope to fly back, Del?"

"No decision yet. There is no such thing as too much cinnamon. I feel I should spend some time with Dutch. Something has a nervous twitch working on me about his decision to just quit working at his business."

"I don't know how long I'll be tied up here, so the bureau will take care of me. You do what you need to do and go back when you wish.

Dutch was waiting for us as we parked by Sparky's hangar. "So glad you came, Del. Where did you find this other guy?"

"He showed up yesterday and said he had business here, so we flew up instead of driving." Dutch, at 6' 4" was the biggest guy on our military basketball team. A strong man, he showed signs of a few too many beers. His curly hair never seemed to need extra care, though it was now mostly white. His face always seemed to smile. His hugs are bear-like and Cliff and I always lose those. He is just too strong. We do not try to beat him.

Leading us to his fifteen-year-old green suburban, he said, "How about a burger and a beer, and we shoot some pool?"

"Let's go. I need some time to relax," answered Cliff.

While we were taking a break from pool and enjoying our meal, I asked Dutch, "Why are you selling out? I was surprised by your decision."

"I'm tired," He sighed. "My son, Eddie, has never been interested and doesn't want to be involved. He does very well at his sales job. I'm thinking about going to Florida for a while. I found a fifty-five plus place in Ft. Lauderdale that rents by month or year. I've been pounding iron a long time. I need to see and do other things."

Smiling at Dutch I offered, "I know what you mean, Dutch. I do my hunting and fishing, some woodworking, but have changed the rest. Being alone wears on you. I like driving and have a long list of places I want to visit. Maybe we should do a camping and fishing trip before you disappear."

"I would like that. Maybe this Cliff guy would go, too."

"I can't for a while," answered Cliff. "I have big deals in the works, and a couple sticky problems to solve, so I couldn't take the time. I would love to have a fish on the end of my line, though."

Cliff left about ten-thirty. Just said he needed to go and shouldered his way through the door into the darkness, letting a gust of wind tell us it was raining outside. That low pressure system brought some rain to Montana. Cliff acted edgy, and didn't play up to his usual game.

"Something bothering him? He was fidgety and nervous," said Dutch as he waved for two more beers. "I've never heard him curse before about missing a shot, ever."

"He told me on the way up, he has an agent problem here, and was struggling with his choices. Sounded serious to me. Do you have a buyer or any inquires?"

"No, I don't. The place looks old and dirty. The building isn't worth much. My customer list is worth more than the rest of the assets combined. I'll keep trying to sell 'till Thanksgiving. If nothing is in the works, I'll sell off the equipment or give it to Kenny. He's worked here over ten years and has good-sized workshop at his house.

I got a little money, Social Security, and a couple IRAs, so I'll be okay. My attorney said if I sell the customer list, I would need to send a letter to every one of them. I don't plan to sell the list."

CHAPTER 10

The following morning, I rose early and flew over the Bob Marshall Wilderness. My route passed over the small valley my son, Curt, and I found many years ago. I go visit my piece of paradise often. That cabin and valley is my hideaway. Total peace exists there.

I covered much of the million plus acres, including a check-it-out pass at the one airstrip in Schafer-Meadows. I smiled to myself knowing I loved flying and being in the wilderness more than anything. I rested the flying wheel on my knees and poured myself a cup of coffee, taking a sip before grasping the wheel again. I looked at many small valleys hoping to see another cabin.

I marveled at the mountains and rivers and the remoteness, being a lazy, but in control flyer. After returning and securing the plane against the wind, I drove to Classic Fifties. There I ordered lunch and a beer, and called Jack with an idea.

"Jack, are you interested in buying Dutch's metal fabricating equipment?"

"When did he decide to sell it? Jason loves that kind of work. We only have one rig here now and Jacob can finish the work needed to get it ready. Next week we'll be full. Jason and I will have to drive up tomorrow to check it out."

"I will meet you at his shop about eleven."

"That works, Del. I'll go tell the boys."

I was at Dutch's shop when Jack and Jason arrived. I did not tell Dutch they were coming.

Dutch greeted them both with his customary bear hug and said, "What gives, Jack? You lost and leading your son astray again?"

"Dutch," Jason answered, "I *always* do what Jack says." Lots of laughs.

"Dutch, I called Jack yesterday and told him you were selling out. These two would like to talk to you about that. Jason wants to do your kind of manufacturing instead of just fixing trucks."

"You serious Jack?"

"Yes, we are. How many employees do you have?"

"Three, but only Kenny can do quality stuff. I already told the other two they should start looking for another job." Dutch always took great care of his equipment.

"Well let's look at the equipment and supplies and see what is worth moving and keeping," said Jack. "We only have an hour or so today."

I excused myself, drove to the airport and took the Cessna for a ride. I needed to think. Cliff was working in my old stomping grounds. Something was nagging at me.

Cliff and I had a financial arrangement allowing me an elevated status with the FBI. They would pay me when I proved to be valuable to them. I gave them three worthwhile tips last year that resulted catching some bad guys and sending them to prison. Also, a mining-claim ring was exposed. I have been also credited with saving a young agent's life.

Dutch and I needed to have a long visit. When I returned to Dutch's shop, Jack and Jason were getting into their car to return to Bozeman. "Leaving."

Dropping into the passenger seat, Jack was all smiles. "Got to get back. Jacob called, we have three rigs assigned to us today. And we are going to look for a place to move Dutch's machines.

It is easy to see Dutch took good care of his machines. I know of a place in Manhattan, that might work. Kenny says he would be happy to move to the new location. Stop by when you get back, Del."

"Drive safely, Jason. See you in a day or so." Dutch and I waved when they drove away.

"I owe you big time Del," Dutch said. "Jason was so excited about the machines and that Kenny was going with them, I thought he would pee his pants. Jason wants his own business, and Jacob will eventually buy the big rig repair business. Then good old Jack can retire and go fishing with us. Looks like we all win." Dutch entered his office and made a phone call.

I watched Kenny work on a two-lane iron gate for a new housing development. His welding skills are the best I have personally seen. He ignored me and concentrated on his work. I decided to put off a talk with Dutch as he acted too happy now that his business is sold.

Dutch returned. "I just talked to Zig Belene. He wants to buy my building to winter-store his construction equipment. He was kind of on hold earlier, while I tried to sell the whole business. In six to eight months, I'll be free as a bird. I can't stop grinning. Kenny and I have an arrangement about the client list."

"I have an idea. We should fly to Florida and check out your place there and see if we can arrange a fishing excursion. I will cover the plane, and you rent the car," I offered.

"I think that's the best idea I've heard in a long time. I already have a rental lined up in Ft Lauderdale. I'll check to see if it's available. When should we leave?" Dutch smiled.

"I have a couple things to tidy up in Bozeman. I will fly down today and take care of them, then come back and pick you up…day after tomorrow."

Our trip to Florida covered three days. We diverted to many places along the way. I did not tell Dutch why I wanted to stop in Lincoln, Nebraska. A lady criminal there needed my attention. I completed a recon of the area around the courthouse. I also tested an escape route. We played tourist enough for me to find a shooting location and set up my preferred escape route.

"Perfect, this will work fine," I uttered to myself.

After landing in Fort Lauderdale, we drove in silence to Dutch's rental. He acted nervous, because he sent a too-big-of a deposit to Bubba. Dutch fidgeted when he was nervous.

I carried my computer along on this trip, so I could discretely check my individual credit report, and both corporations, plus all three of my alternate identities. I studied all with a fine-tooth comb, and deduced all were satisfactory. I noticed the charges for airlines and rental stuff, but expected that. I was pleased.

I called the Daily Chronicle to place an ad saying the range would be open for long distance shooting all of next week. I texted Rick and told him as well.

CHAPTER 11

S ince it was available, we checked into Dutch's rental. Not quite a dump, but close. Dutch was angry. No, he was really pissed, way past being angry. "I've been worried since I sent Bubba the deposit money… We'll look for a better place! This doesn't look *at all* like the pictures Bubba sent."

"I agree. We should first find a place on the ocean and enjoy a seafood dinner." I did not tell him that I had been there before. We went to Captain Dan's, an open-air seafood place, specializing in a big platter of prawns. Dutch sipped a Bud-Lite, while I enjoyed a Lagunitas IPA.

"How can you drink those IPAs? They don't taste like beer," a smiling Dutch teased me. "If I had to drink Lite Beer, Dutch, I would become a teetotaler. Just can't get past the watery taste."

"Del, what did the zebra say to the piano?"

"No clue."

"Hi, Dad," as Dutch laughed at his own joke.

"Weak, Dutch, very weak," but I smiled for him anyway.

Bo was our waiter. He looked nothing like the drug and money carrier I saw on the trail by Priest Lake, Idaho last summer. He appeared to be doing well, sporting a new haircut and not standing with the slouching posture I saw on the trail. He served our platter of fish and prawns.

Looking at his name tag, I said, "Bo, we are new in town and want to do some fishing, then find my friend a decent rental. He is thinking of spending the winter here."

"I have a friend that just bought a fishing boat. He's been crewing for six years and finally scraped enough dollars together and convinced the bank to back him. It's the *Baby Bird* at the Pelican Pier. You can walk from here. Dillon might be around. There are two decent rental places near here, Waterways and Sunny Side."

"Thanks, Bo."

"You're welcome and tell Dillon I sent you." He turned and walked to the kitchen.

Bo helped his new friend, Dillon, realize his dream to own a fishing charter boat, by using thirty thousand of his drug money. Only Dillon knew Bo was listed as a minority owner. Bo worked as a deck hand whenever he could. He liked the ocean and he liked to fish. Bo hid in Fort Lauderdale from Arizona drug people.

Bo and his partner, Zach, lost three million dollars walking south from Canada toward Priest Lake, Idaho. Bo escaped, collected his personal money from a Marana credit union and relocated to Fort Lauderdale. He looked different, talked different, and acted different. He and girlfriend, Stef, were happy. Bo watched out for Rocco. Rocco killed people because he really hated working in the drug culture and being around people he believed to be incompetent.

Bo liked his waiter job at Captain Dan's. He liked his new life. He positively believed no one from his old life knew where he lived now.

Del knew.

Bo gave then Lieutenant Davidson, now running for mayor, a tip that resulted in the apprehension of five drug runners. The newspaper ran a poor picture of Rocco as a person of interest.

I recalled my huckleberry picking day near that trail overlooking the Upper Priest Lake. Bo's partner had a careless accident that allowed me to steal almost three million dollars of drug money. That money was financing my *adventures* and allowed me to own a plane. Only my daughter, Molly, knew about the money.

"Del, what's wrong? You seem to be someplace else. You look distant."

"I was thinking about Amy." I lied. "She always wanted to come to Florida, but cancer ruined all her dreams. I miss her every day."

"Yeah, I miss her too. Always wish I'd found someone like her," said Dutch. A long-term friend of over forty years, we played many basketball games on the same team.

I changed the subject. "You ready to look at rentals and line up a fishing trip."

Dutch pushed his plate away and stood, ready to leave. "I can't eat like this every meal. I'll weigh three hundred pounds in no time."

Walking out the door on our way to Waterways to look at a place for sale, I wondered to myself: *Does Bo know Zach, Little Zap, and Vinney are dead? I bet he does not and could not care less.*

Special Prospector, one of my two corporations, bought a newer two-bedroom modular home, turn-key ready, in Waterways near enough to the ocean to have canal access. The deal included an ocean ready boat and trailer. The ninety-four-year-old lady lost her husband a month ago and wanted to go back to Wisconsin to be with her family. Offering a cash deal and covering the costs suited her fine.

"Del, I can't afford this place. It's perfect, but I don't have that kind of money."

"I would like to come fishing, and there are lots of tourist things here. I too, like it, and each bedroom has its own bath. You pick the one you want, and I will set up the other one for myself. I have a place to stay, a boat, and can skip the motels. We will make the title in both names, so when one of us dies, the other gets it."

"Okay, Del. But the expenses are mine. Not buying a place makes this affordable."

We hauled four boxes to the FEDEX office, for the seller so she could ship them home. We gave her a ride to the airport, and she left Florida. I always feel extra good when life makes someone happy.

"What about the rental?"

"Well, we are going to get your money back. First, we will go to the public library and get a resident card for both of us. Then we will type a letter with an offer he cannot refuse. We will go to a photocopy shop and make copies of the contract and the pictures he sent you." I did not want the ever-watchful librarian to know what we were doing.

"The pictures he sent you are not from his park. Old Bubba Sinclare, a sloppy obese man, will be happy to give you your deposit and rent back. Maybe we will let him keep today's rent."

Bubba first tried to call our hand. Then we showed him the copies and pictures. "Cash Bubba. No checks. Every penny, except yesterday's rent," I said.

After Bubba paid us, I told him, "I want you to know, Bubba, we are going to report this tomorrow. You are through scamming people."

On our way to the car, Dutch laughed. "Jesus, Del. You sounded like a lawyer and scared the crap out of him."

"A gutless man. He did not have a leg to stand on and did not want to risk ending up in court. The pictures of the cockroaches alone, were enough to win our case. We should go see about fishing." He nodded at me with a grin.

"Dutch, you need to have our new boat picked up and made completely ocean ready, so we can use it. Also, buy some ocean charts and the tide schedule. That cost is mine. We cannot just go out not knowing what we are doing."

On our way to the Pelican Pier to set up fishing, we saw a billboard with a smiling Lieutenant Davidson running for mayor. Tough on crime. In bold letters below his name. "We will send an anonymous tip to Mr. Davidson about Bubba," I commented.

"Ain't his real teeth," quipped Dutch.

The Pelican Pier jutted a long way into the ocean, many people fished all along its length. We found the *Baby Bird* two slips from the full-service convenience store halfway down the pier. A young man was cleaning the engine compartment.

"Are you Dillon?" I shouted to him.

"You got him. How can I help you guys?" he asked turning around.

"We were eating at Captain Dan's and asked our waiter, Bo, about fishing charters. He suggested the *Baby Bird*. So, here we are," I answered.

"So, Bo sent you? Great," smiled Dillon. "I have a license test tomorrow, about the harbor rules and need to get a new current ocean chart, but have two open dates after that. I'll go get you a rate sheet."

While he was gone, I asked Dutch. "What do you think? Shall we try this kid?"

"Yeah, I like him. If he is any good, we could go out both days."

"My thoughts exactly, Dutch. I have a feeling we lucked out."

"Did Bo tell you I just bought the boat, and my license is only a month old?"

"Yes, he did. But he also told us, you have been working on other boats here for years."

"I know where the fish usually are, but fishing is fishing. Catching makes fishing more. . . fun. I provide all the gear and bait. One deckhand will assist us. I'll have lots of water on ice. We'll take care of any fish you wish to keep. Some are very tasty. I'll tell you which fish are extra tasty. You need your own clothes, sunscreen, food and drink. The most important item will be a decent wide-brim hat. See you at seven tomorrow."

We had a lot of time on our hands. We stopped on our way to our new abode, for a rental truck to haul away the items in the house we wouldn't need. After returning the rental and stocking up on food for a week's stay, we went looking for a new TV and two new recliner chairs.

"We need to get good hats. I am pasty white and will be burnt to a crisp in an hour. Stuff is too expensive at the pier," said Dutch.

We went to the same nearby grocery store where I shopped during my first trip to Fort Lauderdale. The fishing wholesale store was the same one I visited then, too. The store covered everything else we needed and more.

Back at our house, we stowed our new gear in two new backpacks. We were ready. While we enjoyed our evening meal of spaghetti and meatballs from a prepackaged frozen food company. Actually, it did not taste too bad. I opened a bag of Ruffles potato chips and filled a bowl, then reached into the sack and took one out and popped it into my mouth.

"Why did you take an extra chip from the bag, Del?"

"I have always taken an extra. I never really knew why, but am sure now that I took it just to get under my sister's skin." I changed the subject. "Dutch, you ever been deep-sea fishing before?"

"Nope. Something new to me."

"I have been out twice," I answered. "Lots of waiting for big stuff, but if he finds some schools of smaller fish, there can be a fish on every cast. Ocean fish are strong."

"Wow, Del. I can't believe this. One day I'm sitting on my hands, worrying about what I'm going to do, and the next thing I know, I'm going fishing with my best friend in Florida. Blows my mind. I can never repay you for working the deal with Jack and Jason.

We fished all day, as Dillon's first customers. He was proud of himself. We caught fifteen jack mackerel, but no big fish. Dutch had a shark on his line for a while, but it broke off. While he was playing the shark, I watched him. I could not remember seeing him this happy in a long time. He was not dancing, but he acted close to dancing.

Dillon was fun to be with, but his deckhand was a grump. When I asked his name, he answered, "Blake." Nothing else. He did his work because he wanted to be paid.

Dillon paid him in cash. "See you around, Blake." Dillon turned to us and added, "Sorry about Blake. He was all I could get on a day's notice. He subs around when he needs money, but he never seems to like people."

"You are right, Dillon, he was okay, but not friendly. We will go tomorrow, if it's still open…" Dutch said.

"Open and you two are on! I'll see if Bo can go. I know he gets the day off. Seven a.m. again. I'll ask around about the big fish."

Seafood again at Captain Dan's for dinner. After we returned to our new home, Dutch went for a walk covering every street in Waterways.

The second day of fishing was better. I landed a small shark, and Dutch caught a small sailfish. We took home enough red fish and a permit for a couple meals. We wanted to barbeque some fish on a grill we did not yet own. Handled that on our way back to our canal side house. The yard will take some extra work as the jungle close to the back fence encroached almost a third of the back yard. Dutch left to go pick up his new Traeger.

I made some calls. I could hear the frustration in Cliff's voice as he briefly commented about his undercover operation. "I need to pick your brain when you two come back."

The next morning, Dutch wanted to work on the house. I chose to drive to St. Petersburg and look for a way to make a shot on the second Jamaican drug lord. I formulated a plan, including an acceptable escape route.

Jack called, and we put him on speaker. "You guys are coming back on Friday, right? We have a lease option on the warehouse. So, when you two are here, we can finish everything and move the machines, tools, and Kenny down here. Jason hasn't been this excited since his first date."

Dutch, leaned toward the phone, "We will be back *Saturday*. I'm excited, too. I feel so lucky." Dutch performed a thirty second jig. Fun to watch.

"Jason and I will meet you at your shop on *Monday*," answered Jack.

CHAPTER 12

The same morning Dutch and I left for Florida, Cliff started his plan to check on Johnny. He walked two blocks from the courthouse parking lot and entered The Antique Shop, a cluttered place with something to look at in every nook and cranny. A bell announced his arrival.

Quickly, a short woman about fifty sheepishly greeted him. "Good morning. Let me know if I can help you."

"I'm looking for an old desk, but I'll wander through the store. I'll find you if I need anything."

"Make yourself at home," and she disappeared into her antique collection.

Johnny didn't know Cliff by sight, but could probably peg him as a cop instantly, if Cliff showed himself. An old large rolltop desk was near the front window. Cliff worked at testing it, while watching for his undercover agent to finish his breakfast.

His quarry was in the restaurant across the street. Word had filtered through the grape vine that while undercover, the agent was making some money on the side. Johnny Beckman was a fifteen-year field agent veteran. This was his third undercover assignment. Never had any hints of problems. A three-month old picture showed a small well-built man with full facial hair and a knotted and tied ponytail. A round face with the broken nose look. A real scar at the widow's peak hairline over the right eye, made him look sinister.

Johnny came out and looked straight ahead, then started up the street with a purposeful stride. Cliff did not give himself away. A quick call and a whispered, "He's on the move."

St. Paul Agent, Eleanor Millwood, with the Bureau for two years, was not known in Great Falls when she started following Johnny. Thirty-two-years-old, five-ten and a solid one hundred seventy-five pounds, she carried an air of confidence. She was proud of her black belt in a karate discipline, though hid her toughness behind her ever-ready smile. She was a businesswoman today: power suit, thin briefcase and a second computer bag completed her cover.

Cliff watched her start the tail.

Johnny appeared to ignore her. He was very good at his profession. His undercover experience to date had been stellar. He was an expert at covering his back. If he had lost his way, he would be hard to catch.

Eleanor went into a ladies clothing store and called Cliff using her cell. "He went into the Sparks Hotel."

Cliff left the antique shop, crossed the street, climbed to the second floor of the parking garage on First Avenue South. He positioned himself to watch the Bruisers bar. It was rumored that anything was available there. He noted all license plates he could read and sent the info to his office.

Johnny showed up thirty minutes later. Cliff watched from the shadows. Johnny acted like he didn't have a care in the world. He had been undercover here for over a year. His last check-in was a sketchy minimum report four months ago.

The FBI and DEA knew the Canadian-USA drug pipeline was active. An unknown informant calling from Shelby, had provided some names. But the FBI and DEA wanted to see if they could catch the top players. The informant had mentioned Johnny's name, a player, he said. The informant did not know Johnny found a job at the Country Club.

Eleanor came to relieve Cliff three hours later. "Eleanor, we will watch together for a while. He's been inside too long. I'll bet he went out the back, and went looking for you." Thirty minutes later, Cliff called it off. They ate at the McKenzie River Pizza on the Missouri River. The river is very wide, but the noises of the pizza place drown out the murmur of the flowing water.

"Hawaiian large?" asked Cliff.

"And a pitcher of beer," answered Eleanor.

"Eleanor, . . ." Cliff started to go over the day.

"Please call me E.L. I asked my mom why I got this name. Grampa loved Eleanor Roosevelt and insisted. My middle name is worse, so I started using E.L.

Cliff started over. "E.L. we can't do the same tail again. We will be caught. Johnny has control. He is too good. If he is rogue, we will not get close to him. We're going to need a better plan."

"Do you know where and what he did in his other undercover assignments?

"Not much. Headquarters keeps some secrets about him, I'm sure. We'll need to find something solid or we'll not learn much more. He was last in Bakersfield, California and Memphis, Tennessee before that. There may be others, but that's all I know. Lots of outlaws in both places. After we report in, I intend to ask a lot of questions.

"How are the local police involved? Do they cooperate with the Feds?"

The pizza and beer were gone. "I plan to call HQ in the morning. I need to know as much as they will tell me. I need to know what they actually expect. I know they do not want to lose the progress they've made so far. They cannot use the local agents as Johnny would know in a heartbeat."

"Will they use retired agents?" asked E.L.

"Most likely not. Too much risk with little reward."

"Cliff, we need to find someone who knows the town and the people."

"I have had those thoughts. I know someone to ask." He was hoping Del could help somehow. "We should mull over our options, and meet at Perkins on Sixth Street for breakfast at about nine. I will have spoken to HQ before I arrive. You get there early and find a seat by the window. Watch for Johnny. I don't expect him, but if he made our tail, he may have followed you. Be drinking coffee and writing in a journal. If you see any suspects, write a description in your journal and have it open in front of you. If I see that, I'll keep walking and not enter."

E.L. let Cliff pay, and they walked out together, acting like father and daughter. Driving away in their older red suburban, both looked at everything and tried to show real laughter.

E.L. dropped Cliff at the Heritage Hotel and continued on to the Hampton. Cliff had decided they shouldn't stay at the same hotel. She noticed a car in the parking lot with two people in it, then rode the elevator to the fifth floor. She hurried to the stairs, raced up to the sixth, and watched the floor lights above the elevator door. The one she used, went down, the other rose to floor five and stopped.

"Not a coincidence, E.L., not a coincidence," she whispered aloud.

In her room on the eleventh floor, she sent a text to Cliff. *I saw Sammie today.* Then she called her fiancé in St. Paul. No answer. She left an *I love you* message.

Her phone announced a text from Cliff. *Sorry I missed him. In the morning, go see his sister.* Cliff was getting her out. She would fly back to St Paul and wait for the next step, if any.

Cliff checked out at five a.m., took a cab to the airport, and caught the earliest flight to Salt Lake City. Waiting for his ride to his office, he called SAIC Agent Long. "Regroup."

The answer, "I'll work on it."

Agent Long knew the tail had been discovered the first day. Regroup was going to require a restart after a call to Cliff. He hoped he would get a call from Johnny.

CHAPTER 13

Johnny knew better than to confront the woman. She must be new. Too obvious, and he had never seen her downtown before. Great Falls was too small a town to be new. The drug people here were a close-knit group. He had spent most of his year here becoming accepted, but felt still on the fringe.

He didn't know any of them for sure, but positive that the man who owned the big used car lot on Tenth Avenue South, was one of the players. He knew one screw up, and that one was dead. So far, he had caused them no worries. He wanted to talk to Jeff.

Jeff Springer's favorite saying was, "No worries." He held a position as one of the drug mules using the Saint Mary's route into Canada. Jeff was sort of in. He knew one of the in players for sure. The lady sold real estate and seemed to always complete the cash pick up from Johnny's car. He had followed her twice using a friend's motorcycle. Jeff was a six-foot-four string bean young man from Judith Gap. He could have stayed on the ranch his parents owned and lived a decent life, but he became a dreamer. "Can't stand cow shit and don't like to ride horses." He would say to anyone who would listen.

After coming to Great Falls and becoming a carrier, he let his naturally curly black hair grow longer, added a Fu-Manchu mustache, and long sideburns to the jaw. He maintained a four-day scruff of whiskers. He didn't smoke, drink much, or use drugs and could run a respectable mile or two. He had been the top athlete at his local high school. He knew the drug crowd dealt drugs, but didn't use them. He did not know most of the other carriers for sure. The system was set up to be that way. He was positive about only two.

Jeff knew the route and felt he could follow it even on the darkest night. He always parked in the same spot near a cabin in St Mary village, a cabin -type of resort, with many evergreen trees. Pinecones always littered the parking lot. He picked up a backpack from the trunk of a different car every time. The car had a tiny disco ball with the trunk key laying on the backseat. He never looked to see if he carried drugs or money, but could tell by the weight which item he carried.

He made four hikes per month and received ten grand deposited into his account at the credit union. It really was nine thousand five hundred, but the other five hundred seemed to always show up later. He had one hundred eighty-seven thousand saved. He decided to get to two-hundred thousand and then just disappear. After completing his trip, he needed to stop in Kiowa and call a number to learn which of the two locations in East Glacier he was to use for his pack. He knew he was trusted to a point. Mess up, then die.

Jeff played in a pool league for the Dugout Brew Pub team on the Northwest Bypass Road. Someone, he didn't know, left no perfume smells, but had keys to his car. If it was not where he parked it, he would drive to St Mary's, park and make the hike to the border, meet the other team from Canada, and trade packs. Then hike back. The backpacks had a bottom section containing food, traveling money, and other essentials.

He knew Johnny was part of the system, but did not know what he did. Somehow Johnny knew he was a walker. They never talked about drugs.

"Jeff, Johnny here, burger and a brew?"

Sure, man, I'm at the Dugout. That work?"

"I am at the Queen Club. They have better food. Come when you can," said Johnny.

"Okay," answered Jeff. "Wonder why Johnny never went to the Dougout." Jeff said aloud to himself.

Jeff finished his pool game, pushed his way to the bar, paid his tab, and left the bar. Reaching his car, he saw a note with a T taped to his door handle. He tore the note into tiny pieces and dropped them out his window as he drove to the Queen Club. After crossing the Missouri River, he followed the park road along the river. Then pulled off and checked his car. His cheap sweeper showed a tag. He pulled back onto the park road and finished his route to the Queen.

"Hey, man," he smiled at Johnny offering his hand as he came in.

"Our food is on its way."

"You been here long, Johnny?" asked Jeff.

"Since seven or so, why?"

"Just asking, cause that's when I got to the Dugout." He hung his head a minute fussed with his hair, then told Johnny about the note and what he felt about the tag. "I'm a little spooked now."

Johnny sat back acting shocked. "What does that mean?"

"A tail, I think. Why? I left the tag, so whoever knows I'm here with you."

Johnny leaned over his beer about to answer, when the waitress delivered their food. "Let's eat, think, and talk it through."

After they finished eating, and the dishes were gone, Jeff sighed. "You shoot pool Johnny?"

"Some, but not very well."

"There's an open table in the rec room, let's play a couple games, and talk about things." The pool room was small with only three tables, but in top notch condition. They did not have a team in the league Jeff belonged to.

After the break. Jeff pointed to a couple of balls, then not moving his lips or looking at Johnny, whispered, "You think we are bugged?"

"Doubt it but, did you sweep yourself?"

"I just assumed it was the car."

Johnny shot and missed.

Jeff made two solids, while Johnny acted out a chuckle.

Moving past Jeff to line up his shot, he mumbled, "Go to the can and check."

Jeff made one then missed, propped his cue against a chair, "Gotta pee, be right back."

Johnny made two stripes and missed a third, so he sat and sipped his beer.

"Clean," offered Jeff as he reached for his cue and dropped his sweeper into Johnny's lap.

"My turn." Johnny strolled to the men's room.

Jeff sipped his beer, waiting for Johnny to return.

"Clean," nodded Johnny as he dropped the sweeper into Jeff's lap.

"Did you shoot?"

"No. If I do things right, I can close you out, so I waited." Jeff made his last four solids and the eight. "One more, I still have most of my beer left."

"Okay, one more, then I gotta run," Johnny answered. They walked out together and drove away

CHAPTER 14

Johnny knew it was well past midnight in Washington DC at the FBI headquarters. He also knew Agent Long's special number. He used one of his burner phones and punched the private number. Special Agent Long answered on the second ring.

"This is Johnny, I am almost in. Get rid of the tail. I need a witness protection protocol for a guy. He knows more than me, I think, and it looks like the *in group* has taken an extra interest in him. Johnny hung up, started his car, then threw the burner into the Missouri River when he crossed the Central Avenue Bridge.

Johnny knew the 'T' meant Jeff was targeted for elimination, but someone had given Jeff a heads up. That someone had been Johnny, risking everything.

Agent Long called Cliff the next morning and related Johnny's entire conversation.

"Do you believe him?" asked Cliff.

"Just enough to pull the surveillance for now. That will send an okay to Johnny. It will also give us time to place another agent undercover in Great Falls.

Johnny suspected someone in his building placed a call every time he left the building or returned. He ruled out everyone except the lady in apartment one. She could always see who came and went.

He owned a small receiver, and devised a way to lower it between two interior studs. He went to a pawn shop and purchased a hand drill and bit, which made a hole big enough to lower the receiver attached to mono-filament fishing line. He installed it and checked his phone, immediately hearing her TV. Johnny could check anytime if she called someone whenever he left his building.

CHAPTER 15

eff finished his nighttime trek in a light rain to Canada and back, started his car and drove to the Kiowa location to make his call to learn which drop for his backpack he needed to use. He completed his call, noticing two pretty big guys walking toward him from one of the small shacks. They slowly made their way in his direction.

The darkness covered their purpose. The smaller of the two chuckled, then lifted his gun to shoot at Jeff. "You must be a screw up."

Jeff threw his backpack (which he knew by weight contained drugs) at them and started running. Both men fired their revolvers until they were empty. They did not hit Jeff. He escaped without a scratch, returned to his car and threw wet gravel in their direction, as he sped away. It took every bit of concentration he could muster to follow the rules and drive back to Great Falls. He felt scared to the bone.

When he arrived, he called Johnny, "Johnny, two guys just tried to shoot me in Kiowa. I threw my pack of drugs at them and ran. I'm not harmed, but I'm scared."

"Okay, Jeff, meet me at the boxcar. Make sure you are not followed."

Jeff hid under an elderberry bush just west of the boxcar, above the Missouri River, worried sick Johnny wouldn't show.

"Jeff, you alone?"

"Jesus, Johnny! You scared the shit out of me."

"Jeff, I have two hundred dollars for you, two water bottles, and four granola bars. Also, here's a burner phone to use just once to call Leon and once to call me, after you are in Highwood. You are to walk to Highwood tonight, and ring the doorbell once, then three times at the small gray house next to the school. Leon will take care of you. Stay off the roads and walk south of the air base. You need to move as fast as you can. Good luck to you."

"Why are you helping me?"

"Jeff, you are too nice a kid to be involved in the drug business. When you get to Lewistown, your escort will expect you to use the money I gave you to make a deposit in a bank and transfer your personal money. Then in Billings, he will expect you to have the Lewistown bank transfer your money to a Billings bank. The Billings bank will allow you to collect your money. Your escort will know which banks to use. Leon will explain things. Who are you most afraid of?"

"A guy I talked to over the phone named Bill, and Delvin, owner of Wholesale Car Lot on Tenth."

"Do you know any others I need to watch out for?"

"A lady realtor picks up your money when you park at the Lido, I don't know her name, but she and Delvin both belong to the county club. I borrowed a friend's motorcycle and followed her twice. Once to the Lido and once to the Country Club."

"Thanks Jeff, now get going and hurry."

"Thanks, Johnny, you won't regret helping me. See you." Jeff started walking up hill towards the public golf course and disappeared into the night, then ran over half of the thirteen cross-country miles to Highwood. He called Johnny and left a message.

The US Marshals took over after Jeff left Billings. Jeff became Tommy Bell after traveling with a two-agent escort team to Minneapolis. With all the right papers, Tommy enrolled at

Bemidji State in Bemidji, Minnesota, became a member of their cross-country team, and selected a major of criminal Justice.

Johnny completed the long three mile walk back to his apartment, knowing he would be watched very closely for some time. He called Agent Long. "Jeff is on his way to Leon's. He knows two of the players. I may be done. Please have an agent place ten burners, tomorrow night at 10:00 p.m. at the bus station in Locker fifteen. Then set the combo using successive fives. I know three of the players now." He hung up and threw the phone into the Missouri River, as he walked along the path next to the river. He walked fast enough to minimize the mosquito problem.

Johnny sneaked out of his apartment early, then watched the bus depot from a shadow in a recessed doorway across the street. A slight mist helped keep things extra dark. He saw the agent enter and leave. He did not see a tail.

After waiting over an hour, he then crossed to the depot, retrieved the burners, and stashed eight of them in a sealed double plastic bag, in an old, abandoned car in an alley a block from his 'home'.

The two remaining phones he hid in two hollowed out paper back western novels, he used as a hiding place. He liked to read and traveled to garage sales, often adding to his collection of nearly a hundred books. His bookcase, a beat-up old maple wood relic from a thrift store, had room for thirty more books.

He hoped to be finished in Great Falls before he filled it.

CHAPTER 16

Johnny continued doing his undercover (UC) work of keeping the drug lower-level people away from the police and doing their job correctly. His main job involved making the actual swap of drugs and money using a system he created. He functioned as the teacher, and his people knew to do things right. Johnny did not like spending so much time in bars. He detested the odors.

During his California UC, he performed the drug mule job and the drug/cash exchange. He knew those tasks very well. His reputation as a meticulous operator served him well. A policeman insider in California told him the authorities were watching him, so he talked to his main handler, who recommended going to Great Falls, called a major player and set things up. Johnny made the switch.

After arriving in Great Falls, he studied the current system used to swap cash for drugs and changed everything. He chose all swap locations only if they had an available front and back exit. He made every swap himself, then drove to the Lido bar on Tenth Avenue South. He knew a woman picked up the money. Her perfume possessed a unique smell. If he smelled it anywhere, he would know she had been the one in his car.

Johnny always waited at the Queen Club for his favorite table in the rear southern corner. The staff knew he liked to sit there and saved it for him every Friday night. He placed his order, noticing a man talking to the hostess. He didn't hear the man ask which table Johnny occupied.

The man finished his conversation, proceeding directly to Johnny's table.

"Johnny, call me Bill. May I join you?"

"Why?"

"I wish to visit about Jeff. We know you two were friends and shot pool together sometimes. We believe you have learned that Jeff had an altercation in Kiowa, and then disappeared. We do not know where he is now," Bill paused watching Johnny closely.

"Have a seat Bill," Johnny could use a poker face with the best of them. "Bill, I heard about that problem. Tough to keep it a secret. I don't know where he is. I went to the Dugout where he shoots on a league team and asked about him, and learned he has been a no show for two weeks. The story I heard, someone shot at him. That's all I know."

"Yes, someone shot at him. We are angry about that. Jeff always completed his trips in fine fashion. We are searching for a replacement and have a lead on a young man who worked the Minnesota pipeline. He should arrive here in a couple of weeks. We would like you to train him," finished Bill.

"Whatever you need," offered Johnny, while staring in his eyes. "I understand my role."

Standing to leave Bill finished his mission. "Yes, we know you do. We thank you."

Johnny finished his dinner and key-lime pie for dessert, rehashing everything Bill had commented on. He decided he would be carefully watched for some time. Bill's scotch glass with his fingerprints sat empty two feet away. If he took it, he knew he would have to run or die, because he would bet the farm someone in the bar would notice.

He believed they did not know how Jeff got away, but will watch him to see if he makes a mistake. Johnny proved the tail on him as he drove back to his apartment. Two men followed in a big black crew-cab pickup.

He would make his Helena run tomorrow to Costco and Walmart. He used a burner to call his Walmart contact and arrange to purchase five more burners. They had a system to exchange money for phones using a Mr. Coffee location in Walmart to complete the exchange. He made the swap. The black truck goofed around some, but Johnny saw it wherever he went.

Monday, he would go to Shelby and study the small town for two reasons. He needed to know Shelby, Cutbank and Browning better. He also needed to see if the train could be a viable option if he had to run. The black truck seemed to always be around.

He went to all three towns, and checked the train, and scouted for sheriff and police presence. He stayed overnight in Shelby. His company did as well. Time to check those two.

He walked to the Queen Club the next Friday, noticing the truck parked five times, so they could keep him sight. Leaving the Queen Club, he could tell the men were out of the truck but not visible. Johnny always walked fast then took the alley behind the Russell Museum. He knew two places to hide, so he could see who they were.

They stopped twenty feet away from Johnny's hiding place. Johnny knew the look of every shadow and doorway, as well as every hiding place between the Queen Club and his apartment. He knew how to hide and how to breath softly. Darkness was a friend when you need it.

"He's trying to dodge us. We'll get the truck and put him to bed. That's what Bill wants, so that's what he gets.

Johnny recognized both men. They sat together in the Dugout Brew Pub. One cowboy and one Native American. 'Walton' wore a big black cowboy hat and black boots. He proved to be the cowboy, and 'Jesse' sounded like a native American. He didn't know their last names.

CHAPTER 17

Last summer, I hitched a ride from Columbia Falls, Montana to West Glacier—a ride of 17 miles. My driver was Jody Cummings, a kid from Saco, that dressed in jeans, cowboy boots and a blue paisley shirt. We talked about horses more than I would have, but when Jody found out I had never ridden a horse, he tried to stifle a laugh but couldn't. He immediately invited me to come to his parent's ranch and ride one. I promised I would.

We talked about hunting, fishing, rodeoing, and flying. Our trip together turned out to be too short, so we stopped at Charlie's Bar in Evergreen, where I treated him to one of Charlie's Famous Cheeseburgers. The grease smell covered everything else. Jody's parting words were, "I'm going to hold you to your promise, Del. Let's swap phone numbers now, and we will get you that ride."

It was time to go meet Jody's family. I called him a month or so ago, and he said early May would work as the calving would be finished and the crops planted. So, I punched his number.

"Morning, Del, when you coming?"

"May 9th, if that works for you."

"Great, I'll check with Mom and Dad and let you know if there are any problems with that date. I'll have the guest house ready for you. We even have electricity and running water," laughing heartily at his own joke. Just kidding, Del. It will be great to see you again."

"Jody, do you have a place I could land my plane?"

"Sure, we have a mowed strip between two hay fields. We drive equipment over it, but it is pretty smooth. I'll check it for junk and holes this Saturday."

"Then I will fly up. We can look at your entire ranch. I am not prepared to do that from the back of a horse. How will I recognize your place?"

"We have a flagpole in the center of our yard. Our place is five miles north of Saco. On the east side of the road. Frenchman's Creek runs through our property, about three-quarters of a mile east of our buildings.

"I'll park my red truck beneath the flagpole. Then after you fly over, I'll drive to the hayfield strip. That strip is exactly a quarter mile north of our barn. The outbuildings and shelterbelt form a 'u' around the house. I have some pink wire flags, so will mark the runway with those. You can taxi your plane all the way to the shelterbelt.

"I'm excited for you to meet my family. I think dad has some questions for you. I told them all about you when I got home after giving you a ride."

"Great directions. I will be coming via Lewistown. I am not stopping there, just want to see their runway. I learned I can refuel in Glasgow on my way back. They told me it is a 24/7 service facility. This going to be a special time, I can feel it."

CHAPTER 18

irst, I flew over the Highwood Mountains, then the Little Belts. Both sets of mountains contain quality herds of elk and deer. And, some rugged country, and then flew over Lewistown. The airport was better than I had been told previously. I would land there one day soon and learn the usual arrangements for fuel and overnighting.

I arranged with Jody to arrive about one o'clock. Departing Great Falls at 7:00 am allowed me six hours to explore the Northeastern portion of Montana. I flew over the Missouri River including Fort Peck Reservoir to Glasgow, landing at ten thirty.

I visited a short time with the day manager and refueled. The manager secured a rental car, which I drove the twelve miles to Fort Peck Marina, to check out the boats for rent. I decided I would rather bring my own. I had the time and the extra money.

I always smiled when I remembered how I 'found' the money that set me up for life. Last July, I took a trip to Lionhead Campground at the north tip of lower Priest Lake. To get to my secret/favorite huckleberry-picking spot in Upper Priest Lake, I needed my canoe. I was the only one there, paddling along in nature sounds until I reached my cove. While eating my lunch up the hill, I heard two young men backpacking drug money as they walked on the trail below. One young man lost his balance and accidently fell down the mountain several yards and broke his leg.

While begging his partner to help him, he mentioned the packs contained money. His partner helped his descent to a logging road. While the two men negotiated the steep trail, I located and picked up both backpacks of money. I forgot all about the huckleberries as I canoed as fast as I could back to camp. Quickly I packed up and traveled to another location to count the money.

Returning to Glasgow, I finished my journey to Saco and found the Cummings Ranch immediately. I saw Jody's truck and the pink flags. I made an observation pass over the strip and smoothly landed on the second pass.

Jody arrived and waved a *follow me*. I shut the airplane down a stone's throw from the trees. The weather, warm, sunny, with little wind felt good.

"Nice landing, Del. Looked easy." We piled into Jody's truck. A small dust cloud followed us the way back to the ranch house.

"I really like the openness in Montana and the smell of alfalfa."

"Me too, Del. No other place like it, except Wyoming. But they have a lot of interstate miles in that little state. I should learn to fly. You are smelling the first cut of hay for the year."

Jody's mom and dad strolled down the crushed rock walkway to meet them. "I'm Frank and this is my wife, Meg." Warm and friendly handshakes from nice people were exchanged. "Please come inside, and we'll share some fresh pie."

As soon as I met Jody's parents, I knew this family would become special to me. Frank was a six-foot-tall man with a full head of white hair. He had the weathered cowboy look. Meg was a Jody look-alike. A small oval face, a few freckles with a small mouth and smiling eyes. She was petite, and sun-tanned, with minimum makeup and a professionally cared for hair.

"Jody picked the apples. He does do nice things once in a while," smiled Meg.

"Our family has lived here over 150 years," offered Frank. "Lots of hard work, but it's a good life. Our sons, *The boys,* do most of the work now. I still help during harvest time. We have a retirement villa in Fort Lauderdale, so we get to dodge as much of winter as we wish. I like to fish and go new places, so we make do."

"Frank and Meg, when Jody asked me to come here to visit, I debated it. But my judge of a person's character has always served me well. I liked Jody the minute he said, "Hi, need a ride? He promised me a ride on a gentle horse. He also mentioned two other things that are very much a part of me, hunting and fishing. How could I say, no?"

"He talked about horses as if he was part of one. When he learned I had never ridden one, he laughed and asked, how could anyone live in Montana most of his life and never ride a horse?"

I continued, "Today he said maybe he should learn to fly. I have my plane here, so we can see if he should stick to horses." Then I asked, "Have any of you flown over your ranch?"

Meg answered first, "I have ridden twice in commercial planes, but never in a little one like yours. I'm not sure I would like it. Frank has been in a small plane once or twice."

"I will offer both of you a ride today. Jody wanted to see the entire ranch from the air, and he can go tomorrow. He can try flying then."

Frank and Meg paused, looked at each other, but didn't comment right away.

"I have flown thousands of hours, and the plane I own is in near perfect condition. I promise nothing fancy, just flying and looking."

"Count me in, Del," answered Frank, "But Meg can go first."

"Okay, but I'm very nervous."

I made the takeoff as smooth as I could, and climbed to 500 feet. I could feel a light thermal, so I climbed to 800 feet and things were much smoother.

"Wow, this is great! Things look so much different from this high." Meg pointed out some of the landmarks. Many of the fields looked flat, but Frenchman's Creek drainage was laced with many gullies. Some deep enough to have pine trees and many filled with Juniper and berry trees.

"Are there any chokecherry trees in those gullies?" I asked.

"Lots of them. We don't use them anymore. My mother did, but I haven't canned anything in years."

"Meg, I still make my own jams and jellies and syrups. I grew up on chokecherry stuff. I will bring you some next visit." I could not explain to myself why I felt extra comfortable with Meg in the plane next to me, but I knew those feelings were not just because. They were closeness feelings I had not experienced since Amy passed out of my life. Meg did not just smell extra fine she looked extra fine. I knew I should not have those feelings. They belonged to Frank, not me.

"Wonderful, that will be special. Oh, look at those two mule deer bucks. They are going to be fine specimens. The boys hunt, but not real hard. We enjoy venison if they shoot one, but we prefer our own beef."

"I enjoy venison. I am trying to get a big enough deer to qualify for the Boone and Crocket list. Jody said he has seen some big ones here once in a while."

After an hour of flying, I landed as softly as I knew how. "Thank you, Del, I haven't enjoyed myself this much in a long time. I had forgotten how big our ranch is. Frank and the boys work hard to do everything. We are lucky. My three sons are best friends. Oh, they have had a set-to once in a while, but Gary, our oldest, is very gentle. He sets an example and Jimmy and Jody have learned from that. Gary and Jimmy are at a horse auction at a ranch near Judith Gap. They should be home for supper."

"I am looking forward to meeting them. I can see where Jody gets his good looks and personality."

"Jody said you always know what to say. I'm glad you didn't say no to visiting."

Jody met them halfway up the path. "Del, let's go meet your horse."

"Supper at seven."

"Wouldn't miss it for the world, Mom." Jody and I walked to the coral behind a long stable. There were seven horses acting bored. Most using the three-legged pose. "How'd Mom like the ride?"

"A lot, I am guessing. We can check during supper."

"Good idea. Gary and Jimmy are going to be jealous."

"I can give both of them a ride tomorrow."

"Your horse is the sorrel with the three white stockings. She's just gentle. She likes to run, but will walk all day if you let her. We call her Lucky, but I don't remember why. Dad can tell the story.

Gary called about five thirty saying they were going to stay in Lewistown to look at two other horses, tomorrow morning.

Meatloaf, boiled potatoes steamed carrots and another piece of pie satisfied everyone.

"Too bad, no pie for the absent brothers.," interjected Jody. "I'll show you to the guest house, Del" We walked to the airplane, picked up my two bags, and walked on a narrow path through the trees. We came to an eight hundred square-foot, two-story frame-house.

"We built the new house when I entered third grade. This was the original house. There are pictures showing how you could see it from the road before the trees grew too big. Dad remodeled it himself. You can lock it if you want, but we never do. I'll do the chores in the morning, so Dad can go fly with you. You and I can go about eleven and take a lunch. I know another place we can land. I checked it out on Saturday."

CHAPTER 19

rank was up with the birds. So was, l. Sparrows and blackbirds greeted the day and everyone else, whether or not they wanted a wakeup call. Breakfast consisted of a small steak, scrambled eggs and home-made waffles. All breakfast smells are intoxicating.

"Wonderful breakfast, I feel spoiled. Thank you, Meg."

"You're welcome, Del. What time are you and Frank going for your ride?"

"Whenever he is ready."

"I'll do the chores, Dad," said Jody. "You go enjoy the ride."

"Thank you, son. Let me get a jacket, as the air is cool this morning," answered Frank.

"You are wise. I have mine in the plane and will certainly wear it."

The first half hour, Frank pointed out many landmarks and the boundaries then added, "Only one ranch between us and Canada, the Sutherland's. My grandfather settled on Frenchman's Creek and struggled against all odds to keep his homestead. The original sod and tree dugout is still here, but has all but eroded away. Jody mentioned stopping there when you go for your horseback ride."

A small herd of antelope began racing away, spooked by the noise of the plane. "We have a few antelope, but they seem to just pass through. We never see them in the winter."

I flew over the same gully that yielded the two big Mule deer bucks yesterday. They ran out from the bottom again. "We have too many deer. The boys do hunt them, but don't make a dent in the population. Three deer a year means we lose ground by eight or ten. Coyotes are our biggest problem. They kill a calf or two every year."

Frank was silent for a few minutes, then asked, "How do you know Bill Davis?"

I did not flinch, act surprised, or show any noticeable emotion. "He invited me to join his daily coffee group one morning at Betty's Breakfast Bar in Bozeman. He introduced me to some of his friends. Why do you ask?"

"Bill and I have been friends for over fifty years. My ranch is as big as it can get. The seven parcels we abut are all bigger. The debt to buy any of them would most likely make cashflow damn difficult.

"You also know Sylvia Delany, who still owns her 26,000 thousand acres near Judith Gap. You arranged her finances, so her two sons, one married and the other, not yet, can stay debt-free, while sharing the common watershed. They each have a large parcel. They need to share the water shed or one of them would be without. Either can buy the other's share, but know the debt would be huge. They seem happy.

"I have talked to my boys. Gary and Jody want to stay here and be ranchers. Jimmy wants a marina and fishing guide service on Fort Peck. I am telling you all this because Sylvia recommended you. I hope to hire you, so Meg and I and family can put things together. We have our thoughts, and did talk to an attorney, but neither Meg or I liked his approach. Frankly, all he saw were dollar signs.

"You will meet our other two boys tonight. They are trailering four horses. We will not talk of this now. If you choose to add us as a client, we will start in earnest. We don't expect an answer this trip. We want you to study the situation properly, then come see us again.

"Jody thinks you are special. When he first told us about you, he said, "I don't know why Dad, we just vibe.""

CHAPTER 20

Jody had lunches packed and a duffle with some gear. He also carried a Savage 223 with Bausch and Lomb's best optics.

"Is it okay to bring the coyote gun? I can put it back if you want."

"It is okay with me, but I follow all laws and regs."

"I agree. Dad always wants us to buy all licenses and tags. He won't let us be illegal. We have two neighbors that poach a deer now and then. I have a couple of things to show you from the air today. Tomorrow, we ride the horses to the original Cummings homestead."

"I hope I do not fly into Canada."

"No chance Del, we won't even fly over our northern neighbors. I'll show you where we can land. It's on the edge of a soybean field, right next to the creek." Jody pointed out landmarks, described the crops in each field, then asked me how low would I fly.

"Just off the ground if we need to, why?"

"We're going to buzz *Stinky Hollow*, you'll see. We got rid of a skunk family from that gully, so it is now called, Stinky Hollow." Jody pointed out the largest gully on the ranch. "Let's fly over that draw and watch what happens."

I turned the plane and lined up, making a pass from the opening to the narrow point at the top of the low mesa. I stayed close to tree top level. "Wow!" he yelled, as twenty Mule deer raced out of the draw. One magnificent buck and three others that would be shooters for any hunter.

"That big one did not get that big by being dumb. Next time I visit you, I will study his movements. Have you seen him before, Jody?"

"Not sure, we always see some nice ones, but he could be here because we got maybe forty does around, and he would be king of the hill. Let's fly north to the end of our property and then follow the creek back to the house. After a few minutes, he suggested turning south and following the creek about a hundred feet above ground level.

I am 120 feet above the altimeter reading at your house."

"Perfect. We might see some whitetail along the creek."

"Any fish in that creek?" I asked.

"Not much, because it gets too muddy. We are pretty careful not to pollute. Still, it is very muddy from spring runoff to late fall."

We saw a dozen whitetail deer, but no quality bucks, then a wisp of smoke caught our eye. "Is that a wisp of smoke up ahead at the edge of the trees? Sure, looks like it to me."

"I think so too, Del. Can you land on the strip between the trees and the alfalfa?"

I landed into a light breeze at 55 knots. The touchdown was as slow as I dared, and a soft start the wheels rolling landing. We taxied back far enough to be ready for a takeoff.

Jody was out and running toward the origin of the thin rising smoke. He stayed at least fifteen feet from the small campfire. "They didn't do a good job of dousing the fire. Looks like two small tents were here, and both people wore hiking threads. These bastards come through here once or twice a month. They hike at night carrying drugs or money.

"We tell the sheriff every time we have evidence. He comes out, takes pictures and snoops around, but we never get a report of anything happening. The Sutherlands live between us and Canada. They have written the governor. We have never heard of any arrests. For the most part, they just trespass—don't cause trouble, steal anything or vandalize. Dad won't let us boys go after them. He says that would only bring trouble."

We stayed away from the evidence, and Jody called the sheriff. "Sheriff Dolan please. Jordan this is Jody Cummings. I am standing next to a drug runners camp on our ranch."

A short pause. "Yes, sir. We can wait. Come along the creek fence. That will bring you right to us." Turning to me, "Sheriff says twenty minutes. I hope you don't mind, 'cause this is the freshest camp we have ever found. Maybe there's some evidence he can use."

"It is just fine to wait. How long have you had this problem?"

"We saw the first camp about three years ago. Gary took a quad to the creek about then. An old dead cottonwood tree had blown down and blocked the creek. Water was overflowing into the alfalfa, and it was time for the first cut. He used the quad to break the tree loose, so the creek could return to the channel. He walked downstream a-ways, to make sure the water was going where it should, and found this camp that had been used more than once. It's about an hour walk from here to Highway 2. Since that first time, we check when we can, and have seen other camps, but never any people."

"I hear a car, Jody."

The sheriff arrived driving a dark gray Buick Enclave. "Howdy, Jody. Thanks for waiting for me."

"Afternoon, Sheriff. This a family friend, Del."

"Nice to meet you Del. Where're you from?"

"Nice to meet you as well. I am from Great Falls. The plane is mine."

"I knew you were around, got a couple of calls the last two days. Let's take a look."

Sheriff Dolan used a ruler and took some pictures of footprints and the entire scene. He motioned us closer to where the tents had been. The sheriff tried to look professional. Toby and I looked at each other and smiled. The sheriff appeared to us to be lost. He didn't video anything.

"We can look closer now." They were about to end their investigation when Jody called to the sheriff and me.

"Sheriff, I think that cigarette butt is fresh," pointing to a used cigarette on the ground.

The sheriff examined the butt, took an evidence bag out of his pocket, and using tweezers, picked it up and sealed it in the bag. "This is a hand-rolled marijuana smoke. This may help us catch someone," he remarked as he studied the camp more thoroughly a second time.

"If the same people come through, and we catch them, we will have proof they were here at least once before. This is as close as we have ever been, I doubt they are still around. We think a traveler comes to pick up the walkers up. There is a turnout by the bridge. They must be gone in minutes."

They all walked to the patrol car.

"Jody, thank you again. I'm going to head back and process this evidence. Nice to meet you, Del."

After the sheriff was gone, Jody said, "He's from Salt Lake City, or so he said. He ran against both deputies after Sheriff Williams retired. He barely won. The two deputies have decided to work together to get rid of Jordan. He's nice enough, he just never arrests anyone and refuses to go on the reservation. He drives around a lot. The deputies have agreed, whoever gets the biggest buck this fall, will get to run for sheriff.

I did not tell Jody that I took a really good picture of the sheriff while he was snooping around the campsite. I will ask Cliff to check on this guy.

"Is Sheriff Doland based in Glasgow?"

"No Malta, as our ranch is 80% in Phillip's County. The rest in Valley, that's Glasgow."

"How far is Malta?" I asked.

"Thirty-three miles to our ranch, why?"

"He arrived here in eighteen minutes. He had to know we would notice."

"He could have been on the road somewhere close, Del."

"Yes, he could. We should get back to flying."

1 noticed Sheriff Jordan took a sip of coffee from a convenience store type of paper cup, barely tipping it to take his drink. He had to be in Saco at the gas station when he took the call. Will be interesting to see what the FBI says.

CHAPTER 21

inally returning to the airplane, we started a short flight over Fort Peck Reservoir and the marinas on the lake.

"I didn't realize how big the lake was, with so many bays. It would take a lifetime to fish all of it. Jimmy wants to be a guide here. He has been studying all kinds of places to fish, all over the world. He watches all the fishing shows on TV. My other brother and I love ranching and want to stay at home. One person working the ranch could not do everything to keep things operating like it should."

"Have you and Gary talked about sharing the ranch and the work?" I asked.

"Some, but we haven't gotten to the final stages yet. Kinda hard to know what to do and what is fair."

"Jody, I hope to trailer my boat and fish a week or so on this big lake. There are at least fifty bays around the perimeter of Fort Peck Reservoir with lots of walleyes. And I want to catch at least one *paddlefish*."

"Me and my brother never got into fishing. Jimmy has started and is hooked. Get it? Hooked." Jody laughed at his joke. He likes to laugh. I find I am enjoying my stay here with the Cummings family more than I ever expected.

"Maybe when you bring your boat to fish in Fort Peck, I'll go with you and Jimmy. Jimmy told me he isn't going to do rodeo anymore. He says he's tired of being sore all summer. Gary and I knew he just tried because we love rodeoing. Gary rides broncs pretty well and wins money at almost every rodeo we go to. I do broncs and bulls, but only won money twice. I'll know when it's time to quit. Gary and I like to travel together." Jody paused to just watch out the window.

"You want to try flying?" I asked.

"Sure, I'll give it a go," he answered with a big smile.

"Just one rule, Jody. If I say, 'I have the plane' you let go of the wheel."

"Sure thing."

"*Smooth* is the word, Jody. Have some fun."

"God, I'm all over the place. You make it look so easy."

"I have the plane." Jody let go, and I proceeded with a two-hundred-foot climb, then back to level at five hundred feet above the ground. "Your turn."

A serious side that I had not witnessed before appeared. Jody started his climb, barely moving the wheel as he had seen me do. "Man, I only missed by a hundred feet, and then back to level by fifty."

"Really not too bad for your first try. We will fly straight and level for a while."

Jody kept the plane within fifty feet of level, but was in a slow right turn. "I'm turning some ain't I?"

"Yes Jody, easy to do with a dominate hand. I have the plane."

Jody let go, then I flew for about ten minutes, putting the 182 through many maneuvers. Sharp turns, climbs and descents, then climbed to four thousand feet and did a soft stall. "This is a stall, which means the plane is not really flying. If you do go take some lessons, you will learn how to recover from those." Jody let out a gasp and reached for something to hold on to.

"I do not have enough power for the nose angle of the plane. Power on. Nose down and instantly the light stall is gone."

"Gee planes can do a lot. I'm going to talk to dad and then go to Glasgow and give learning to fly a go."

After parking the plane, Jody smiled and said, "Let's go saddle the horses, so we can ride a while before supper. Gary and Jimmy will be home around six or so."

CHAPTER 22

Jody saddled both horses, put his foot in the left stirrup and easily slid into his saddle. I watched and followed suit. Jody went through the basics, showing me how to use the reins and knees, then uttered a clicking noise and both horses started a leisurely walk. We silently rode straight to the original homestead.

"Not much of it left, Del. We talked about repairing it, but decided we wouldn't. It's hard to imagine surviving the long winters. They had enough wood it seems, but it had to be so damn cold."

"Yes." I answered. "Those early settlers had a lot of challenges. Today we have drug hikers."

We rode for two hours, with Jody talking about ranching, horses, cows, and rodeos. Turning back toward the buildings, he said, "How are you holding up as a cowboy? Let's go back and drink a beer on the porch."

"I am holding up fine, but might be a bit sore tomorrow, I do see why you like to ride. That beer sounds great." I dusted off my new gray cowboy hat and put it back on.

Jody directed me to the porch as he took care of the horses. He selected two beers and joined me, sat down, picked up his beer, and took a sip. Frank and Meg returned from a grocery trip to

Glasgow. Jody helped haul things into the house, doing the lion's share. After everything found its designated place, Jody, Meg and Frank also selected chairs on the thirty-foot long porch that spanned the entire front of the house.

"Not many mosquitos around," I commented.

"There are only some in early spring," answered Meg. "We spray once in late spring and do not have stagnant water around. That seems to take care of the pests."

A dark maroon 4X4 Ram truck arrived near 5:30, pulling a four-stall horse trailer and parked near the stable. Gary and Jimmy unloaded four animals that seemed eager to be out of the trailer and touching the ground. The brothers paraded them into the stable.

Then they approached the house. Both greeted their parents first, then offered their hands as Jody introduced me. Firm handshakes from two more sons that looked like their mother.

Gary barbequed the steaks, Jimmy prepared the potatoes and carrots. and Jody took care of the table. Meg just watched.

"My boys take good care of me, Del. When it's calving season, haying season, crop gathering season, and sometimes hunting season, I do *all* the work. Otherwise, I get spoiled. Are you leaving tomorrow?"

"Yes, I must. I am mostly retired, but till have nineteen clients. I am scheduled to meet with two of them on Friday, so I need to get back to Great Falls tomorrow and get my act in order. This has been a special few days for me. I will return, if you will have me, to fish Fort Peck and do some hunting.

"You will always be welcome here," pipped up Jody.

"Thank you for the plane ride. I may wish to do that again," beamed Meg.

"We can have a little fun next time and let you fly some."

The flight back to Great Falls was uneventful. As soon as I landed, I called Cliff. I will need his help with the drug traffic problem on the Cummings Ranch.

CHAPTER 23

When I called Cliff on the special number that only we shared, Cliff answered on the second ring. "Afternoon, Del. How was the trip to Saco?"

"It passed by too quickly. They are wonderful people. I will be going back soon to fish Fort Peck."

That said, I have a name for you. When you check, it must be 200% secure. If he is what I suspect, someone somewhere will tip him off, and he will know it came from me. Worst of all, it would put a beautiful family at risk." I told him the whole story about the camp, the history of the trespassers, and the sheriff. I detailed his clumsy attempt to gather evidence, also mentioned the coffee cup used by the sheriff taking a minimal drink.

"Very thorough, Del. We do a regional listing of drug dealer's names. The whole drug community knows this list, and believe being on it can help them. They know to be extra careful, or go to ground. They know the list is not an arrest on sight list. Who is the possible?"

"Jordan Dolan. He is the new sheriff of Phillips County in Montana. He beat out the two local deputies because they split the vote, and he barely won. The word around town is he said he is from Salt Lake City, but he could be a plant from anywhere."

"Just a sec, let me see if he is on last month's list. Charlene checked all of the Western US, and he is not on any list."

"Let me send you the picture of him, as I am 99% sure he did not see me take it. He is near the bottom of the drug culture," I answered. Then I sent the picture and received a 'got it' answer.

"Del, I will be in Great Falls for at least a week, possibly more. I am hoping you can stay as well. The Bureau will put you up, and cover everything. Keep good records.

Back in Great Falls, I stocked up for a week. Then went to the Queen Club for the seafood special. As soon as I sat at my table, I noticed a Lion's Club friend, Murray Lawton and his wife Zoe, sitting at another table. Completing my order, a strode over the greet them.

Zoe spoke first, "We heard about Amy. Please accept our condolences."

"For sure," echoed Murray. "A beautiful lady. We haven't seen you around."

"I couldn't stay here, so moved to Bozeman. I still have a few clients, but am mostly retired. I like it there. I spend some wintertime in Arizona. You remember Dutch?"

"Sure do. We heard he sold his business."

"Yes, he lives in Florida now." Murray was a realtor, so I asked, "Could you find me a duplex in Great Falls, preferably around the Russell Museum?"

"Glad to, Del. I should have a list of options in a week or less. Here's my card. Call me anytime." We exchanged phone numbers, and I returned to my table when their food arrived.

Johnny occupied a table behind the Lawton's. He looked just like the picture Cliff had provided for me to study. Cliff's picture showed only his face. The rest of him would be a handful. I did not know anything about his processes or his habits. Cliff and I needed to share some information. Johnny did not look unfriendly, just serious. Cliff told me about Johnny, but I had not expected to see him during this stay in Great Falls. Johnny is the UC Cliff was fretting over.

I realized he had heard my entire conversation with Murray and his wife. Johnny knew nothing about me until now. I wondered if our paths might cross again.

CHAPTER 24

The next morning, I left the motel dressed to spend the day fishing the Missouri River south of the city. Reaching one of my favorite spots, I parked at the pullout. Then carefully I negotiated the rocks down to the river. I cast my line into the fast current, letting it drift into an eddy. A strike on the first cast. I reeled in a twelve-inch rainbow, then released it, and cast a second time. No strike this time, so I let the current move the salmon eggs, hoping for another fish.

I decided to call Cliff. He answered on the second ring. "Morning, Del. How's the room?"

"Perfect. I am stocked up for a week's stay as you asked, and ate at the Queen Club. Their seafood special is one of the best meals I have ever enjoyed. Cliff, I am not sure why I am here. I noticed a realtor friend eating there with his wife, so visited with him and asked him to find a duplex that I could buy to set up as an office. I could cover my costs by renting the other half. Also, Dutch would have a place to stay when he visits from Florida.

"Cliff, I saw your undercover person, Johnny at a nearby table. He looks very fit. Do you have anything on the Malta sheriff?"

"The picture you sent us looked a bit blurry, but I directed an agent to look back at the election and found six better pictures. We are using some software to compare those to known criminals from Salt Lake City. We think Jordan Dolan is an alternate ID. We will know in a week or so. How long can you stay in Great Falls?"

"I can stay 'till next Wednesday, but then must return to Bozeman. What am I to do for you, Cliff?"

"I'm not prepared to involve you yet. Things did not go as I hoped. I will come see you in Bozeman when we get reorganized. You should check-out and return to Bozeman. How big of a town is Malta?"

"Around 4,500 or so," I answered. "Cliff, how would I go about finding a person from 8-9 years ago?"

After a very long pause, he asked, "Why?"

"I may have a tip for the FBI. I want to practice my detective skills, before I do anything. Could be nothing or a smuggling group."

"I have to think about how much access I can let you have to our data bases. We monitor those types of inquiries. If I gave you my entry codes, I would have to know, who, what, where and why. I suspect you aren't ready to do that."

"You are right, Cliff. I am not. Could you have Billy provide me with a list of long-distance commercial drivers in Montana by city for say six to ten years back? Also, one person attorney offices."

"Consider it done. Mail to Bozeman?"

"Perfect Cliff. Thank you. If I am right, I will need you."

"Be seeing you soon. Godspeed."

"Always." I will abandon the motel and return to Bozeman.

CHAPTER 25

"ood morning, Meg. I just wanted to call and thank you again for having me at your home and in my own special house. Thank you."

"You're welcome here anytime. Jody has taken a deep liking to you. He loves his parents, but seems to really like having another older friend. Everyone likes Jody. I'll bet he didn't tell you he is Malta's most decorated athlete ever." I felt I could see the smile on Meg's face.

"No, he did not. He only talked about rodeo riding."

"Del, thank you for the call. Jody is in the kitchen would you like to speak with him?"

"Yes, please."

"Hello, Del. I rode one of the new horses this morning, and he tried to throw me. Made me laugh 'cause he didn't know I do rodeo bulls. We are friends now. A question. Do you think we should put up some game cameras?"

"My first thought was to say no, but if you do, you must do four or five, and put up a tree stand or two. Have you ever used cameras or stands?"

"No, we haven't. We just ride quads or a horse to the draw we want to hunt, we know where the deer spend their time."

"Do you know where the coyote dens are?"

"Generally, but we don't take the time to hunt them. Why?"

"I think the drug teams are used to not being watched. They just hide if some of you show up to do crop work. They mostly pass your place in the dark. They may know the lay of the land better than we believe." We thought about that for a sec.

"If you do put up cameras, they cannot be where you have seen camps. You can only put them where deer trails are. Buy decent stands with ladders and put two by the creek and one by 'stinky' hollow. Put them up soon. I feel it is imperative the walkers see them in place long before hunting season. Then go shoot at a coyote once in a while. Start carrying a rifle with you whenever you are out alone. Gary and Jimmy should carry the same gun, and shoot at a coyote a time or two.

"Did you tell your family what we saw, and about the sheriff?"

"Yes. The whole story. We don't have secrets in our family. My mom was upset, and my dad was angry. We can't come up with a solution. So far, the hikers have not vandalized, bothered the family, or stolen stuff. They just sneak through. The law never catches our trespassers."

"Jody, talk to your family about my suggestions. If it were me, I would avoid the walkers, just as they avoid you. They want to be unnoticed. You can show signs that you check the cameras, with quad tracks, and footprints. Try to be casual and nonchalant. Go check often on a schedule, say every week on a Wednesday. They will notice that. If a camera is stolen or damaged, just replace it. Keep a couple of spares at your stable or on the quad.

"Start a log of everything you see, only dates and facts. Do not bother to include the sheriff. How well do you know the deputies?"

"I wrestled with Bronte Williams. He was a year ahead of me. He's Sheriff William's nephew. I like him, but we don't run with the same crowd. Darell Booth is the other deputy. I don't him know well, as he is from Glasgow. Wow. Del, that is a lot you came up with."

"Yes, it is, Jody. I have a cabin on some acreage near Lincoln. I made it a point to become acquainted with the local game warden. A couple of trespassers stole a camera from my property. The game warden came up with a plan similar to what I just gave you. Then my camera caught them coming through a second time and recorded good pictures. Two young men from Lincoln. The warden showed them the pictures and warned them. Later, they came up to my table while I ate breakfast at Lambkins in Lincoln and apologized. They also handed me a new camera.

"Your walkers are criminals, low level ones, but criminals just the same. Criminals are not stupid. They just do stupid things. Most don't want to spend a moment in jail."

"Del, I can speak for my family. I will talk to the family and let you know what we decide to do. We are damn lucky to have you as part of our family. Keep the sun at your back, Del. Dad said to tell you he will call you in a week or so."

"And friends beside me. Jody, take care and call me anytime."

CHAPTER 26

I needed to travel to Casa Grande, Arizona before the daytime temperatures started reaching 90 degrees. I wished to check on the progress of the tutoring arrangement for local children that I established eight or nine months ago. I will fly this time, making a stop in Cheyenne, Wyoming, then on to Mesa to park the plane, then rent a car.

I called Ernesto.

"Holla, Del. Are you coming to our little town?"

"Si, Ernesto. I will be there Sunday evening sometime. Will you let me take your family to dinner at Dos Tacos on Monday at six-thirty?"

"Si, I will arrange that. We have much to talk about."

CHAPTER 27

I left Bozeman, Thursday at nine a.m., taking my time to fly over the mountains of Yellowstone Park. You can see lots of geysers from a thousand feet above them. Two erupted during my short flight over the park.

Landing in Cheyenne, I checked on a rental car. The only one left smelled like smoke. I declined, then took a cab to the Best Western Motel across the highway from my storage rental. I changed my appearance to become Spencer Morgan at the storage unit. At dusk, I walked the mile to the Cowboy Brew Pub. My alternate identity, as Spencer, was based in Cheyenne, and plays the role of a cowboy. He looked thirty pounds heavier than me. I kept enough items in the storage unit to easily make the change.

A Lagunitas IPA and a Reuben sandwich with tots, served by a twenties-something young cowgirl, spiced up my day. I sat at the bar as the place was packed. The bartender remembered me. "You haven't been here in months."

Looking at his name tag, "Quill, I don't live in Wyoming. I stop here when I fly from Montana to New Mexico or Arizona. I like your place and the food. I very much like the airport."

"Glad you stopped in. I forgot your name."

"Spencer. Quill, would you consider giving me a reference or two that I could use to hunt antelope?"

"I can do better than a reference. I have a typed list of seven outfitters I would use. Let me get you one." Returning with the list he added, "Everything you need is on the list. Being close to the airport, I get this question so often, I decided to make the list."

"Thanks, Quill, got an errand to run. I hope to be back in a couple of weeks."

I went to the storage unit that contained a used gray Ram truck and enough essentials to allow me to hide there, if I ever needed to.

Last fall, I stopped at the Cheyenne Regional Airport on my way back from a pheasant hunting trip to Madison, South Dakota. An alternate ID, Sven Hansen, owns a small house there.

While securing my plane, a small Hispanic man walking briskly came out of the general aviation office and approached me, acting unfriendly it seemed to me. He asked me why I parked my plane next to his new Bonanza. He acted tough, and I was positive he was carrying. He told me he would watch for me. His Bonanza 36 was not here today. I will check my plane before I leave for Mesa in the morning. I believed this new plane to be involved either with drugs or human trafficking, just because he disturbed my worry meter.

I drove my Ram to Safeway, gave my storage unit supply of water to a Hispanic couple. I purchased a fresh supply of water for Spencer's hideaway, and the fixings for a sandwich for the flight tomorrow. I checked in at the Best Western, watched a fishing show, then slept like a baby. No, I do not snore.

A beautiful flying day greeted me. I would cover Western Colorado enjoying the scenery and the solitude. I could smell

Meg's presence in the plane and it excited me. In Mesa, I arranged for fuel, secured the tiedowns and walked to the casino to check in. I rarely gamble, but do get my casino card and donate enough to get special room rates. I sat at the bar, nursing an average IPA and playing a poker machine.

After half an hour, I was ready to cash out and call it a day, when I hit a jackpot royal flush for $4,500. Most I have ever won in any casino. Smiling is easier sometimes.

I always have my rental car delivered the morning I need it. I could have just picked it up when I arrived. I have over three million dollars, but still cannot spend money I do not need to spend. Arizona winter weather is mostly perfect. A TV lady predicted a high of eighty-two tomorrow. Sure, beats Bozeman's chilly thirty-eight degrees.

My car showed up right on time. I wanted to stop at the main library in Mesa and check the newspapers for possible *adventures*. Ajani Bustamante, a Jamaican drug dealer, lived in St Petersburg, Florida. He received a notice that he will be deported. His court date to be determined. The word on the street says no more than two weeks. I had all the details worked out for him, as I did complete an *adventure* there last year. But I located a new hidden spot for the shot and a safer escape route. Two policemen at my door, after I shot Diaz, scared me deeply.

My best friend, Dutch, moved into a modular house we own together. I will get to see him, and go fishing. The *adventure* in Lincoln, Nebraska will happen soon. The lady coming to trial there had a string of killings in at least five states.

After a week, I flew commercial to Fort Lauderdale, and set my *adventure* plan in motion. I kept a locker for fishing gear in Fort Lauderdale. It also held one of my best long-distance rifles. I have collected five newer rifles to date, all from private sources. Most new shooters find long distance shooting to be too difficult to learn, so they sell their rifles at a discount. Only one asked to do a bill of sale.

My chosen shooting location was in a run-down vacant building in a room on the third floor, exactly 982 yards from the target. May have to clean my shooting location after I shoot, as there is evidence of people camping here. This will be my longest shot not on a range.

The location in that vacant building has a window opening with a broken pane that allowed the rifle to be positioned far enough back to contain most of the sound in the room. Rick found me a high-quality new suppressor that should help with the noise. I believe he senses I am the new shooter of bad guys.

One of the busiest highways in all of Florida, passes just below my building's window. Almost every car going by will be using air-conditioning with their windows rolled up.

The rental car was to be parked on the street, occupying the first spot next to the alley facing the traffic light. No one can park in front of it. I intend to drive to the light and enter traffic. If any hitch shows, I will go down the alley instead. Getting to the car only exposes me for about twelve seconds.

My plan was in place. If I am too late, there will always be other opportunities. They said the court date was set for the twelfth, a Friday. I did not believe it would be on a Friday. They must have learned from the first dead Jamaican, and were setting up a safe day. I will hide out in my vacant room starting Wednesday morning. I stayed all day until six p.m. no action Wednesday.

My car was parked. It was Thursday nearing six a.m. After a long tense wait, a police-caravan arrived at nine-thirty, two cars and a van. Bustamante stepped out of the van onto the first step. I checked to make sure it was him using my spotting scope, then rechecked my numbers, knowing precision about my numbers was critical. I pulled the trigger. Bustamante fell to the concrete sidewalk. He did not move. *Number 6, Curt.* I packed my rifle in its backpack case. Cleaned up after myself and descended the stairs to the broken back door.

A glance both ways proved me to be alone. As casually as I dared, I walked to my car, dressed as Spencer. Placing my rifle in its backpack on the back seat, I started the car and entered traffic on my side street, three cars back waiting for the green light. I felt totally stressed, a slow crawling itch nagged deeply. I was unable to get used to feeling scared about going to jail. I was not ready to stop the *adventures*, but may need to take a break after the Nebraska one. Stopping at a convenience store with an outside restroom, I changed from Spencer to myself.

I entered the busy throughfare and blended into traffic. An hour later, I secured my rifle in the locker after another renter departed. I could not have anyone see me storing a rifle. Sure, it was in a soft case, but people know about those. Ten seconds of exposure could mean someone mentioning what they saw to the police.

I decided I could not press my luck for a long time in Florida. Too many other places to use for my adventures.

Later, Spencer flew commercial to Phoenix. Then, I called Dutch in Florida.

CHAPTER 28

"Hello, Del. When you coming down to Florida? Word is the Tarpon are around."

"I will be in Fort Lauderdale late this evening, Dutch, so see if Dillion can take us fishing soon, I can stay three days. Cliff has a job for me next week."

"I'll talk to Dillon right now. I found a used car. So tell me when you arrive, and I'll pick you up,"

"I arrive at nine-thirty tonight on United 2323. It will be good to see you."

When I arrived at the airport, I watched a news story explaining that Bustamante had been killed at nine-thirty-eight this morning, by persons unknown.

Dutch arrived as soon as I walked out with my bag. A quality handshake in the car, and a nervous Dutch found his way back to our house.

"I got a couple routes I know kind of well. But this is way different than little Great Falls."

"You will be a pro in no time Dutch. It is great to see you. How's your job?"

"Del, helping these kids learn the stuff I took for granted is the best job I've ever had. I love it. I now work four days a week, and net enough to cover all my expenses. I don't like the humidity much, but I am happy, and that's what counts in my book."

"Well, Dutch, seeing you happy, counts in my book."

CHAPTER 29

aptain Colton Peterson of the St Petersburg Police Department called a late afternoon meeting, which included all department heads.

"How did we lose Bustamante? We told the media his court date would happen on Friday. He was killed today! We are not going to publish court dates anymore. The media won't like that, but we cannot lose another, and look like we are incompetent."

A voice in the back of the room asked, "Do we feel it is the same shooter?"

"We can only guess, but I'll bet some big bucks it is. Too much is similar. We never found a lead on the Diaz shooting, and we are not going to find a lead on this one. This shooter is a quality planner, and shoots from big yardages. There must be thousands of shooters that could do this. I don't even know where to start."

"Captain, is it okay for me to check some fight data around both shootings?" asked Betty Sellers.

"Go ahead, if you have time. But I think this shooter plans things to avoid seeing his name on flight lists. That could make him vulnerable, and he knows that. I'll bet the shooter is disguised, and if anyone saw him, he would look a hundred percent different by the time he traveled an hour away from the shot.

"He is a risk taker, but very capable. He knows guns and how to use them. He shot a bad criminal, and he knew all about that before he risked even coming to Florida. I'll bet he was here days before he made the shot. Before I called this meeting, I reread everything on the Diaz shooting. It looks the same to me. I think he will avoid us for a while. Let's get back to work. We will work any leads we get, but we have so much on our plate now that we can't keep up. Be careful as always."

Betty did look at all the flight manifests. No names surfaced on inbound flights that matched outbound flights. She filed the many flight-lists away.

CHAPTER 30

utch and I fished two days with Dillon on the Baby Bird and both of us caught a tarpon. They were smallish at thirty pounds or so. The weather shined perfectly both days. No real big fish, but Dutch caught a ninety-pound tiger shark. He was so happy, he just danced and hugged everyone. Bo was our deck hand and treated us extra special. Seeing Dutch so happy made me smile.

Dutch was my, *I will* help you at all costs—*no questions asked, go-to friend.* I hope I never have to ask.

"Del. You seem a little on edge today," a smiling Dutch said as we drove away from the pier after fishing the first day. "You need a joke? What's a deer's favorite ice cream?"

I didn't respond.

"Chocolate chip cookie doe?" Dutch laughed.

I ignored the joke, "Yes, I noticed that myself. I think I have forced myself to stay busy, since Amy died, and avoided coming to grips with her not being with me. I will change that. I need to affect that closure as soon as I can. Hopefully, I have many years left to live. Staying in the past is detrimental. I know Amy would understand. All of my friends, old and new will help with that. Thanks for caring…Where are you getting these lame jokes?"

"Yes. I care, and you are welcome. I'll never be able to thank you for all the times you've taken care of me. Helping to sell my business alone is off the chart. If you ever need anything, you'd better call on me…A kid in welding class brings them."

"Dutch, tell him those lame jokes could affect his grade."

Two days of fishing gave me a lot of time to think, and I released most of my stress. Dutch and I used the third day to drive to Cape Canaveral and watched a rocket launch. Witnessing that kind of power was mesmerizing and beyond spectacular. After learning to fly the Air Force way, I applied to become an astronaut. I received a nice letter declining my application.

I would commit to the Nebraska *adventure*. Then I would study the Seattle one, and the Little Rock one. Taking care to bring myself back to the unstressed Del, would become more important than the *adventures*. I felt at peace more than anytime, since I embarked on my *adventures*.

Amy would notice that I held her hand the whole time I was on the boat.

CHAPTER 31

The first morning after returning to Bozeman, I rode the bus to the library, but detoured to buy a scone and coffee. Mable was at her table and waved for me to join her.

"How have you been, Del?

"Just busy, I guess. You look extra spiffy today."

"Well, It's my 88th birthday."

"Happy birthday! Can you let me buy you a treat today?"

"If you insist. I have not had anyone to share my birthday with in 21 years, so thank you. You have been gone."

"Yes, I still have a few clients, and see them when I go fishing, hunting, or traveling. I am mostly a private person."

"So, you won't tell me your life's story."

"No, Mable. Something tells me we will become good friends. But I am sure you are not ready to tell your story and did not expect me to. Right?"

"Yes, you are right. I like you, and do feel we will become better friends."

"I cannot stay long. I must go to Arizona, so I need to make my library stop. Again, happy birthday. I think we should go for a walk next time I am here."

"I will look forward to that walk," she answered with a nod.

At the library, I checked on the four possible *adventures* I was tracking. The Nebraska one will be soon. I must be ready. St. Petersburg is now in the rearview mirror. I called Cliff and left a message with Charlene. I had a plan about the twins and Michelle.

CHAPTER 32

I called Cliff. He answered on the second ring. "Morning, Del. What's up?"

"Where are you regarding the note I sent? Are you in Salt Lake? And can you disguise yourself as a homeless person, and try to get on my city bus, in Bozeman?"

"I have an agent at the Bureau working on it, but haven't checked lately. I am in Salt Lake, and I know how to look homeless. What do you need me for?"

"If you can include a bodycam, you could get some good pictures of the twins and even Michelle. The twins ride the same bus I use every Tuesday, and are already on when I board at nine a.m., sitting in the back of the bus.

"Sanford, the regular driver will not let you ride for free, so I could offer to pay your fare. I will offer you a breakfast sandwich at the Daily Coffee, across the street from the library."

"I like it, when should we do it?"

"Will next Tuesday work for you Cliff?"

"Perfect," he hung up.

The following Tuesday, as I boarded the bus, I glanced casually at the passengers, and the twins were sitting near the back. "*Good.*" I mumbled to myself. I needed Cliff to see them. It is tough to remain casual when a plan is working.

The twins, sat in separate seats. They never looked happy about anything.

"Morning, Sanford, how are you today?" I greeted the regular weekday driver.

"Fair to middlin', library for you today?" he asked.

"Yes, as the new books are available today," I answered. "I could use a couple."

"Well, then we should coast on down there."

Two stops later, a scruffy, disheveled man asked to ride the bus. Cliff looked the part, everything in tatters.

"The city won't let you ride for free," scowled Sanford.

"I don't have any money, I'm just tired." His shoulders dropped, and he started to turn away.

"Sanford, I will pay his fare, and we will both get off at the library."

"Okay, Del, it's your call, but I don't like those homeless guys getting things for free."

"I will talk to him about his plight, over a cup of coffee at Mable's."

"Thank you, sir. Thank you," he uttered as he selected the first seat behind Sanford.

I paid his fare, and on my way back to my usual seat, I said to the homeless guy. "We will get off at the library, and I will buy you a breakfast," (making sure Sanford heard me).

Just a nod of understanding. He not only looked the part, he smelled it as well. I almost changed seats to move back out of smelling range. I could tell Sanford did not enjoy Cliff directly behind him.

The twins liked to be first off the bus. I told Cliff that during our planning. They were already standing when we reached the library. I fussed with my newspaper like always, and let them pass my seat. Cliff stood and entered the aisle just as the twins went by, bumping into the lead person of the pair.

"Sorry," he grunted, and backed out of the aisle, to let them pass in front of him. The hidden bodycam captured them both.

The twins ignored him and hurried off the bus.

There is often a soft breeze whistling up the street from the south, so I directed Cliff to the northern most outdoor table, then went inside.

I returned with a breakfast sandwich, a cinnamon roll and dark roast coffee for each of us. Cliff didn't look up, just acted uncomfortable, took a sip of his coffee, then a bite of his sandwich. He pretended to weakly smile at me.

Zella showed up with a refill of coffee for both of us. I knew she was being extra nosy and smelled this morning like Michelle did the day she held the door for me. I am now positive she's a good close friend to Michelle.

"Who's your friend, Del?"

"He boarded my bus and looked like he could use a breakfast, so I am being the good Samaritan today."

"We get homeless looking people once in a while. Mable will help them if they don't cause trouble, but never lets them become regulars. She just walks up to them and talks to them nicely. Enjoy your treats. Mable will be here next Tuesday." Zella briskly walked away.

Cliff just ate. No more conversation. The twins sat at their regular table and ignored us. Michelle arrived, wearing her traditional jalabiya. She entered the café and returned with coffee and breakfast for herself and the twins. They talked softly using Farsi, I guessed. Cliff recorded everything they said.

I stood up, looked at Cliff. "I am going to the library. You are welcome to stay and finish your coffee. Take care."

The gruff answer, only a mumbled, "Thank you."

I selected a chair next to the window at the library, so I could watch while reading the Journal. Cliff finished his breakfast, put his empty paper coffee cup in his pocket, fussed over his clothes, walked past the trio to the corner, crossed the street and shuffled away.

Waiting until Cliff left the area, Michelle reached into her plain brown jalabiya, gave each twin a small six-inch square black cloth packet. She returned to her apartment across the street. I took a phone picture of the exchange, but doubted it would prove useful.

A library employee pushed the new book cart into the aisle. I selected a Lee Child and a James Patterson, checked them out and left to catch my bus home. I knew Cliff would be at my house. I hoped he recorded everything possible.

Cliff was sitting on my patio when I returned.

"Interesting morning. I enjoyed being a rookie today. I have many good pictures and recorded most of their conversation. I will send all to the lab and see how much we can use."

"You want to clean up here? You sure came across as homeless and stunk worse than a skunk. How did you create that smell?" I asked.

"Great idea, you came up with, Del. The smell is real stuff rubbed into the clothes, then it's sealed up to use when needed. I'll need a ride to Walmart," as he packed his homeless clothes in a large plastic sealable bag.

"Full-service hotel here. The shuttle will take you when you are ready." I smiled at him with my hands spread wide.

Cliff paused, "Your plan may have provided enough information to find out what this group is up to. You surprise me often. You could be a mastermind criminal."

I did not react. This my first real sense, that Cliff suspected me of criminal activity.

Just a knowing smile, as he went into the bedroom he used every time he stayed here. Like, always, Cliff hid in the back of the crew cab and sneaked away in the parking lot.

"Godspeed."
"Always."

Late the next afternoon, Cliff called. "We now have all three identified and cataloged. We're working on a lot of things. But the traffic noise was too intense sometimes. They did mention Billings twice."

"Cliff, I have been meaning to go to Billings and see if a rancher or two will let me hunt pheasants and maybe whitetails along the Yellowstone River. I also hope to locate a guide service and fish for trout. I can do that next week, and see if I can find any connection to the codes in the note I found a few weeks ago. If they mentioned Billings, maybe the note refers there and not Bozeman. It is only 150 miles east of here. Nothing really military around Billings, but will use the library cross-reference book to work the numbers. I may check the internet, but those old cross-reference books should have what I need."

"They'll recognize you, Del."

"I have a solution for that. I will use one of my alternate ID's." Cliff helped me get those, but told me he has yet to ask for those facts. He does not know James Colbert owns a condo in Billings. I will stay at the four-unit rental apartment building Del owned, and James will canvas the town.

I did talk to two ranchers along the Yellowstone River. One already had a group of hunters coming opening day. The other told me I was very welcome to come and hunt., The rancher said, "If you are comfortable, I could join you."

"I would welcome your company," I answered.

"I have not had a hunting partner in five years. Both my hunting partners passed away then. We will find many birds. Thank you for stopping."

"I am excited to hunt those beautiful birds. See you on opening day." I drove back to Bozeman grinning from ear to ear.

I did travel to Lester Bryce's ranch and hunted with him four days. He lost both his hunting partners and his wife the same year. He and I agreed I could come and hunt every year for as long as I wished.

The last day his son joined us, Truman looked just like his dad. Six-foot-one, very lean, with a prominent nose and a narrow mouth. He liked to laugh and seemed to know hundreds of jokes.

I came back to Bozeman with nine cleaned birds. I had a wonderful time. Lucky for me to find Lester's ranch. I hoped to have Cliff join us next year.

CHAPTER 33

I drove to Billings, Montana, stopped to stock up my apartment for a week's stay. I did plan for James Colbert to operate out of his downtown condo and be the sleuth. I will have to use fake whiskers, so I can do some of the leg work.

"Good morning Mr. Colbert."

"Good morning, Johnathon. You have two small parcels for me?"

"I have them in my office, just a moment." Returning with both, he added, "I chose not to try to put them in your unit. I don't know your entry codes."

Ignoring him, James asked, "You have military bearing, Jonathon. Would you mind telling me what branch you served in?"

"I should have known you would guess. I was a procurement officer with the Coast Guard."

"Just answering questions in my mind, Johnathon. You seemed to be extra careful choosing words."

"James, I retired seven years ago and wanted to do something not tied to the military. I also wanted to live in Montana. I never visited this part of America. I landed in Billings, and the Sunday newspaper listed this job. I applied, and it became my new career. I like to know my tenants."

"What do you tell yourself about James Colbert?"

After a too long pause, he continued. "You are a self-made man, who likes things a certain way. You have military experience, and presently are not married, but have been. I sense you have a higher IQ than most. I don't have a complete picture of you yet."

"Pretty close. I will take my packages up to my condo, and see about some errands I must do. Thank You." strolling to the elevator, I revisited his comments. I worried he knew I was not as I wished to portray. His comment about me being married meant he had checked things about me.

I will sell the condo later this year, ask Cliff to arrange another alternate ID, and choose a different city for the new ID's residence. I would also move the hideaway money from Cancun. I will not stay in Billings as James again. Too risky.

I also will quit referring to errands as an excuse to move on; cannot have people noticing the similar wording.

I purposefully waited until after eight a.m. to go down to the car. I wanted to talk to Johnathon and confirm my suspicions.

I ambled out to my small veranda, sipped a dark roast coffee and ate a cinnamon roll, while watching the city come to life. The exhaust smells carried up to my third-floor mini patio, ruining the cinnamon roll smell. Nearly eight-thirty, I stepped out of the elevator. The last occupant had to be a woman who used expensive alluring perfume.

Johnathon sat at his desk, talking on the phone. He waved.

I proceeded to my garaged car and drove to the main library. Stopping at the front desk, I asked about the city cross-reference directories. The clerk directed me to a section near the front door.

I first checked the Little Rock *adventure*. Connel Cashman allegedly had a system where he picked up women at randomly selected bars. Eventually taking them to his apartment, he then drugged and raped them, sometimes keeping them for a week. He never believed he would be caught. But one of the women he kept for a week turned him in. Eight others came forward about their suffering at his hands and the terror they experienced.

He planned to spend his last dollar to stay out of prison. 'Cash' as he preferred to be called, retained a big-name attorney. I felt this *adventure* would be a long while before I needed to fly there. But I would complete my planning phase and fly there anyway to look around.

Spreading out my copy of the city map for Billings, I looked first for anything like 'Red Bottle'. Two items surfaced, a motel near Walmart and a bar near the freeway. Nothing anywhere used 'watermelon'. Looking for places with 225 in address, listed five residences and one industrial address east of the refinery.

My rental vehicle was an older white pickup, which I drove to Walmart and parked far away from the front door.

A few grocery items were in my cart, when I turned toward the coolers hoping to find some Lagunitas IPA. The twins and Michelle pushed two heavily loaded carts away from me towards the checkout area. I did not look in their direction, just slouched behind my cart, wearing my baseball cap and my sunglasses. Then hurried to finish my selections adding my treasured Lagunitas. I wanted to be at the checkout area and finished, so I could follow them.

I stayed way behind them, as they pulled out of the lot and drove directly to the Red Bottle Motel. Michelle went into room 11 and the twins unloaded all the groceries into room 12. I drove past the motel, committing the license plate on their car to memory. The FBI would check that. Felt really good to find them.

I decided they would not go by the Red Bottle Bar, so for now, I would skip that stop. I drove the old white truck past the industrial complex housing the 225 building, a huge older metal sided building, with a large overhead door, faced the street. The padlock looked new.

I made a trip to Cabella's and purchased a 20-60-85 spotting scope. Much better than my current hunting model, I could watch the warehouse from the five-hundred-foot cliff above the city near the airport. It included the attachment for taking pictures. I could not watch 24/7, but felt I needed to start today, covering traffic if any. I drove to the top of the cliff, located a parking lot and a trail along the rim.

Three large spruce trees in a cluster with branches touching the ground, allowed me to hide from possible hikers, and watch without exposure. After two hours, Michelle and the twins arrived, unlocked the door and entered the warehouse. "Bingo." I muttered to myself. I did not think much about the passengers at the time, but it looked like there were three and the driver. One too many. I guessed Zella was taking a vacation.

The FBI needed to learn what I now knew. I called Cliff, left a message, and returned to my apartment.

Cliff called an hour later. "Evening, Del, are you in Billings?"

"Yes." I relayed everything I learned since arriving.

"You have been busy. What do you think the FBI should do?"

"Start active surveillance at both sites and assume they are in extra alert mode and they will notice, if agents are careless. The agent you put in charge, needs to visit with me, because that warehouse is big enough to hold many van-sized vehicles. I will bet the 225 location is their central area to store everything they will use to do whatever they are planning. I have not been exposed. I will send you the pictures I took of them today at Walmart and at the warehouse. Let me know the name of the agent you will put in charge.

"Desmond Sandoval will be in charge. Is it okay for him to come to your apartment?"

"I will meet him nine a.m. tomorrow, but at the Starbucks on the corner of Eighth Street W and Cook Ave. What does Desmond look like?"

"Got it. He is a small olive-skin man, five-foot seven, one-hundred sixty pounds, and always wears a tie. He also always acts nervous, but he is a top organizer. You will like him. Please ask him to call me before he sets the surveillance program."

"Okay, Cliff, after I brief him and describe my lookout point, I am returning to Bozeman."

"We'll take it from here. I'm amazed how quickly you found all this."

"Cliff, I know Montana. I have visited and played tourist in every city over five-thousand population, making sure to see all that this beautiful state has to offer. I will be very interested to know what your team learns."

"Drive safely, and Godspeed."

"Always."

Cliff called Desmond and started things in motion.

I became James and went back to the condo. Johnathon was not there, and his office was locked. James cleaned out the condo of all his personal possessions, stowing everything in his SUV. He also wiped the place with disinfectant to completely erase any evidence of his ownership, covering everything he could possibly have touched. When I walked out of that condo, I felt positive I left no evidence behind.

I carefully handled the two parcels Johnathon had kept for me, hoping Cliff's team could check Johnathon's fingerprints. I remained quite nervous about that check. I believed Johnathon to be much more than a 'supe'. Cliff did check Johnathon's prints. He was in intelligence during his career with the Coast Guard. Cliff passed on what he learned to me.

l felt glad to be away from Johnathon.

I moved all of my personal possessions from the condo and transferred them to my apartment for safe keeping, then returned to Bozeman. I needed to check on the Nebraska *adventure*.

CHAPTER 34

liff called the Billings FBI office and detailed his surveillance plans for both sites, making the warehouse the top priority.

"Desmond, we received some very creditable information about a possible terrorist activity in Billings. I want you to set up the surveillance plan for both sights, pictures if you can get them. You'll need to expect your subjects to be extra alert about law enforcement. I am asking for daily reports. We already know they are using both sites. We completed a satellite search and located a vacant house for sale across the street from the hotel a block west of it. One room shows a useable window.

As of now, we will watch 24/7 at both locations for at least three weeks. You are to meet Del Sanderson at Starbucks on the corner of Eighth Street W, and Cook Avenue, at 9:00 a.m. tomorrow. Del is in the new program working with me. He is responsible for all of the intel we currently know about."

I met with Desmond and outlined everything, including the rimrock vantage point.

"Desmond, I have watched her about four to five weeks. I am positive Michelle will have some type of security at the warehouse. I saw Michelle and the 'twins' drive their SUV onto the building. The car held a fourth person, I am positive. I could not determine who the fourth person could be. I will be out of town for three days, and will call you when I return, and meet you here again."

"See you then." A firm handshake and Desmond walked to his car. I drove back to my apartment to prepare for the trip to Miles City.

CHAPTER 35

I called Cliff and left a short message. "Call me as quickly as you can."

I completed most of my prep work for the trip to Miles City, before Cliff returned by call. "What's so urgent, Del?"

"I checked the farmers market information. The word 'watermelon' in the codes means the farmers market in Billings. Because the 88, on the coded note I found, is the exact number of days from the day I found the note to the first day the market opens. I expect Michelle to do something. That does not guarantee Michelle is going to do what they have planned on that day, but thousands of people are expected to attend. I do not believe the 88 is a coincidence. If I were a betting man, I would expect something to happen that opening day. That is fifteen days from today."

"I agree, Del. It's not a coincidence. I'll have Desmond keep watch at least through opening day. Hopefully, we will know about vehicle traffic at the warehouse. Thank you, my friend. If we are right, maybe we can save some lives."

Desmond started the surveillance at noon. His agents recorded three new-looking white vans entering the warehouse at two-thirty-seven p.m.

Michelle and the 'twins' arrived at ten p.m. No lights were on in the main building. One of the twins unlocked the padlock, the big door went up, so the door had to have an automatic system. Michelle drove the SUV into the dark interior. The office lights came on immediately and the blinds were lowered, but enough light filtered through to reveal the attendees at the meeting.

The area surrounding the building remained in total darkness. Evidently, the abandoned look was to be maintained.

FBI Agent Steve Wilson called Desmond and received permission to have an agent approach the building and attempt to record the office conversation.

Jeremy Shackleford silently walked along the fence, then crossed twenty feet of open space. He crouched by the front window, and stayed in position nearly an hour, afraid to breathe. When the light went out, he sprinted to the western corner of the building, eight feet to his left. He watched as the SUV sped away, confident he escaped being seen. He ran to his car in total darkness because clouds covered the moon and called Agent Wilson. Shackleford was instructed to bring the recording to the office.

Agents Wilson and Shackleford listened to the recording and believed at least six different voices made comments, two of those voices were unmistakenly female, hinting some people were staying inside the warehouse. Jeremy wrote in his report he could see the back of the head for the second female. She sported bright purple hair. They decided not to approach the building during daylight.

All the conversation happened in a foreign language, so Agent Wilson forwarded it to FBI headquarters. They relayed to Cliff what they had done. Cliff called HQ and asked for expedited study. They agreed.

CHAPTER 36

Billy Crocker's computer list of commercial drivers in Montana arrived three days after Cliff asked for it and sent it to me. I printed the list then deleted the computer version. Joel William Cantelay (Cindy's father) still lived in Miles City.

I drove to my Billings apartment and changed out of being James. I called to reserve a room in Miles City. I left, covered the one-hundred forty miles and checked in. I chose the Tilt Würks Brewhouse known for its good food. Joel stood around with a group of eight guys shooting pool. He wasn't quite drunk, but closing in fast.

I noticed them, but stayed by myself on the last bar stool. I could watch the pool game in the bar mirror. I heard Joel say, "I gotta pee, then go home. A long day, and I'm bushed."

I paid for my food and beer and followed Joel out the door to his home. His rig sat safely parked in the long driveway. The shop would hold the cab, but not the whole trailer. The house was a double wide mobile home, and the yard looked neat enough. No sign of a mailbox just a slot in the door.

I made one pass, taking a picture, but not stopping or slowing down.

CHAPTER 37

hile in Miles City, I decided to try and find a rancher who might let me hunt on his property. I parked in front of the Montana Fish, Wildlife, and Parks and paid them a visit. A young woman asked, "How can I help you?"

"I would like to visit with a warden, if one is available," I said, smiling back at her.

"Our supervisor is in the back, let me see if he can see you." She picked up an old dial office phone, cycled two numbers, then said, "Sir, a visitor would like to talk to a warden." Listening to the reply, she continued, "Thank you, I'll tell him."

"Warden Bligh will be right out."

"Thank you, Jennifer," I answered using her name, from the desk name plate.

While waiting, I selected a copy of the current year's hunting regulations.

"Good afternoon. How may I help you?" The greeting was offered by a mid-fifties very fit man wearing the traditional tan and green uniform. He looked like he could walk all day, and never look tired. Just shy of six-foot, maybe 175 pounds, with an angular face, brown eyes, and neatly trimmed brown hair, he offered his hand. He acted proud of his role, and the smile real.

"I am Del Sanderson. I live in Bozeman now and studied the deer harvest records. Many of those record animals come from this area, so am hoping to purchase maps for the area and find some public land to hunt, and maybe locate a rancher who will let me hunt on his property."

He turned to Jennifer, "Jen could you locate those maps for Del, and bring them to my office?"

"I will bring all four."

"Follow me," he turned to the door he just came out of.

We strode down a hallway to a small office. I sat on the chair he offered, as he sat behind his desk. The room was just like the man, neat and functional. A very nice antelope and mule deer mount decorated one wall, and a framed Charles Russell print hung on an opposite wall. His window overlooked the Yellowstone River. A clothes rack in one corner held an array of items to cover every kind of weather. A locked gun cabinet occupied the other corner. His desk used a glass plate to cover a map of his area of responsibility. Everything looked neat and tidy.

Jennifer was right behind us with the maps.

"Thanks, Jen."

"You're welcome," she answered as she exited and closed the door.

"How long are you going to stay in our area, this trip, Del? By the way, my name is Mervin Bligh. Just call me Merv. The maps are free, courtesy of the great state of Montana."

"I have a room at the Comfort Inn and paid for a week, so I would have time to scout around. This a huge hunting area. I own a custom big rig set up to haul a small car and a quad, and a room for me. I hope to park it remotely and hunt from there. Thank you for the maps."

Merv studied me for a minute, remembering something. "Can you return around four-thirty today? I would like to work on something for you."

"Sure. You have piqued my interest."

They walked to the front together. "Jen, Del will return near four-thirty. Please bring him back to my office."

"Yes, I will. See you later, Del."

I drove around the entire town, stopping at a house for sale across from Joel's. I had a copy of the sales brochure in my hand. I studied the entire block and the residences, then turned to walk back to my car when I heard a voice behind me.

"Can I help you?"

I turned to see a small older woman emerge from the house south of the one for sale. "Sure, I am new in town and am looking at properties I could fix up for resale. This one has potential and a view of the river."

"The owner wants out. The last flood *put the final nail in the coffin*, he said. I have a key if you want to look at it," she added.

"I am supposed to see another property in twenty minutes. So, may I come back tomorrow, if that is okay with you? Does the river flood every year?"

"No, Mister, but it can. And when it does, we have repairs."

"Thanks. I may see you tomorrow. I can tell you are a great neighbor, how about the others on this block?" I continued.

I saw a beaming smile. "We are all good neighbors, only Mr. Cantelay isn't here much. He drives a big truck, and came back today. We all know his patterns."

"Thank you, you have been very helpful." I nodded.

I'm Beatrice, and you are welcome." She retreated into her home.

Lunch called, meaning a trip to Tilt Würks. The Reuben tasted better than any other, ever. The clam chowder soup matched the sandwich. I needed to learn to make my own clam chowder soup. No beer right now, as I decided to drive around the rural area using my Honda Civic. I used the maps, but finding the BLM land was not easy. Too often, it appeared those parcels were immersed within private property.

I covered a lot of miles, but did not locate any public lands. Ranch buildings were often a quarter mile off the road, only one seemed to be in disrepair. Maybe they would let me hunt on their land if I paid them. The name on the mailbox said, *Wellington.*

I formulated the outline of a plan to deal with Joel and Tyler. I knew where Joel lived. To learn about Tyler will mean a trip to the library in Billings.

Tyler Spivey showed on Billy Crocker's list of one-person attorney's offices, with the office address. I would locate his office and work on a way to teach him a lesson for severely abusing Cindy.

It was getting close to Thanksgiving. Last year, I hosted everyone. This year, Madeline and Jack are covering Dutch, Sally and Dave, and Jack's twin boys, and Cindy.

Molly, Trevor, Cliff and I are flying in my Cessna 182 to the Cummings ranch from Great Falls. The Bolton's are also going to Saco. Things are arranged.

CHAPTER 38

Merv waited for me when I arrived at his office later that day. "Del, I made some calls. You drive back to the Comfort Inn. And I'll pick you up. We have a place to go."

Merv picked me up and drove the northern route out of town, crossed over the interstate, and headed east toward Baker. Merv carried on a one-way conversation about area hunting the entire trip. He even talked about paddlefish. After twenty minutes he turned south and crossed a cattle guard under a huge log entry way.

I noticed a very small camera high on a western post. No one comes through here unnoticed. While Merv turned, I sneaked in a comment.

"I hope to catch a paddle fish next May." I stared straight-faced out the front window after I glanced at Merv.

Merv ignored my comment, just smiled as he drove the ten minutes to a beautiful log home, surrounded by six or seven buildings painted forest brown.

A short block of a man, wearing all black including a big Stetson, greeted us. "Merv says you want to hunt. Del, I'm Clark Abercrombie. My wife, June, is visiting some grandchildren in Las Vegas."

"Great to meet you, Clark. Yes, I love to hunt. I hope to shoot a trophy mule and whitetail deer, and a trophy elk. Harvest records show many of those records come from Eastern Montana. So, I came out here to see about hunting."

"Merv and I have been close friends since we were kids. I inherited this ranch and Merv has hunted every inch of it. He liked you immediately, and he, like me, trusts those feelings. We are going to get you a shot at a big one or two.

"My son will be here for dinner, and we will put a plan together. We have three regulars that hunt here. One is an archery hunter, and won't shoot unless it is a surefire Pope and Young. We do have some Boone and Crocket mule deer here, but they don't get that big by being stupid. My other two regulars have already booked their hunts.

"Merv says you have a self-contained big rig, and your own quad."

"Yes, I do. It can travel from the highway to your ranch," I replied.

"Del, after dinner we will show you where you can park, then set things up after you arrive to hunt. By then we will know where the big ones hang out. Apply for an antelope tag, you will get one as there is so much private land here, most locals don't apply. Let's go eat."

"Merv, this over the top. What can I say, except, thank you very much," I said trying not to over smile.

"You are welcome. I remembered your name is on Bill Davis's list. Clark belongs to the same group that Bill Davis started. Their main purpose is to make Montana a better place to live. Clark lists himself as retired. I know about them and support them any way I can. You let me know if you need anything, ever."

Rett Abercrombie rode into the yard on a beautiful chestnut gelding, three white stockings and an air about him. Rett was a bigger version of his father, four maybe five inches taller and at least thirty pounds heavier. "Howdy. You must be Del. I'm Rett. It's great to have you as our guest."

Clark interrupted. "Let's eat then go for a ride. Del, the washroom is the first one on the right."

An Asian woman, near sixty years old, served us a beautiful western style dinner consisting of a salad, cream of broccoli soup, baked potato, and a beautiful T-bone steak.

She topped it off with a brownie and chocolate ice cream.

"I like to eat, but will need to walk a lot of miles to work off this beautiful meal," I said.

"I knew to skip lunch," added Merv.

Both Clark and Rett laughed. "We do our best to work hard enough to eat what we want," said, Rett.

"Let's go for that ride," Clark offered as he directed us to a Chevrolet 4X4 crew-cab camo painted, with huge off-road tires. "Rett will drive."

We covered a third of the ranch. Rett showed me where I should park. They glassed a huge, irrigated hay field looking for game. Two separate herds of antelope played and ate alfalfa. Mule deer were evident near the tree line by two smaller canyons facing the large alfalfa field. Only three whitetail deer appeared.

They all talked hunting when back at the house. Everyone had a favorite story to tell, creating lots of laughs. Clark excused himself, then returned with a calendar. "The week of November 3-10 is yours, if you can make it."

I checked my phone, made an entry, then answered, "It is on my schedule. I will be here. I just hoped to find a place on public land to maybe get a shot. How long of a shot should I expect and prepare for?"

"Two hundred minimum, but a shot at a big mule deer could be closer to five hundred," said Rett. "I use a 308 with elite optics. I hit the target on most shots."

"I have a 308 with elite optics as well. I will be ready. This is going to be special." I could not stop smiling.

"We should be going," Merv interrupted. "I'll call Bill Davis and tell him you will hunt at Clark's."

Merv talked of his relationship with Clark and his job as warden. He also explained how he knew Bill. The last topic covered fishing for paddlefish. "I did hook one once. That was enough for me. I watch people hook one after another. People do know that we wardens operate that if you break the law, you pay. Nothing is free."

I agree with you Merv. If a person breaks the law, he or she should pay.

Merv dropped me at the hotel, long after dark. "See you in November, Del." The air smelled of rain as I got out.

"Absolutely Merv, thank you very much." A few drops of rain caught me before I could enter the lobby. I decided to make sure Joel stayed home before settling in, so I drove past his house. All looked quiet.

CHAPTER 39

Frank attached the horse trailer to the maroon Ram, said a short goodbye to Meg and traveled to Billings. He intended to find two bulls to add to his herd, to see his mistress, and to follow the courier.

Four months ago, as he passed through the lobby at his hotel in Billings, a woman approached him, "Frank Cummings, correct?"

"Yes, how may I help you?" he said, smiling at the woman.

"I have a picture for you to look at, followed by an ultimatum," as she handed him the picture.

"I don't understand," a nervous Frank said.

"Look at the picture first, then listen to me very carefully as you have no options. You must do as I tell you." She faked a smile.

Frank looked at the picture of he and his mistress entering a motel room in Billings.

"Why?" asked Frank.

"We have a half-dozen pictures of you two. We know you are part of the WIM group. We are telling you to pass any and all information decided at those meetings. Are we clear?"

"I can't do that. It would betray my friends."

"If you don't comply, your wife, Meg, will be told. You can count on that," another fake smile.

Frank looked for a place to sit down, as his heart started racing. He buried his face in his hands, trying to control his emotions. "What do you want?" Frank worried about his heart.

"I already told you that. You will be told where to give the courier the information. You must comply," a third fake smile, showing wrinkles in her brow.

Frank finally agreed to do his best, feeling trapped. For most of four months, he passed enough information to keep them pleased, but never everything. He decided it was time to quit betraying his friends. He also decided not to call any Montana FBI office, as they night know who he was. He chose to call Salt Lake City FBI instead.

Cliff and Charlene listened to Frank on speaker. Frank told them everything about how he ended being trapped with no way out. "I just don't want to betray my friends and my wife anymore. What must I do?"

"What are you presently trapped into doing?" asked Cliff.

"I belong to WIM. I am to pass information from the meetings to them via courier. They never use the same person."

"Okay Frank, I happen to be in Billings now. I will meet you at the airport terminal restaurant tomorrow at 9 a.m. Can you do that?"

"Yes, I will be there, wearing a much-used straw cowboy hat."

After the call ended, Charlene thoughtfully added, "I sense he is so scared, he will be of little use to us."

"You are exactly right. I wonder if Del knows about WIM, whatever that refers to. I'll bet he does, so I'll call him. Del needs to know what Frank Cummings is facing in case he is asked to help," replied Cliff.

Cliff called me. "Del, do you know what WIM stands for?"

"Sure, it is the acronym for Wyoming, Idaho, and Montana. It is a group of retired people who are trying to influence things in their states. I have been asked to join, but have not been to any meetings as of yet. I have been asked to attend their first one in January next year. They primarily try to stop drugs, but do not work closely with DEA. I do not know why that is, but will ask at that meeting. I have much to learn. Why do you ask?"

"Del, could you ask a principal in the group to meet with me and explain their process and direction."

"I can ask Bill Davis next time I am in Bozeman and set something up, if he is willing."

"That works. I'll wait to hear from you."

"Godspeed."

"Always."

Frank arrived at 8:30. Cliff came in a Gallatin Land Management truck with a company employee driving. He went to the lounge and removed his disguise, entered the cafe and sat opposite of Frank.

"How can we help you, Frank?" inquired Cliff.

"I cannot continue betraying my friends. I want to help you catch the couriers and maybe their handlers," answered Frank.

"Why are you in this jam, Frank?"

"I am ashamed to say I have a mistress, and they have pictures. My wife doesn't know. I have a bad heart and can't live under this pressure. I intend to follow my courier today and hopefully learn of a handler."

"Have you been threatened?" asked Cliff.

"Only by saying they will tell Meg, my wife." Frank started to lose control of his emotions.

"Frank, it took a lot of courage to call and to tell me everything. We will help you, but you need to let our people follow the courier. Let us take it from there. Is this drug related?"

"Some of it is, yes."

"Then we will include the DEA, but you will never know what we plan with them.

"We will teach you how to let us know when you are going to pass information to the courier." Cliff explained to Frank the subtle deception needed to let the agent follow him, and know when Frank is going to pass on the information. Just a simple stop and look in a store window for five seconds."

"I will do that," answered Frank.

Cliff returned to the locker, added back his disguise, and joined the company employee for breakfast. Frank didn't notice, while he sat and worried. He barely possessed the courage to set up the courier for Cliff's agent, but he did it.

After the exchange, the agent followed the courier to a small office with a painted sign on the door window, *Business Solutions*. Then he continued back to the local FBI office. They would start surveillance.

A disguised agent using a Simon Crossfire business card, went to Business Solutions asking if they could help his new company. The young woman gave him a brochure to study, outlining everything they offered. He thanked her then left.

Business Solutions moved the next day to a location on Grand Avenue. They were watched. The FBI knew and the DEA as well. Now it was a waiting game.

Cliff had expected Business Solutions to find a new office.

CHAPTER 40

helia Mason killed men for fun. She *was* a big woman, somewhat like her abusive dad.

She killed the first man during her last year in high school. Frequenting the seedy bars, she was known to be extra friendly. Her mother obtained a prescription for *the pill* when Shelia turned twelve. Mom didn't trust Dad. Shelia missed a lot of school, but should still graduate.

Shelia left the Lantern Bar with a man called Chuck. He planned to keep her a week, then let her go. He would go to Chicago and never be found. "*Not the first and not the last.*" He uttered to himself. He took her to a small run-down apartment over a garage, behind a shabby boarded up house. Using a key, he unlocked the door at the top of the outdoor staircase and held it for her.

"Not much of a place, but the stove and frig work. I hope to get a better place in a couple of months. There's beer in the frig and bourbon in the cupboard over the sink. I'll take a bourbon and water."

Shelia fixed two bourbons and sat on the faded sofa. A new TV perched on an antique end table. She could see into the bedroom. The bed was neatly made. After a night in the bedroom, Chuck rose early and made coffee. He brought Shelia a cup.

She drank it eagerly. It tasted a little off, but she drank it anyway. He started frying the bacon. Shelia liked breakfast smells and felt extra hungry.

When she woke up, she was in a small single room with no windows. She walked to the door to leave, but found it locked. She noticed big blisters on her heels.

Her reaction was to scream, but she didn't. She didn't scream at her dad, so no reason to scream now.

Hours later, Chuck arrived with a fast-food meal. "Here is your dinner." He put the food on the bed and a poor excuse for porta-potty on the floor.

"What's going on here, Chuck?" Shelia asked.

"I'm going to enjoy you for a while. No more questions." Then he left locking the door.

Shelia started working on her escape. In her mind, Chuck was dead. He just didn't know it.

The small cot bolted to the floor, and supported by one pipe at the open corner didn't offer any weapon. No way to remove the pipe. Chuck returned, carrying a small wooden bat.

"You can take the clothes off or I'll take them off, pointing the bat at her. She took them off. He laid the bat by the door, and after an hour, left and locked the door. The same process happened for three more days. The fourth day, Chuck returned mean and drunk. He hit her twice with the bat, though Shelia turned and absorbed most of the blows on her back. He dropped the bat on the cot and reached for her.

Shelia hit him as hard as she could on the point of his jaw, kneed him in the crotch, then picked up the bat and furiously beat her jailer to death. She rifled his pockets and took everything. She calmly put on her clothes, picked up the bat, walked out the door, and locked it.

She went back into the little jail and cleaned up everything, but didn't lock that door. Her fingerprints were not on file anywhere, but she watched enough TV to know about prints and

DNA. Then she went back to the small apartment and cleaned everything there as well.

She used her sweatshirt when she opened every drawer in the place, stole everything she could, finding his cash stash of six hundred dollars. She put everything in two pillowcases, added the new tv and cords, climbed down the staircase, got in Chuck's little black pickup and drove to a convenience store on the southern edge of Fargo, North Dakota. There she pumped a full tank of gas, purchased enough food and drinks to make it to Sioux Falls, South Dakota and started south. She skipped so much school she would not be missed.

Shelia was now on her own. She called her mom and told her she was leaving.

Five years later, she believed she would never be caught. She had killed eleven other men. She loved killing. Loved it! She knew she was a different person now. The killing felt so satisfying. Her dad occupied a place on her list of people to kill, but she still feared him. He was a lot bigger than her. She believed she could shoot him, but he terrified her. She decided if she ever got up the courage, she would buy a shotgun and shoot him.

Waitress jobs in bars and restaurants were easy to get, and she was a good worker. She stood five-foot ten one hundred eighty-five pounds. She often bested men in arm-wrestling contests. Flawless skin, with high cheek bones on an oval face, and steady blue eyes made her look younger than she liked. So, she often wore wigs to look older. She looked smooth, but her regular trips to the local fitness center kept her toned. She worked hard toward earning a black belt, but finding a woman to match her strength was difficult, so she often worked with men.

She pushed her cart in a grocery store, in Davenport Iowa. She watched a man berate his entire family and swat two of the three children. Obviously, the whole family was afraid of him.

Shelia felt differently watching him, knowing she wanted to kill him. She never completely understood the feelings she experienced seeing men abuse others, but always noticed the powerful strength of those feelings. No fear, just power to act. She decided to kill the bastard after following the family home. No plan, yet, just a need.

Shelia liked off-the-grid bars, and liked men enough to fit them into her life. She sat at the bar in the Spike & Nail sipping a lite beer, when the mean man from the grocery store came in very drunk. He ordered a beer. "Just one, I have to get home."

Shelia left, sat in her small black truck waiting, and finally followed him home. Getting out of her truck she called to him, "Hey, Mister, I'm lost. Can you tell me how to get to Williams Boulevard?" She closed the distance to within ten feet.

"Miss, I ain't sure, but it's a block or two from the courthouse."

Shelia was now only three feet from him, holding the ten-inch serrated hunting knife out of sight by her leg in her left hand. She lunged, stabbing him just below the ribs, then jerked it upward as hard as she physically could.

He fell to the ground, moaned a couple of times, then died.

Shelia wiped the blade on the man's shirt. She wore thin latex gloves, to take everything out of his pockets, stealing the money and noting his name, Bart Button. She wanted to see what the newspaper said.

She hummed as she walked to her truck and drove away. She didn't know a neighbor watched. She loved killing. She believed she left no clues, but actually left some at every killing. Detectives worked the cases in every city she completed one of her crimes. They knew they searched for a big woman. They also knew she was a traveler.

The detectives working on her first killing of Chuck, sorted his timeline. Chuck's truck was gone, and finding the little jail room he used, proved he imprisoned women. They learned that Sheila left the bar with him, and no longer attended school. This made her a person of interest. All of Shelia's killings were cold cases, as she always moved to a new town after she killed someone. Shelia, flashed a little skin when she hunted, causing men to notice her. "*I can always find a man*," she told herself every day.

CHAPTER 41

S helia now worked at a very busy truck stop on the western edge of Omaha, Nebraska, her twelfth town since killing Chuck. She knew she was changing, as she no longer needed to kill a bad man, since any man would do. The day cook at the truck stop was a man. She fantasized how to kill him. She processed those thoughts about male delivery drivers and sometimes a patron or two. She felt the need. It was time to act.

She went to the Barnyard to hunt. It was a cowboy establishment on Highway 92, on the Platte River near the small town of Venice, Nebraska. Less than a hundred people called Venice home, but the Barnyard was popular. The cheap beer, and the rib basket attracted a full house most nights.

Shelia sat by herself, after waiting a half hour to secure a table. Her order of ribs, tots, and slaw arrived just as she started her second lite beer. The packed place was filled with people she didn't know. She did not then know, the two couples at the table next to her were two male homicide detectives from the Omaha police department, out with their wives for dinner. Jerry and Lyle took note of the stranger sitting by herself. Lyle said, I'll do the recon." The ladies knew what that comment meant. Jerry just nodded.

Shelia decided there were too many people who would remember her. *"A great meal, but a poor hunting ground,"* she said to herself. After asking for her check, she paid and left.

Lyle heard her ask for the check, stood and asked the ladies if they wanted their coats. They both answered yes, so he left.

Shelia walked to her small black pickup shivering in the cold wind. "Brr, it's cold." She smiled at the young man who held the door for her.

"Yup, it is going to rain hard tonight, they say," he answered politely.

Lyle was close enough, sitting in his car, to see the North Dakota plates and mentally noted the number. He and Jerry would check the plate tomorrow. Most likely a dead end, but both of them thought it a bit strange for a woman to be dining by herself. Jerry and Lyle took their wives to the Barnyard almost every Friday night. She had never been there before—Lyle and Jerry always checked new faces.

Shelia drove, back toward Omaha, looking for her kind of place. Out of the way, seedy, and looking not too crowded.

She pulled into a gravel parking lot, with many water-filled potholes, belonging to the Hayloft Inn. A Rainer beer sign flashed on and off in the front window. She paused after entering the door, adjusting to the dimness. The tobacco smell took her breath away. Four young cowboys played pool and smoked cigars, hardly noticing Shelia. Four other men occupied one table, and a lone man sat nursing a schooner of beer.

Shelia, the only woman, felt the scrutiny and decided to leave and find another location. Walking past the tables, she heard the single drinker say, "Care to join me?"

Shelia paused a moment, then sat down. After all, she was hunting.

"I'm Sara."

"I'm John. Nice to meet you."

The short conversation, devoid of anything memorable, stalled.

"Sara, are you hunting companionship?"

"No. John, I need to get home. I have been out longer than I intended." Shelia noted he had been half right. She was hunting.

"It's okay. See you."

Shelia left quickly—out of the lot, down to a dark corner, and parked behind a big gray pickup, hopefully hiding her little black truck.

John left the bar thirty minutes later. He looked around extra carefully as he unlocked his car door. Acting like he dropped his keys he surveyed under every vehicle. Seeing nothing out of the ordinary, got in his car and drove toward his apartment, passing Shelia without seeming to look.

Arriving at his apartment building, he parked in his numbered spot, and started walking to his door. Shelia walked quietly right behind him saying, "I changed my mind."

"Glad you did, Sara. Follow me," he answered without turning his head.

Shelia trailed behind him and stabbed him two times in the lower back. He fell to the sidewalk and punched the panic button on the key fob he held in his hand. His car started honking loudly.

Shelia ran as fast as she could to her truck and sped away. For the first time ever, the huntress felt scared.

A neighbor came to the rescue and called 911. John survived.

Shelia aimed for the kidneys but stabbed above them. Hearing the sirens, she followed some side streets and made her way back to Highway 92. She was in panic mode, so decided to go to her apartment, take everything that was hers, and head for Denver. She cleaned the apartment thoroughly, but missed much as she was *out of this world* scared.

Jerry said to Lyle, "She doesn't know her little black truck is on camera at the bar and the apartment building." As they walked down the hospital hallway the next morning to Alfred Bodine's room.

CHAPTER 42

At the hospital, Jerry and Lyle took the victim's statement. Alfred Bodine would survive Shelia's attack, telling the detectives he used John at the bar. He described her and listed the clothes she wore, and mentioned her size.

Jerry and Lyle made copies of both videos, split up and canvased the bars and truck-stops. Jerry scored at a truck stop restaurant on his third stop. Shelia didn't show for her shift that morning. The manager gave him Shelia's address. Jerry called Lyle and they met at the apartment complex. The resident manager opened the door.

"She's gone," said Lyle. Let's get the lab people over here and maybe find some evidence. I'm guessing she has done this before. She is on her way to a big city to get lost. We will ask the chief to issue an all points. Maybe we can catch her before she gets out of state.

The lab people arrived, and the detectives went to talk to the chief. The APB was issued at eleven a.m.

A Nebraska state trooper followed Shelia about three miles before he received a reply from dispatch to stop the vehicle. A few miles east of North Platte, he called for backup, then turned on his lights, and caught up to Shelia. He noticed what looked like blood spatters on the sleeve of her shirt. He drew his nine mm, stepped back, and ordered Shelia out of the truck. His backup arrived. (The partially washed knife lay on the floor on the passenger side of the truck.)

After reading the Miranda statement and cuffing her, they placed Shelia in the back of a patrol car, behind the shield. She never said a word while being transported to the county jail. The sheriff called Omaha as Shelia's driver's license listed Omaha, and spoke to the chief. The chief asked, "Is she about five-ten, 170 pounds, wearing a dark-red western shirt, Lee jeans and baby blue cowboy boots?"

"Exactly!" said the sheriff.

"Beautiful, we got her. Good work over there. Please hold her, and I'll send a team to pick her up. We will drive the black pickup back here. Lucky for us. I'll call you and tell you the story after we get her back here."

Lyle and Jerry were the designated pickup team. After they processed Shelia and issued her a baggy set of men's jail clothes as they didn't have any woman's jail cloths to fit her. They secured her in a jail cell, and started trying to backtrack her. Her size and hunting methods led them to six other possibles and every one of those cases added traceable clues. She just looked too unique. They felt they had her on seven cases.

Shelia would meet the judge in federal court in Lincoln, Nebraska. Maybe four other states would line up to try her as well.

1 read the story at the Bozeman library, and started planning a new *adventure*.

CHAPTER 43

helia and her court appointed attorney were doing everything they could to keep the trial in Nebraska. The 'John' she tried to kill survived, so she wasn't facing murder one, just attempted murder. They were hoping for a deal. Shelia believed she could easily handle a short prison sentence.

She met her attorney in the bare minimum counseling room with yellow painted walls almost every day. She knew the plea, if she could obtain one, would happen at the nearby courthouse. She already had three rides in the transfer wagon, but she knew of no possibility to escape. The chains were too much of an obstacle. The walk from the van to the courthouse covered 22 feet.

I flew using visual flight rules to Cheyenne, Wyoming. There I refueled and continued on to Grand Island, Nebraska, about one hundred miles west of Lincoln. While enroute, I arranged to rent a small SUV after landing at the Central Nebraska Regional Airport. While waiting for the car, I visited with a young woman about things to see and do in Nebraska. I planned to stop at the Veterans Home and the State Museum of The Prairie Pioneer.

I drove to Omaha and rented a motel room on the western edge of the city, on State Highway 82. I changed over to Spencer and drove as him back to Lincoln. Spencer went directly to the courthouse, completed his survey of options. Escaping should be easy, but a lesson in St. Petersburg proved at least one Plan B should be prepared. Spencer completed a Plan B, a much longer trip through the city. But it seemed likely that Plan A.—to get on the freeway after the shot, would work.

The almost daily westerly breeze would make working out his shooting numbers extra critical. He walked all the side streets and found a two-story building measuring 1004 yards from the paddy wagon's reserved parking slot. (This was another personal best distance away from the range.) Spencer knew his numbers would work, but understood exact precision would be necessary, to minimize the effects of the extra distance, the wind, and the humidity.

Three small one-person offices on the second floor were available. Spencer rented the only one facing the target area. The bare walls were painted robin's egg blue. He received permission to construct a desk under the front window. He rented a small table saw, two sawhorses, and purchased enough wood to make the desk. The saw was loud, but the desk started to come together.

The first-floor hair salon manager wearing very thick glasses came up and asked him to please work after five. He agreed. He became a tourist, visiting the state capitol building, and talking to the tour-guide. Then he played golf at the local public course.

Shelia would be visiting the courthouse every day while her attorney processed the plea arrangement. Spencer did not like being seen by the salon manager lady. He finished making the desk the first night.

The office ceiling suspended below the actual ceiling enough to hide his rifle. He included his new extra-long, almost soundless suppressor. The *adventure* was a no go without it. He worried about the noise, being seen by the manager, and sneaking down the back stairs with two landings each creating a change of direction to his car.

He returned the rented tools, driving past the courthouse entrance in both directions. Watching the weather report in his motel room, the promise of light wind pleased him, but after tomorrow, the wind would freshen, making the risk of a miss too great. Tomorrow must be the day.

Spencer was ready. The police van came on time. Shelia pretended she needed help getting out of the van to start her short, exaggerated shuffle. He checked with his spotting scope, confirming it was Shelia. He pulled the trigger. Shelia fell face first, smashing into the top step and spraying blood everywhere.

The small office smelled from the shot. The two-person police escort jumped behind the van, never looking west. The sound suppressor worked beautifully. *"Number seven, Curt."* I said aloud.

I traveled on I-80 west in less than four minutes after the shot. Still wearing Spencer's get-up, I drove the speed limit and followed all the rules of the road. I hoped the search for this shooting spot would never take place.

My worry meter maxed to the hilt. I trembled and felt nauseous. *"I must reduce the stress in my life,"* I told myself. *"I cannot keep operating at this level. Retirement should be things I like to do."* But I knew I *enjoyed putting* together all the many parts that make an *adventure* successful.

Arriving in Grand Island, I made a point to chat with that young woman again and thank her for helping me to see the local sights. The Pioneer Museum was quite interesting to me; they have many good exhibits. I'm especially interested in learning as much as I can about Native cultures.

I unlocked and entered my plane. After takeoff, using visual flight rules again, I followed the Platte River toward Cheyenne. I believed I would take a sabbatical from the *adventures*.

While flying back to Cheyenne, I decided to take from my safe the list of participants in the melee that transpired the night my son, Curt, and Curt's best friend, Nick, were killed. I remember that night vividly and still shed a few tears whenever I think about it. Time to see if there was anything I could do about those young men. Sometimes I feel I should have addressed that issue before now. No ideas in my head, just maybes. But I wanted a brass plate and granite rock memorial to those two boys.

I needed to work on the caper involving Michelle and the twins. They were up to something bad; I was positive. I wanted to be the one who solved it. By the time I reached Cheyenne, most but not all of my anxiety drifted behind me.

It was necessary to visit with FBI Agent Sandoval soon. I needed to learn what intervention might be planned and how they expected to stop the vans, once they were out of the gate and on the highway.

CHAPTER 44

Lincoln Police Captain, Shirley Thomas opened the Thursday morning meeting, with a question. "How did Shelia Mason die on our watch? She was exposed for less than two minutes, with only twenty feet to the entry of the courthouse. No one heard the shot. No one has come forward from anywhere with any kind of tip. Suggestions, please."

Sargent Bitters sat in the front row at every morning meeting. He offered, "Since no one in our detail guarding Shelia heard a shot, it must have been made from a long distance. This woman appears to have a history of killings in other states. If it is a long-distance shot, we will need a tip or we will have nothing to work with. Those types of shooters can be accurate from at least a thousand yards."

"You are probably right, Tim. We need to see if we can find where the shot originated. We will use range finders to potentially locate possible sites. Everyone needs to try that today. Enjoy a safe day."

Shelia was just page three news in Nebraska's capitol city. No leads were found. No way to tell the next of kin. Shelia died alone.

CHAPTER 45

Bryan Kellerman, a computer specialist with the Marana Police Department, loved his job. When he had free time, he helped to solve cold cases. He currently attended the University of Arizona, taking two classes every semester, working toward a master's degree in forensic science. He often meshed his cold case work into his classwork.

Bryan received three anonymous tips about unsolved cases in Priest River, Idaho; Spokane, Washington; and Fort Lauderdale, Florida. All tips identified Arizona criminals, allowing Bryan to receive credit for solving two 'lukewarm cases,' and to learn about Jose Zapata landing in a Florida prison.

Class for Bryan was held Monday, Wednesday, and Friday at two p.m. He always returned to the station after class, to make sure his work was current. The Marana Police Department allowed all officers the opportunity to go to class and tried to schedule their work around school. When his degree was finished, he hoped to find a top-level administrative position in Arizona.

For now, Bryan was a single man, who went to the gym a lot and worked. He was at his desk working on a twelve-year-old cold case about a murder in Eloy, Arizona, when his desk phone rang.

"Bryan, you have a call on line two. He wouldn't ID himself."

Bryan picked up the phone and heard, "Kellerman?"

"Yes. Who is this?"

"Rocco Welty is in Miami. You have a picture?"

"Only an old prison photo, nothing current. How do you know where he's at?"

"Put a picture in the Star. You find a way to get it done," said the anonymous caller.

"Why?"

"Do you want to catch him?"

"Yes," said Bryan.

"Do the picture. I will be in touch and ask you some questions. Maybe you could help me."

"Wait!" Bryan said to dial tone.

Bryan hurried down to dispatch and asked the woman on duty, "Luanne, did you by chance copy the number from the call you just gave me?"

"509 something. I thought you would want it, so I did copy it for you." She handed him a note.

Back at his desk, he dialed the number. "The number you dialed is no longer in service."

"A burner! I was so hoping it was a good number."

He placed a note on the chief's board. 'Two minutes, request for the Star.'

He neatened up his desk and went to the gym, then to his apartment to do homework.

"*Another tip, and I have no idea who is helping me or why,*" he moaned.

CHAPTER 46

The following morning, he returned from the coffee room about 9:30. Before he could sit down, the chief called, "Two minutes."

Bryan related the phone call verbatim, asking if he could work something with the Star.

"Let me see it first. What do you think he is up to."

"Really, not a clue. We haven't seen Rocco since Pepe was released from prison. Maybe he is afraid of Pepe, or is looking to become a bigger player in our part of the woods. I think the drug bust in Fort Lauderdale hurt his status a lot."

"I feel you're right. Few people would know exactly what he looks like today. You know Pepe does. Would he tell us? They are rivals."

"Chief, can I talk to Savino and see if he has a decent picture. I know he and his partner watch the drug world a lot, maybe they have a good picture. We should ask our artist to take the old prison picture and age it some."

"Talk to Savino, and see if he can arrange something. Let me know. Your two minutes are up. How did you learn Rocco was in Florida?"

"The call today, sir. I believe he is going to call again and want something. He hinted twice now that we could help each other. The first time, he only asked, 'Who's Rocco?' I told, him a player in the drug world."

"Bryan, I feel he knows about some other event and wants you to earn another star. Long two minutes, but worth it. Keep me in the loop."

Back at his desk, he called Savino, explained the issue and arranged to meet at IHOP for breakfast the next morning.

Bryan sat in a booth drinking coffee, when Benito Savino arrived. Benito had been a successful Golden Glove welterweight. He chose the police academy over a possible pro career. He didn't like getting hit. He loved clothes and enjoyed being the best dressed person in the room. He and Bryan were often at the gym together, not really friends, but respected each other's work.

Benito's undercover days in California were behind him, but he seemed to harbor contacts deep in the gang and drug world, as well as an enemy or two. Benito harbors personal plans to become a very rich drug-dealer. Pepe owed him. Benito saved Pepe's life, but they are on opposite sides. Pepe was a little Hispanic man, who acted like he was the biggest man in the room. He practiced his swagger everywhere he went.

"Morning, Bryan. We doing breakfast, and is the chief buying?"

"I'll buy and turn it in. If he turns me down, you can take a turn."

"Fair enough," Benito answered.

After ordering their meal Bryan started, "I received my fourth tip from an unknown whose information has been spot-on every time. Two days ago, he called and told me Rocco was in Miami. We haven't seen much of Rocco since Pepe was released from prison. So, maybe he is in Miami putting something together to take his job back from Pepe.

I talked to the chief yesterday, and we are hoping there is a decent picture of him around. I brought a copy of a prison photo and our artist's age enhancements showing what he may look like now. We are asking if you could comment on our work. Also, can you give us anything better?"

Benito took the mug shot and the artist's three projections. He held the pictures and laid them upside down just as their food arrived. They talked shop and gym stories, and asked for more coffee when the waitress bussed their dishes away.

He picked up one of the artist projections and said, "This one is closer than anything I have, just add a small scar over his left eye like this. He proceeded to draw a neat scar on the artist drawing."

"Benito, we know Pepe owes you. We also know he hates Rocco. Do you think we could bring him to headquarters on some pretense and get him to give us a better picture?

"Nice thought, Bryan. If I did that, all the progress I've made with him would become worthless. He trusts me some, but nobody else on the force. He's the kind of guy that's paranoid about everyone now. Another man he trusted caused him prison time. The one you have is close enough for the Star article."

"Benito, thanks. We will use ours. You and I should visit each time we are at the gym. My tipster is going to give up something, just a feeling I have…"

"Bryan, sounds good. Ask me anything." Benito stood and offered his hand. "You and I should be better friends. Let's work on that. Maybe we could talk privately about undercover and drugs."

Shaking hands, "I'd like that, Benito. See you." He couldn't explain why he felt a deep chill when he shook Benito's hand.

Bryan, drove back to headquarters winding his way through the high crime area of Tucson. Small groups of younger people loitered in the usual places. Bryan didn't see anything unusual. Not even any new graffiti. Things were quiet.

Arriving at his desk he wrote a note 'five minutes' and pinned it first spot of the chief's board. He decided not to make a written record of his meeting with Benito.

"What have you got?" asked Chief Robinson, watching Bryan intensely.

"First, I did not make a written record of my meeting with Savino. I doubt he will either. He offered to become better friends. I felt a chill when he said that."

"Benito picked out one of the drawings, added a scar and told me it was better than he could offer. Pepe won't ever come to headquarters or tell us anything. Benito thought we could get away with the article and the artist drawing. He wanted a heads up when the picture will be given to the Star. He promised to pass any information he received from the street."

"Okay, let me see your work before you give it to your contact at the Star."

Bryan called Benito. "The picture will be in Sunday's paper."

"Thanks, I'll be in touch."

CHAPTER 47

Benito returned to his apartment and quickly changed his clothes to look like everyone else in the Hispanic community. He parked near Nico's and entered the bar. He sat in the back booth, so he could watch the front door. The bartender brought him a Tecate; no words were uttered.

Thirty minutes later, Pepe arrived, acting like he came alone. Benito knew he had extras watching everything. Pepe nodded at the bar tender and walked directly to the back booth and sat facing Benito.

"You have something for me?"

"Si. The Star is running an article on Rocco. It's a police-based story, using a prison mug shot, and an artist projection of what he might look like now. The picture is not very good, the police are asking for information, nothing more. They got an anonymous tip saying Rocco is in Miami. He hasn't been around much, but I don't think they knew where he hid.

"I wanted you to know before the article and picture were published. Rocco's friends are going to tell him. He is going to be pissed. He may come for you, and I wouldn't like that. I will leave now. Please tell me what I need to know before it could embarrass me. See you."

Pepe pondered what he learned. He stood, nodded to Benito. "Si, I will."

Benito walked out, not paying for the beer. He held a position of importance there.

Pepe made three calls, then left.

Benito returned to his apartment, changed back to his dapper duds, and called Bryan. "I talked to Pepe. He is preparing for war." He knew Pepe would only tell the bare minimum. Benito's friendship could help Pepe, but they really didn't trust each other. Though Pepe owed Benito, his position in the drug culture came first. Pepe would go find warriors. Benito had secret plans of his own. He intended to become very rich.

Pepe was thinking of a strategy, but knew he did not have enough people. Benito would help by telling him what the police might plan, but Pepe needed to take care of himself. Alejandro was a Rocco man. Jose Zapata would die for Rocco. Zap's older brother, Jesus, was killed in Spokane, Washington last summer after his boss, Vinny, lost three million in drug money. Vinny is now dead and Rocco took over his job.

When Pepe went to jail, Vinny got Pepe's job, and when Vinny became a victim, Rocco got Vinny's job. When Pepe finished his time, the big boss gave Pepe his job back, and Rocco lost out. All of these changes happened in less than two years. Rocco hates better than anyone. He swore he would get his job back. Pepe stood in the way.

Rocco traveled to Miami by car, to find some help. He did not trust anyone in Arizona. Most loyalties in the drug world were fragile at best. He knew he owned a voice in Marana, because Alejandro owed him bigtime. He sent a package to Alejandro's sister in Marana. Coded instructions and two burner phones. The last thing he expected was Alejandro selling him out.

Alejandro worked for Benito. He and his sister, Margarita, needed the extra money. He used his own burner phone and called Benito with news. "Rocco is in Miami buying help. He will tell me when he is ready. He will not tell me when he plans to come back here. He will go to the Jeminez hacienda first, but I will not know. I'll try to call if there's no risk to Margarita. We will need to get away very soon."

He hung up. Alejandro possessed a cheap sweeper that Benito provided him. He felt his small apartment was clean, but he cried himself to sleep most nights worrying. He did not trust Rocco. He would go to all of Pepe's meetings, but he didn't trust Pepe either. He expected to leave Marana as soon as the coming war ended.

CHAPTER 48

enito called Bryan. "Lunch at Applebee's."

"I can't get there until near 1:30, I am waiting for a call," Bryan replied.

"Fine, I have another place I can stop first."

Beth Booth called Bryan at 12:30. "Chief Booth would like to meet with you. A local citizen will fund your entire trip to Idaho."

"Really? I would love to visit your part of the world. I'll talk to my chief and see if I can make it work."

"Great, Bryan. When you get here, I will be your guide." Bryan could hear her smile.

Bryan put a note on the chief's board, 'One-minute update'.

Benito was working on a cinnamon roll and some spiced tea when Bryan arrived.

"You weren't supposed to see the roll," smiled Benito.

"I would love one, but I had a lemon filled Danish with my coffee this morning. One a week is my limit, Benito."

"I eat one cinnamon roll each week like you, but behave otherwise. I know I have extra workout time when I eat my roll.

We got a couple of 'Brothers,' as the chief calls us that need to cut back on the sweets. Does the chief know you are here Bryan?"

"Don't think so. I never told him. He isn't real computer savvy, so mostly he leaves me alone. He seems to know who earns their pay, versus the slakers."

"Yeah, you are right about that. I got a call last night. Rocco is in Miami buying help. I may get a call when Rocco comes back, but Pepe will know as well. I don't trust either of them. I don't think the combined Tucson and Marana Police will be able to stop what's coming."

"Benito, do you think the police will let things play out?"

"Yeah, I do, unless things overflow and innocents are involved. Chief won't put us in harm's way, if the two sides stay after each other. Pepe will tell me some things, if it will help him. He used two cars with guys, when I met with him last week. That means he has between five and ten soldiers.

"Rocco will bring a few, well-armed and well-paid guys, but won't have as many as Pepe. He is a sneaky bastard and will try to ambush Pepe first. There's going to be some dead drug people...My guess is he's making a deal with Miami. He wants to get the Idaho and the Florida pipelines up and running again. Jose Zapata didn't stay in jail long, because the others arrested with him said he only arranged the boat. He is loyal to Rocco, so will be player in the war."

"What do you and I do, Benito?"

"I hope to get as much as I can from Pepe. I will not get messed up in his problems with Rocco. I need to come out of it with my contacts still good."

"Benito, you know we get tips sometimes."

"Yes, I do."

"Maybe we get a heads-up that way. Is your source reliable?"

"Yes, but he is so far down the ladder, he may not hear in time. I am sure Rocco doesn't trust him. He won't tell someone that low what he's doing."

They agreed to meet again soon.

CHAPTER 49

hief Johnson called Bryan. "Can you come to the DA's office for a short visit? I'm not going to be done by five."

"Ten minutes, sir."

Traffic slowed Bryan's trip. The chief sat on a stone bench in the courthouse hallway, slouched over holding his face in his hands waiting for Bryan. He tried a smile when Bryan arrived. "What do you have?"

Bryan passed every detail he knew, then asked about going to Idaho.

"A free trip. How does your work schedule fit?"

"I can take a lot of my work along and manage, if Rocco doesn't show. Both Benito and I feel we are less than a month away from Rocco's return."

"Take the trip, enjoy your time. Call Benito and ask him to see me if the shit hits the fan before you return."

"Thank you, and I'll call him."

The chief walked back into the DA's office and closed the door.

Bryan called Beth, then Benito, leaving a message.

"I'm so glad you are coming. We will show you the crime scene, and Chief Booth wants to pick your brain about cold cases," said Beth.

Bryan realized he was smiling and humming while he packed for his trip to Priest River.

Beth's e-mail directed him to fly to Spokane, Washington, where he would be met. His flight ticket to Spokane would be at the Southwest Airlines counter in Tucson.

Bryan studied a Spokane cold case. A Russian mafia leader, who was killed on the courthouse steps while being processed for deportation. He also wanted to touch base with Sgt. Wilson that helped with the Jesus Zapata killing. He arranged a Tuesday departure, so Wilson could meet him at the airport. Maybe he would learn his first name.

Bryan's world included Tucson, Marana, and Phoenix. One trip to San Diego and one to Sante Fe, New Mexico.

Now, he was going to Idaho.

CHAPTER 50

Bryan tried not to act excited while waiting for his flight out of Tuson. He heard an announcement of a Miami arrival, so walked down to the announced gate. He could spare the time to walk to the nearby gate, then watched from a full boarding area across from the Miami arrival.

About a third of the passengers deplaned, when he noticed a slender, well-built, very dark black man come through the portal. He looked neat and crisp. Six foot two, he carried a maroon briefcase with gold locks. He looked at the direction signs, then managed a quick sweep of his surroundings, and turned toward the baggage claim.

Bryan didn't look much like cop. When the man looked at the signs, Bryan didn't watch, but fussed with a Velcro strap on his carryon bag. There is a large Air Force Base by Tucson, so he could be an airman, but Bryan didn't think he looked the part.

He heard his flight called, so he called Benito while walking to the gate.

"Benito, I am at the airport and may have just seen one of Rocco's players." After describing the man, he added. "I didn't get a picture, but will write everything down and give it to our artist to get a rough outline."

"Bryan, we have two cars here now and Tucson has four. We are looking for some teens roaming between parked cars in the long-term lot. We often send cars to help at the airport. We haven't found them yet.

"Bryan, I will call and ask a car to watch the cabs, and let us know which one your man takes. Maybe we can locate where he goes. I don't think Pepe knows about him. He will have a place to hide if he is a Rocco man.

"I'll get things going here. Have a nice trip, Bryan."

"Thanks, Benito, I will touch base when I return."

CHAPTER 51

ryan stowed his carry-on, nodded to the boy next to him, buckled in and opened his window shade. He wanted to watch outside the entire flight. He recognized the Grand Canyon, and the Great Salt Lake, but enjoyed the snowcapped mountains the most.

He was one of the first ten passengers off the plane, and noticed a young man holding a sign with his own name neatly printed, as he approached the baggage carousel. Bryan started walking toward the man, who put the card away, removed his sunglasses, then walked toward Bryan. "Mr. Kellerman. I am George Swanson. I will be assisting you for the rest of your trip to Priest River and the to the lake."

After gathering Bryan's bag, they proceeded through a private security door, after visiting with a security guard, and walked to a white with yellow trim Beach Craft Bonanza 36, six passenger plane. George stowed the bags in the last two seats, and invited Bryan to ride in the copilot seat.

"You a pilot, Bryan?" asked George.

"No, this is my first non-commercial ride. I'm excited."

"I'll call ahead, but Mr. Shelton wants you to see the entire area from altitude, so you have a perspective of the logistics and the policing difficulties. We'll fly over the two crime scenes, and both of the Priest Lakes. You'll meet my boss and owner of this beautiful plane. You may like his little cabin on the lake."

George landed smoothly at Priest River, then transferred Bryan's bags and some supplies to transport into a very new red Chevy pickup. They traveled through a scenic wonderland, sometimes along the Priest River, on a well-maintained road to Coolin and on to Austin Shelton's "Little Log House." (George's description.)

They strolled together to the front door. George rang the chimes, waited a few moments, until the door opened revealing a smiling Hispanic woman.

"Hello George, this must be Mr. Kellerman."

"Si, it is Juanita."

"Come this way, Mr. Shelton is on the patio.

CHAPTER 52

They walked through the most beautiful home Bryan had ever seen. A view of mountains and the lake filled every window. Sunsets will be spectacular off the lake.

A six-foot four man stood as soon as he heard them coming. "Mr. Kellerman, glad to have you as my guest. I'm Austin Shelton, call me Austin."

"Bryan Kellerman, sir. Just call me Bryan. George hinted I would like your little log cabin. This is beautiful."

"George, I would like you to fly to Bozeman to pick up Mr. Davis. He is to be a guest while Bryan is here. Then you can fly them both on their journey home when they are ready for that. George will drop Bryan off at the Great Falls Airport, on his way to Bozeman. Sergeant Wilson will meet you Tuesday at the airport. Will that work for you Bryan?"

"Perfectly." Before he could say more, Austin continued.

"Help yourself to a refreshment of your choice." He lifted a countertop revealing beer, soft drinks on ice, and iced glasses. Excuse us, now as I must give George the information for his trip to Bozeman. Austin and George disappeared down the hall.

Bryan selected a Kalispell-brewed IPA, poured it into an iced glass. He took it forty-five feet to the patio railing, on a beautiful deck covering the entire backyard view of the small tree lined cove. He took a sip of his beer and watched Mother Nature at work.

"What is going on here?" Bryan asked himself. "This is over the top."

Austin returned, selected an IPA, poured it into an iced glass, and joined Bryan at the railing.

"Bryan, I sense you are wondering why. It will take me sometime to explain. Please be my guest for these few days. Juanita takes care of things here. Beth and her uncle Keith will join us for dinner. Inviting you, was Beth's idea.

"Let's get comfortable." Austin pointed to a soft leather chair under the covered portion of the patio, selected a similar chair and sat down. Bryan sat down in a firm dark maroon chair with oak arm rests.

"Beth did all the work regarding asking you to come here. She completed a detailed log of all your phone calls and actions about the young man found in our sheriff's jurisdiction. She coordinated everything with your chief, asking him not to alert you. She made all your arrangements for the Spokane visit. She is very efficient.

"Her Uncle Keith is the sheriff here, and a close friend of mine. I am paying for all of this because I learned you like to solve cold cases. Am I right?"

"Yes sir. I have four successes so far, but the Priest Lake one wasn't really cold, and I did receive a tip. I would never have made any connection without that tip."

"Yet, Bryan, you look at many Western US unsolved cases."

"How do you know that?"

"Beth will need to explain that. I am not sure how she knows all she knows. Seven years ago, my wife was found sitting in her car, between here and Priest River. No visible signs of struggle or trauma. Her car sat parked in a vista turnout. The police never found any useful evidence. She went to Spokane to shop, but when she did not arrive by nightfall, as she usually did, I called

Keith. Deputy Brandon Scribner found the car and called the ambulance, though he knew she was dead.

Beth will bring the case file. Keith and I would like a new perspective. We hope to learn how you would proceed. Keith and his staff will do all the work. It's an old and cold case. Mary Jo was Keith's sister. Beth is our niece. We don't expect you to magically solve it."

"Austin, new procedures and quality forensics are used to apply to cold cases. I am the computer person in the Marana Police Department. When I find a new lead, I enjoy following up and seeing new results. I will be happy to review the file."

"Fair enough. You shoot pool, Bryan?"

"Some, but I'm not a good player, Austin."

"I am not a good player either, but like the game. Not many chances to play pool living out here. We have about an hour before Beth and Keith arrive for dinner. I am allowed one more beer, how about you, Bryan?"

"I would enjoy one more."

They descended to the basement level, with two pool tables and a very large wall mounted television. One table regulation pool, and the other billiards. Bryan never played billiards before. Bryan walked to the window and gazed at the lake. Do you catch any fish from the shoreline or dock?"

"Always some smallmouth around. I don't fish much, but Keith's son owns one of the charter services. We go sometimes on days he doesn't have paying customers. Some big lake trout swim in this lake.

"Bryan, we don't expect a lot. A new mind, new procedures, experienced thinking. We published a plea for six months hoping for some helpful information on Mary Jo. We never received a call."

Bryan could see the anguish written on his face. This conversation is dragging up memories. "Eight ball is the only game I know."

"The guest gets the first break. Winner after that." He gestured at the table.

"I can live here, and George will take me anywhere I wish to go. You made the four on the break. I owned a little over one thousand acres of farmland where Boise wanted to build an industrial park. It belonged to my grandfather, then my father, and then to me. I still own eleven thousand acres south of Nampa.

"That city is asking to buy some, and a developer wants a chunk, too. I don't have any direct heirs. Beth is extra special to me. She will be some part of what I decide to do. It is time to sell more of the farm. A corporation farmer wants the rest of the land, to keep it out of development. I am sixty-two, so I have some decisions to make." Austin looked down at the table as he talked.

"Your shot Austin, I left you a couple easy ones," then added, "Since we will visit some crime scenes tomorrow, will your Bozeman guest be here for that trip?"

"No. he is coming here to meet you, Bryan. Bill Davis and I have been friends for more than forty years. We met at a farm expo in Kansas City and became instant friends. We talk farming, and hunting. He comes here to fish.

"Beth's notes indicate you knew the man found above the lake here. He carried drugs or money on the Canadian pipeline. Bill is deeply interested in reducing those pipelines in Montana. Those drug people must drive past my driveway on every trip. Bill hopes to reduce the Montana pipelines. He wants to hear your thoughts. Your chief speaks highly of you."

"Chief Johnson and I get along well. I like that he lets us do our stuff, go to college, and cross paths with detectives, and share ideas. I only know of two officers that are not fans."

"Beth and Keith should be here soon. Junita will show you to your room. Dinner is at seven. Mary Jo preferred that time, so I have never changed it."

Juanita met them at the top of the stairs. "This way Mr. Kellerman." She led him to the last room at the end of the hall on the second floor.

"*Wow.*" Bryan whispered. His bags were on a bench at the foot of the bed. *"Damn, I need some cowboy boots. This Beth seems to do what she wants. I hope she's not going to be trouble."*

After putting his few items away he danced down the steps, selected a leather chair near the fireplace, and became engrossed in a book of Charlie Russel paintings, when he heard new voices.

"Hello Jaunita. So nice to see you, again." Juanita and Beth shared a hug.

"I am happy you have come and bring Uncle Keith. I have his favorite dinner planned."

"You spoiling me again?" Keith said with a smile.

"I am so, Uncle Keith. We can share a hug, and then you meet Mr. Kellerman."

Bryan rose from the chair and moved to meet Beth and Keith.

"You are a handsome one, Bryan. I am so pleased you could come to our little community. She reached out and presented a distance hug and a soft peck on Bryan's cheek.

Yes, Bryan blushed. "My imagination is perfect, I'm lucky to dine with a beautiful woman."

Beth was a five-foot-seven, slender woman. Her thirtieth birthday was a week away. Professionally cared for short brown hair revealed a high forehead, light blue eyes, and narrow eyebrows. Her narrow face, nose, and chin highlighted smile lines at the corner of her eyes. She smiled enjoying Bryan's silence and lingering appraisal.

"Bryan, I am Chief Keith Booth. Happy have to you here," shaking Bryan's hand.

"My pleasure, chief. I didn't expect anything like this. I am blown away."

"Let's go find Austin."

Bryan quickly offered Beth his arm.

"Handsome and a gentleman—that's refreshing."

"Welcome everyone," Austin greeted them at the dining room entry.

Austin sat at the head of the table, Beth and Bryan on one side and Keith and Juanita on the other side. Mary Jo's place was set the napkin neatly folded over the plate.

After the meal, Beth, Keith, and Juanita bused the dishes. Austin directed Bryan to his office. He pointed out his prized Charlie Russell painting and a Bob Schriver sculpture. When Beth and Keith joined them, Austin started the conversation.

"Bryan, there is an organization in Montana, Idaho, and Wyoming, that operates behind the scenes, trying to make our states better. We look at everything from elections, environmental issues, and Federal and state actions, but our main goal is to curtail drug trafficking." Austin paused, seemingly deciding how much he should say.

"I know you have questions about being invited here. Your contact to Beth, triggered many discussions. We were aware of the Idaho pipeline using walkers. We know of at least three in Montana. When you identified the young man found by Priest Lake, and the dead man in Spokane, we learned more about the route, players, and scope of their operations than we previously knew."

He turned to Keith, who said, "Bryan our department covers a large area. We will never have enough people, cars or money. The Priest Lake area is especially hard to manage. The labyrinth of roads and trails is so extensive, there are places we have never been.

"Your Zach Erlinger, died at the end of a little-used logging road. It joins a steep portion of a well-defined, hiking and game trail to the Canadian border. We sent a team of hikers to walk the trail. They found three well-used camps. A Canadian law-enforcement team hiked from Creston to the same border crossing. That trail has been temporally abandoned. We have not found a new one yet. We are hoping you have ears in your area, and can tell us where any new drug trails might be."

"Austin, Keith, I really don't know any specifics. I will need to ask when I get back to Marana. We have contacts in the drug culture. We believe they haven't reopened it. We learned they lost about three million dollars. One of the two mules escaped. The autopsy on Zach showed two bullet wounds in the back of his head and a badly broken leg.

"The dead Hispanic man found in Spokane, proved to be an enforcer and bodyguard for one of Marana's top drug dealers. That dealer's body was found in the desert two months ago. The new dealer just uses the Mexican pipeline. That cartel also used a Miami location, but five major players were arrested, so that source is not being used to our knowledge."

He paused, deciding to keep Pepe and Rocco out of the discussion. He felt out of his element here, and wondered how much they knew about him. He decided he would visit with chief Johnson at length about this meeting.

"Enough about drugs," interjected Beth. "He needs to know why and how we have developed so much information about him."

She handed him a file. No names anywhere in the information. After a brief silence while Bryan scanned the file. He made sure he remained calm, then said, "Who and for what reason did someone give you permission to develop this file?"

"Bryan, please don't be upset. The three of us spoke to your chief, using a zoom call on a secured port. He listened from his home, and we were here. This place is swept every day. I compiled the information during that visit. He is expecting a private conversation after you return. He wants to develop an organization like ours. We did not know our drug issues were so closely tied together with Arizona. We do not have a copy of your personal file. Only the three of us know about you."

Beth then handed Bryan their department case file on Zach Erlinger. "Your copy—it includes everything we have. We ask you to read this and give us anything else we should know."

She gave him another file, labeled Mary Jo Shelton. "We are asking you to read her file and add your comments. Anything and everything you think of. Take your time, but keep a record of everything you do. You will be paid for this consultation.

"Tomorrow you will go with Austin and Keith to visit both crime scenes, and then take a super nice boat ride. Also, be prepared to hike in the mountains.

"Uncle Keith, will you help me with dessert?" asked Beth.

"You bet." They both walked to the kitchen.

Austin watched Bryan throughout Beth's comments. He liked what he saw, a young man very dedicated to his profession. His politeness and calmness told him. Bryan was the right man.

Beth and Keith returned with a piece of carrot cake for each of them.

"This should put us to sleep," offered Keith. Chief Booth looked about 55 years old, with mostly salt and pepper hair, cut short. Maybe five-foot-ten, weighing near 235 pounds. He didn't look overweight. A round, clean-shaven baby face, with a small roundish nose, made him look younger than his age, especially when he smiled.

"Bryan, shall we go for an evening stroll and watch the sunset?"

"Wonderful idea, Beth."

"It will be cool down by the lake. I will grab my sweatshirt and meet you in the rec-room."

"Perfect, I'll be ready."

"Do you have a jacket, Bryan?" asked Austin.

"I looked up the weather here, so I brought a sweatshirt and a windbreaker. Just like the desert, it gets cold after the sun goes down."

Beth and Bryan met in the rec-room, then started down the path to the lake.

"Bryan, take your time with all this. Chief Johnson supplied everything we know about you. We do not intend to put you in any position you don't want to be in. Neither I nor Uncle Keith are in this organization Austin referred to. We both help Austin, no questions asked."

They walked along the lakeshore for most of an hour talking about their lives.

"I have lived here all my life. My parents were killed in a boating accident the summer after my freshman year in high school. I am an only child, and now live with Uncle Keith and Aunt Thelma. At my parents' funeral, Uncle Keith said, "You can come live with us.""

I do not have a boyfriend. Haven't found one that puts my body 'in a tingle,' as Aunt Thelma says."

They stopped at the boat dock, sat together on a bench, then Bryan started to tell his brief story. "I am a Tucson native, live alone, go to the gym a lot, and attend most of the 'U's sports games. Chief Johnson encourages everyone to attend college, and makes sure our schedule makes school work. I am pursuing a master's degree in Forensics. I like it, and hope to find a position in homicide admin. when I finish. I love my computer career and plan to stay current, but I want to learn more detective procedures."

He paused and looked at his shoes. Beth told him about her status so must want to know his. "I have a girlfriend, but we both know it isn't going anywhere. She wants a career in politics and has an internship at the state capitol. Beth have you ever been to Arizona?"

"I've been to every state west of the Mississippi River and once to New York. I drive wherever I go, except New York. Uncle Austin takes good care of me. I am quite spoiled. I love my job here. Always something new. Having you come here is exciting for me. You will enjoy your day tomorrow. Brr, it's getting chilly! Let's go back."

Beth took Bryan's hand, led him from the dock, past Austin's Glass-Ply boat and back to the rec-room. Keith and Austin were watching a baseball game, "Gentlemen, I have returned him safe and sound." She let go of his hand, gave him a peck on the cheek and hustled up the stairs.

"See you three men in the morning."

Bryan started up the stairs. "I think a shower is in order, then I will read both files at least once. I expect I will have some questions in the morning. Goodnight."

CHAPTER 53

After his shower, Bryan read both files twice, and made a few notes. He felt the crime scene may add something, but neither file contained much to study. Marana department files would be much more thorough. He decided these two files were window dressing, and not the real purpose of his visit. A pretense really. He thought about Beth. She certainly wasn't trouble, as he feared. He liked her.

The next morning, Bryan showered and dressed for a hike as suggested, then hurried downstairs, meeting Keith and Austin in the dining room already eating breakfast.

"Morning Bryan, sleep well?" asked Keith.

"Very well. Thank you."

Juanita appeared and offered eggs, hashbrowns bacon and toast. "How do you like your eggs Mr. Kellerman?"

"Over medium."

"How many?"

"Two would be perfect, Juanita, gracias."

Austin said, "Good morning." Bryan sensed he wanted to hear about Mary Jo's file. "I read both files, and will send you ours on Zach. I'm eager to visit both crime scenes. Austin, If I may ask, I didn't see a time trail of Mary Jo's, day in the file. Just the note about the calls.

"Yes, she always called from Macy's when she arrived in Spokane and from O'Leary's when she started back. There were no other calls on her phone. I believe we lived in a happy marriage, and trusted each other. I never checked the milage, so don't know how many miles she drove in town. She brought home two packages in the car, receipts for them and lunch."

"Austin, I'm not—"

Austin interrupted immediately. "A critical question, Bryan. We have no way of knowing. I would bet everything she was faithful, but we may never know. You are right to follow that timeline. I expected it. Keith went to Spokane personally and checked everything, including the house where the Marana henchman met his demise."

Keith added, "The Spokane people didn't have any leads to work with. Clerks in the two stores she shopped at remembered her, but didn't have anything else to offer. Both said she shopped alone."

"Well, I'll keep thinking," answered Bryan.

Jaunita appeared with Bryan's breakfast. "Thank you, Juanita, I couldn't eat like this every day."

Austin chimed in. "Juanita is showing off today and has another planned for tomorrow."

"If it's okay with you, Bryan, Keith and I will go with you to the crime scenes. Beth will join us for the boat ride."

"Whenever you're ready."

"We will leave around ten. We have over an hour. I have two calls to make, and Keith wishes to contact his office before we go. You're welcome to cast for some bass off the dock if you like."

"I don't have a fishing license."

"You will be fine. No one will bother you."

Bryan suspected he was not wanted in the house. He selected an ultralight rig and a small tackle box, walked down to the dock and started casting. The fourth cast produced a solid strike. A nice smallmouth bass dangled at the end of his line. "*Not skunked.*" Bryan mumbled to himself. He continued to cast the line for a time, feeling only one more strike. Changing to a three-inch worm, jigging close to the edge of the dock produced three more nice smallmouths. He released all the fish to grow bigger.

He cleaned up the gear. Returning to the rec-room, he poured himself some coffee. He leaned on the fully stocked bar, puzzled about the files. Why? He had nothing to add. Austin and Keith must know that. At ten, he climbed the stairs, thinking, "*I could live here. Wonder what the winters are like?*"

At the top of the stairs, he met both of them coming out of Austin's office and followed them down to the car.

They piled into a dark gray Acura SUV. Austin drove the nine miles to the vista where Mary Jo's car was found. Keith pointed out the exact location of her car and where the deputy said he parked.

"The file indicated she occupied the driver's seat. I wonder why she didn't fall onto the other seat after she died?" Offered Bryan, noticing a furtive glance between the two men.

"The deputy told us she leaned against the glass in the door. She didn't respond when he tapped on the glass. He further stated, he backed away and called dispatch, asking for an ambulance and a second patrol car. The second car arrived in twenty-eight minutes, the ambulance a minute later.

"She was pronounced dead at the scene. Her body was already cold," explained Keith.

Austin never said a word. He stood off to the side, trying to control his emotions.

Bryan looked at Keith. "The only other thing I will ask now: could she have been killed somewhere else and driven here, and a second car picked up the driver? Then stage this spot to look like a murder scene."

Keith answered. "We never determined any positive cause of death, or evidence of other vehicles here. The coroner felt she had been asphyxiated but could not or would not determine how. We couldn't find any leads. No one called about the car for at least two hours. Austin went to look after the deputy called him. If someone killed her, why come all the way to this spot to leave the car."

"Good point, Keith. I will ask our homicide people about that. I sense the killer wanted it to look like Austin killed her."

When they reentered the Acura, Bryan wanted to steer the conversation away from Mary Jo. "How far to Zach's scene?"

"About forty minutes," answered Austin.

After they traveled nearly half the distance to Lionhead Campground at the northern tip of Lower Priest Lake, Bryan broke the silence. "What kind of fish are in Priest Lake?"

"Most charter boats fish for lake trout," answered Keith. "There are other trout, yellow perch, kokanee salmon, and smallmouth bass. Some others. But lake trout can get to forty or fifty pounds, so that is the fish that generates the money, we will welcome you to come fish with us.

"We do lake trout fish fries often."

CHAPTER 54

They arrived at Lionhead Campground near one p.m.

After passing the campground with a long, large beautiful sandy beach, they followed a rutted, overgrown, barely usable, logging road for nearly three miles. The road ended abruptly at a cliff showing evidence of a trail. Keith walked to the stump where Zach's body was found. "His leg looked badly broken, so he must have taken an awful fall. There was a poor crutch next to him, so his partner tried to help him. He had been dead about three days when his body became too decomposed, and someone found him."

"Is it okay to hike the trail a bit?" asked Bryan.

"Sure, just be careful on the steep part," smiled Keith.

Bryan climbed to the top and walked along the trail for a hundred yards or so. (He then sat on the very log Bo used to hide the backpacks of money.)

"This is beautiful." He took many phone pictures to show the desert folks. Back at the bottom of the cliff, Bryan commented. "Beautiful setting. How far is it to the Canadian border from the top of this cliff?"

"Seventy miles, give or take," answered Keith.

They walked to the car in silence. After driving back to the cabin, they moved to the patio to get a beer. Austin's patio covered about two thousand square feet. The entire deck surface used an elegant looking artificial surface in a light tan color.

Austin decided to take a nap. Keith needed to call his office, so he showed Bryan the small boat with electric motor, detailed where to expect fish and how to catch them. Austin then left for the office, saying, "Beth, will be back about four."

Bryan found Jaunita, made a small lunch together, and Bryan started for the dock.

"You find some perch. I will take to my family," said Juanita, as she waved to him. He slipped into the small boat. Juanita remained on the dock as she continued the conversation, waiting for Bryan's comments.

"Gracias," Bryan continuing in Spanish, "I hope to find you some. Where is your family?"

Answering in Spanish, "You use our language. They live in Coolin. Five miles. My husband, Pablo, fixes boats. He is good. We have one child but hope for one more. She goes to school. We are very lucky. Mr. Austin and Beth helped us become American citizens. They help us with our English. I take care of this beautiful house. It is much work. You catch me some fish."

Switching back to English Bryan continued, "I have little experience as a fisherman. I will need some luck."

Juanita smiled and waved Bryan away to go fishing.

The small boat would not do well if the wind came up. Bryan wore his life jacket. Only a slight ripple greeted him as he set out to try the spots Keith mentioned. He caught three small lake trout and released them, then tried the perch spots.

Bryan realized he felt relaxed and enjoyed everything he was exposed to. But he still did not have a handle on why he was here. He caught two ten-inch brook trout, saving them for Jaunita, then lucked into a school of perch. He motored back to the dock with an even dozen ten-inch perch.

Juanita, saw him coming, so met him at the dock. "You have some fish for me? I see you catch them."

"Watching me, Juanita? Do you want the two-brook trout as well?"

"Si, my family will like them. My work is done till I must start dinner."

Near the back of the patio a fish cleaning area allowed Juanita to make quick work of the filleting chore.

"That was quick," smiled Bryan.

"It is easy to learn, and Mr. Austin lets me fish if I am free. I always do my work first."

Bryan went to his large bedroom, sat in the recliner by the window and started to reread the files. They could learn much when he sent them how the Marana police do their files.

He decided the Mary Jo file did not reflect a drug test in the autopsy report. No cause of death included anywhere. A well-to-do person with all the connections Austin maintained, would imply that no stone would be left unturned. He decided he could jeopardize the entire arrangement, but he would ask about both items. He may have to hitchhike to Spokane and buy his own ticket to Tucson, but he felt used.

Halfway through Zach's file, he fell asleep. He awakened when he heard Beth's voice in the hallway. After he heard her door close, he went downstairs.

The first person he saw was George. Juanita was serving him an early dinner.

"Hello George. Back from Bozeman?"

"Yes sir, Byan. Mr. Davis is here, but plans to rest until dinner. It has been a long day. I have another trip for Mr. Shelton."

Austin came into the room carrying an IPA. "Thank you, George. When you come back, if the weather is good, could you land at Cavanaugh?"

"Sir, I will fly over the strip. If it looks clean, I will use it. If I prefer Priest River, I will fly over the house on my way back to Priest. Very often the Cavanaugh strip is too great a risk for your plane."

"Whatever you decide, I trust you," answered Austin.

"Bryan, please join me on the patio for a beer."

"Sounds great. I'm beginning to enjoy being spoiled like this."

Out on the patio, beers in hand, they sat side by side, but those dark maroon chairs were turned so they could look at each other.

"I am interested in your one hundred percent appraisal of Mary Jo's death."

"You may not like it, sir."

"I have never liked it, so speak your mind."

Bryan took a sip of his beer, wiped two small drops of spill from his chin and nervously began. "First, sir, I am very nervous about this."

"Don't be, I have a reason for asking."

"Okay. The file seems very small for a death involving the wife of a prominent citizen with close and intimate friends and relatives in law enforcement.

"I believe other people could have seen Mary Jo's car, and would have known who owned it. Someone should've stopped.

"The deputy would have recognized the car and parked closer not suspecting anything, until she didn't respond to his tapping on the window. He should have tried to open the door to help. He wouldn't have been concerned about fingerprints.

"The autopsy report is very brief. No sign of a drug analysis, say to detect if she drank wine with lunch. There is no mention of a cremation or burial. I didn't see a record of the check receipt and what she ate and where she dined.

"It appears little or no effort was made to determine where she went after lunch.

"The delay from when she called you saying she was starting home and the delay before you called the sheriff, could be considered excessive in a court room.

"Forensics has come a long way in the time between her death until now. Keith isn't as good a poker player as you and Beth. A couple of his comments didn't relate to the information I received.

"If, and I mean if, a second car played a part in whatever happened, that is a minimum of two people who know the real facts. Driving almost to your house, leads me to feel that was designed to implicate you. Before I go on, any comments, sir, and is this being recorded?"

Austin stood up. "Another beer, Bryan?"

"Sounds good, sir." Austin brought two beers in frosted glasses, then set one in front of each chair. He sat down and sighed heavily.

"I don't record things here, and you have a right to ask. You don't know us. Our hospitality is tops, that is how I live. This place is mine, no pretenses.

"The organization I spoke of exists. It is not secret, just very exclusive.

"You did not miss much about the file on Mary Jo. Beth will have the rest of the documents when she returns. I wanted to save a couple documents for you to study after reading the basic file. We do think forensics has a place, but do not have the facilities here.

"I will pay for anything you need or do. We cannot trust anyone here. The general population does not like rich people owning everything on the lake. We ran into many blank walls. Deputy Scribner's story is not well thought out. We suspect most of it is a lie. We also suspect he knows exactly what happened and how. The time frame doesn't match. We have not been able to fill the gaps.

"We suspect she saw something she wasn't supposed to see. Someone killed her and drove her to the pullout. We are only guessing, but I feel a tiny sense of vindication after hearing your remarks. After you read the rest of the file, we will speak again. Then I will make you an offer. Fair enough?"

"Fair enough. I hope I did not cause you pain. I am still spinning things around in my head," uttered, Bryan.

"You keep those thoughts spinning. You have a date tonight, and here she is."

CHAPTER 55

eth came down the stairs looking like a cowgirl. Black jeans and boots, a paisley long-sleeve muted multicolored cowgirl shirt accented with a dark green lacy neck scarf. She looked stunning to Bryan.

"Bryan, we are treating you to a dinner at Hills Resort. You get to drive, and I get to show you where to turn."

"I need to change my shirt, but I don't have a cowboy one."

"I am just showing off Bryan, because I'm sure there will be a few people at Hill's that know me. I get to brag about my new friend from Arizona. We will use the Acura."

Bryan changed his shirt and followed Beth and Austin to the car. "Drive safely and enjoy yourselves."

Hills resort was a rustic sprawling place with twenty or so cabins, a marina, a long-sandy beach, and a fine dining restaurant. Beth reserved a table by the biggest picture window.

"Hi Beth, I'll show you to your table. We saved the best for you and your date." She removed the reserved placard and filled the water glasses. "Would you like a drink before ordering?"

"I will have the house chardonnay, and the Kalispell IPA for my friend.

"Austin told me to select that beer for you. I come here every chance I get. The two young women at the back table know me, so the word will be out about you. Tell me anything about your family, work, or anything you feel free to talk about."

"Beth, I don't talk about my family much, I will tell you my biological father left the family, when I was ten and my brother, twelve. My mother is a mail-carrier by day, and a bar waitress by night. My brother is in prison—maybe until he dies. I visited him once. He told me not to come back.

The wrestling coach at my middle school talked me into trying the sport. He became my savior. I finished middle school and wrestled in high school well enough to earn a scholarship to Arizona State. I did okay, but was never a state or conference champion. Coach Spaulding came to all my high school matches and home college ones. I actually lived with him my last two years of high school. We are still super close friends.

"I graduated from ASU with a law-enforcement degree with honors. The first position I applied for, the Marana Police Department, hired me. I'm better than most at computers, and that was what they needed.

"Chief Johnson is my mentor. He would probably deny that, but we get on very well. He lets me tag along with homicide detectives whenever it works. For some reason, he hasn't shared with me, he watches my cold case work closely. I'm thirty years old, and have been with the Marana Department for the last six years.

"I attend the University of Arizona, working on a master's degree in forensic science. I have thirty-two credits remaining. When I get to the last eighteen, I intend to apply for a sabbatical and finish the last semester. The Tucson department has two of their top forensic specialists retiring in three years. I hope to secure one of those positions."

Beth didn't say anything immediately, as she studied Bryan and sipped her wine.

"That is a remarkable story. Chief Johnson left out some items. Coach Spaulding must be quite the special person."

"He is that and then some. He had two Hispanic boys that lived with him when I also lived there. Both wrestled in high school and were tough little guys. Neither went to college, but one was on the Mexican Olympic wrestling team. Coach kept us out of trouble and taught us much. He often picked kids at middle school to try wrestling, many of them wrestled at some college level. He took it personally, if he lost one of his hopefuls to bad influences."

He paused, sipped his beer, then smiled. "Your turn, Beth."

"I'm twenty-nine and have worked for Uncle Keith since my sophomore year in high school. I told you about my parents' accident. I still live with Uncle Keith and Aunt Thelma. He jokes, he will just will the house to me, so I never have to move. I have traveled to lots of places, including New York, but I like it here.

"I am now the office manager and daytime dispatcher at the department. We have eight policemen, one policewoman, and a semi-retired jailer. Any guests in our jail know I don't have keys for anything, except the front door. I am slowly working on a business degree from the University of Idaho. At the rate I'm going, I'll retire the day I obtain my degree. That's my story."

"Do you ski or do other sports?" asked Bryan.

"I don't seem to have an interest in such things. I ran for a short time, but didn't enjoy it. I love to dance, so I go out with the girls when I can."

"You go fishing with Austin and Keith?"

"I have, but fish are slimy. If you come fishing, I might let you talk me into fishing, then you could take care of me."

"I don't know if I'll be invited back, Beth. I'm not sure I can be much help to Austin."

"I'm sure you will be invited back. Uncle Keith asked me to copy the rest of the Mary Jo file. You will find it quite interesting. Austin will want to hear everything you have to say.

"Uncle Keith appreciated your help on the Erlinger case. We know you received a tip about Zach, and the Spokane homicide. But you knew what to do, did it on a weekend, and followed through with us and the Spokane Police to close those cases. Keith said few would have been as decisive as you.

He, spoke of you to Austin, who talked with others. They want to stop as much of the drug trade as possible They believe having a go-to person in Arizona will be a game changer. That's why Bill Davis is here. Let's order. I skipped lunch, so I could splurge tonight. Austin is buying."

Bryan chose the shrimp with scallops meal. Beth polished off a nice rib-eye and fixings. They talked of school and the different climates, and found themselves laughing often. When the waitress removed their dishes, Beth said, "We will have the huckleberry pie á la mode. Heated please."

"Nice choice. I'll bring them right out."

"You ever eaten huckleberries, Bryan?"

"Never."

"You are in for a treat."

They finished the desert about the same time. "Well?" smiled Beth.

"That is the best piece of pie ever. I don't eat a lot of sweets, but those berries are superb."

"I knew it. You are hooked. How much do you think a gallon of them sells for around here?" Beth asked.

"No clue, maybe five to ten dollars," was Bryan's guess.

"Between forty and sixty dollars depending upon size and quality. There are people who use their vacation to pick and sell them. Some keep their spots a secret within their families. Often unemployed people hike well off the beaten path, pick and sell to places like Hills. All who sell berries are supposed to have a permit, but most don't."

"When are they ripe?"

"Mid-July through mid-August depending how early spring is and the altitude of the bushes," answered Beth.

"The only berries I have ever picked were from the shelf in a store. Something to put on my bucket list," smiled Bryan.

"It's getting late. We should be getting back," said Beth.

Only evening night lights greeted them as they reached the cabin.

As Beth stopped at her door she turned to Bryan, "I had a lovely time. I don't kiss on first dates, but maybe we will have a second one soon."

"I would like that. Good night, Beth," and he entered his room.

Juantia cooked up a breakfast that consisted of ham scrambled eggs and whole wheat pancakes with huckleberry glaze syrup.

"Mr. Kellerman, you like, no?"

"Wonderful Juanita, a super meal."

Bryan took his mug of coffee and headed for the stairs to read the rest of the Mary Jo file. Bill Davis entered the dining room as Bryan was leaving.

"Good morning, Bryan. I'm Bill Davis, from White Sulfur Springs, Montana. I own a ranch there. Let's visit after I eat breakfast."

"Nice to meet you. Juanita's breakfast is super." He reread the Mary Jo file and listed the questions to ask.

Bryan strolled slowly down to the dock and made a few casts with the fake worm. Three bass out of six casts. He released all three fish. He felt nervous. He heard someone walking on the dock and turned to see Beth walking toward him.

The water reflected the morning sun creating glistening ripples over the lake. He could see three bass swimming below the dock.

"Good morning, Bryan. I am on my way to work. I hope to make it back before you leave tomorrow."

"Good morning Beth, you look extra nice this morning, drive safely, I do hope you make it back."

"Thank you, Bryan. See you." She smiled and reached out her hand and held Bryan's for a few seconds, then turned quickly and climbed the path to her car. She turned and waved.

"Beth, I will keep this pretty picture of you in my mind."

"So will I, Bryan, so will I."

CHAPTER 56

It was almost ten when Austin called Bryan to join them in the study.

Bill started the discussion. "Bryan, I started and organized our three-state group. We either have a unique skill, some level of influence, and a long-term standing in our community or state. This is our card. The logo is WIM, Wyoming, Idaho, and Montana. We don't advertise or allow just anyone to participate. A person must be referred, and receive a yes vote from at least ten members," he paused before continuing.

"We are not asking you to join, as you don't live in our three states, and you are still employed. All of our members are retired. We hope you can find time to help us tackle the drug problem plaguing our states. You know about the Idaho pipeline, which is temporarily shut down. We have learned of a similar Minnesota pipeline that was recently shut down.

"We are working to include North Dakota in our group, and wish to stop the hikers in Montana. We have prepared a list of possible criminals for you, to see if they are in your databases. Monitoring the dealers and their products at a larger scope than we presently are able to is critical to us. We are hoping your computer expertise can help."

Bryan looked down at his hands, then offered, "This whole thing is overwhelming. I would like every dealer in jail, but they are difficult to catch red-handed. We know lots of them. Catching them is not easy. Undercover doesn't work, as they are always killed. If the bad guys suspect someone, the suspected is killed by the drug culture henchmen. This culture is big in our area, and we have walkers, too. You know I work full time and go to college part time. The Chief will not let me add a lot more."

"We respect that, Bryan. We are well-funded and will pay you well for your services. We will not let you use your own funds for anything. Maybe you will be able to help get names and pictures into the hands of watchers, who in turn can allow law-enforcement to catch them, *red-handed* as you say."

Bill sat back in his chair. "Thank you for listening."

"You're welcome. I can say today, I will try to live up to your expectations, but will not violate my law-enforcement protocol," said Bryan.

"We would expect no less. Our research told us about your outstanding character, or you never would have met any of us. I will give you the list of names for you to test. None of the named parties are known to be above the law. All are possible criminals. We just cannot prove it. Please, Bryan, do not do anything illegal, ever."

"Not a chance, Mr. Davis."

Austin interrupted. "George has landed at Cavanaugh, and asked that you leave by one p.m. to complete his return by dark. Bill I'm so thankful you were able to travel here on such short notice."

Bill held Bryan's hand. "We will advance you five thousand dollars to purchase what-ever you need. A separate computer, and separate communication devises as well as the software you need with the best security protection you can find." He handed Bryan a leather wallet containing the money, and five contact phone numbers. He added one thousand for Bryan's work while in Idaho.

"We should gather our things and go to the plane," Austin said.

"Bryan, when you are ready, call Austin. He and I will fly to Mesa, and we will meet in the casino. When you have a good start, call Beth, she will know what to do," added Bill.

Bryan turned to Austin, "I have some ideas about the new information I received about Mary Jo I need to touch base with a friend in the Tucson Police Department, before I visit with you about my idea, If that's okay with you. Will you tell me if Mary Jo was cremated?

"Perfectly. I have waited a long time for any progress. I can wait a few more days. Thank you, Bryan. She is buried near-by," Austin answered.

CHAPTER 57

eorge dropped Bryan at Spokane International, then left immediately to fly to Bill Davis to Bozeman. Bryan called Wilson at the Spokane Police Department.

"Wilson,"

"Bryan Kellerman, I'm at the Spokane airport and was asked by Mr. Shelton to call you. My plane leaves in three hours."

"I'll be up to see you in thirty minutes. I'll wear my Dodgers baseball cap." Click.

Bryan wandered the spacious lobby, noting the western art, and sculptures. He saw the baseball cap and hurried to meet Wilson.

"Bryan, Dennis Wilson—lunch and coffee on me. Let's go get a table."

Both selected a club sandwich, coffee, and a piece of apple pie. Dennis produced two files. Both said Mary Jo Shelton.

"You don't have this information yet, check page two. Austin wanted you to have this. The third file lists some bad people you may want to check. Bill Davis's son and I grew up together. Bill is like a father to me. I would do anything for him. If anyone asks, I will deny giving you anything. I know I was not followed today."

"I understand Dennis, you can count on me."

They talked about the Zapata killing. Dennis took the lunch check.

"Thank you for taking the time to meet, Dennis. I hope our paths cross again."

"You are welcome. Austin is paying. I am positive our paths will cross again. Call if you need anything about the files explained."

Bryan and Dennis shook hands, then Bryan sauntered to his boarding gate. Southwest gave him a smooth ride home. He was at a loss to figure out what was really going on. The two lists of names only listed one person Bryan knew about. This was something new that may change his career. He knew Chief Johnson would not interfere, but he was the boss. Brian decided three things:

1.To see Beth again. Before he left Priest Lake, he and Beth exchanged phone numbers. He sent her a short text. "Back in Marana. Thank you for the date, a special time for me."

Her quick reply, "Very special, be seeing you."

2. To relay only about the files to the chief.

3. To travel to Mesa and learn everything he needed to know, find a suitable storage place to keep the WIM items, and study access codes and passwords. He did travel to Mesa, purchased a top-of-the-line computer and three cell phones, then ordered the enhanced security he felt he needed. The storage unit was only two blocks from the casino.

He figured he could arrange the meeting with the chief and some principles from WIM and get things in motion. Just needed to keep everyone posted. He still had money left, so he purchased the entire Microsoft office package. Lots of ways to keep track of things.

Bryan danced into his apartment, talking to himself, *"That Beth woman has stirred me up. I am humming to myself. I may like that first kiss."*

He needed to call Benito.

CHAPTER 58

Before going to his desk, he put a note by the Chief's door, 'three-minute update.'

Then he called Benito. Voicemail. BK at IHOP tomorrow at seven a.m. if it works for you.

Benito walked into IHOP at exactly seven on the dot. He was wearing khaki slacks and a pink polo shirt, sporting the not a hair out of place look.

"Bryan, how's the trip?"

"Interesting. I met a lot of people. Some new friends."

He told Benito an abbreviated story how it all happened, and about the unknown tipper. He told him he believed it is also the same source who told about Rocco.

"How did he know to call you?"

"Benito, I work cold or unsolved cases that I find in newspapers, when I have spare time. It helps with my college classes. My tipster answered, *yes,* when I asked if he saw my inquiry about the Spokane case. I leave my open number at the police station. He called that number. I am sure he disguises his voice, and he knows his way around Arizona."

"I get tips too, Bryan. Some are really good, others are just testing me, I think. I have one good source, but I know he stays alive working both ways. He doesn't lie, just forgets all the facts.

"Bryan, we got a picture of the black guy you spotted at the Tucson airport before you left on your trip. Chief didn't want to alert Miami yet, because he didn't want a leak there to give us away. I am guessing he is going to call someone he knows in Miami and check things himself. We are 100% the black man is from Miami.

"Benito, how much time do we have before the power play begins?"

"Chief asked me the same question. I told him if that black guy is a part of things, we have a week or two at most before someone dies. Then if Pepe is still alive, he will hire some muscle from Mexico and unleash them."

"Are the police vulnerable?"

"I think, no. Bryan. They will fight with each other until an innocent is killed, then who knows? I may move my informant to Williams next week. Rocco won't like that, but will wait until things are over. I think Rocco wants to take over, or be dead."

"Are you at risk? Pepe sort of trusts you."

"He will tell me things if he thinks I can help him. He doesn't really trust and neither do I. We will always be on opposite sides. He will never tell me who his boss is. If he did, he would end up like Vinny did. Buzzard food."

They finished their meal, paid their own and left together.

"Bryan, you going to the gym later?"

"Yes, about four."

"I will join you then," smiled Benito.

Bryan didn't make it to his desk, before the chief waved him to the office.

Bryan, by now you know I played a part in arranging your trip. Chief Booth wanted you to go. He is hoping we can coordinate working on the drug traffic. Can you come to my house for dinner tonight? Nothing special just BBQing some burgers."

"That would be great. What time?"

"Come about five-thirty, and park in the driveway, not on the street."

Benito and Bryan did a workout together. Bryan noticed Benito wanted to be the best at everything, not a word about business. Benito acted stressed and edgy. During his boxing days he was known as an aggressive combatant. Bryan let him be the best.

CHAPTER 59

ryan parked in the driveway as expected. The chief's home was a modest three-bedroom rancher painted light yellow.

Before he could ring the doorbell, it opened and a pretty young black woman introduced herself. "I'm Vanessa. Dad is on the patio. I am supposed to get you a beer and escort you out there." She opened the refrigerator, and Bryan selected an IPA he had never tried before. "Follow me." She was enjoying herself.

"I am a senior. I don't eat burgers. Two of my friends are coming over. We get vegan pizza." Pointing to a woman in a wheelchair, this is my mom, Rose. She just is."

"Thank you, Vannesa. Nice to meet you," offered Bryan.

She leaned close and whispered, "He likes you."

She vanished into the house and Bryan knew she smelled extra fine, almost like fresh roses.

"Welcome, Bryan. How do you like your burgers."

"Medium, sir."

"All of mine are medium, and you can drop the sir."

"Vanessa will be in college next year. I will have a tough time when she is away. I am sure she knows how to be a teenager, but she is an absolute treasure. She does everything here and has a chance to be a valedictorian of her class.

"Rose had an aneurysm when she was home alone. I had gone to watch Vanessa play volleyball. We didn't get home until after ten. She survived the surgeries, but has been in a vegetative state ever since. The Dr's say she does not have much time left. Been tough."

"We have a couple of things to talk about, but we eat first. Vanessa and friends will join us when the pizza arrives."

Vanessa came dancing out with the pizza. "Bryan, my friends—Belle and Chelsea." Belle, black, and Chelsea, white. Five around the table. All three girls were over six feet tall. The girls dominated the conversation with school and teen topics. Some teasing of Vanessa about a nameless boy.

The chief acted happy. Vanessa fed Rose a small slice of pizza and a few sips of tea.

"Are you all volleyball players?" asked Bryan.

"Just Vanessa. I run track and Chelsea has a scholarship to ASU in basketball," answered Belle. The girls cleaned up everything, while the Chief cleaned the grill. Belle pushed Rose into the tv room.

"You need anything, Dad?"

"No, Vanessa. You have done more than enough."

"You are welcome. We are going down to Belle's. I'll call when I start home. How long will you be tonight?"

"Maybe until eight."

"I will plan to be back by eight-thirty then, I need to finish some school stuff."

She planted a kiss on her dad's cheek. "Nice to meet you, Bryan. See ya."

And with a skip she took off.

"We have two topics to talk about. I did not want us to be overheard. I sweep my house every day. Vanessa knows how to do it, too.

"Should I buy a sweeper?"

"It would be a good idea, Bryan. I'll get you a catalogue." Returning, he handed Bryan a one-inch-thick telephone book-sized catalogue from Brisbane Industries in Las Cruzes, New Mexico.

"Page 93 has the best deal. How are you and Benito getting along?"

Bryan looked at the chief and decided two things. Something deeper bothers him and he is planning to take a big risk with a trusted colleague. Bryan felt privileged to be that colleague.

"I feel he wants something. He could have worked at friendship before. I saw a mean streak at the gym today. He can be charming, but I seem to remember he was often too aggressive as a boxer. "

"Bryan, I can't tell you all. You will have to guess some. Benito tries to be a good cop. We are sure he knows, few in the department trust him. His undercover work in California won some commendations. A lot of criminals saw jail time. His grades at ASU were tops, and he earned a degree in criminal justice. He applied everywhere. The board hired him. I wasn't asked. He works hard, but his logs have too many missing events.

"I sensed that you seeing the black man from Miami angered him. He acted that way when he briefed me. That man knew to go to ground as soon as he arrived. Benito hinted he couldn't find him."

He paused a full minute. "About six months ago, we received a tip about a drug deal at a certain place. We set up an arrest. When we arrived at the location, everything was gone. A family of illegals huddled in the back room. They were allowed to reenter Mexico. The bad guys must have been tipped off. Then a week ago, while you were in Idaho, 'Smith and Jones' (code names for undercover) arranged a buy. When they got to the house, the door was ajar. They entered and found a young Hispanic man, brutally tortured and very dead. The only name on both police lists was Benito.

"We know that is not conclusive, but it is enough to set things in motion. The two undercover cops were exposed, and have been reassigned. I am telling you this, because you could be in danger. I am ordering you to stay away from Pepe. I am asking you not to get too close to Benito. I am not able to tell you what we are planning."

"Wow, sir. I will follow your order and your suggestion. I do not think I will become aloof, just close enough to find out what he wants from me. I have a file on a cold case concerning the three bodies found on Superstition Mountain. Now that you raise the questions, I am sure he started talking to me a lot more after I made some calls regarding that case. That case is over four years old and never a suspect. I will bait the file, and leave it on my desk. If he reads it, I will put a note on your door asking for eleven minutes. That will mean he looked at the file."

"Good plan. Now for item two. Your trip to Idaho. Chief Booth, at first just wanted you to see the crime scene for Zach. Then they asked if you could talk to them about how you work cold cases, including how you handle new leads. Then they wanted to see if a relationship could be established to make further progress stopping the drug pipelines. They offered to pay all expenses. I sense there is more involvement coming, so felt it would be a beneficial trip. You tell me what I need to know."

"I am not sure yet what all is to happen. They gave me two lists of possible criminals to compare. I only recognized one name. I can't start looking, as that would tip someone somewhere. I made no promises, and wasn't asked to. I feel I need to do something, because they are serious about trying to stop the drug trade. We know that's impossible, yet our job dictates we try. I will keep you in the loop asking for six minutes, Chief, if I have something. Do you want to meet any of them?"

"Yes, if approved by them. I will not do anything, if I'm not wanted."

"Let me study this and get back to you. I will ask for fifteen minutes."

"Fair enough, Bryan."

It is almost 8:30, so I'll run along. Thanks for the burger. Your Vanessa is special."

"Yes, she is, and you are welcome. Only one other person knows we will watch Benito. Do watch your back, he is very capable."

CHAPTER 60

ryan studied the catalogue first after returning to his apartment. *"Wow, this stuff is expensive,"* he said out loud. He decided to order the best sweeper and chose a medium-priced remote camera system. He also decided to buy a metal window screen to cover his only window looking out into the courtyard from his kitchen, and a deadbolt locking system for the door. He would just install the items and not ask permission. He needed to minimize the risk to himself.

The info about Benito, disturbed him. He wondered where in California he worked undercover. He believed the chief knew.

He hoped his apartment wasn't currently bugged.

Turning on some music, just in case, he started the homework for his college classes. Two hours later, he closed his books, and started to rehash everything he and Benito had talked about. He decided not to write anything anywhere. He realized Benito knew way more players in the drug business than he did.

Benito could list all of the real players in the Tucson/Marana drug culture. His contacts were that complete. He knew no one else knew them all. He would continue his planning. He believed he could trust Bryan, but would be on opposite sides if his planning came together.

Bryan trusted Chief Johnson.

CHAPTER 61

I landed in Mesa, just in time to enjoy dinner at the casino. I picked up my Honda CRV rental and drove directly to the casino. After the dinner buffet, I completed my journey to my park model in Palm Creek Resort in Casa Grande. Making a quick stop at the grocery store on Pinal Avenue, I stocked up for a week stay.

As soon as I had my treasures stowed, I called Ernesto.

"Hola, Del, you are here, no?"

"Si. Ernesto. I am here. Will we have dinner at Café Taco's?"

"Si, it is arranged. We have much to discuss."

I reached the Café five minutes early. The Sanchez family already occupied a table. Ernesto stood to greet me, and waited for me to sit, then he sat.

"Elena, thank you for coming. Emillio, Maria, Anna, and Lupe, thank you for coming to see me."

"We came to eat and not have to clean lots of dishes, Senior Del," smiled Lupe.

Elena scowled at Lupe, "It is not respectful."

"Mr. Sanderson," said Emillio. "I have an A in math now, thank you for helping me."

"I am very pleased, Emillio. How is the rest of school going?"

"I have *all* A's now."

"I will shake your hand after dinner," I promised him.

Turning back to answer Lupe I said, "Well Lupe, I do not like to do dishes either, but I must if I am to eat," I grinned.

Consuello brought me, a Dos XX's amber and a Modelo for Ernesto. "Your dinner is almost ready, Senior Del."

"Gracias, Consuello."

"Poor nada." she answered looking over shoulder, as she turned away.

"Will you come to Helping Hands soon, Senior Del?" asked Ernesto.

"Tomorrow, early, about nine a.m.," I nodded.

"We have much to show you."

Two hours passed quickly. I liked the Sanchez family very much. I knew they liked me in return. We were all standing, when Macho arrived. "Senior Del, it is good you are here. There is no paying for you here ever, we say thank you."

"You are welcome, Macho. I like coming here, and I love the food."

Just after nine, I arrived at Helping Hands, to see how the community tutoring project was doing. The old church sported a new paint job. Desert tan. The entire inside also looked better, with new paint as well. Nine tables now instead of the original three, and sixty plus chairs. Lucas and Michelle were helping children, so was Peter Sullivan.

Lucas saw me and approached him, "Del, we could use two more tutors."

"I will bet you have a couple in mind."

"Si, Senior Del. I have an unopened letter for you from Sarah. We are all interested in what she has to say." Peter replaced Sarah a couple month ago.

"Can you arrange to have your prospects meet me here around four tomorrow, afternoon?"

"Consider it done."

My tutoring project, that I started nine months ago, occupied an old church. That musty barely clean, abandoned building, now looked fresh, clean and modern. My total investment so far, was near thirty thousand dollars, but two of my investments have earned that and more. We employed six tutors, soon to be eight.

I sauntered over to watch Peter. "Morning Peter, you have a new family member yet?"

"Morning, Del. Yes, a son, Connor Liam Sullivan. He and his mother are doing well. The adult citizenship classes are full, 60 students. They work so hard to get things right. I hope it's okay to hire more tutors, because I'm here forty plus hours every week."

"Perfect, Peter, we are lucky to have you. I want to visit with you about your schooling. Would tomorrow morning work for you?"

I can't tomorrow. I only have one car and need to take Connor and his mom to the doctor for his three-week checkup. Can we do breakfast the next day?"

"That is fine, I will be forced to play golf somewhere. Tough life. Breakfast at the Big House the next morning?"

"Thank you, my family will be there," smiled Peter.

I met with Dominic and Candi, so now they had eight tutors. Jordan knew the type of person to ask to be a tutor.

Sitting in the rental car, I read Sarah's letter.

Mr. Sanderson, I cannot thank you enough for asking me to be a tutor at Helping Hands. I am now in my second year to complete my teaching certificate, and have been to four different schools so far watching other teachers. I am happy. You have started a very special program in Casa Grande. Few people try to make a difference like you have. I plan to finish as soon as possible going to summer sessions as well. I will write again, and you will receive an invitation to my graduation. I know how lucky I am because three of my friends are just still spinning their wheels. Thank you.

Sincerely,
Sarah

Sarah will become a decorated teacher, I thought to myself.

The next morning, I gave Sarah's letter to Lucas to share with the other tutors.

CHAPTER 62

I played golf at Dave White Municipal near Casa Grande, a tree-lined okay course, with hard to read greens. First time out in four months, I will take the 88 score.

After golf, I drove to Marana, and called J.C. He is the custodian at the Marana Police Department where Bryan Kellerman works.

"Howdy. Del, you in Arizona?"

"Yes. J.C., I am in Arizona for at least a week. Since you bought dinner in Kona, I thought I could treat you at the Texas Roadhouse, tonight."

"I'll be there at five-thirty, Del. It will be good to shake your hand."

I had a couple of hours to kill, so drove into downtown Tucson, located a parking spot near a traditional Mexican restaurant. I first ate there waiting for my Lorenzo *adventure*. My first long distance shot, not at a range. I ordered only two tacos. The half-rack of ribs coming later will put me over my calorie limit. Lots of expensive art in downtown Tucson. I did not find anything special enough to spend Vinny's money on this time.

A short jaunt to Marana and the Texas Roadhouse, allowed me to sit and a enjoy a Lagunitas, and wait for J.C.

He arrived right on time. "Hello, Del. So happy to see my friend."

Shaking J.C.'s hand, I answered. "Yes, it is special to shake your hand again."

We talked about the fishing trip in Kona, boasting about the big ones we caught. We agreed to fish together again this December in Kona. J.C. agreed to get our tickets, and we will leave Tucson together, on December 15th, four months away.

J.C. talked about growing up in Tucson, how he obtained his job, and a little about the Sweepers, a group of four custodians who meet regularly. After two hours, and the meal finished, I surprised him by asking, "What would you say about the two of us setting up a drug rehab facility in Marana."

He shifted around a little then sighed. "That would be fine, but the cost to keep one open would be substantial. I looked into starting my own. There is one in Tucson, where one of my Sweeper friends cleans it for free. I talked to the manager for a couple hours, and he gave me a copy of his operating costs. You will need to see those numbers. The room and board per person alone was a surprising amount. If you are serious, we have people to talk to. Could maybe act as a satellite in Marana to the Tucson one. I will set up a meeting with them. I would love to save some people."

"Let me know when you have the meeting set. I will make every effort to attend."

We visited another hour, then left together. We noticed a few people sort of watching us. A skinny old black man and a younger-looking white man having dinner together, looked out of place. J.C. started walking down the street. "You want a ride J.C.?"

"No, sir. I like to walk. I live only a half mile from here."

"Be seeing you J.C." Just a wave of his hand. I started my sixty miles back to Casa Grande.

J.C. and I visited with the director of the Tucson rehab center for over three hours. The costs were staggering, but I was forewarned. Pursuing a satellite facility in Marana, would be a possibility. J.C. and I agreed to try. J.C. would scout around for a useable building.

We did fly together to Kona, Hawaii, fished with our good friend, Captain Noah, five times and rode the bus tour around the whole island, something J.C. had never done. We caught lots of fish, but no big marlin. J.C. ate dinner at my condo twice, and we dined at the Kona Brewing Company often. We walked all of downtown together many times.

Molly and Trevor also came for five days. Trevor surfed every day. Molly and I lazed on the beach watching Trevor and talking of things.

We did get to see the Green Flash.

CHAPTER 69

eventy-two degrees at breakfast time in Casa Granda at the Big House Cafe, so I chose to sit outside in a corner location, and stood when Peter, Shelly, and Connor arrived. Peter was everything blond, about five ten, with a never work out, but fit appearance, blue eyes, and large cheek dimples. Shelly was everything red. Thick, naturally long red hair, all the freckles, blue eyes and a ready smile. Little Connor had mom's red hair.

"She greeted me with a soft smile, and a firm handshake. "Good morning, Del. Nice to meet you, Peter has told me about you."

Peter carried Conner in his carrier. His eyes, unblinking, watched everything.

"Good morning, Del. Meet our son, Conner."

I offered him a finger. He grabbed it, held it a few seconds, let go, and finally blinked.

"We can order when you wish, whatever you like. My treat."

We each ordered a different breakfast. Conner seemed happy with his bottle. The Big House is a street front restaurant with a second outdoor seating area near the alley. They are known for their special French toast and super large breakfast burrito.

"I would like to ask you two some personal questions. If you do not wish to answer, that is fine. I also have a proposal for you.

"How many credits do you still have to take to finish your degree, and what will your degree specialty be?"

"Del, I have forty-four credits left and hope to teach math and Spanish in high school. I want to find a small school and maybe teach physics as well."

"How much would that cost, Peter?"

"We live with Shelly's mom. She works full-time and pays Shelly to make life easier for us. I can only go to school part-time, until I start student teaching. We hope to have enough saved to not need to work then. It will cost maybe twenty thousand dollars to finish school."

"You have three semesters to graduate. Correct?"

"Yes, I would need to take one class over summer to get the prerequisites completed. A math and physics teacher at Casa Grande Union has agreed to mentor me."

I paused before offering his proposal, "I would like to help you reach your goal without missing a semester. You can also work at Helping Hands. You can help us find a replacement when you graduate. Jordan is quite capable and could cover as well. Our breakfast is here, so we should eat.

"We can talk of other things and get to know each other. I would like that. Please think about my offer and see if you can make things work. Take the time to prepare a budget for each semester. I will be around through next Wednesday. We can visit again then and finalize an arrangement.

"You should be a teacher now, not three or four years from now."

"Why are you offering this? You hardly know us."

"I like what you are doing at Helping Hands. You are good with the students. You will only get better as a teacher. My judge of a person's character has served me well all my life. I am not wrong about you."

Shelly fussed with Connor. She tried to hide some tears.

"Shelly are you in school too?"

"No, Del, I have dyslexia. School is hard for me. I will do something fun when we find a school that fits Peter's goals, after our children are in school. Peter hopes to live in a small town and be involved. He wants to become a principal eventually.

"I am an only child, so hope we have at least two children. My mom and dad have been divorced a long-time. I never see him. Mom is a bank branch manager. She owns a three-bedroom home free and clear. She and I are close and comfortable. We would have a hard time paying you back and the student loans at the same time. Shelly stood and took Conner for a walk."

Peter added, "The school cost will be over $15,000, maybe $20,000. We can never pay you back."

"Peter, do the budgeting process and agree to meet again next week, and listen to my entire proposal."

"Okay, Del, we will do that. Will next Wednesday after work be okay?"

"Perfect, for now this conversation is just between us," I answered. Shelly returned with Connor. Peter took a turn.

"We can't tell Shelly's mom?" a frowning Peter questioned.

"Not yet, I have my reasons. I am lucky to have some extra money. I would like a better fish locater for my boat, so better get shopping. You two take the time and prepare the budgets. We will meet next Wednesday and see what we need to do."

Both tried to smile, but their minds were working overtime.

I left the meeting with Conner and Shelly and drove through Phoenix to the north two-o-two to walk around the Bass Pro Shop-Cabela's.

I needed to find a more sophisticated fish finder for my boat. When I go to Fort Peck fishing with Toby and Jimmy, I wanted to use the full lake map. There are big walleye and yellow perch in that lake. I found exactly what I wanted, so I spent some of Vinny's money. It was time to call the Cummings family and set up the fishing trip.

Peter, Shelly and I met the following Wednesday, and after many questions, Peter agreed to my proposal. He would enroll this next semester and finish his degree, after three more semesters.

I told him about my two requirements: to never tell anyone where the money came from, and to help someone in need when he learned of that someone, after he could afford to help.

I'm sure Amy would approve. I still miss her and sing favorite songs to her, but I am starting to accept her absence.

CHAPTER 64

I called Toby. Perfect time to go fishing. I towed my boat to Saco, via Havre. It was the shortest way that allowed me to bypass major road construction from Hobson to Lewistown.

I arrived at the Cumming's ranch close to three-thirty. Jimmy barely said hello before taking the cover off the boat. "I love your boat. We have our gear ready. Toby is coming. Gary laughed telling us we will owe him for doing all the chores. Your bunk is ready, and Mom says dinner is at six-thirty. Dad is in Lewistown, at a meeting. I think Gary will try fishing at least once," offered Jimmy.

"We will leave early *tomorrow*. Give us more fishing time," I answered.

Meg stood on the porch, hands on her hips, smiling that soft coy smile she used when she was pleased.

"Welcome back, Del. Frank won't be here tonight. He is in Lewistown with Bill Davis and other friends."

"Be right back," I retreated to my truck, selected my package, hid it behind my back, and continued back to the house. I stepped up on the porch and handed Meg the gift sack.

"What do we have here, Del?" She carried the heavy sack to a chair by a small log table sat down and opened it. She retrieved all three jars, one chokecherry syrup, one huckleberry preserves, and one huckleberry jelly. "Now this is a big surprise! You bring gifts like these, and you can come back anytime! I hoped you would remember."

I stood nearby, and she gave me a long hug. "Jody proves to be quite right about you. Please come in."

I followed her inside and into the parlor. "Frank doesn't expect to be back before you need to go back. We wish to know if you thought about his inquiry to help us."

"I would be happy to help, anyway I am able. I work with an attorney in Great Falls, whom I trust. To do things as they should be done will require full disclosure. You and Frank must be comfortable with that. Your sons must know a lot now, but will need to be included. I believe the future transfer of all things is much easier if there are not any surprises."

Meg answered, "We have talked about the process, as you call it, to finish our estate plan, with our boys. After you left, we started going through every paper and have an understanding of how we see the process working."

"Meg, I feel comfortable here. I have told my daughter about the Cummings family, and she wants to meet all of you."

Meg just smiled. "They are welcome here anytime. I will tell Frank of your decision, and arrange getting started. I need to finish making dinner. You go have fun with my boys," Meg hummed as she turned toward the kitchen carrying the jars. I walked back out into the yard.

Jimmy had the cover entirely off and was sitting in the driver's seat. "I want one of these."

"Make me an offer."

"This one is yours, Del. Wait till you see the one I have picked out at the marina. Shep Remington owns the Marina and has four Lund Tyees that he uses for the guided trips. He promised to teach me the ropes, how to be a guide and let me work there. He is seventy-three and his only daughter doesn't want to take over.

Dad and I have talked some, but the risk owning the marina would be huge. Guiding will help to decide if we should go for the marina. Guiding will be more work than ranching, but the ranch won't support three of us brothers. I just don't know much about Shep's client list.

"I think being a fishing guide would be special. Boats and airplanes are softer rides than horses."

I whispered, "Maybe we should look at a deal together."

Jimmy looked at me and whispered back, "Never thought about having a partner."

"Jimmy, we should keep that to ourselves," I whispered again.

After a long pause Jimmy whispered, "Del, maybe you're right, just between us. I have only fished the reservoir twice. There is so much to learn. I hope to work there this summer as much as possible. They can use me for haying and harvest, but the rest I can work at fishing."

"Where is Toby?"

"He is out checking the cattle and the cameras. He'll tell you the details, but we got a really good video of the drug mules. They camped in the same place you guys found. We saw where they cross the creek. He will be back for supper, in another hour, anyway."

"I'll put the boat under the pull-through lean-to on the west side of the machine shed. When I finish, it will be veranda beer time," I suggested.

"We have some Lagunitas, for you Del."

"Spoiling me, I like that," I smiled.

Jimmy talked fishing non-stop until Gary joined them. Then ranching took over.

Toby arrived a little after six.

"You were out a long time, anything special?" asked Gary.

"I found a coyote den, and reduced the population by five, the female and four of five pups. I also found another well-used camp, almost to our northern property line. An adult coyote ran into the chokecherry thicket, so I rode over and sat for a while, but he didn't come out.

"There's a deer trail that crosses the thicket, so I armed the 223 rifle and followed the tracks. They went right through the camp. I used my glove and wiped out my tracks and started back. I rode along the ridge top all the way to the hay field. Looks like 90% of the cattle are bunched near the spring. I will take the quad tomorrow before we go fishing and try for the other two coyotes. I need to clean up for supper." Gary headed inside.

Supper conversation centered around ranch things. I politely listened. Meg interrupted, "Boys, your dad asked me to visit with Del for a few minutes."

Toby answered first, "I'll clean up here and go help Gary and Jimmy with the chores."

"Thank you," her smile showed warm and real.

"Del, I spoke to Frank before supper and relayed your comments." He smiled. "I could tell we are going to ask a favor of you."

"Anything," I answered.

"Jimmy is so wrapped up in fishing and the marina, that we worry he isn't seeing the pitfalls. He uses all his free time on the subject. Frank and I have always supported our boys, and they are respected young men.

"We aren't sure how, or if we should support him. When we are no longer alive, technically the ranch would belong to three owners. We don't think that's wise. Our favor of you is to use your expertise to access the Fort Peck situation and tell us what you think."

"I will gladly do that. Jimmy already said the property is forty plus acres. Maybe some expansion possibilities. I will snoop around. Should be fun."

Meg stood and so did I. We looked at each other a long time without saying a word. Finally, Meg spoke. "Thank you. Our family is lucky you are part of us," she turned and walked into the kitchen.

After breakfast, Toby, Jimmy and I left for the fishing trip on Fort Peck Reservoir.

Jimmy asked, "Toby, did you get the coyotes?"

"Yup. I left at first light, picked off both, and hurried back. The thin rise of smoke, tempted me, but I stayed with our rules and that means no contact."

"Did you see them?" asked Jimmy.

"No. They had to have heard me. Too bad, there were only two coyotes, so I could shoot some more. They must have been watching and saw me load the dogs on the quad. They know we know about them. Yet they still come through, maybe more often than we think.

Oh, I saw Ritchie yesterday. He heard me shooting, so came to check to be sure things were okay. He has decided to put his ranch up for sale this fall. Ritchie is the only heir, lives by himself and he just wants the money. Too much work for one man, he said."

"I called Dad, and he said he would look into the process, and maybe find someone to front for him."

"Wow. That would double our ranch. The Sutherland place is at least 460 acres more than ours, said Jimmy. "

"Dad asked to keep to this news to ourselves. I think he has something up his sleeve. The Sutherlands do make a little money, but are not efficient ranchers. Most of their equipment is old and the buildings are only fair. I expect dad will talk to us all when he returns," commented Toby.

I just listened to the two brothers as they discussed the possibilities. Both seemed to like the idea of a bigger ranch.

We arrived at the reservoir about eleven, topped off the fuel, added ice to the cooler and put the boat in the water. While in the marina store, Jimmy introduced Toby and me to Shep.

"The kid says he wants to be a fishing guide, so he has a copy of the lake with GPS markings of the better spots. What kind of fish-finder do you have in your boat?"

"It is a Helix 10 mega Si+GPSG4N," I answered.

"Super, Jimmy can add the map apps he has to your system and be all set. The best walleye spots are listed, the three best bays for big pike, and the two bays that seem to always have decent perch. Button Bottom has been hot for walleye. Jimmy knows where that spot is. You guys have a nice day."

"Thanks, Shep. We will park next to our cabin and get to fishing," a smiling Jimmy answered. The cabins all looked freshly painted dark brown, and just a look in the cabin we were to use told me Shep runs a nice clean business.

I let Jimmy be the captain. He smiled all the way to Button Bottom, maneuvering through a small light chop of waves. He looked so excited, doing something he believed he loved. He followed the mapping app. We marked fish at 23 feet. We caught several walleyes, but none over four pounds. We saved three for a shore lunch. Jimmy produced a fruit salad and cheese and crackers to make the walleye lunch extra fine.

Then we went to another walleye spot and caught three 8-to-9-pound fish. Next, he took us into a small bay with lots of weeds along the shore. Toby hooked a nice pike and used thirty minutes of our day, landing a twenty-six-pound Northern Pike. He acted like a kid with his first candy bar: 'Whoopee' and 'Look at him take line' with the biggest grin ever. Toby has fun at everything he does.

"Guess you are hooked now Toby," laughed Jimmy. While Toby played the pike, a plane flew low over our boat. It was the Bonanza from Cheyenne. I recognized the color and the tail number. I started thinking of how I could check where it had been. Maybe Cliff could supply an app to let me check flights.

Three days of fishing passed too quickly. Float planes took off and landed often.

"Very expensive to fish from those planes," I commented.

Jimmy answered, "lots of planes bring in people to fish remote spots with kayaks and inflatables."

I did not comment about the Bonanza. I wanted to work on that myself. I decided to see if it made sense to obtain a float plane rating.

Then check with Cliff about float planes moving drugs. I wondered if the walkers through the Cummings ranch, received a ride to Glasgow and someone with a floatplane then hauled the drugs to places unknown.

Frank needed two more days.

CHAPTER 65

oby and Jimmy joined Gary to complete the evening chores. Meg and I sat silently on the veranda for a few moments. Meg asked, "What did you think of the marina?"

"The marina looked in good condition, I expected more rigs and boats. The land is forty acres but leased from the Corps of Engineers. I would need to see the time frame of the lease. The docks look a bit old, but my main concern is the low water level. That will change fish habits. A good guide would know what to do. I would let Jimmy guide as often as he can to see if that is what he really wants to do. All fishermen and women expect the guide to get them over fish. No fish and they tell others.

"We would need to see the full set of books and the profit and loss statements, and the list of repeat clients, in order to help you make a decision. It is big water, and wind is an issue in Montana. The terms of the lease of the forty acres, could be really good, if any rate increases are tied to some benchmark that is attainable. The merchandise in the store is very pricey. I would not buy my fishing gear there.

"I liked the looks of the facility, and if everything checked out, I feel the place makes money. That is my first impression,

Meg. I see hard work, but can see how a passion could be turned into something fun to manage.

"Thank you, Del. I know Frank will want to visit with you, but has already advised Jimmy to work there and see if that's what he really wants to do. The Sutherlands selling their ranch is an even bigger life-changer. We, and that includes you now, need to study that closely."

"Jimmy piloted the boat, all three days. We caught fish trying new places, then worked proven places. We caught fish but not I great numbers. I could tell that bothered Jimmy. We fished our way into the Big Dry Arm and stopped at the Rock Creek Marina. It is also for sale. We topped off our tanks. Expensive. I could not see how that location would make money, and year around access would be problematic. I enjoyed our three days and would go back again."

"Del, please be open with Frank, and let him discuss things with Jimmy."

"Yes, Meg, I will leave my boat here with Jimmy, so, I can fly here next time."

They sat together in silence, then Meg rose, and turned to look at me for almost a minute, and went inside. "Good night, Del, and thank you for your information about the marina."

"Goodnight Meg, and you are welcome." I walked to the guest house.

After a shower, I went back outside and called Cliff. "I feel I have something for you, when can we get together?"

"I'll be in Great Falls three or four days starting tomorrow. I'm still trying to solve my UC issue."

"Is your UC involved in the drug culture?"

"Yes, why do you ask?"

"Cliff, then we need to meet on the QT. I do not believe we should be seen together. You should bring along anything the FBI has about float planes moving drugs."

"Okay, I'll have someone make me a quality report. Breakfast, Saturday at 0800 in Belt at Frans."

"See you then, Cliff."

"Godspeed."

"Always." I enjoy the Montana openness.

CHAPTER 66

Toby made breakfast the next morning.

"Over medium, Del."

"Perfect."

The young men and I were almost done with our meal when Meg joined us. All three said. "Morning, Mom." She nodded with a smile at them.

Toby placed her plate on the table, then busied himself with the cleanup. "Smells so good in here, thank you Toby. Morning, Del."

"Morning, Meg."

"Sorry I am so late. Frank and I were just on the phone. He is going to come home tonight and has arranged to go back to Lewistown in the morning. He is hoping you could stay one more day." said Meg,

"I can do that, but must be back in Great Falls on Friday. Maybe Toby and I can go horseback riding again," I answered.

"Meg, does the Sutherland family know you might be interested in buying their ranch? Do they have a price in mind? Could Toby and I ride over some of it?"

"Let me make a couple of calls."

"Good, I can go learn how to do the chores. How long will the chores take?" I asked.

"Forty minutes or so," answered Toby. The chores consisted of feeding and watering a dozen horses. Then cleaning the stalls, and adding straw for bedding. Each horse also received a good brushing.

Toby and I did go on a second horseback ride once the chores were done. I saddled my own horse, and Toby checked things, giving me a thumbs up. We actually rode at a faster pace a couple of times. I wore a smile the whole time. "We will do that again, Toby."

When Frank returned, they discussed the possible purchase of the Sutherland property, and he quizzed me about the marina. I related what I told his wife yesterday. The family would go over their options and call me later. Frank left early the next morning to return to Lewistown, to continue the WIM meeting.

CHAPTER 67

ary, Toby and l, drove into the Sutherland's ranch at ten to three, returning to the Cummings ranch near five-thirty. During a roast beef, potatoes and steamed carrots meal, Gary began summarizing what they had learned.

"They have 4998 acres. 70% in crops, with 15% or so in alfalfa. The rest is either unused or dotted with buildings. A rarely used gravel pit is about four acres. The quality of the gravel looks quite good to me. The house is livable, but most of the rest of the buildings are teardowns. Only one decent tractor, but it is leased.

"Richie said he hired out the planting, and the small pasture is also leased. The few cattle look okay, but he didn't know about medicines and shots.

"He says he owes a little over $397,000 to a Glasgow bank. A full balance sheet from his accountant will cost $1,200. I told him to order one and send the bill to us.

"He hinted a cash sale plus assuming the loan would be his preferred option. He has no livestock of his own. He said, and I quote, 'The buildings ain't much, we just couldn't afford to keep 'em up.'"

Toby chimed in, "You even sound like him."

"What did you see Toby?" Meg asked.

"Gary and Richie did most of the talking. Del and I walked around and looked at the buildings. Most of the machinery is worthless, by our standards. We could sell the wood from the old barn and three outbuildings. One machine shed is a keeper, but with lots of rat evidence.

"The farmyard trees will be fine after a cleanup. A person could live in the house, for a time, but a new double wide modular house at the south end of the trees is the replacement answer. I have read about kit log homes, so I need to study that more. It would be nice to have a long-term real home.

"Del commented the crops did not look as good as ours. He is right, they are late and will produce about 70% of ours. The hay field is mixed and may do two cuttings. No sprinklers. Del and I drove all the roads nearly to Canada. It felt like wilderness."

"I sense we all are thinking about the drug trafficking problem, so I will ask a question."

l watched all their expressions change. "Would you be comfortable, allowing me talk to my friend of fifty years for guidance? He is the director in charge for the FBI in Salt Lake City."

Toby spoke first, "Do you trust him, and why would you do that for us?"

"Toby, those very good questions. I would trust him with my life, and all of you. I think we need some real law enforcement help," I answered.

"Dad is not here, but I think you should get us that help. We need to know how he would want us to deal with that drug traffic," nodded Gary.

"I agree with Gary, we are rancher-farmers. That kind of help is essential to us now, especially if we end up buying the Sutherland place," commented Meg.

l turned to Gary, "How computer savvy, are you?"

"I am not a gamer, but use a computer a lot following farm prices and costs. I also work spreadsheets to help decide about selling or buying. I make a little money in commodities, but I only take small risks, why?"

"Could you take the financials and bank loan and forecast how long it would take to pay off the loan and a timeline of income needed to at least break even? You may wish to pay for an appraisal, of the land, skipping the buildings. You can guess their value if you decide to buy,"

"Yes, Del, I can easily do that."

"Meg, I believe the financials will show they barely scratch out a living. I think you have a beautiful opportunity buying the Sutherland place." I stopped talking.

"Richie said we have first chance. If we don't strike a deal. He will advertise and go for more money. I think, Del, you are right about the opportunity. Their place is about five hundred acres larger than ours. Those acres are near Canada are not even in production now," answered Gary.

"Gee, Del, wait until we teach you about crops, you'll be a rancher in no time," laughed Toby.

Frank came back very late, but rose early. When I arrived at breakfast, Gary was relating everything they had discussed in his absence.

"Perfect, Gary. Very nice. You covered everything. I am proud of you."

"Morning, Del, how was fishing?"

"Very much fun, I cannot wait to go again."

Frank, Meg, and I took our coffees to the den. Frank and Meg outlined their thoughts about the entire process of arranging the estate planning. I listened and took notes, making no comments. Agreeing to obtain all the financials for the Sutherland property and see about assuming the bank loan seemed to put deep furrows on Meg's brow.

I explained about offering a structured payment schedule verses a lump sum payment. The furrows disappeared and a smile replaced them. "Our estate plan is going to take some deep thinking, right Del?"

"Yes, it will, Meg." He then suggested they get a guided tour of the entire acreage, especially the Canadian border markings. He also suggested they visit in depth with their sons.

"Frank, get Richie's permission to fly over his entire ranch, after you get a complete guided tour,"

"I will check with the Canadian authorities about the rules regarding their border," I finished. We had our plan of what to do next.

CHAPTER 68

I flew to Great Falls the next morning. Then rose very early the following day to begin the drive to Belt. Traveling eastward from Great Falls allowed me to watch a beautiful yellow Montana sunrise. The breakfast tasted as perfect as the aromas told us to expect.

Cliff gave me four typed pages outlining what the FBI suspected about float planes moving drugs. To date only three arrests this year had been processed. We walked to our cars, shook hands.

"Godspeed."

"Always."

After meeting with Cliff, I returned to Great Falls, and continued on to Lincoln and my cabin near there. The next morning, I traveled to the Monture Creek Trail head, planning a week-long stay at my hideaway in the Bob.

Enjoying the scenery, I turned onto the gravel road to complete the last 20 miles, hoping to hike about a third of the way. I'll be camping off the trail, so I could fish Spotted Creek's two beaver ponds. Curt and I knew the brook trout were bigger in those ponds. I hoped to treat myself and fry up two of them for dinner.

After only two miles on the gravel road, an all-black, big-tire motorcycle passed me traveling noiselessly along. When I arrived at the trail head, the rider worked at setting up his tent, then selected a spinning rod and walked to the creek to fish.

I locked the truck and shouldered by backpack to begin hiking the trail. I have a security camera in the dome light of the truck. The camera took a picture of the young man as he looked into the cab and bed as he returned from fishing. My phone alerted me. Perfect picture, as he looked but did not touch. I expect people to look, but not take a picture of all the license plates at the campground.

I disguised my exit from the main trail, walked to the first beaver pond and set up my camouflaged tent. I side stepped along the second larger beaver pond to find an opening to cast for some trout. Two casts later, two brook trout completed my dinner plans, with a side of angel hair pasta and two brownies homemade by me. "Perfect." I said to the family of chickadees watching me.

I wrote in my journal, covering what to do about the bike rider looking into my truck and taking pictures of all the license plates at the campground. His mannerisms said *trouble* to me.

Then I turned in as darkness settled over my private camp. The wilderness feelings, calm me, like no other place in the world.

Chickadees watched me eat my small breakfast at five a.m. Yes, the birds sitting on a branch within reach got a handout. They would not risk taking the offerings out of my hand. The pine smell and odor from the newer wood chips scattered by a beaver family, brightened my day. I felt at home. The morning breeze filters up from the Danaher River, past my small camp and into the valley, away from the main trail.

After ensuring my camp showed minimal use, I hiked back to the main trail, walked down to the Danaher and threw a rock into it. Curt always did that. I miss my hiking companion.

When I crossed the main trail, I noticed the new set of footprints, smaller than my size twelve. The motorcycle rider looked about five ten and one-hundred sixty pounds. I guessed he walked ahead of me. He began early.

I started down the trail, knowing I would reach Small Falls Creek around five p.m. allowing for some fishing time in the Danaher on the way. There was a stretch of meadow at least three-fourths of a mile long parallelling the river halfway to Small Falls Creek. Before reaching that meadow, I wanted to climb a small knoll and study the trail. Cliff believed the drug culture was using this trail now, so I needed to keep track of this man. Maybe he was just here fishing, but then why did he take all those campground and license plate pictures?

At the knoll, I stepped off the trail and climbed the 60/70 feet to the top. Standing behind an alder bush, I looked over the whole valley using a small pair of binoculars.

The motorcycle rider sat on a log just off the trail a quarter mile ahead of me, eating something and drinking from a canteen.

I decided to watch him. He only lingered a few minutes before putting on his backpack and heading north along the trail. I returned to the main trail continuing as though I had stayed on that trail.

The cabin Curt and I found in 1979, on Small Falls Creek, was well hidden. The valley just south of my hideaway, framed a similar valley around Willow Creek. Last fall while hunting for deer and elk, I located a game trail, linking the two valleys.

I decided to turn off the main trail, disguising my exit, and using that backdoor entrance to my valley. I have a system for disguising my exit from the trail. I always set up two exits toward the Danaher River, then scuff the ground as though I am undecided. Might not fool a true woodsman, but few others would check for better evidence. Cedar branches work quite well to erase footsteps, but I rarely use them. Deception works better in my opinion.

Arriving at my cabin, I stowed my gear. I located and retrieved my two air drop canisters. I climbed the escape trail to overlook the Danaher River and the main trail. The bike rider was setting up camp near the bridge. I watched him catch a nice cutthroat. He prepared his trout dinner and read a book for a time, before entering a small orange tube tent.

I returned to my cabin, ate my steak dinner, and softly sang a couple of Jim Reeves songs to myself.

The next morning, I greeted the sun as it climbed over the continental divide. I sang a song softly to the birds, and smelled the coffee brewing. Filling a carry cup, I have always sniffed my coffee before taking a drink, makes the coffee absolutely taste better. I took my coffee along as I climbed the ridge to see if the camper might be leaving.

He packed his tent as I peeked over the ridge to watch. In ten minutes, he faced north and hiked up the trail. I watched him take a few pictures of his campsite. That meant the stand next to his tent was a solar charging station for his electronics. And he could show the south bound hikers where to camp.

After my breakfast of ham, eggs, hashbrowns, and toast with huckleberry jelly, I climbed down to his campsite, took a few pictures just of the camp, climbed back to my valley and called Cliff. I fed my birds.

"Morning, Del."

"Morning, Cliff. I have a picture for you and a story to tell. We need to know who he is."

Cliff listened to the entire story, without making a comment. "Send the picture, and we will carefully check. Are you on the trail we talked about that the drug people might be using?"

"Yes, but you need to have an agent go the Meadow Creek trail head, south of Hungry Horse Reservoir and hide out to see who picks him up. Starting early as he did means he intends to make that location today."

"Okay I will try to get a Kalispell agent over there."

"Cliff, you need to have a second agent drive him to the trail head and let the watcher out. You do not want a vehicle there.

Too visible and you do not want him taking a picture of your vehicle or its plate.

"Right, I'll set it up. Can you call me tomorrow morning sometime?"

"I will." I sent the picture.

"Got it, Godspeed."

"Always."

CHAPTER 69

liff called the next morning. My phone was set to silent vibrate, as I was on the ridge behind my cabin watching two hikers with large backpacks, at the camp by the bridge. My satellite phone alerted me to their arrival last night about eight p.m. They must have met my bike rider half-way and visited.

A spotting scope with camera attachment provided pictures of both men, and the backpacks. They prepared a trail meal that looked like spaghetti, only opening the smaller bottom part of their pack. They each used a similar small orange tube tent. No fire, just a small butane stove. I watched them crawl into their tents near nine pm.

Returning to my valley, I called Cliff.

"Sorry I did not answer earlier, I had company." I told him everything and sent the face pictures, I took using my spotting scope, being extra careful not to reveal anything about the campsite. Just the faces.

"About your bike rider. He's Simon Castleman. Originally from Lincoln, Nebraska, he is now living in Ogden, Utah. He's a part-time student at Weber State, working on a technology degree. He has a full-time job at Walmart, near the college. He owns two motorcycles, the one you saw and a VIX 1800 cc. It's a double cradle type two-cylinder bike capable of one hundred miles per hour and maybe could do the one hundred fifty the speedometer shows. He paid thirteen thousand dollars for it. A very good deal.

We know he's the primary supplier of cocaine at the college. He uses a quality system with trusted distributers. We know who they are, too, but have never seen a transaction. They have us perplexed. Every attempt by an undercover person is a no show by his team. Somehow, they know everything we're doing.

"Cliff, I am sure you have looked into leaks at your office. My guess is that person is someone who hears things, but is never part of actual operations. Could be, someone has stolen and is using an agent's entry codes.

"Do you know how many people you are asking us to look into?"

"No Cliff I do not, but I would start today. It has to be someone with tenure, well thought of, who is always around. He has to be taking dollars for info, and has for some time. You also need to do a study about agents checking whatever they normally check.

"How long have you known about Simon?"

"Five or six years."

"You should look at everyone hired since then. One of them knows Simon and is a closet hacker."

"Del, we have sort of looked for leaks, but not in earnest. You surprise me sometimes, coming up with all of those options based upon a short phone conversation. You could be a very successful criminal."

My second warning. "I doubt that, Cliff. Too many ways to get caught. Jail does not appeal to me."

"I am going to start as you suggested. Just Charlene and me. I have about 60-65 people to check, including agents."

"I do not see it being an agent, unless the insider stole an agent's entry codes. Agents are not always aware of each other's assignments, and could be out of the area when a buy is scheduled. Look at tech people and computer access people first. I bet that will be as far as you need to go. One of them will know a lot more than you realize.

"Back to these hikers, you need to have a couple or ten agents. Meet them at the Monture Creek trailhead, and stop the pipeline. You can describe them for the agents, as you know the color of their shirts. Use horses as your cover. Have a watcher a half mile up the trail to alert the posse. I am guessing the two-legged mules are used to arriving, loading their packs into an unmanned vehicle and driving off. They should arrive as early as six p.m. If I hike that distance with a light pack that is the best I could do.

"Okay, Del. I'll put it in motion. We have a Missoula agent who has horses and a small ranch west of Ovando. I like your idea."

"Cliff, the walkers need to believe they were compromised in West Glacier, and have been under surveillance for some time. No reference to the Bob, *ever*. I cannot be exposed."

"I agree. You're out of it. I will let you know what happens. Godspeed."

"Always."

I peeked over the ridge at sunrise. The hikers left at just after seven a.m. An hour after they left, I called and reported to Cliff. He said they were ready.

I worked all day at increasing my wood supply. I have a quality one-man saw and a special pack just for carrying as much wood as I wished. I use a solar one burner grill for most of my meals, so my wood supply lasts a long time.

I worry the smoke from any fire I make in my cabin stove could give me away. I store the wood in the cave and have routed the cabin chimney into the cave, and the smoke rises nicely out some-where on the ridge above. I hope to check and find that opening tomorrow.

The following morning, I started a fire in the stove and climbed the ridge, edging south to locate the smoke. I smelled smoke before I saw the very light tendril, sifting out of the ground close to a large a Douglas fir. I felt certain the smoke would never become visible from the air. I cleaned the area where the smoke came out of the cave, to make sure I never cause a fire. Satisfied, I moseyed back to the cabin, making a mental note to check the area often.

Cliff called about eight thirty p.m. "We arrested both of them, and have the backpacks of drugs. I told the agents the tip came from a source in West Glacier. So far, neither walker has said a word. They are young and very frightened. We will transport them to Salt Lake. They should get there late today. We owe you again."

"Glad it worked out. I do not want people like that using the wilderness."

"Del, I sense they will abandon the route."

"I agree, Cliff. I will study the camp today and then know if it is ever used again."

"Call me when you are back in civilization."

"I will."

"Godspeed."

"Always."

CHAPTER 70

Billy Crocker was a young FBI agent, who, started working for Cliff in Salt Lake City. He was assigned an undercover job at a shooting range in Manhattan, Montana. He met me there, but we were not close friends. His undercover name was Tony Marcelo. He came from New Jersey, yet worked hard at getting rid of his accent.

I had related information to Cliff about the threats to Tony's life, so Cliff arranged to ship Tony to Minnesota in a drug undercover position. Billy studied undercover ops and the drug culture every day. He hoped to become tops in both areas. He was going to make a name for himself.

He was a member of a shooting range near Litchfield, Minnesota, learning to handle firearms better. He finished a shooting a session of rifle practice and started back to the office. The owner, Bud Anderson called to him, "Phone call, Tony."

Tony hurried to take the call. "Thanks. Bud," as he picked up the phone. "Tony here."

"A development." Is all he heard before the dial tone. He knew he needed to go enjoy lunch at the Wendy's three blocks from his apartment, at noon tomorrow.

Tony arrived early at Wendy's, so he could practice watching people. He looked at everyone and decided no agents where in the building. His undercover assignment as a drug hiker, into Canada, meant he worked five times a month, and looked the part. Long black curly hair and a three-day growth of whiskers, thus he sort of looked like a college kid. Always carrying a backpack, he rode buses often, but used a scooter to travel to the shooting range. He knew no one had ever seen him talk to an agent.

He finished his meal and worked on a medium chocolate Frosty, noticing Eleanor arrive and order her lunch. She purchased a baked potato and fixings, and a small drink. Then sat in the booth behind Tony. With only three spaces available, it was a logical choice.

Holding her drink to her face with the straw in her mouth she said, just loud enough for Tony to hear, "The raid will be Friday. You are to be arrested with the others, if you are working. More." She ate some of her lunch, picking up her drink, she continued. "If you are not working, call someone and tell them you are *going to ground*. Be totally safe and go back to Ohio."

Tony did not acknowledge her, just continued eating his Frosty with a long red spoon. Eleanor finished her meal and left.

He walked back to the counter and ordered a large cup of coffee. He stayed two more hours working on some notes for a class he attended at a Community College in Saint Cloud. He left, hopped on his scooter, started south, and made an immediate U-turn at the first light. Still no tail. He stopped at the library, the grocery store, and the Subway near his one-room apartment.

Tony had been undercover for six months. His reports were enough for the FBI to set up a raid. Great, Cliff will be proud.

He liked undercover and would ask for another undercover assignment. His mom and dad would not approve. They didn't want him working for the FBI.

Friday morning at six a.m. the FBI and DEA raided fifteen locations in the Saint Paul metroplex. Forty-seven individuals were arrested. Tony worked as an automobile salesman at 'Twin City Wholesale.' The lot owner and three of his employees were part of the forty-seven.

The three hundred square foot stand-alone office had a closed sign on the door, and an agent waited until a Saint Paul police car arrived. He handed the two policemen a list of instructions, then left.

"Babysitting job, Gregg."

"Beats traffic control, Brownie. The list says, keep our car out of sight, and photo every car or person that comes into the lot."

"Gregg, I'll watch and take pictures. You can go get breakfast at Mc's. Two Mc-muffins, two hashbrowns, and large coffee. He handed Gregg a twenty, then watched him drive away.

Brownie took nine pictures standing beside the office, before Gregg returned. None of the people looked suspicious to him.

The lady in the silver Lexus missed her arrest by fifteen minutes. She saw the sort of hidden police car, fussed with her makeup, and backed up some so they couldn't see her face or get a picture. She called Tony.

"Tony here."

"Good, they didn't get you either. Come to the Big Flower Nursery, I have a job for you."

"Twenty minutes," he answered to the dial tone.

He went to the nursery. Sherry Jensen gave him the keys to the Lexus, a thousand dollars cash, new South Dakota plates, and the address of where to deliver the car.

Tony loaded his scooter in the back of the SUV, changed the plates, and started his trip to Kansas City. He stopped at his apartment to gather his belongings. Next, he drove to the college to arrange completing his two classes over the internet. He used the bank drive-thru to close out his account, then called the landlord and said he could keep the deposit. Lastly, he canceled the Tribune newspaper. He then started the process to go to ground. But he had to get rid of the car.

He believed the lady's Lexus had a system to listen to everything he said, so he started talking to himself. "Wow I'm lucky. Never been to Kansas City. May stay a couple days, then go to Florida. I can sell cars there. Since there's no critics in this car, I guess I'll find some country music and sing along." All that anyone listening heard was Tony singing in a key all his own. Sometimes close to the real song. Tony knew he couldn't sing a lick, but loved country music.

He arrived in Kansas City, about twenty hours later, after one short nap. He purchased two duffle bags and transferred his belongings to them. Stopping at the airport, he secured the bags in a locker. Then he locked his scooter in a special lot just for two wheelers. Finally, he delivered the car.

"Can I get a ride to the airport?" he asked as he handed over the keys.

"Seve." The owner of the car lot yelled over his shoulder.

A short, well-muscled young man entered through the rear door of the office, "Yeah, what do you need?"

"Take the Buick and give Tony a ride to the airport."

"Sure thing."

Thirty minutes later, Tony rode his scooter out of the lot. His phone GPS located a motorcycle shop. He sold the scooter and caught a ride back to the airport with a salesperson.

He didn't feel or see any tail. He bought a ticket to Miami, checking his bags to New Orleans. He departed the plane there, picked up his two bags, and bought a ticket to Columbus, Ohio.

Exiting the plane in Columbus, he stayed by the terminal exit until all passengers were also out of the plane. He didn't recognize anyone from Kansas City. He called the FBI office. "Billy Crocker here. I will wait for a ride."

He decided to wait two hours before he called again. They picked him up in just over an hour. He hoped he could influence his new assignment somehow.

CHAPTER 71

illy met with the agent in charge, Bart Fellows, three days after arriving in Columbus, Ohio.

"Morning, Billy. I'll get right to it. On your reentry debriefing, you asked to be reassigned to undercover. Your reports on the Minnesota drug pipeline allowed us to shut it down. You will get a commendation or two."

"Those are always nice, I hear. I don't have any yet. Yes, I like undercover and have learned a lot about the drug trade. I'm studying everything I can get my hands on about UC."

"Billy, I have options for you. Great Falls, Montana, Bend, Oregon, or Albuquerque, New Mexico. The New Mexico location prefers someone with fluency in Spanish," Bart waited.

"Sir, I only know thirteen Spanish words. The other two are intriguing, so I'll ask who the supervisors are and the nature of the UC assignments."

"Bend is gang related, so blending in may take some time. Janet Steiner is the supervisor. Those gangs wouldn't last a week in big cities.

"Great Falls is a drug pipeline similar to your last UC. The supervisor is Cliff Rawlins. You know him, I understand. There has been some violence in the Montana drug culture lately. A pipeline walker is now in witness protection."

"I would have less to catch up on in Great Falls, and I believe I earned Cliff's respect, for the work I did there. That would be my first choice," answered Billy.

"You have two weeks off, starting today. When you return, I will have it set up for you."

"I'll go see my parents and some old friends. I know how to avoid bragging about what I do." Standing, he shook Bart's hand, "I will be back in a week or so. See you then, sir, and thank you."

"You're welcome, Billy. The bureau thanks you for a job well done. Enjoy your stay at home."

Billy rented a car and traveled to his hometown in New Jersey.

CHAPTER 72

illy's dad, a lifetime New Jersey resident, was a retired Newark homicide detective. A man of few words. He didn't approve his son working for the FBI.

Billy knew he couldn't stay two weeks; he would maybe last one. *"Back to Montana, wonderful."* He, uttered to himself. He pushed the doorbell on the house he lived in as he grew up. It sported a new roof and new coat of an almost white paint. His mom answered the door.

"Billy, Billy, Billy! We don't see you enough!" They shared a long hug. "Your dad is in the kitchen."

"I like the new roof and paint," offered Billy as they entered the kitchen.

"Good to see you, son." They shook hands. "How long are you staying?"

"I have five days, then back to the Salt Lake region, not totally sure the nature of the assignment they have in mind for me."

"As you know, I don't like you doing UC, but if you are staying in the Bureau, you should talk to Red Larch. He just retired from Newark Police Department, and was undercover over half his years. Want me to set it up?"

"You bet, Dad. I would love to meet Red."

They joined Red at a place called, The Plain Bar. "Hey, Crock. Long time, no see. So, this is little Billy."

"Say, Red, what you up to? And yes, this is our *not-so-little* Billy."

"Up to 225, that's what I'm up to," he said as he patted his round stomach.

"Nice to meet you, Red. Dad told me a few stories about you. I have done two UCs, but the first one didn't go so well. The bad guys made me as a cop. The second one worked well."

"What did you do on the second one?" asked Red.

"Confidentially, drug and money mule in Minnesota." Billy then related the complete story about the job, the raid, and his exit back to the real world.

"You felt trusted?" queried Red.

"Very much so. I've almost lost my New Jersey accent." He explained about the nursery lady and the car.

They talked over three hours. Billy made detailed notes of Red's dos and don'ts, Red avoided answering direct questions, but did give Billy four typed pages of information.

"Red, I can't thank you enough for sharing all this information. I especially like the statement, *practice lying while telling the truth.* I didn't do that on my first UC, I thought I should learn to fit in," smiled Billy as he shook Red's hand.

Billy, drove back to the house. On the way, his dad said, "You know I don't like you risking so much as a cop. Our State-Farm agent needs a new man to take over his business."

"I don't want to be an insurance agent, Dad. I intend to stay an agent in the FBI."

"I know son, that's why we talked to Red. You will benefit from his info."

"I will expand my notes, and start working on a book covering UC for rookies. I want to pass on everything I learn."

"Billy, I don't want you to think I'm not proud of you, because I am. I couldn't sell insurance either. Your mom is a worrier, but I heard her bragging about you to her church group. She has no clue what you really do for the FBI."

Three more days passed quickly. He said his good-byes, at the house, turned in his rental, and passed through the gates to board his flight to Salt Lake City.

Cliff's phone disturbed his concentration. He finished rereading Johnny's under cover report dictating Jeff's need for a safe exit from the Great Falls drug pipeline, before picking up the phone.

"Morning Cliff, Bart Fellows from Columbus, Ohio. If you are in the middle of something, you can call me back. No hurry."

"It's okay Bart. I am studying a sketchy undercover report from a UC agent, saving a drug mule in Montana."

"UC agents have a lot of freedoms, but take some horrendous risks. Speaking of UC, Billy Crocker is coming back to your region. He will be the replacement for the walker your agent saved."

"I like Billy, I read about the Minnesota raid."

"Billy's reports allowed us to set up that raid. His escape was facilitated by one of the top players, who also escaped arrest. We didn't know she played a part, but we are watching her now. Billy handled his role quite well.

"Neither the Bureau nor the DEA has yet to debrief the young man who was funneled out of Montana. The kid is still making his way east, with a two-agent escort. We want to see what he really knows about the Montana drug culture. I am to be the AIC asking the questions, then the U.S. Marshalls will put him in the witness protection program. I will call you personally after each session. I don't know Billy well, but he used his days off to visit his parents, and cut that short to leave for Salt Lake. His flight number is United 88."

"Is he in UC mode or regular?" asked Cliff.

"A little of both, neatened up, but still not looking Bureau status."

"I'll send a new lady agent to pick him up. Thanks for the heads up, Bart. I will wait to hear from you. Charlene will know where I am and give you a number to use."

"Great, take care."

Cliff started to file Johnny's report away, then decided to make a copy himself for Billy, then filed the report.

CHAPTER 73

liff sat in his office leather executive chair in Salt Lake. His posture, leaning back in his chair with his eyes closed, masked his worried state. He couldn't decide what to do about Johnny Beckman.

Charlene entered his office and saw Cliff's eyes were closed. She started to leave when he said, "I'm just studying what I must do about Johnny. What do you need?"

"Remember when we went to dinner and talked about Del."

"Yes, I do."

"Cliff, I sense we should do that again tonight. I have an idea."

"Perfect, it's a date. I'll call Agent Long about Johnny, then we can go to Maridux."

Cliff and Charlene ate their meal, talking about non-work things.

"Charlene, did Del tell you he asked me to let him obtain another alternate identity?"

"No, he didn't."

"I okayed it. He plans to go to Choe in Apache Junction, Arizona. He will have four, but acted intentionally vague. He plans to pay her extra to never tell a soul the facts about ID # four."

"Why do you think he did that?"

"My guess, Charlene, is something scared him to the core."

"Do you know what that might be?"

"No. When Del returned from Florida after fishing with Dutch, he told me he would be making some changes in his life. He didn't even hint at what that meant.

Last fall, I mentioned that I felt he was the shooter of some bad guys. I am now convinced he has done that. I don't have a single bit of proof. No evidence. I hinted twice that he could become a mastermind criminal. He didn't react either time.

After a short pause, Cliff continued. "He sees things and categorizes them. He sorts out the facts better than I do. I have always felt I sorted with the best of them, but he is twice as good. Every time I ask him what he would do, he surprises me. I would never want him for an enemy.

"You and I are a team, Charlene. We share many secrets, and both know Del's tips helped me get the top job here. I believe with all my heart and soul he is avenging his belief that the justice system let him down big-time after Curt was killed. He told me about talking to the judge. That judge said, *'my hands were tied.'* Del stared the judge down and said, *'Bullshit!'* and stormed out. Those were Del's words. I feel certain he could shoot people. I am going to tell you a story about Del. That story will remain between you, me, and him.

"He met me in Helena late last fall, telling me he killed two Russians in a hanger in Great Falls. He then dumped the bodies out of the plane into the Bob. He acted nervous, but did not show remorse. He has become tougher than I ever believed. I love the man like a brother. I will never betray him."

"Cliff, I could grow to love him, too. I only met him once. He portrays himself as a nice guy, and knows how to be a gentleman. I didn't see any of the traits you just described. This secret is safe with me."

"Charlene, you and I have been together...like forever. I trust you completely. I may need to help him in some way. Lately, he has been working on what we both believe is a terrorist plot of some kind. He is working to solve it. I am blown away by how much he knows so far.

"Do I need to treat his calls and information in any special way? My idea won't work, in light of our conversation tonight," she said.

"We treat him as he expects, unless he says he needs something extra. I believe he wants to solve the Michelle caper himself. Charlene, I think Del should meet Caroline."

"You do? Well, I agree and will arrange that when we see each other in December."

They walked to Cliff's car holding hands. While driving back to Charlene's car they talked of planning the training process for Charlene's two new office helpers, Charlsie and Morgan.

CHAPTER 74

While talking to Jody on the phone, I rose from my recliner, walked to my front door, and peered through three very small windows at the top of the door out to the neighborhood. Martha lived across the street. She admitted she spied on me for *the Noses*, the gold dealers, but added she wasn't doing that anymore. Still, I could not trust her.

Boris Spovok lived across the street in the corner house. A Russian with dual citizenship, he owned a semi and was gone much of the time. He hosted some unexplained activity every 90 days or so. This was the pattern: Two trucks arrive and three bigger white guys, from each truck, enter the dark house, stay for four to five hours, then leave with two large duffel bags each, and drive the trucks away. The FBI was watching, and so was my neighbor Ben. He's keeping a log of everything he sees.

I noticed a single lens telescope aimed at my house, through a narrow slit in the drapes. Boris came to the first monthly coffee meeting of our block residents, but no other meeting. I am positive he is up to no good. So, in my new role with the FBI, I wanted to see what he was up to.

That telescope meant he did not trust me. Well, I did not trust him either. I will talk to Cliff and Ben before I try anything.

Ben first. He will always join me on my patio when food is involved. I ordered two pizzas from Domino's.

I saw Martha Sutherland come outside her house to water the plants, so I walked over to visit.

"Martha, may I ask where in Montana you lived before moving to Bozeman?"

"Sure, I lived in Malta and attended school there. I had an uncle that owned a ranch near Saco, but he is dead now, and his son lives there. Richie lives by himself, but is not a hard worker."

Martha, I have two pizzas coming, would you like half of one?"

"Yes, that would be very nice. Thank you."

"I will bring it by as soon as it arrives. And you are welcome."

"Thirty minutes, sir," a young female voice told me.

I called Ben. "Absolutely, I'll help you eat that pizza. I'll bring the beer. I know you like Lagunitas, I'm getting partial to that beer myself."

"Ben, come over when you see the delivery car show up. I will meet you on the patio, and add some cookies from Aroma's."

The pizza delivery car arrived. Ben hurried to my patio with the cold beer, before I finished paying and carrying the pizza to the backyard. I removed half of one pizza and added it to the second box. Then I carried the remaining half in the box over to Martha.

"Thank you, Del. You are a nice man." I retreated to my patio, wondering a little about this neighbor, Martha.

"You sure know how to treat your neighbors," said a smiling Ben as he plopped into a chair. "I see you gave Martha some. I don't think she has much money."

We helped ourselves to a slice and washed it down with a sip of beer.

"Tastes great. I brought my Boris Log along. I kept records of every day I thought he might be here. I have all the pizza deliveries and all three times the six guys showed up in their trucks, since we saw them last Thanksgiving. I am sure I have everything. Always at midnight, and gone by about four a.m.

"Ben, what do you think we should do?"

"I'll go get us another beer." Returning, he continued. "We don't have enough stuff to call the cops. People can visit. I don't think we have enough to give a judge for a warrant. If they really are bad guys, and we tell the cops, we will live in fear. I don't want that, I'm too old to worry like that."

"I agree with you, Ben. I do not want police worries either. I do not believe Boris sees us as a threat, so we should keep it like that."

"I'm sure he uses a small telescope to watch your house and mine. I believe he saw us last Thanksgiving night, my light was on, and you hauled out garbage. He knows we saw the trucks."

"Ben, we just keep good records. If we hear about an arrest, we can come forward with our info." We polished off the pizza slices, four of the cookies, and two beers. We talked about the next neighborhood coffee, as it was Ben's turn. For the record—Ben ate three cookies, me only one.

CHAPTER 75

After Ben left, I called Cliff.

"Working late, Del?"

"Not really. Ben was over, and we visited about Boris Spovok and the activity there. The two trucks you and I saw last Thanksgiving have been back three times. Also, Boris uses a small telescope sticking through his drapes to watch Ben and me. Ben is somewhat scared and nervous. Do you have any news?"

"Some, but not enough. We know where he stops in Sioux Falls, South Dakota for his delivery there. Our agents don't think that delivery is a problem. He always goes somewhere else within 300 miles. We know of four cities, Kerney, Nebraska, Davenport Iowa. Alexandria, Minnesota, and Wahpeton, North Dakota, where he picks up some of his return load, before adding the rest in Sioux Falls. We think those cities are pre-selected, so he doesn't always use the same location.

"We have started tailing him when he leaves Sioux Falls, so we can then alert agents to watch the where, what, and when of his stop. He stops at the same hotel in each city, picks up a return load at a warehouse and returns through Sioux Falls. Every agent swears no one ever touches his rig."

"Well Cliff, I am sure your team has worked through everything, but my take is this. The contraband is either in the motel room, or hidden in the return load before Sioux Falls. He has to have inside help at each remote location. Agents should check employes at each warehouse, and I will bet you find a one-time felon at each place. Maybe you can luck out and get a UC at one location.

"Back in Bozeman, I sense he secures his stuff at the abandoned gas station until he has enough, then arranges the pickup people. The four hours tell me the drugs are cut at his house.

"When he is home from his long-haul trips, he makes excursions often. Maybe a disguised agent could tail him and see where he goes. When he comes to the house, the garage door rises, he enters, the door comes down. When the pizza delivery arrives, he meets the delivery person at the front door."

"I feel you are right, Del. What would you do?"

"Have an agent with good equipment watch long distance loading of the truck, at the four remote locations, taking pictures if possible. Run the pictures. The tainted ones will be easy to sort out. If all are clean anywhere, I will be surprised. How things are done have become routine, so your agents will recognize the pattern. Then give agents a heads-up all along the route home, so you can check each stop he makes. I am sure he uses the exact same stops everywhere. Video every stop if safe. Next time he leaves.

"Arrange to watch the abandoned gas station covering the entire action when he arrives. I think beyond a doubt, he stores his whatever it is there. You cannot arrest him at his house, as Ben and I will be blamed and singled out for retaliation."

"You need to arrest him when he picks up the goods and then the carriers when they stop at the gas station to get the trucks."

"How do you know the trucks are there?"

"Well Cliff, I disguised myself as homeless, walked to the nearby McDonalds and got a two-dollar burger and coffee. Then I walked over to the gas station. Lots of people saw me sit on the old pump island without any pumps to eat my burger and sip the coffee. Then after dark with gloves, I tried all the doors and looked in the windows. The trucks are there. I do not know when the carriers pick them up. You need an agent to watch and figure that out. No guessing. No maybes."

"Cliff didn't answer for a long time. "We will stay away from his house. I agree we need to keep you and Ben out of it. I will set some things in place now. And work with the other FBI people to try most of your plan. Do you think he uses the same reserved room at each outlying city?"

"My guess is yes. I always did when I could on my long hauls. Usually, to be able to see my rig."

"I will ask to have his room checked ahead of time, where we can. Again, you surprise me. I asked three other agents the same question, I received some of what you said, but not a whole plan like yours. Thank you, my friend." Then he changed the subject. "You going to be home Friday night?"

"Yes."

"I'll bring chicken from Martha's. You have the beer and coffee," Cliff answered.

"Deal. It will be good to see you. You are welcome to stay the night."

"I will, Godspeed."

"Always."

CHAPTER 76

I t took a while, but I finally tracked down the name of the attractive black lady who prepared the set of papers for alternate identity Sven Hansen. Cliff approved my request over a month ago to have a fourth alternate identity. Sven owns a small house in Mitchel, South Dakota. His next-door neighbor takes good care of the yard and plants. That neighbor also planted a lot of annuals that need water every day. Many dahlias.

Choe Sampson will completely create my fourth alternate ID. I called her and arranged the necessary appointment.

Randall Morrow will be unrecognizable by all my friends, including my daughter, Molly and grandson, Trevor. After I have that fourth ID, I will test it on Molly and Trevor.

Choe greeted me with her beautiful smile. Randall is not really a slob, but looks a lot like one. Del prides himself as a very fit person. Wearing some expensive extra pieces of body shaping items, and a full, but trimmed white beard, I smiled back at Choe.

Choe sort of kept smiling, but it was not easy for her. She finished the papers quickly, took the $12,000, and the extra $5,000 to never tell a soul, including Cliff. As I walked out her door, I uttered, "Ya sure, Choe," her smiled returned. I needed her to hear me sound like Sven. Choe completed the alternate ID papers for Sven Hanson.

Disguised as Randall, I left Mesa Gateway Airport at 0500 the next morning—destination: Portland. I rented a car and drove directly to Molly's office. I visited with the receptionist, watching Molly talk on the phone. She glanced at me, then returned to her call. Next stop was at Trevor's school. I sat on a bench in the lobby. Trevor passed by on his way to lunch, ignoring the visitor. Satisfied, I returned to the airport and flew to Santa Fe.

Randall bought a used white GMC 4x4 crew cab, and rented a truck sized storage unit near the Santa Fe Airport. He leased a 1000 square foot two bedroom, first-floor condo in a downtown gated community, complete with a covered parking space by the front door. His Costco bed, complete set of cooking pans, and smart TV were delivered that afternoon. A used furniture store delivered a battered roll top desk, a wooden maple table with three chairs, an old maple bookcase, and an old oak nightstand. The new recliner finished setting up this new residence. The older wooden items would be refinished to look like new.

He browsed two thrift stores for enough kitchen utensils, and found four wall pictures. "*Done.*" He uttered to himself, especially pleased with a picture of seven running horses.

Randall visited the library only four blocks west of his condo and obtained his card. While there, he checked out three books from authors he had never previously read.

I believed if I could safely sneak into Santa Fe, I could stay quite some time.

I sang a couple of Jim Reeves songs while I put things in their place.

My supplies were running low to create these alternate IDs. I used my computer lists to order fifteen sets for each one. Seven different businesses agreed to ship via express delivery to Santa Fe. Total cost, just over $18,000. The body padding for Spencer and Randall is very expensive.

I will wait for the delivery of everything to Santa Fe. I stopped at Home Depot, purchasing glue, a quality palm sander, and five different grits of sandpaper. The bookcase and nightstand now looked new again. The table and chairs were sanded, but not finished. The rolltop desk would be a project next fall during hunting season.

Three days passed quickly. Santa Fe is an enchanting place. Things in much of the downtown showed their history. I could sense the oldness. The aromas from two Mexican restaurants dominated the smells. I could smell them from my new condo's patio.

The Rancho Villa restaurant hired a young man to dress like a vaquero and pose for pictures beside a beautiful black horse, decorated with a silver studded saddle that would be used by a that traditionally clad vaquero. They did this once a month throughout the year.

When all alternate identity items arrived, I sorted them out. I took items for Spencer and Sven and loaded all in the airplane after dark, leaving just enough room for Randall. The next morning, I flew to Cheyenne making a stop in Mesa so I would arrive there just after dark. I unloaded Spencer's stuff. Then filed a flight plan to Sioux Falls, South Dakota.

I do not mind flying in the dark, I know the stars and constellations and their relationships in the night sky. I do believe there are other planets like earth elsewhere in the vast universe.

After landing, I rented a car and took five disguise sets for Sven to a storage rental and the rest to Sven's house in Mitchel SD at midnight. I left one set of body shaping items in Mitchell, for

Spencer and Randell. Turning no lights on in the house, I just locked everything in the hall closet, and drove back to Sioux Falls.

I rested in the pilot's lounge there, before flying back to Cheyenne, Wyoming, then to Bozeman, Montana.

A tired me was happy with himself.

CHAPTER 77

Time to hike into the Bob from my Lincoln cabin. I will drop two canisters of supplies first, then start hiking the following morning.

The Lincoln cabin electronics showed no sign of visitors. I used the quad to get to the end of my property. The U.S. Forest Service land between my boundary and the Bob is not a large parcel, but it does have one creek to cross. Using my chain saw, I dropped an old tamarack snag across it two weeks ago, creating a log bridge. That old tree looked like it belonged.

A Lincoln tire shop put studs in soles of a pair of old boots for me. They were two sizes too big, so I could wear two pair of felt inserts to cushion the bumps from the studs, making a safe way for me to cross the log. I stored the boots in a camo painted plastic buckets with lids buried close to the ends of the log bridge. If critters harmed them, I could replace the boots.

I knew this creek emptied into the Danaher River, but walking next to any creek is impossible. I found a sparsely used game trail going in the right direction about a third of the way along the ridge line. I marked my trail discretely using a system my son, Curt, and I would recognize. We vowed never to tell anyone our system.

I also placed nails with heads at strategic places along the trail. I only tapped them in each location, so they will be easy to remove. They would glow back to me when using a black light. Once I know the route perfectly, I will remove the nails. The path I had chosen did pass over two ridges, but I could see the Danaher from the second ridge. I was pleased.

Hiking from my cabin to Curtis Castle would take seven to eight hours. I carried three meals with me, so I camped behind two large alder bushes near the Danaher. I walked back nearly to the main trail, looked back at my camp to prove it was not visible. Perfect.

I did not see anyone at the Danaher camp near the bridge when I made my drops, but I fly so low I may have missed them. No one notices canisters come out of my plane, I am positive. Since Cliff warned me about possible hikers, I will climb the hill by Willow Creek and check the camp before going all the way to Small Falls Creek.

After climbing that knoll I saw two people sitting by a small campfire.

I climbed further up the ridge and found a flat spot hidden from the trail. I pitched my camo tent behind a huge Douglas fir tree. A trail meal would suffice. No fire, so smells, no noise, and no footprints. Early morning, I slipped out of my sleeping bag and greeted the sun, no song this morning.

I saw the hikers trekking by, traveling to the south. I sat for an hour, just me and my trees and birds, while I updated my journal. I love the wilderness.

I was ready to shoulder my pack, when I noticed two very nice whitetail bucks cross the Danaher, then the main trail and disappear along Willow Creek. I did not move, as they passed twenty feet below me. Both would be shooters. I could smell them.

Not Boone and Crockett, but worth the work, I have a system to make jerky on my wood stove.

Wood smoke smell is unique.

I used the satellite phone and told Cliff about seeing the hikers.

"You in the Bob?" he asked.

"Yes, two campers last night. The packs look the part. One guy and one girl. Girl is wearing a purple fleece, and the guy, a dark-maroon and gray flannel shirt. They are experienced hikers."

"Hold on a sec," answered Cliff.

"Del, Things are in motion, a helicopter will take the agents to Ovando, the horses are already there, when should we expect them?"

"Near five p.m., no later than six. They are carrying big packs," I answered.

"Thanks, Del, we owe you again, and I will let you know. How long you staying?"

"Five days. I need to gather some wood and saw a nice buck to check out."

"You be safe, my friend. Godspeed."

"Always."

Elk sneaked through my valley, while I slept. They left some deposits, and their distinctive odor. My gray jays watched me make breakfast, hoping for a handout. I tried to get them to eat from my hand. Maybe next time. They were lucky, as I must feed my friends when in the Bob. I planned to see where those bucks disappeared to after a night of foraging.

First, I needed to retrieve the two canisters. I put most of the contents in the cave, noting that my new tree saw, without the wooden handle, survived the drop when lashed to the outside of a canister. The handle was inside.

My canisters contained everything I needed to roll the bunk back into the cave side and lock it in position. If anyone ever found my spot while I enjoyed it, I could hide in the cave, and no one could pull out the bunk.

That sharpened beauty of a saw would make keeping up with the wood supply much easier. It took a long time, however, to rip through a six-foot log to make the two halves of the shelves in the cave pantry. Using rocks from the alluvial fan Curt and I found in 1979 I finished propping and arranging rocks so the two newly sawed shelves fit nicely in the new pantry.

Before catching a brook trout dinner, I sat on my log bench by the beaver dam, and sang my favorite song to my feathered friends. Three gray jays arrived making their distinctive *wheoo* sound. A family of chickadees politely listened.

The wilderness soothed my soul. I have no stress here. I felt born to be in the woods. I believe that time spent in the wilderness does not count as part of one's lifespan.

The fish were willing. A dinner of two brookies and pasta with a slice of sourdough bread topped with huckleberry preserves satisfied my appetite. Those fish do not know how good they taste. I enjoyed my beer, but it is never part of my wilderness experience.

Day two. Today I find where the bucks go. I made a large lunch, as I will be out most of the day. I have learned to drag a cedar branch over my footprints, to mask when I leave the main trail. It is my stop-gap method as I prefer deception best. An experienced woodsman may notice, but most would not. I took extra precautions leaving the trail where the two bucks crossed it.

I made too much noise, but the going was difficult. I climbed higher on the north ridge. The meadow looked small and marshy. I did not see any deer, so sat on a log and studied what to do (lots of deer tracks here, compared to my valley). I changed and acted like I was hunting. After two hours of hunting, I had not seen an animal. I sat on the hillside again with lots of birds. Finally, a family of blue grouse walked between me and the deer tracks. Using my binoculars, I studied the marsh inch by inch. The only trail I could see went into the marsh through the water.

My second pass through the marsh, I saw some movement. A deer stood on dry land in the middle of the marsh. Then I saw three more, one of the bucks for sure. Next, I studied every inch again counting nine deer and three bucks. Finally, one of the bucks stood up, looking directly at me. He wore a four-by-four set of antlers.

I finished my lunch then moseyed back to the trail. The deer didn't move. I planned to return an hour before sundown and watch. When I returned, the deer were gone.

After two afternoons of watching, I saw them stand, then in single file leave the island and exit. I never saw where they went. I will bring my journal tomorrow at noon and log what I have learned about these deer, and wait them out. I always need to solve things. Playing in my wilderness is extra fun.

I am compelled to see where they go. After they were gone, I went down to the very cold water. No way to reach the island without swimming or bringing my waders and staff. Tomorrow, I would have them.

I waded carefully into the water. Only three-feet-deep, though it looked much deeper and the bottom felt like a stream bed. The deer used a deep cut through a gap through the next ridge, easterly into a larger valley. There were fifteen to twenty deer roaming in that bigger valley. While glassing the whole valley, I noticed two steep-looking valleys on the southern edge of the meadow. I made a note to check them during hunting season.

A decent game trail led northwest toward my valley. I followed it, taking me through willow creek valley and into my little piece of paradise. Another backdoor to my hideaway. Wonderful. Next time I drop canisters, I will pay more attention to my backdoor route.

I hiked out using my newfound route to my Lincoln cabin. No more driving to a trail head.

CHAPTER 78

received two more notices declining applications to hunt deer in Kansas and Oklahoma. So, I decided to use my modified semi, and travel to New Mexico. They have over-the-counter methods to hunt deer and elk. I arranged a spot in an RV park in Socorro, then followed I-90 to Buffalo, Wyoming, using I-25 to Socorro, and visited most tourist spots along the route. I parked my rig in my reserved pull-through in Socorro, unloaded my E-bike, then made my way to pick up my four-wheel drive rental truck.

The San Mateo Mountains would be my choice to locate a quality elk. And the lowland plain northeast of Socorro, for trophy mule deer. My rental truck would easily carry my e-bike and small two-wheel trailer that Kenny made for me. Jason, one of Jack Fletcher's twin sons, opened his metal fabrication business in Manhattan, and has enough business to pay the bills. Kenny worked for Dutch in Great Falls, but moved to Bozeman, when Jack and Jason bought Dutch out. Dutch retired to Florida a while ago.

I took my rig back to Love's truck stop, topped of the gas tanks and washed the road grime away. Then I returned to my designated spot. The cashier at the truck wash, directed me to the

Beef and Brew. "Good beer and food," meant I should give it a try. The interior decor surprised me, many shades of gray, lots of mirrors, and thirty-eight TVs. I had time to count them waiting for my food. On the walls, many impressive mule deer and elk heads. One beautiful antelope mount looked out of place. Three hamburger sliders, with tots and a very good local IPA, filled me up and raised my spirits.

I studied the mounts. If they represented the animals in the area, I was impressed. Two mule deer racks were bigger than any I had ever seen.

Four uniformed Border Patrol agents occupied the table next to me. Three men and a woman were visiting quietly about illegals passing through the mountains, often referring to local landmarks. The woman said, "They must be able to see Socorro when they walk the trails west of here."

"You could be right, Bernie," replied one of her friends. "My guess is they walk 24/7 and cross Highway 60 at night."

"I agree, Scottie, but when we hike around in those mountains, we rarely find evidence of their passing. We are sure supporters have places to stash food and water, but if we find one, they seem to know and stop using that place. If they hear a vehicle, they hide, and we never see them," answered one of the other men.

I decided to ask if it would be safe hunting here, while I waited for my food. "Excuse me, I couldn't help but hear some of your comments. I am on a scouting trip to locate a few places to hunt elk and mule deer. Will it be safe to hunt alone in the San Mateos for elk and east of here for mule deer?"

Bernie spoke for them. "Shouldn't be any problems unless you actually run into them. They try to sneak through. Where are you from?"

"Montana, I have places to hunt there, but am alone now, and read about the trophy's around here, so wanted to see if I could find one."

"People here talk about hunting in Montana," piped in Scottie, "and you came all the way here to hunt?"

"Montana is a great place to hunt, and I have places to hunt, but can afford to hunt non-resident. I love the challenge of big game hunting, plus you have over the counter licenses available." I answered. After a short pause I asked, "Do you have a tip hotline to let locals tell you if the see anything out of the ordinary?"

Bernie reached into her shirt pocket and retrieved a card. "All you need is on the card. Where do you plan to go?" Bernie wanted to know everything and worked to get as much information as she could.

"I plan to try the San Mateos for elk and northeast of here for mule deer, in Socorro and Lincoln counties. Unless you have a better suggestion."

"Both are good places. None of us are hunters." She continued, "Do you mind telling us why so far from home?"

"I like new places, but hope to find a trophy elk and mule deer in as many western states as possible. I want to do the work myself. My Montana hunting is set up for late in the season.

"There are also places I have not visited, so I plan to be a tourist as well." I answered with a grin.

Bernie seemed to be the spokesperson for the group. "Enjoy your stay here."

"Thanks. If I wanted the best Mexican food and breakfast in Socorro, what would you suggest."

Scottie answered, "Buckskin Rider for breakfast, and either Ana's or Cactus Taco's for Mexican. How long do you plan to be around?"

"Three to five days. Maybe six. Why do you ask?"

"Just curious," he replied.

I studied the older looking fourth person for a second, as he did not speak. I thanked all for their help, and returned to my table as my food arrived.

I casually watched them leave, noticing a hat on the floor by the chair used by the person who did not comment. I picked it up and started toward the door, hoping to catch him.

Before I reached the door he entered, and I held out the hat. "Thanks," he offered as he donned the hat. "You a Fed?"

I studied him long enough to make him flinch. "I am Del Sanderson from Bozeman, Montana. I lived most of my life in Montana and worked as a financial planner. I have never been involved with any level of law enforcement. Why do you ask?"

"I have been in law enforcement all my working life. Your story doesn't ring true to me," he answered.

"Really, I cannot see why you would say that, Mr....ah?"

"I'm Westly Kimberly. I'm the senior officer at the Border Patrol Station in Socorro."

Turning quickly to the exit, he finished his comments with a, "You take care."

He knew I sensed he deliberately, left the hat on the floor. I had to figure out why.

I decided to do the mule deer scouting first. I drove through some very remote countryside. The map I purchased was very precise. Access through some well-marked Bureau of Land Management (BLM) property took me to the top of a rocky outcropping, giving me a panoramic view of many acres.

I set up my spotting scope and systematically studied the entire vista. I saw two quality bucks, though neither would make the Boone and Crokett trophy room. After two hours of study, I moved to the eastern-most point of the ridge. This new location offered a better view of the rugged valley below. No roads or trails.

At noon, I ate my lunch with a bottle of sweetened tea. Thought about a nap. But nixed the idea. I am not a timewaster.

Near the center of the valley, I noticed a patch of green juniper trees at the beginning of long gulley. Turning the scope to study that area, I found myself looking at a set of beautiful antlers. Easily a Boone and Crokett trophy and then some. About 800 yards, the range finder said. He watched me without believing he gave his hiding spot away. I savored the sagebrush and outdoor smells, then quietly retreated, dodging prickly pear cactus as I hiked to my bike. I wondered how many other hunters knew of this big buck. It was near sunset. Watching the orange sun disappear behind the San Mateos was a beautiful scene.

Returning to Socorro, I went to the Cactus Taco's for some Mexican cuisine. The place looked full to overflowing. The only open spot, the last seat at the end of the bar became mine. The wait would be worth it. If the food matched the aromas, I knew I picked the right place.

Her name tag said *Maria*, her smile real, and the Dos-XX's amber beer, cold. She presented a one sheet laminated menu.

"Maria, which combo meal is best?" I asked.

"Number two, senior," she answered with passable English.

"Number two it is. Gracias," I answered speaking in Spanish.

She gave me a big smile then turned in my order and continued helping others. I could use my wait to watch others. No Border Patrol people in uniform, but the two young men at the table by the window looked out of place. I think Westly is keeping an eye on me. I would go visit him in the morning.

The next morning, I joined the crowd at the Buckskin Rider for breakfast. A Border Patrol truck pulled in behind me. Bernie, Scottie and two new faces followed me in. The coffee and bacon smells greeted us.

"Good morning, Del." offered Bernie, then Scottie said the same.

"Good morning," I answered. I sat at the counter, and the group took the furthest table from me. Guess I am not to overhear anymore conversations.

After breakfast, I drove to the Border Patrol office, filling my gas tank first. I also patronized the Safeway store, and purchased my lunch selections. I saw Westly come to work at 0700. I parked next to his truck and caught up with him as he entered the building.

"Westly, would you have a minute?"

Without tuning to see who asked the question, he said, "Of course, Del. I expected you. Let's go to my office."

Passing the receptionist, he added, "Julie, hold everything until Mr. Sanderson leaves."

"Yes, sir."

A government issue office, with two plaques on the wall and a two-foot framed picture of an Apache warrior were the only extras. As he sat down, he noticed me looking at the picture.

"A local artist gave that to my mother many years ago, Mr. Sanderson. I know why you are here."

I sat in the chair he offered and waited for him to continue.

"One of my longtime co-workers, retired four years ago, and accepted a job as Sheriff in Forsythe, Montana. He wanted to be away from the desert heat. I owe you an apology. You are as you said you were."

I waited for him to continue.

"I am guessing you are an accomplished woodsman and hunter. I sincerely hope you find what you came to find. The San Mateo do have some trophy elk, but not a lot of roads. About 22 miles west on Highway 60, you will come to a poor Forest-Service-road leading south. There are some four-wheel drive trails branching off that road to the east and west. Test a couple of those trails turning east or west. Then hunt that area as you usually hunt."

"Thanks for the apology, Westly."

"Wes is enough."

"An interesting day already, Wes. I hope we can share a few moments before I leave."

"Here is my card. The second number is my personal cell. Call before you plan to leave and we will see if anything works. Some days are off the wall here."

I followed his directions and began hiking up a ridge by eight a.m. After I hiked high enough to get into the pine and fir forest, the cactus plants gave way to bushes that looked like alder, but I could not be sure. I made a mental note to find a book of native plants.

Elk sign increased, but only after I reached the highest third of the ridge. I felt I needed a better alternative than my first try. This far away from the truck told me, I could only shoot a 7X7 bull elk, if I saw one.

Returning to Socorro, I went to the Beef and Brew for a Rheuben. A group of eight Border Patrol personnel occupied a long table in the back of the room. No familiar faces, so I ate my meal and studied my new book of native plants. The Reuben, tasted better than average.

Day two of scouting mirrored day one. Day three evolved into a different scenario completely. Both days I just traveled further south along the forest road and used a trail to the east. The side trail I chose on day three, turned into a short steep canyon. A ninety-degree turn after only a fourth of a mile marked the end of the road. I positioned the truck facing down-hill, but kept it hidden from the main trail.

I followed a well-used game trail for two hours, arriving at a small saddle, showing evidence of a campsite. Whoever used it, left the site as clean as they found it. A rarity from my experience.

Another trail perpendicular to the one I used, angled south along the ridge. Continuing my climb, I followed the new trail. I traveled no more than a couple hundred yards, when I noticed small footprints on the trail. I stepped off the trail on the high side, and studied my options for some time. Using my binoculars, I checked the trail to the south. Many more footprints.

I felt they were not today's prints, but could not be sure. Leaving the trail, I ghosted my way higher until I confronted a rock wall too steep to climb. I wore camo clothes and hat, so I added breathable gloves, and a face and neck covering, placing my camo backpack between my feet. My worry meter buzzed, and I trust that feeling.

I slipped my 9MM Smith and Wesson and spare clip out of my backpack, putting the extra clip in my shirt pocket, then hid the gun in my hand behind my backpack. I would wait. I felt hidden.

I tried to stay awake, but did nod off at least twice. I decided to wait another hour before returning to the truck. The cliff prevented any further climbing.

I nodded off again, but awakened to a sound not natural in the woods. A compact file of ten people, men and women traveled north along the trail I just abandoned. The leader and the last person carried assault-looking rifles.

If the leader noticed my footprints, he certainly did not change his purpose. The group acted in a hurry. I worried about my truck. Waiting another hour proved to be difficult. I itched to risk it, but waited as I planned. I could not match the group's firepower.

Finally, I shouldered my pack, returned to the trail and on to my truck. Reaching the campsite, I could see evidence of use, but no scraps of anything. Their footprints showed them going north. Continuing, I reached my truck, looking just as I left it. I counted my steps and timed my decent. I knew I needed to pass everything I saw to Wes.

I coasted my truck downgrade to the forest road, started it and headed to Socorro. Wes did not answer, so I left a call 'asap'.

The party of ten, did stop at the saddle camp site, but only for ten minutes. The leader did notice Del's footprints. He said to all in English and Spanish. "Only one-man hiking. Not Border Patrol shoes. We not see him. We not worry. We go. Must get to highway soon, so can cross tonight."

CHAPTER 79

Wes called after fifteen minutes. "What do you need Del?"

"We need to visit privately, so I can tell you what I saw today."

"Okay, meet me at Starbucks, next to the Safeway across the street from our office."

"Be there in ten," I answered.

When I drove up to Starbucks, Wes already occupied a stool, drinking coffee and watching the lot through the window. I ordered a dark roast coffee adding a slice of pumpkin bread. I sat next to Wes.

"We meet again, Del. What did you see?"

"Are we being recorded, Wes?"

"No that is FBI-CIA stuff. We only record actions with people we retain for questioning."

"Good," I replied, then related what I saw.

"Interesting. Did you take any pictures?"

"No, Wes. I was out gunned and could see no reason to risk it."

"Excuse me, I need to call and set up a trap on highway 60. May even work." Wes spoke at length to two team leaders. "We will know in the morning. I do hope the hiker leaders don't use their rifles. Meet you at the Buckskin at seven-thirty in the morning."

After meeting with Wes, my entire afternoon looked free. So, I drove south, exiting to try unimproved road 107. I tried two side road trails on a westward beeline. Both side trails looked better that the first three I tried. I hiked one trail most of two miles and saw plenty of elk sign. I decided I will return tomorrow, prepared to hike all day. I will hunt here, unless there are too many hunters. Most hunters are not skilled woodsmen just think they are.

I met Wes at the Buckskin the following morning.

"All ten are in custody. We are thankful no shots were fired. Our people were on both sides of the road and executed the plan to perfection. It's rare not to have a glitch or two."

"What happens now?" I asked.

"Mostly, that is up to others. The illegals will probably be given a ride back to Juarez, and will be back in Mexico with nothing. The two with guns will be detained for a while, but are so far down from the top operators, that they are little use to us. If they say anything they know, they are dead. We thank you for the lead. Which trail they used to get to Highway 60 is important to us."

"Just lucky to be hiding, I guess. I just wish to be a hunter," I sighed.

"Del, if you had continued hiking, you could have been in serious trouble. Noticing the very different footprints, and having the wisdom to hide far off the trail, may have saved your life. Most people hiking in the woods would not have thought to do what you did. I know I wouldn't have been able to sit and wait as long as you. I think elk and deer are in trouble when you are hunting," added Wes.

"I am starting back to Montana tomorrow. I will let you buy my breakfast, when I come back to hunt."

"You have a deal. See you in October," said a smiling Wes. "We owe you more than that for the tip."

"A thought, if you do not mind. Could I get a satellite phone that would let me call you from remote areas."

"Why, Del?"

"I will be in the San Mateos, and remote areas of BLM land, northeast of here. My cell showed 'no service' most of the time. I think your people have a way to call for help."

"Yes, they do. I will need to think about that. We will talk about it when you come to hunt," he answered.

"Perfect, Wes. See you in the fall." I may have overstepped the line, by asking, but I felt concern about my safety. Hiding saved my life. I could not shake the scared feeling. Being lucky is one thing, running out of luck is another. I may never encounter illegals again. But I should not depend upon luck to stay safe.

Driving back to Bozeman through West Central Colorado, provided scenic beauty seldom witnessed by most Americans.

I sang every song I knew, most of them to Amy. I still miss her, but sensed I was drifting, aside from the *adventures*, I do need to simplify my life.

I thought about Meg. Thoughts of her spin around in my head. I wonder about these new feelings I have. Am I leaning toward not being alone? Meg is a married woman. Yet her family has become extra important in my life.

I felt certain this New Mexico fall hunting trip would be one to remember. Either a trophy, or another eventful exercise in the mountains. Maybe both.

CHAPTER 80

Molly, Trevor and I bunked at my Lincoln cabin, then started our planned hike to Curtis Castle.

"How much shorter is this route than the Hungry Horse one?" asked Molly.

"If we hike right along, we will reach Small Falls Creek near sundown. So much shorter and easier. I will point out how the trail is marked, but that system must remain a secret between us. We will cross the creek only once. I made a log bridge, but you can use the special boots if you wish," I answered.

Only I chose to use the boots. When we reached the main trail, I did not see any recent footprints. We should be alone on the trail. We let Trevor lead the way, along the main trail from the creek junction with the Danaher River. Trevor will want to be first to arrive.

Seven hours later, we erased our tracks and faked three trips to fish the Danaher River. Then let Trevor go first up the falls. We passed him our gear, finished our climb, and proceeded to the cabin. After locating the two canisters with our rations and stowing all in the cabin, Molly and Trevor caught three brookies each from my small beaver pond. There is evidence that my beaver family has been working on their dam. Lots of new branches tucked skillfully into the dam.

I just watched them standing side by side. Their laughter made me smile. Having my daughter and grandson with me in my hideaway created a specialness few fathers get to enjoy. Difficult to control my emotions, feeling lucky came to mind. We all slept in the cabin. Molly got the bunk, and Trevor and I used air mattresses and slept on the floor. We swatted the only two mosquitos flying around.

We stayed five whole days. We climbed the rock wall, past the pool that fed my stream, and climbed to the source of the gold. I told them a shortened version of taking the gold to be assayed. Nothing about the crimes *the noses* committed.

"Grampa, are you going to mine all the ore, you can find?"

"Most likely not, Trevor. I do not want to pack the rocks out. I thought I could break the quartz apart more and may try that this hunting season. If I ever need the money, I will break it down more, and do that up here by the gold. No one can hear me from the main trail."

Molly knew why I did not need the gold money. She was the only person I have told, about stealing the drug money.

I showed them the backdoor trail to the hide-away. We saw a dozen deer in the Willow Creek meadow. One sported a five-by-five set of antlers. He would be the deer I would watch for during hunting season. Might get lucky. We hiked into one of the canyons I noticed, while watching the deer last time I visited this valley. A small creek meandered out of the narrow valley into Willow Creek, but after reaching the end of the box canyon we saw no evidence of previous use, only the spring source of the small creek. We did not have time to check the other small canyon.

I let Trevor cut some wood and pack it back to the cabin. "Why don't you cut the wood in the valley, grampa?"

"I do not want anyone ever to find this place. But if they do, I need it to look abandoned. I cleaned up the inside old stove pipe, so I could mask most of how it is diverted into the cave. Not perfect, but they would have to study closely to notice.

"Months ago, using my drop system, I added some old pipe from the old, abandoned cabin on my Lincoln property. I have located where the smoke exits from the cave. I try to keep evidence of me being here to a minimum, but a decent woodsman could figure it out.

"I intend to continue exploring many of the side canyons with creeks flowing into the Danaher. I am positive there are other places like this in the Bob, but after exploring five valleys so far, now six, I have not found one. We need to do another hike tomorrow. I have something to show you both.

"You two are the only ones alive who have been here, besides me. I have no intentions of ever showing anyone else. Not even Cliff." Trevor listened intently to every word as he took a sip of water from his insolated travel bottle.

The next morning, I showed them the trail up to the top of the ridge behind the cabin. Then we returned to the main trail and hiked to the cache near the Young River where it joins the Danaher. I showed them my cache, while replacing some food items.

"Why do you need this, Dad?" Molly asked.

"I helped Cliff catch three bad criminals. They have contacts all over. I am good at checking things, but know I cannot be perfect. If I ever have to leave here floating from this location with a paddle, will get myself to Hungry Horse Reservoir. I can hide everything then and hitch a ride to Evergreen," I answered sitting on the big old log.

Our special time passed too quickly. We said few words as we hiked through my version of paradise. All of us were at peace with ourselves. Words just interrupted that peace. Taking both to the airport, left me feeling alone.

On the way back to my house, I thought about the Cummings family in Saco. Meg stirred deep in my soul.

CHAPTER 81

I called Cliff. My phone alert showed two intruders near my Lincoln cabin with guns.

"Morning, Del, you back in civilization?"

"Yes, I have a story and a request." I explained about the trespassers with guns, and that I had pictures.

"Send the pictures. I'll have someone see if we know about them."

"Cliff, I will be at my Lincoln cabin a couple of days, then back to Bozeman. I am going to slow things down. I am putting too much on my plate. I need to reduce the stress."

"Go see Dutch. I talked to him the other day. He asked about you."

"I will call him, but will not go to Florida right now."

Cliff interrupted, "I'll be in Bozeman Friday, so I'll pick up Chinese and come to your house about six p.m."

"Great idea, I can enjoy a visit and an update.

"Godspeed."

"Always."

Cliff called back an hour later. "Your trespassers are from Salt Lake City. They are an assassin team, hired by the drug culture. Our prison snitch said Bully hired them after his try for Rick failed. Bully decided *you* could be part of things.

"Those two bad guys are holed up in Augusta, but don't realize everyone in that little town knows about everything they do. Two locals followed them to Lincoln. We have asked the sheriff to let us know the next time they leave for Lincoln, so we can give you a heads up."

"Something has to be done about Bully, Cliff."

"You are right, but we can't just kill him."

"You could, but you will not."

"Let me work on things, Del. Godspeed."

"Always. Thanks for the heads up."

Returning from a grocery trip to Lincoln, I reset the camera system. While preparing my dinner, I heard my phone.

I checked the cameras. Two visitors, with their guns at the ready walked down my two-track lane.

I immediately grabbed my 9mm and four clips, hurried behind my woodpile, leaving the radio playing country music. After buying this cabin I risked trailing a long antenna up a tree at the back of the cabin, so I get five or six good radio stations.

Using the woodpile for cover and watching the duo on my phone, I backed into the forest. I knew where I wanted to be, if they forced me to confront them. I hurried to the creek crossing, making enough noise to ensure they followed me. Then using my studded boots, I crossed the creek, crouched behind a huge Douglas fir and waited.

Hearing them coming, I loaded a shell into the chamber. They reached the log together. I was twenty-three feet away. When the first one started to cross the log. I called to them. "You have two choices, lay your guns down now, or die. I will not ask twice."

"Shoot him, Bugs," cried the man on the log.

I shot the man on the opposite bank, and a second later, shot the man on the log. I knew they were dead. I practice my 9mm way more than my long-range shooting.

"Not again," I murmured, *"Not again!"*

I cannot just drop these two out of a plane like I did the Russians! I now had two bodies and a suburban to get rid of. Using the quad, I transported the bodies one at a time into the suburban, returned to my cabin and readied my backpack for a two-day hike. Gloves prevented me from leaving any useable evidence in their vehicle.

I drove the thirty miles to the Monture Creek trailhead, arriving after dark. Parking in the most remote camping spot, I shouldered into my pack, locked the vehicle, then hiked two hours along the trail. Reaching my turnoff to the cabin, I left the trail, disguising my exit. I hiked a hundred yards or so, and camped, not pitching my tent. I just dozed leaning against a big fir tree. I nodded off a couple of times, but my emotions got the best of me. I did not like being hunted. I did not like being scared and I felt more than scared.

I shivered most of the night my phone told me the nighttime temperature to be forty-three degrees. Before sunup, I continued the hike to my cabin. Reaching the cabin, I sat on the outside bench and coped with exhaustion, mental and physical.

Cliff's people needed to clean up in Augusta and at Monture Creek. I called him and told the whole story.

"I will take care of things, Del, so glad you are safe."

I checked the tire tracks and destroyed all evidence of the assassins' visit. Taking my metal-detector, I found my two shell casings. I would add them to my used casings next practice session at the Rick's range.

I felt shaken to say the least. Retirement should not be this dangerous. I must change some things.

CHAPTER 82

Tuesday was Rick's-day to train and evaluate Army teams wishing to be part of special ops. I called and asked if he could spare some time for me.

"Come on out, Del. I have only one team this week. I'll go unlock the gate. Be good to see you."

"I will arrive about eleven."

I stopped at Aroma's and paid for cinnamon rolls and a dark roast coffee for each of us. Rick rarely eats sweets. I am trying to corrupt him. We sat in his office eating and sipping.

"You haven't been around in a while, Del."

"I have been in the Bob, riding horses in Saco, fishing in Fort Peck and doing some financial planning work in Great Falls.

Rick, I have something to tell you. I related the entire story about the two assassins, including Cliff's comments about the prison snitch.

"Bully is still in our lives," interjected Rick. "What does Cliff say?"

"Bully is not up for parole anytime soon. He seems to have connections and money. Cliff does not know of a way to get to Bully in prison. I do not want to live in fear."

"I hear you, Del, but I do have some good news. Sig Sauer has hired me to rep for them and agreed to let me rep for an optics company. I haven't had a real job in 25 years. I may even like being around people. Mostly, I'll be setting up stations at top level gun shows."

"You will do better than you think, and will get to see some old friends. I am happy for you."

"I only have three friends I would trust you and Cliff are two of them and Art is the other. I would have shot those assassins, but I would not have given them any options."

"I felt I needed to, knowing I put myself in more danger. The guy on the log had nowhere to go and his pal did not know where I hid. I only waited maybe two seconds before I shot the first man, and another before shooting the second. I told Cliff, and he cleaned things up at the trail head and Augusta."

"Rick, I need to hustle along now, but I will return in an hour when you finish with your shooting team," I paused. "Rick, I shot two Russians in Dutch's hanger last fall. I dumped the bodies in the Bob. I told Cliff about that, too." Then I told Rick that whole story.

"You saved your life by shooting them. They followed you because Jim stole some guns. Revenge, I guess, Del. I'll never tell a soul. You and I are the deepest kind of friends. I need to teach you some things. I know you and Art set up security at your house and cabin, but you need to know some better tactics of survival and ways to attack an enemy. We will start the lessons today. You must trust me."

"Rick, I trust you and then some. I also feel the deep bond. I know I had a little luck both times, but sense I cannot rely on luck. I recognize the obvious and am able to react."

"Del. If you're hunted, you must always believe it's for keeps. It is never a game. Remember those-kind of hunters have killed before. You're only money to them. Shooting the trailing man first was the right choice. The guy on the log should've dived off the log and hunted you. When you return, we'll start the lessons. I will be done with my Army team evaluation."

When I returned to the range, the trainees were driving away. Cliff called and reported the Augusta site had been sterilized. "The local sheriff sat in his car and let the FBI do everything, only asking if the shooters had been apprehended. The agent in charge assured him they were in custody. The sheriff learned we got anonymous tip from Augusta.

"A cowboy team cleaned up the suburban and bodies from the Monture trailhead. Our team did find some drugs and weapons in the suburban. The report reflects a tip from a local bar in Ovando.

"Also, we did apprehend the man and woman hikers with their packs of money. We expect that trail to be shut down. Del, you are the reason we have four drug hikers in custody.

"Cliff, I will watch for some time to make sure it is shut down. I do not trust much these days. What about Bully?"

"Not much we can do. We believe his attorney is the go between, but if he is, they have a very good code system. That attorney has many clients in that prison. Can't do undercover. Too risky."

Rick listened to everything Cliff said. "Cliff, Del and I need to know if Bully is ever released. "I guarantee someone from my office will contact both of you, if he is released," Cliff assured.

CHAPTER 83

Time for a trip to the grocery store. I have visited every grocery store in Bozeman, usually going to my two favorites. My list is short, so will stop at those favorite stores. Returning with my treasures, I raised the garage door, drove in and parked.

With an armful of items and key in hand, I reached to insert it in the door to the kitchen. It stood slightly ajar. I follow a strict security checklist whenever I leave my home. The door should have been locked. That meant I had company, or someone has attempted to break in, yet my phone had not alerted me.

I did not know there were gadgets that could bypass my security system. I must solve that problem.

I will check on that, but must find a safe course of action now. I returned the items to the truck, walked stealthy out the side garage door and checked my back door. The window looked completely destroyed, pieces of glass littered the steps down to my patio. I deduced my company hid somewhere in my home.

My office is in the first of three bedrooms facing the basement stairs, only fifteen steps from the patio door with the broken window to the office. I retrieved my 9 mm, an extra magazine, from the bottom desk drawer. Grabbing the suppressor, I then hid in the office to wait and see about his intentions. I fitted the suppressor to the pistol, stood behind my office closet door, positioned myself sideways, gun in hand, and waited for any sound.

Last Thanksgiving as I sat in my office reading, I noticed when someone passed in front of the soft glow of the furnace thermostat, it created a brief shadow. I decided he must be in a back bedroom, so would need to pass by that soft light. If he came up from the basement, I could shoot before he could stand high enough to aim at me.

So far, I had not heard him, but I am positive he knows I am here, so believed he will start advancing. He must be getting closer, but still no sound. Yes, I felt totally scared about being shot. An experience I never wished to feel.

I heard a scruff of clothing scrape the wall, then immediately saw the brief shadow. He was four steps from my office door. My heart skipped a beat or two, then started beating much faster. I heard another scruff. The hallway mirror revealed a small man, slinking slowly along. He had to notice the mirror, but kept his focus on the open office door.

Without checking if I sat in the office chair, he placed two shots through the back of it.

I shot twice through the wallboard, one at shoulder height and the other about a foot lower. A muffled cry, and he fell in a heap. He tried to raise the gun, but I kicked it out of his hand. I frisked him for a second gun, not finding one. A small Hispanic man, with a huge noticeable old scraggly scar over his right eyebrow, labored to breathe.

"Why are you here?" I demanded.

"To shoot you," he whispered.

"Who sent you?"

"Bully no like you. I work for him," he gasped and died.

I called Rick, he said, I'll be there in twenty. Don't say anything but the facts to anyone, and call your attorney. Get rid of the suppressor." I waited until Rick arrived then dialed 911.

I hid the suppresser. The police probably knew I used one, but I did not offer to tell them, and they did not ask. After I explained things as I saw them, they checked the intruder for a pulse, then the back door, and the bedroom hiding place, but did not like that I insisted Rick stay. One said to me, "You should have just called us, before entering your house."

"He said he intended to shoot me and had been paid. I cannot prove that, because he is dead. Sure, I could have run away. I did what I believed I should do. Putting two shots into the chair proved his intent."

"You were lucky, sir." I read more than dissatisfaction in his voice.

The two shots through my chair missed my computer by two inches. Lucky for me.

I called Cliff while the police worked.

"Del, I'll be there in the morning. Call your attorney."

"I have, and he is on his way. We have to do something about Bully."

Cliff didn't reply.

My attorney solved most everything, and I could remain at my home. The police accepted that the intruder fired through the chair before I dispatched him. My concealed carry permit made a lot of difference.

The police team that processed the crime scene were not happy that I shot the intruder. Each of the three of them chastised me in some manner. I did not appreciate their comments or the constant berating tone. Little curtesy, something I felt to be out of line. Maybe they were right, but I believed they could have treated me with more tact.

I did have presence of mind to get my groceries from the truck.

Cliff spent two hours with the prosecutor behind closed doors, making sure I wouldn't be charged, and that there would never an article in the paper. The intruder had a long list of offences covering many items.

No charges were filed, and no pictures in the paper. I told my neighbor Ben, the police came because of an attempted break in, and my security system alerted them.

Cliff made some calls and learned someone figured out how to remotely delete apps. Cliff also learned there is a blocking system. I purchased that blocker and an upgrade, and studied how it worked.

I also purchased a new phone security system to triple my protection.

CHAPTER 84

ew Mexico hunting was open, so I drove my semi straight through to Socorro. I called Wes my last evening on the road. We scheduled to eat at the Buckskin Rider the second day after I arrive.

I hunted five days, but never took a shot. The exceptional mule deer I had seen during my scouting trip never materialized. I saw five decent bull elk, but being much too far from the truck meant, I could not do the work to pack it out.

Wes did give me a satellite phone, to be used only in emergencies. Wes and I shared breakfast the morning I left. He covered much about the problems at the Southern border.

"Del, do you plan to return next year?" he asked.

"Yes, I will. The trophies are here I just need to find them."

Wes paused, then offered, "Let me work on a couple of things before you make the trip. Call me a week or so in advance. How complete are your living quarters?"

"Wes, if I stock up after I arrive, I can stay in my rig at least a week, maybe two. My holding tank is not real large. I transport a quad and a Honda civic."

"Good, I will have a remote place for you to park and a map of the area you need to hunt. Could be other hunters around, but you may never see them. It is a known area to have larger elk, but you will be walking a lot."

"Thank you, Wes. I am already excited. Is it okay to use quads there?"

"Yes, it is, but there are few places that can be called flat. Drive safely home. See you next season," we shook hands, and I started north.

I love to sing songs I like and know. Sometimes I sing along with the radio, but usually prefer to sing the songs that come into my head. They all have meaning to me. Music is important in one's life, especially mine.

CHAPTER 85

ick called a lot of people (many he called previously were helping him locate Bully). He finally located Selmer 'Bully' Varnel. He was in the Federal Correctional Institution in Littleton. Colorado. So was Bowen Bowie. Bowen, a retired Army special ops shooter, and long-time friend of Rick's, couldn't adapt to civilian life. He became involved in the drug culture, and then found himself arrested when trying to transport a large quantity of cocaine.

Bowen needed to feel safe and prison provided everything for him. He didn't feel safe, but he lived as comfortably as he could. Outside life always made him feel everyone hated him.

He lived in a cell, in the same block with Bully. Rick knew Bowen lived there, but had to call a lot of people to find Bully. Rick visited Bowen once or twice a year. They talked along the edges of their special op's times, but used coded conversations and never mentioned names. Bowen owed his life to Rick, so when Rick called him and said, "I have a favor to ask."

"You ask and you get, my friend," Bowen answered.

"Remember last year when we visited?" queried Rick.

"Yes."

"He will get a call in four."

"Gotcha." Dial tone. Bowen knew to subtract three from Rick's number.

Rick waited the exact hour allowing time for the transfer, then called the prison asking for Selmer Varnel.

The loudspeaker blared interrupting Bully's evening meal, "Varnel, call on the blue phone." Bully paid handsomely for the phone privilege.

Bully stepped to the window by the guard's office and picked up the phone, "Yeah, Varnel."

"You're dead," Rick said through a voice changing devise. Then hung up.

Bully went back to his meal wondering why and who.

A few minutes after lights out, Bully fell to the floor in his cell, dead. Bowen put something slow acting in Bully's coffee, while Bully was on the phone.

Bowen received some small favors by busing tables and sweeping the floor. The first week he lived in the prison, he had to fight twice. No one bothered him after those two fights. Putting something in Bully's coffee, simple.

Cliff called both Rick and I with the same message. "Bully died in prison last night. Prelim believes it was a heart attack. Be talking to you."

"Godspeed, Del."

"Always, Cliff."

"*Great for us.*" I uttered to myself.

CHAPTER 86

ary and his fiancé, Stacy, often took early morning horseback rides when she visited the Cummings ranch. They enjoyed the lanes near Frenchman's Creek, and the deer trails through the many gulleys and ravines. Both loved to ride horses.

They met at a rodeo in Billings. Stacy was an accomplished barrel racer. Gary rode broncs and bulls, and he often won money. It wasn't love at first sight, but after two or three casual evenings with their rodeo friends, they realized the spark was worth a real date or two. After six months and the customary meet the family days, Gary asked her to marry him. Her answer an enthusiastic, "Yes, yes, yes!" They scheduled the wedding for a September date.

Today's horseback ride began early. They hoped to be above the largest ravine and watch the sunrise, and the deer return from the fields. They crossed the creek using a worn deer trail.

A shot rang out, and Stacy fell from her horse, raising a small dust cloud when she met the ground. Her horse ran off about fifty yards then stepped on the end of the reins and stopped. Gary jumped off his horse and ran to her side. She laid unconscious and bled from just above her right breast. Gary tore at her shirt and saw the bullet hole. Turning her slightly he didn't see an exit hole.

Using pressure, he tried to stop the bleeding. Removing his tee shirt and belt he covered the hole with multiple layers of cloth and secured the cloth with his belt. He hoped the belt wasn't too tight.

He called 911, told his story and a Glascow ambulance was dispatched. He called Meg.

"I will wait by the road and lead the ambulance to you. You take good care of her. I'll call the sheriff. We know he isn't much of a sheriff, but he better get this right."

"Thank you, Mom. I think she is coming back to me. I'm trying not to become wild."

"Toby is at the north hayfield. I'll call him to come help you."

"Great, mom, I think I have the bleeding stopped."

Toby skidded the quad to a stop, and rushed to help, "what do you think, Gary?"

"I think we disturbed the drug people and one of them panicked."

"I have the 223-rifle, Gary. I'm going to check things, I'll be careful, they could go a long ways in fifteen minutes. I'll be back." Back on the quad he hurried to the fence road and sped to the highway in time to see a car drive away, *"That's the sheriff's car!"*

Toby surprised himself. He felt in control. He went to all the known camp sites. The third one still had a small fire. He videoed the entire campsite, then took about thirty pictures. He saw a spent shell casing, taking an extra picture. Then he returned to Gary and Stacy.

"They shot from the chokecherry camp, Gary. I photographed and videoed the whole camp site. Our super sheriff needs to get this right.

Meg called Gary. The sheriff is supposedly at a meeting in Billings, so both deputies are coming out together. I hope they will do a decent job. Dad is in Lewistown. You should ride with Stacy no matter what. Toby and I will direct things, then call you.

"Thanks, Mom. Stacy is conscious, but is hurting bad, I think we should call Del, he has FBI contacts and will know what we should do."

"I agree. I will call him—the ambulance is here. We'll be there in a couple of minutes.

After Stacey was loaded up, Gary told the ambulance driver he would be with Stacy on the trip to Glasgow.

"I'm not supposed to let you, but I would insist if I was in your shoes. So, okay."

Gary gave his mom a hug then sat next to Stacy, "I will call you." The ambulance left in a hurry, making lots of noise.

As soon as the ambulance reached the Glasgow hospital, Gary called Stacy's mom, telling all he knew.

Meg called Frank. He didn't answer. She called Del. "Del, Stacy was shot while horseback riding this morning and is on her way to the Glasgow hospital. Gary stayed with her. Stacy's mom lives near Harlowton and is working on finding a way to Glasgow.

"Meg, I have an appointment with a client who will understand that I need to reschedule after I explain. Call—"

"Evelyn," interrupted Meg.

"Evelyn." I continued, "Tell her I will fly over and give her a ride to Glasgow. I will need her phone number. Suggest she take enough for five days. Plenty of room in the plane. I am already on my way to the airport."

Meg gave me the phone number.

After she hung up, she called Gary. "Del is flying Evelyn to Glasgow in his plane. He will call you after he has her in the plane."

"Wow, he is like family. Thanks, Mom." He hung up and softly cried privately.

I called my client and received an enthusiastic, "Absolutely."

I called Evelyn. "Hello. This is Del Sanderson. I talked to Meg. Do you have transportation to your airport, and is your husband coming as well?"

"Yes, I have a car, but Thorney is in Billings. I have called him, explaining about you giving me a ride," answered Evelyn.

"I should arrive at your airport in an hour and fifteen minutes. There is plenty of room to bring what you need."

I hung up and called Cliff on the 'NOW' number as soon as I left the runway. I pushed the plane to the max that I dared.

"Morning, Del. Cliff here."

I related everything I knew.

"Let me work on things. I'll call you back as soon as I can arrange everything.

"Thanks, Cliff. This changes things about the drug mules."

"Yes, it does. I can assure you we will discuss this at a very high level and include the DEA. You counsel your special friends to be extra careful."

"Will do. Cliff, keep me in the loop."

"Best I can. Fly safely. Godspeed."

"Always."

I landed smoothly at the small airfield. I greeted a very shaken Evelyn.

"Evelyn, I am Del, let me get your things." I loaded her items into the back two seats, strapped her in, and asked, "Have you ever been in a small plane like this one?"

"No, Mr. Sanderson. I am not a big fan of flying," sighed Evelyn.

"Call me Del. I will do my best to make it a soft ride. We should be in Glasgow in a couple of hours."

Landing at the airport in Glasgow, we saw Gary waiting for her.

Turning to me she spoke through tears, "Meg said you're special. She is absolutely right. I will never forget this. I did enjoy the ride, seeing things from above and even relaxing some." Giving him a long hug, she whispered, "Thank you so much."

Gary took Evelyn's arm and offered, "Stacy is out of surgery and doing great. I even got a small smile from her. She's expecting you."

"That is such good news. You're a good man, Gary Cummings."

"Thank you, Evelyn. It will take fifteen minutes to get to the hospital."

Shifting to me, he offered his hand and looked me in the eye. "I will quote my little brother, Toby. 'Gary, Del is a special man. Giving him a ride last summer will change our lives.' He is totally right. Thank you."

"You are welcome, Gary. I learned early in life to help others. Helping is special to me."

I called Meg. "Evelyn is on her way to the hospital. Stacy should recover nicely. Gary is holding up okay. I have a car and will stop and talk to Gary to get his story. Then I will start for the ranch. Please ask Toby to watch everything and video the camp. I called the FBI and expect an answer quickly. See you soon."

"Drive safely. The deputies are here with Toby. They act lost. Toby has already videoed the campsite. See you soon."

I called Cliff.

"Del, I have talked to everyone under the sun. The DEA is now deeply involved, we do some things together, but mostly go our own way. They will both tell me the name of the agent they're dispatching. They're expecting you to be at the ranch and understand about your relationship with me. "

"Great, I am an hour away from the ranch now. I will talk to Gary and get his story. Then I will call you after I get there."

"Godspeed."

"Always."

CHAPTER 87

I stopped at the ranch house and noticed a small note pinned next to the door. Meg and Toby were out with the deputies, so I continued to the campsite.

Meg and Toby greeted me, introduced the deputies, and asked again about Stacy.

"She is out of surgery and doing well."

Toby spoke next, "I told the deputies I videoed the camp and took pictures. They asked if I would video everything they did, so I complied. They wanted copies. Is that okay?"

"Let me make a call."

He called Cliff.

I told him what I had learned so far, and asked about the videos.

"That should be okay. I'll give you a contact for the DEA and FBI, so he can forward copies to them as well. DEA Agent Leland Lemire will arrive in the next hour. FBI Agent Georgia Kolker is also about an hour away. Give them everything, and let them do their job. Keep the family immune, keep them out of everything."

"Thanks for fronting this. I will do my best."

"That's what friends are for. It's also my job."

I turned to Meg and Toby and related what Cliff asked me to do. They all sauntered over to watch the deputies. I told them about the government agents soon to arrive. Meg excused herself and returned the mile and a half to her house using a quad.

"We will be happy for the help and guidance. This is above the norm for our little county," said Bronte.

Agent Kolker arrived first. Meg directed her to the crime scene. Agent Lemire showed up twenty minutes later and received the same directions.

Meg remained on the front porch and tried calling Frank again. The call went to voicemail. Her terse message, "Please call immediately!"

CHAPTER 88

A gent Lemire followed his agency's procedures, and Agent Kolker followed hers. Both took many pictures and videoed the scene. They had worked together before.

Toby transferred everything he had videoed to both agents.

"We should both drive to Glasgow when we're done here and get Gary's statement. Georgia, this is very strange to have a drug mule shoot someone. That person must be new, or extra violent. I'm sure those walkers are told to slip through and never disturb anything."

"You're right, Leland, but we're dealing with the bottom of the barrel here. Word is the woman will survive, so at least we aren't dealing with a homicide, but maybe attempted murder. I'm guessing this route will be abandoned for a time. We need to ask the residents to inform us if it starts up again. We're done here, so on to Glasgow. I'll follow you," said Georgia.

Both stopped and thanked Meg, left their contact information, then continued to Glasgow, to meet with Gary.

CHAPTER 89

heriff Doland was the driver of the car Toby saw leaving the bridge. The sheriff didn't know he had been spotted. His Deputies believed him to be in Billings. After he heard the story about the shooting and the shooter's comment, he became scared.

"Such an easy shot, bet she's dead."

"Chip, you are supposed to just sneak through, no hint of violence," chastised Sheriff Doland. "Your action will shut this route down. The boss isn't going to like that."

"I'm not doing this again anyway, not my idea of fun. I'll just go to Fargo, North Dakota and do something else."

Sheriff Doland had called the FBI a month ago about offering to tell them all he knew and get a new life. Now was the time. As soon as this drop ended, he would be gone. He called the number he had been given, after completing the exchange and getting rid of the walkers.

"How may I help you?" a female voice said.

"I was told to call this number. Today was the last straw for me. One of the drug mules shot a resident. I know if I don't disappear, I'm dead, too. Tell me what to do," Doland uttered, his voice cracking. He shook for a full minute then tossed his cookies in the restroom.

"Where are you?" he heard the female voice ask at least twice.

"In the restroom at the Dairy Queen in Glasgow," he finally gasped.

"What make and model and color is your car?" she questioned.

Another gasp, followed by more cookies. He stuttered, "a one color dark gray Buick Enclave that belongs to the Sheriff's Department in Malta," he answered. "The gun used to shoot the woman, is in the car. I know the shooters name is Chip Nelson. I am sure his prints are on the gun."

"Drive Eleventh Street to the dead-end sign, turn left, park on the right side of the street, exit your vehicle, and walk south. Someone will find you. Leave the gun and keys in the car."

"Okay, and thanks," he answered trying to sound professional and failing.

Sheriff Doland followed the instructions. He met an older white-haired man walking a large beautiful Irish Setter, "Morning, sir. That is a beautiful dog," he said as he bent to pet the animal.

"Morning to you. Sig is getting old. He used to be a great hunting dog. Are you Sheriff Doland?" The man asked. "Keep petting the dog, he likes the attention."

"Yes."

"I'll walk you back to the old red Subaru. Keep talking and smiling as you get in the car," He sat in the back seat noticeably shaking.

Agent Kolker, dressed in a dark business suit, started the car and drove silently to a tourist vista near Fort Peck Dam. "Please go get in the white van."

Returning to the small FBI office in an older one-story bungalow, Kolker noticed the sheriff's car already parked in the driveway. The gun had been removed. The prints processed and checked.

Inside the white van, were three DEA agents, one woman and two men. The driver was a hulk, at least 250 pounds, sporting a blond buzz cut and a serious face. The other older man, looked frail, with a narrow face and receding widow's peak hairline.

"Thank you very much," Doland said, trying not to cry.

The woman spoke. "We are going to Bismark, North Dakota for processing. If you can provide useful information, we intend to take good care of you. Do you know what the DEA is?"

"Yes. Drug Enforcement Agency."

"We are part of that agency and will do most of the processing. The FBI wants to solve the shooting of the woman. We will keep you safe. We know you took a huge risk today. Did you leave personal items in your apartment?"

"Ma'am, I decided a month ago to do this, and Chip shooting the woman proved I needed to do it now. Too many people know about the pipeline. Chip thought the shooting was funny. I have his picture. I rented a small storage unit in Billings a month ago and moved everything important there.

Anyone can have what's left. I positively know four or five of the drug world people in Salt Lake City, and two in Sparks, Nevada. I also know the location of the drop in Glasgow." He stopped talking abruptly, knowing he should learn what these people were going to offer before saying anything else. "I have not slept well in a while, so could I rest as we complete the drive?"

"Just two more questions. What do you expect us to do for you?" the lady agent asked. "And please give us the backpack drop information in Glasgow."

"I only know the address, but have never seen the person."

"The address will do."

Sheriff Doland gave them the address.

"Agent Driscoll, the agent I talked to in Salt Lake, hinted I could get a new life if my information was good. I have no idea what that could mean for me. I'm not a user. I just want out. I don't want to feel scared all the time."

"Fair enough. Take your nap." When she saw the sheriff's jaw drop, she texted the frail passenger.

His answer, "We could get a top name or two, but at least we will get a starting trail we can follow. Great job, he trusts you. We will nurture that trust. It is nice to catch a break. We need to talk to Georgia and Leland to get their take on the shooting."

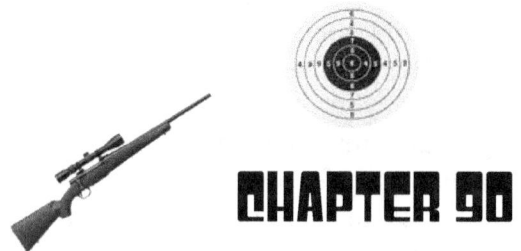

CHAPTER 90

The hospital released Stacy after two nights. Gary drove her to the Cummings ranch, assured her comfort, then completed the evening chores. Toby was working sunup to sundown to complete the first cutting of hay and doing all the chores. Jimmy completed one guided boat excursion then came to help.

I flew Evelyn back to Harlowton. She offered little conversation until we landed.

"I can't thank you enough for your kindness. I enjoyed flying much more than I expected, seeing things from the air. Seeing Fort Peck was really a treat. Meg told me you are a financial planner."

"Mostly retired, Evelyn, though still work with about twenty clients."

"Meg suggested I ask you to look at our situation and advise us on what to do. We have yet to plan anything. We are not sure how to proceed. We can't use a local lawyer. Then everyone will know more than they have a right to."

I listened intently, and weighed my options. "Evelyn, I travel a lot, and do wish to stay retired. I will do two things for you. I will look at your financial statement, assuming you are willing to allow full disclosure, and if you and your husband will come to Great Falls, we can meet privately to see what your next step could be. If I can be helpful, I will do my best to show you how to arrange things.

"I have your number. When I get to Great Falls, I will look at my schedule and call you this evening,"

I offered my hand. Evelyn ignored it and gave me another meaningful hug. "Meg is right about you. Thank you so much." She slipped into her car after we loaded her suitcases and drove off.

I called Evelyn and arranged an appointment for the following week, then called Meg for an update.

"Del, thank you for taking care of Evelyn. I have come to love Stacy as if she were my own daughter. Evelyn and I will be more than good friends. Stacy's one brother, Dean, who works in the North Dakota oil fields, drove all night to visit his sister in Glasgow. Dean and Gary get along nicely.

"Stacy is in more pain than she lets on, but is doing well. It's Gary I'm worried about. He believes he needs to do something more."

"Meg. I will call him if you wish. Did Frank talk to him?"

"I doubt that, since he didn't call me until yesterday, then came home, but didn't go to Glasgow. He was more concerned about the authorities and their actions. I'm afraid I was more direct than he expected. We've only quarreled twice throughout our marriage. He seems extra troubled lately."

"Meg, my wife Amy and I always talked directly if something was troubling us."

"I believe I shall. I probably waited longer that I should have. Frank and I do need a direct talk. He has heart trouble, but he should have called me much sooner."

"Let me know if I can help. Your family has become important in my life," I could not tell Meg what he had learned about Frank. My heart ached, but knowing what I knew about the blackmail was not my business.

"Thank you, Del. You have become a part of our family. I will visit with you soon."

I did call Gary. We visited thirty minutes or so. Gary expressed his gratitude and agreed with me it was best to go about his normal routine.

CHAPTER 91

Frank had returned, but mostly sat in the book-lined study brooding about his options. Jimmy went back and fished at Fort Peck as a guide, Toby worked to finish the haying, and Gary finished the evening chores with Stacy at his side.

Stacy took Gary's hand, looked him in the eye and started crying, "Gary, you saved my life. What a beautiful way to start our life together."

"I felt totally scared for you. I love everything about you. We are so lucky to have each other."

Frank sat alone in the study, not finding any answers. Meg joined him, but remained standing. "Frank, I have known about your mistress since the beginning. My boys and family always came first. I don't want a detailed explanation. I want the estate plan completed as soon as possible, and the purchase of the Sutherland's ranch completed as well, and my boys set up for the rest of their lives.

"I plan to stay on the ranch as long as I am able. Gary and Toby will each have a ranch of their own. I will find a way to help Jimmy make his way. You may stay here and keep the family intact. When the Sutherland deal is done and the estate plan completed, you can do what you wish, but all the property stays in the family. Good night."

Meg walked to their bedroom and sat down to cry, but couldn't. She shook with anger and worry.

Frank came to their bedroom, "Meg I am so sorry for the deception. I know I can never repair the damage to your heart. Do the boys know?"

"Yes, they have for some time. But I did not tell them."

"I will call Del. Will you come with me to Great Falls to finalize everything?"

"Yes, finishing everything is critical now. Please come to Gary's wedding."

"I wouldn't miss our son's wedding. I will stay as long as you will let me, so we can finish everything."

He returned to the study, crying, relieved, yet terrified. He felt it all come crashing down. He blamed his weakness, hating himself. His heart began to race. He took a pill to slow it down.

After two weeks-time, the Sutherland property purchase was completed, and their estate plan copied and filed, which allowed the family to move forward. The family sat together and Frank explained how each of the sons would be taken care of. They talked late into the night.

Meg told Gary about her conversation with his dad. Gary admitted all the boys knew about Frank's mistress. But didn't know what to do about it.

CHAPTER 92

rank needed to be alone. He saddled his horse the next morning and rode through the pasture to his favorite place above stinky hollow. His heart still raced. He dismounted, sat and cried. *"How could I ruin such a beautiful family?"* He muttered. *"I am such a fool."* He started to get back in the saddle. The heart attack solved all his problems.

Toby and Gary went looking for him that afternoon. He had been gone six hours. They found him lying on the ground next to his horse, his heart broken in many ways.

Gary called his mom. "We found him, Mom. He must have had a heart attack. . .he's dead. I am so sorry, Mom." Toby and Gary returned with their dad draped over the saddle.

"I'll call Jimmy, Mom," offered Toby.

"I'll call Del," said Meg. "What should I ask him?"

"Mom, ask him to please come as soon as he can, he knows how to sort this stuff. I think he'll say, 'I will arrange things and leave as soon as I can,' suggested Toby.

"I agree, we are going to need his help," echoed Gary.

"Look, we should sit down together now and get our ducks in a row. I loved your dad. We all knew of his weakness. But for now, I would like to be alone."

"I'm going for horse-back ride. Gary, do you want help with the chores first?" Toby gave his mom a long hug. "I loved Dad. But he made a big mistake." He tried not to cry but failed.

"Go on your ride, Toby. The chores will allow me to be busy."

Gary walked over to his mom, gave her a long hug, too. "We all loved him. He did most things right. We will miss him." Gary cried privately as he completed the chores alone.

1 flew to the Cummings ranch to help the family cope. I fronted much of the legal processes. I watched the Cummings family cry together, yet felt a powerful resolve to be strong. My last act before getting in the plane, was a long hug with Meg as she cried, setting my heart into a spin. After the funeral, I flew back to Great Falls. My feelings for Meg were real, and it scared me.

A week later I called Meg. "If you need me for anything, just call. I know I have become close to everyone in your family."

"Del, we will call soon. We will welcome your input to get the Sutherland property ready for Toby. He is so excited to get started. Jimmy is liking his summer job, and all three trips he has guided went 'okay' to use his words. I would like to ask you to help Jimmy study the marina business in great detail. If it will make money, especially after you explained to Richie Sutherland the benefits of a structured payment plan to buy his place, we could cover the marina as well. We, as a family, have learned much about ranching business finances."

"Meg, I am a phone call away, followed by a short flight. I would love to see the Cummings family soon."

I hung up, knowing that seeing Meg was what I wanted most.

CHAPTER 93

ary and Toby drove to the Fort Benton rodeo. They talked about getting the Sutherland property ready for Toby. "Gary, as the oldest, you should stay at the Cummings house. That is perfect in my mind. We should do all crops next year using our own machines, so we can see what we need to add. I want to clean up the home site, especially the trees, so we can decide about adding on to the structures, or tearing them down."

"I agree, Toby. We three brothers can work at the cleaning together. I think we should make sure Jimmy feels totally welcome at both places. He's taking dad's death very hard. I sense he will be okay, but I worry some. Mom is struggling. I'd bet Del shows up one day soon."

"Gary, Del has been in love with Mom since that first plane ride. I don't have a solid feeling about her yet, but she loves him too, I believe, she at least trusts him."

"I'm surprised you said that. I'm positive you're right. I didn't see her after the plane ride, but her hugs are extra-long. Dad made a huge mistake and hurt Mom's heart. I don't see them rushing into anything, but they will start testing those feelings. I have always loved our mom, and have come to respect Del a lot. Both know they need someone. I'm happy for them.

"Stacy and I will be married next month. We plan to use the old farmhouse, for now. When Del comes, he will get the guest room."

"Gary, glad we are on the same page. Del has changed our lives for the better. I know I love him."

When they parked at the rodeo grounds, they looked at each other and clasped both their hands together in front of their belt buckles. Gary spoke," we need to keep these feeling and thoughts to ourselves. They may not see things like we do. We will show both complete respect."

"Agreed. Let's go win some money," added Toby.

Gary took second in bronc riding. Toby took first in bull riding. "If I liked to drink, I would tie one on. Never won a *first* before, just two third place medals. We'll celebrate at the ranch when we are home."

CHAPTER 94

Benito believed he shouldn't get too close to Bryan. Bryan and the chief were good friends, not just chief and computer man.

He knew Pepe was going to start shooting Rocco's people. Pepe owned a Rocco spy. But still lived because he didn't trust anyone. He wanted his money and needed Rocco gone. Pepe's airport security person told him about the black man from Miami, and where he was hiding. He would send his three best shooters.

Pepe's shooters parked three blocks away from the black man's lair. Two went into the alley, and the third dispatched to knock on the front door. No real need for details. Two minutes later, all three were dead, and the black man was gone. Rocco paid for the best.

When Pepe learned his shooters were dead, he went into war status. He didn't know if Rocco was still in Florida or back in Arizona. He sent his twenty-year old son, Tomás, to Mexico to recruit expendables. Pepe needed to win or die.

Pepe knew about two of Rocco's safe houses. He sent two shooters to the first location armed with automatic weapons. They approached the small single-family house from the front and rear, expended two thirty-round clips each and hustled away. They didn't pause to see if they were successful.

Rocco lost three soldiers to Pepe's daring attack. The same two shooters tried the same tactic at the second house, but did not kill any others. Those people were warned.

Rocco had returned to Arizona, but told no-one. He knew Pepe's son was in Mexico recruiting, so he sent the black man to take care of things. The black man crossed into Mexico. It was easy for him to find Tomas, who left a simple trail. He followed the young man into a seedy cantina and shot him; he also shot the other two patrons and the bartender.

He left through a small narrow alley. The smell bothered him. He was meticulous about his looks and clothes. Smelling like an alley in Mexico would not be acceptable. Back in Arizona he purchased new clothes, rented a motel room and showered before donning his new clothes, and leaving the soiled ones on the floor.

He called Rocco, explained about Pepe's son and the collateral damage. Then negotiated a new financial deal. His next task would be Pepe. Rocco sent the money to a third safe house in Marana. The black man collected his money. Walked back to the bus stop and boarded the downtown Tucson bus.

Pepe used a small adobe house in North Tucson with a surrounding wall, topped with razor wire. He felt safe. The Tucson police knew about Pep's place, but nothing bad ever happened there. Pepe was incensed about losing his three shooters. He waited for word from his son.

Benito learned about Tomás before Pepe did, so arranged a meeting. They sat facing each other in Nico's. Benito relayed what he had learned.

"How is it you know this?"

"Pepe, I have an informant in Nogales. He heard about it and learned the shooter was a tall black man, who killed everyone in the cantina. Four people. Your son trusted too much."

"I must check myself, yes?"

"Pepe, I would if I were you," answered Benito.

"Gracias, I will call you, if you give me some number."

Benito gave him a burner number, telling it was good for two calls.

"Si, I call you."

They went their separate ways.

CHAPTER 95

The Miami assassin suspected a group of kids were watching him. He just had fun losing them.

He didn't know they had ties to the police department. Sgt. Hernandez paid the kids from his rent-a-cop job at a local brewery. Sgt. Hernandez trained them to see things and the rules about bad guys.

The kids rode bikes and worked in groups of two or three. They knew where the assassin lived and shopped. They had only one rule, no risks.

Hernandez told the chief, and the chief told the rest of the force. Chief remained fearful of the coming feud.

"Anyone hear anything, I want to know. We need to catch Rocco."

"Pepe is going to be wild when he hears about his son," added the chief. "I've visited with the mayor, and he agrees. We stay out of this mess unless confronted. Do not engage unless forced. Be careful out there."

The war grew cold for most of a week. The kids offered nothing new. Everyone believed Rocco hid somewhere in Tucson. No visuals anywhere

Nobody believed the war had ended.

CHAPTER 96

B ryan saw Benito at the gym. Benito followed the same routine each day, always using free weights in some way.

"Have you heard anything about Pepe and Rocco?" Bryan asked when they were alone.

"Pepe's son got himself killed in Mexico. My informant said Rocco is already in Tucson," was a short answer from Benito.

"I heard about Pepe's son, Benito. Street talk pins the killing on the Miami black dude."

"My Rocco informant is scared to death. I think I should call him in now and not wait."

"Chief is sure more deaths are on the horizon. I sense he's right. I agree, Benito, you should save your informant and his family. That black man does not care who he kills. Word is, he shot everyone in the cantina when he dispatched Pepe's son. My guess is he will shoot cops.

"You know, Benito, I hope this war stays away from the police. If they do involve us, we will have some dead police men and women. Chief knows Hernandez's son and his friends are at greater risk than they believe. You and I don't know everything the chief knows. But that Miami man is totally aware of everything. He knows those boys have been around too often."

"I agree, Bryan. The chief needs to stop those boys, now. I will get Alejandro and his sister safely out of Marana."

"I will talk to the chief today," Bryan answered.

"I'm done for today, Bryan, so I'll clean up and see if I can find Pepe. See you."

Bryan did talk to the chief. Hernandez received orders to keep the kids away from the drug war. Benito secured his informant in a safe house in Williams, Arizona.

CHAPTER 97

Bryan called Beth in Idaho. "I have six days off, starting Thursday. Austin invited me to stay with him, as my chief wants to get a program started that is similar to Mr. Davis's WIM. I'll be there early Thursday, and must fly back the following Wednesday. Austin said a fishing trip will be planned. I am excited to return to North Idaho. Where should we go on our second date?"

"So nice to hear from you, Bryan, and that you're coming north. I'll have the second date all planned. It's too early for huckleberries, so you'll have to come back in July or August."

"I'd like to make that work, Beth. I'm happy to have a second date with you."

Bryan called the chief after talking with Austin. "Austin, Bill Davis and Sylvia Delany will come to Mesa and stay at the casino by the airport next week, after I return home. They will bring everything to help set up a three-state group like theirs."

"I'll arrange two days off to meet with them, Bryan. I hope to learn exactly how to make a similar system work here. Enjoy your working vacation. We will have another BBQ as you'll need an update on Benito."

"Anything I should know now, Chief?"

"Not really, I just want you to know our next step, as it will not involve you. See you for that BBQ when you return.

Austin arranged everything, and Bryan flew again to Spokane. There he met George then flew to Priest River.

Beth did go fishing with Keith, Austin and Bryan. Keith's son bought Bryan's license. Austin caught the biggest lake trout, thirty-four pounds. Bryan caught one weighing twenty-two. Beth didn't catch anything, saying she enjoyed just watching the scenery.

Beth and Bryan returned to Hill's for their second date. After dinner, they did eat another piece of Huckleberry pie. Arriving reasonably late, they shared that first kiss. *"Perfect,"* a smiling Bryan said to himself. They walked to their separate bedrooms, and shared a second kiss before parting. Bryan laid awake a long time, processing his feelings. These were new to him, as he shared none of these same feelings with his current girlfriend. What to do? They lived miles apart.

CHAPTER 98

Pepe and the last four of his henchmen that he believed to be loyal to him, were at his adobe planning what to do to avenge his son's death. "We don't have enough people. We cannot get to Rocco with the people we have now."

"You are right, Angel, so I need a volunteer to go to Mexico to buy the help we desperately need."

"He will be killed like your son. We should go to San Diego tonight by car with money to buy some help. We can sneak out of here. They cannot watch everyone," said Angel.

"Okay Angel you go. I give you fifty thousand to buy help. Tell them I pay double if they come. They need their own guns. Everybody, leave together to help Angel to escape."

Pepe was left alone. He locked everything, rechecked the locks twice, then prepared a batch of tacos. He liked to cook. He loaded three rapid fire guns, placed one by each door and carried the third. He did not plan to sleep until Angel returned. He waited for the last three of his players to come back.

Angel did not know he had followers. The five toughs he hired were ambushed and killed. Angel did not know about the ambush. He expected these new people to arrive at Pepe's safe house.

CHAPTER 99

The black man waited until all of Pepe's help were gone, then scaled the gate using a blanket over the razor wire. He crept to the front door, placed a small explosive by each lock. He then backed to the side of the house and triggered the explosives. Both locks failed and the door fell inward, leaving Pepe exposed. Pepe panicked and emptied a full cartridge of thirty rounds through the open door. While he reloaded, the black man shot him three times. Pepe died alone.

Just like that—Rocco took over. When Angel returned, he became the last of Pepe's allies to die, the other three were also victims of the war. The black man took Angel's remaining cash from his satchel. He chose not to tell anyone about the thirty-five thousand that was now his. The war never involved any police department.

Benito learned everything within minutes. His master plan was almost completed. Only Rocco stood in the way. Benito knew the black man's name, but Rocco didn't. The black man, Raphael

Diaz, would now kill Rocco. Raphael's brother met his maker when Spencer shot him from long range in Saint Petersburg four or five months ago. Benito felt on top of the world. *"At last,"* he said aloud to himself.

The chief's surveillance team took pictures of every meeting with Mr. Diaz, Rocco and Pepe that Benito participated in. Cameras can take pictures from a long distance, with great clarity. Raphael worked for money, no other reason. He planned to take over from Rocco very soon. He met Rocco at Rocco's safe house and killed him.

Bryan attended a second barbeque at the chief's home. "Benito will be arrested soon, Bryan. We can't let him get away."

Policemen following policemen is not a duty the cops relish. Catching a policeman doing a crime causes distrust between the rest of the men and women on the force. The chief will have department repair on his agenda.

The chief wanted Benito and the black man badly. Some things are not meant to be. The black man disappeared driving a rental car back to Florida, and Benito went to prison for a long, long time.

Benito never revealed the black man's name, and left Bryan out of every discussion. He knew he needed an ally. Chief Johnson warned Bryan to watch his back. He knew Benito to be a powerful enemy with many contacts.

Bryan finished his class at the University and drove back to headquarters. He saw a small Hispanic man approach him as he started to walk from his car into the building. The man waved to Bryan and stopped in his tracks. Bryan stopped as well. The Hispanic man beckoned Bryan closer.

Tentatively, Bryan complied.

"Si, Mr. Kellerman, I am Alejandro, Benito says he is sorry to deceive you. He asks you to come see him, if the chief approves. I will come here next week same time to hear. Gracias," and he turned and walked away.

Byran did ask, and the chief suggested he decline. But Bryan could accept a delivered note.

The following week Alejandro asked Bryan what the chief told him to do.

"I am told to decline, but I could accept a message from you."

"Si. It is what Benito expected. I will see what comes next. Gracias, Senior. I will return next Wednesday," he walked away.

Bryan felt many emotions wondering what Benito could possibly want from him.

CHAPTER 100

Bryan sat at his desk, sorting information about the Superstition Mountain cold case in Mesa. He had lots of new data, but found it difficult to match the data to Benito's report.

His phone chimed, "Bryan, is Rocco still in Florida?"

"No, he is back in Tucson. Why do you ask?"

"I need to know about Rocco's assassin." I learned about the assassin from J.C. I visited J.C. most days about our possible drug rehab satellite facility in Marana.

"How do you know about that?"

"Answer…or we are done."

"I have a picture."

"Publish it in the Star with a bolo."

"Why?"

"Do it," dial tone.

"*Wow*," murmured Bryan to himself. "*How does this guy know so much?*"

I saw the picture in the Star. I would recognize the man, if I saw him. "*Jamaican*," I told myself. Time to visit Dutch in Florida, and go fishing. He needed to be very lucky. Spencer would find a suitable room to shoot from and be the shooter.

CHAPTER 101

After calling Dutch, telling him I would be in Florida next week, I flew commercial to Miami. My research told me the Jamaican community was called Pembrook Pines. It was easy to find.

Spencer watched traffic for two hours. Passersby asked if he was all right, three times. He worked in a crossword book the whole time. No black man. After the second inquiry, he visited an upscale clothing store to see if he could trade his plain jeans for Jamaican style.

The sales lady showed him ten different options. Not a fan of bling, he chose one with only back pocket accents. While he paid for them, the black man walked past. Spencer returned to his bench. After seeing the man turn into a clothing store, Spencer walked to his car, preparing to leave. His quarry exited the store, turning back, the way he came. His car turned out to be a neat red-Alfa Romero. Luckily, Spencer's car faced the same direction. He kept the red car in sight, seeing it as it turned into a gated community, and proceed to a driveway of a front row condo.

No way I could get to him at his residence. The clothing store may be an option. So, I needed to find a room facing the street more than five hundred yards away. I set about looking.

This man killed for money. That was slime in my book. I did not have a shooting location yet. The search proved very difficult. I looked too white. Many doors opened slightly, then closed. At last, a small elderly black woman asked me into her living room.

"Why do you need a room?"

"I want to taste some Jamaican cuisine. I will only be here a week, so I must find a top restaurant," I said.

"One week will cost one hundred dollars."

"Sorry then, I can't afford that much. I'll have to find a cheaper room. I can only pay fifty."

"Fifty it is," she answered without a smile.

Looking out the window, I realized I would see him for six or seven steps. My landlady seemed to be hard of hearing, so Rick's new silencer will barely be heard. I will need to use extra precision with such a narrow window of opportunity. Maybe he would not come back to the store. I may have the crossword book done. I ate out every evening, enjoying the food. Some extra spice at times, but tolerable.

The fourth day, the black man entered the store, stayed twenty minutes, purchased something then started back to his car. After checking with the spotting scope and opening the window, Spencer shot him. *Number eight, Curt.* He did not twitch.

I returned to my car before anyone risked stopping to look. He will not kill anyone else. I did not feel any remorse or stress this time. My simple plan worked. I left no evidence in the room then drove back to Fort Lauderdale. Time to go fishing after removing my disguise.

Shooting the black man hardened me. I felt almost nothing. No trembling, no nausea, no fear, just a job well done. I realized the change while traveling back to Fort Lauderdale. Realizing I was not trembling, I actually smiled. "I have finally mastered some of the fear. Now I think I know what Cliff meant about becoming a criminal mastermind."

The scared feeling never surfaced. I knew changes were happening in my life. I knew I would do something now, about the young men involved in Curt's death.

I also knew I felt strongly about Meg. I worried about that change and possessed no foggy idea what I should do about it.

Maybe Meg did not have those same feelings.

CHAPTER 102

I visited the Cummings family, almost every week. The boys had the Sutherland buildings cleaned up, the trees trimmed and lawns mowed, and tested all the equipment. Two decent rains assured an okay crop on the Sutherland property.

Jimmy guided four days a week. During his off days, he tested other fishing spots. He found two super perch spots, and one where a client caught a 44-inch thirty-five-pound pike. He liked every trip on the water. His tips were improving. He didn't miss ranching, but helped his brothers anytime he could. He talked to his mom after nearly every trip about owning the marina.

I carried all the papers needed to buy the marina, so I visited two other marinas near Bozeman, asking tons of questions. I went with Jimmy and Meg to the bank in Glasgow holding Shep's loan. I worked a detailed structured payment plan, and the three of them presented it to Shep. They waited to hear Shep's answer.

Meg and I did go flying again, but she did not try to fly. However, Toby started a flight program in Glasgow. On his solo flight, he buzzed the ranch, smiling the whole time.

After the second flight with Meg, they sat on the porch together, "Meg, I do love you completely. I have wanted to say that for a long time."

"Del, I know I love you too, but I am not ready to follow those feelings."

"If and when you become ready, I will be the happiest I have been since Amy died. I will never completely get over losing her."

"I will never get over losing Frank either Del, he made a big mistake in his life and hated himself for it. I have to come to grips with that as well. I think the boys know about us. When, we are ready, we will know," sighed Meg. They sat in silence, both smiling.

CHAPTER 103

I needed to check on Michelle. During his call, Agent Sandoval told him the surveillance had become boring. The suspects traveled back at forth between the two locations, but nothing new ever happened. The first day of the farmer's market season was only a week away. The three white vans were still in the building. "Cliff asked us to keep watching until a week after the market opens."

I flew to Billings, checking on things for myself. I planned to stay until the first day of the market. I would bet the farm Michelle would be ready and do whatever she planned on that first day.

I did not go the Billings condo as James. Instead, I called my lady realtor and asked her to offer it for sale, giving her his entry codes and the procedure to create a reset.

I asked Agent Sandoval what plans were in place to prevent Michelle and crew from any terrorist act.

"If the vans leave the building, we have two large sand and gravel trucks ready to block the road either direction. A helicopter will be airborne less than ten minutes away. Four cars of agents will then hopefully surround the building."

"Desmond, I am positive Michelle will detonate one or all of the vans if she is thwarted," I interjected. "Word is, she is a hater. She will kill all of her people, try to escape, and start over. My guess is she is going to leave early and be in position to blow up the vans anytime. We should not trust her to be part of the van convoy."

"What do you suggest, Del?"

"Not sure, but we need two cars with two agents, to very carefully watch her if she leaves separately, as I expect her to do. Those cars have to be nondescript, and cover both the front and back of her building. I will volunteer to be in one of them. I am a better than average shot with my 9mm."

"Will Cliff approve letting you act as an agent?" asked Desmond.

"I have no idea, maybe."

"Del, I will ask him. Will you abide by his decision?"

"One hundred percent, Desmond. But I do want to be part of the arrest."

Tomorrow the market will open. We needed to catch Michelle. I remembered her icy treatment of me as I held the door for her 87 days ago. Cliff approved allowing me to be in the car facing the gate of the business behind her building.

The vans exited the overhead door, and drove out at the gate. The two big trucks effectively blocked the road both ways. Michelle raced out the back door, used a tarp to scale the back fence, and started to cross the business lot behind her.

My station to watch from, fronted that back building and the open gate. She stopped at the entrance and triggered the explosives in all three vans. The explosions were horrendous and partially damaged both gravel trucks. Neither agent received any personal harm. I chambered a shell, waited until she came out from the gate, and yelled at her to surrender. She started to run through the gate, so I shot her in a leg. She cried out and fell. I sent my partner to attend to her. I did not want her to see me.

Cliff called me after hearing Desmond's report, "I will come to Billings tomorrow to hear your report. Amazing."

CHAPTER 104

While I waited to meet with Cliff, I worked to move my offshore money to Beliz. I do not intend to return to Cancun. I will still use James Colbert if I needed to hide in plain sight, but will not return to the condo as James.

I opened the account with nine thousand dollars, then arranged to transfer the 1.6 million from Cancun to the Belize Bank Limited. The Belize bank will pay me 9% to keep my money. The Cancun bank paid zero.

The confirmation of the transfer arrived in two hours. I asked the new bank to then transfer $50,000 to my Bozeman bank, as I needed to pay for the supplies, I ordered for all the alternate ID's.

I enjoyed a dark roast coffee and a pumpkin bread treat at a Starbucks on Grand, while waiting for Cliff. He called and hinted another hour would expire before he would arrive.

I greeted Cliff with a complete hug. It felt like we were brothers.

"I have Desmond's complete report. I do need yours. Michelle has not said a word. She just hates everything. She doesn't seem to care she killed at least seven people. We must rely on small pieces of her victims, to see if we can identify them.

"We sent two agents to Michelle's apartment building to search both apartments and confiscated everything and sent it to headquarters to be analyzed. We also processed the warehouse at 225. The occupants left much proving the quality of the explosives in the vans."

"Cliff, I felt positive Michelle would either leave early or remain in the building until she could follow them to the market and detonate the explosives. If she left early, my partner and I were to follow and hopefully stop her. After she blew the vans, I needed to shoot her so we could catch her. I did not miss."

"Rick says you rarely miss, using the 9mm or your long-range rifle, even from a thousand yards."

"What will happen to me now that I shot her?'

"Del, I'm supposed to confiscate your gun. You are supposed to fly to headquarters and be debriefed."

"Cliff, my gun is secured where only I can get to it. I think an agent can come out here and do the debriefing. I have done nothing wrong. If my wounding Michelle means I am under the microscope, then I am out of the program."

"I have some calls to make. I bet Charlene a nice dinner you would not go willingly to headquarters. Let me run interference, and see how this plays out."

CHAPTER 105

liff called his boss, Special Agent Randy Long. A female agent answered the phone, and placed Cliff on hold.

"Good morning, Cliff. I've been expecting your call."

"Good morning. Randy, as you may have guessed, this is about Del Sanderson wounding Michelle in the leg. He has secured his pistol privately. Michelle will recover. She detonated the explosives in all three vans, and we have that action on video. We believe she killed at least seven of her own people. The explosions destroyed the vans. We may never know who died in them. If they had reached the farmers market, many more innocent lives could have been lost.

"Del expects an agent to come to Billings to conduct any debriefing. He will surrender the pistol if two things happen. One, he is to be given a new Smith & Wesson 9mm to replace the gun he surrenders. And two, he expects to be declared not responsible for any breach of protocol.

"I want to keep him in the enhanced program. He single-handedly learned every location and process related to this terrorist attempt. I believe he is due compensation for a job well done. He is not guilty of any criminal act. I firmly believe he saved many lives. I approved allowing him to partner with an agent in the car. The agent reported he called out to Michelle before he shot her in the leg, which stopped her attempt to flee.

"Cliff, I can go to Billings and conduct the de-brief myself. Please have the partner agent available and yourself in attendance," stated Agent Long.

"More than fair, sir. Thank you."

"Cliff. I do want to meet Del. In your year-end report, you credited Del with three of your criminal arrests and saving an agent's life. He is a person I need to know," added Randy.

"You will like him, sir. He is my very special friend. I love him like a brother."

"I will arrange to book a flight today and call Charlene about the timetable. I am looking forward to this trip, as I haven't seen you in four or five years, that is too long. I will bring Del a new Smith & Wesson 9mm, maybe even better than the one he used."

"See you soon, sir."

Cliff smiled to himself and called Del.

"Del, my boss, Randy Long, is flying out to Billings tomorrow to meet you and complete the de-brief himself. He's bringing you a new pistol."

I walked into the Billings FBI office with Cliff and Agent Williamson. Randy rose from his chair, and greeted Cliff.

"Cliff, thank you for coming. Agent Williamson, I thank you as well," Long said shaking the hand of both men.

"Del Sanderson, it is my pleasure to shake your hand. We have a most wanted terrorist in custody because of you. We have some procedures to complete this morning. First, here is the new pistol you requested. I understand you turned in the one you fired to wound Michelle."

"Yes sir, Agent Long," I said.

"Please call me Randy, Del."

"Randy, I am quite nervous about today. I have never had to explain why before."

"Del, I have reviewed everything about this action, many times. Cliff's reports are always the best in a technical sense and well thought out. Agent Williamson's report confirmed you asked Michelle to surrender. He added she started to run through the gate to escape. He had the presence of mind to catch her triggering the explosive devises.

"The FBI is here today to thank you, Del Sanderson, for a job well done. I wish I could return your personal gun, but may not. We have some paperwork to complete. Please read each page before signing them, ask any questions you may have."

I read every word twice, as Cliff suggested before they entered the room. "I did not fire in self-defense, Randy. Michelle was not armed. I am not sure what is correct in his blank."

"We understand that, but you were too far away to know what she held in her hand. It means you could not be certain, as she could have produced a gun. When you sign that last page, you are free of any action by the FBI. Cliff speaks highly of you. You took a note, located everything and ended up facilitating the capture of one of our most wanted terrorists.

I signed all required pages.

"Cliff has submitted a claim on your behalf, and it will be honored. His previous two claims will also be honored. So will any future ones.

"We will never get Michelle to tell us what her target was, but your analysis of the note and the exact date of the farmers market as her target, proves to us enough of her intent. Sending the vans out on the market's first day as she did, is quite conclusive," Randy stood and shook each hand, holding Del's a bit longer.

"We believe lives were saved. I don't like to dine alone, so am asking you three to join me at six in the hotel restaurant."

Cliff answered for all, "We will be happy to join you, Randy. That will be special, right Del and Stew?"

Randy talked to all, but spent most of his time visiting with me. Cliff just smiled. He enjoyed my directness with Randy. He asked about my skill with pistols. Randy shared he shot competitively, often winning. There was no real laughter, just friends enjoying things. "Why don't you shoot in competitions?" asked Randy.

"Do not think they are for me. I enjoy competitive actions. But do not relish shooting against others." answered Del.

Stew Williamson smiled while recounting my shot. "She started to run and refused to stop, so Del hit her leg. I might have shot all my shells and never hit a thing."

"I was just lucky, Stew."

"Bull. Only one shot and she's down, but not dead, ain't luck."

"Well, I do not wish to shoot at any more people," I finished.

"Gentlemen, I must fly back to DC tomorrow. So, I will call it day, one of my most memorable," Randy stood and shook everyone's hand one last time.

CHAPTER 106

I attended three weddings in late September.

A proud father, Thorney Bolton gave Stacy Bolton's hand in marriage to Gary Cummings during a church wedding in Malta. Over one hundred people attended. The reception filled everyone's expectations. Gary and Stacy released a dozen red and white balloons after Gary said, "I am sad my dad could not be with his family today."

I stood with Meg during the ceremony, because Meg insisted.

"Congratulating, Gary," I said. "First time I have ever seen you nervous."

"Yes, for sure. Happy to be married now though."

Back at the ranch, Gary and Stacy disappeared. Toby and Jimmy took a quad each and left the yard to go work on the Sutherland place.

I sat on the porch with Meg.

"Del, thanks for standing with me at the wedding. I asked Gary if that would be okay. He gave me a hug and said, 'Absolutely, all us sons know you love him.'" She took my hand. "I would like us to go on a trip somewhere together."

"I would love that, Meg, what do you have in mind?"

"I have never been to San Francisco. I researched it and found lots of fun things to do there."

"I have two more weddings to attend this September, but could arrange much of October. Let's find a waterfront hotel, and enjoy the sights," I offered.

I attended Dave Cummings marriage to Sally Knox. A lifetime bachelor, Dave finally found his lady. My friend for fifty plus years, Dave and I worked in a Forest Service camp together. Dave is not related to the Cumming's family in Saco.

I also attended Jack Fletcher's marriage to Madline Bellinger. Jack acted so nervous he could barely say, 'I do.' Another friend of fifty plus years. Jack and I played many basketball games together.

CHAPTER 107

Johnny didn't really like to play golf, but could play at bogie golf level. He searched in three pawn shops before he found a decent set of golf clubs made by the Ping Corporation to purchase. They fit okay, and the price was right. As a teen, he worked at a municipal course and learned all the tasks. He could mow greens with the best. After a stint at the range, he decided he would play once in a while.

He called the Meadow Lark Country Club to ask about working there. The lady answering the phone told him the greens keeper, Terry Foust, handled hiring workers and rang his extension.

"Terry here, how can I help you?"

"Terry, I'm Johnny Beckman. Do you need any morning help? I worked at a municipal course as a teenager, so wouldn't need a lot of training."

"We are short two bodies, Johnny. When can you come talk to me?"

"Right now, sir, if that works for you. I can be there in fifteen minutes."

"Come to the side door facing the ninth green, Johnny. I'll be in the maintenance building. We can do the paperwork and have you show me what you can do."

Johnny arrived a minute early and knocked on the door. He met Terry, who covered the three steps, and greeted him warmly. "I have the paperwork ready for you to fill out. I need to talk to another worker, so I'll be back in a few minutes."

Johnny completed the papers in short order. He looked around the neat office and noticed a couple plaques for ten and fifteen years of outstanding employment with Terry's name on them.

Terry returned, quickly and studied Johnny's application. He soon suggested," Let's get a mower and see what you can do."

Johnny mowed three strips of the tenth fairway. Four women waited on the tee after Terry explained what he wished to do. As Johnny walked past them, he smelled the same kind of perfume he smelled in his car after he parked at the Lido. One of these women had the key to his car.

Terry beckoned him back to the tee box. "You can mow the practice putting green next, then treat the two sand traps by that green. Thank you, ladies for letting us mow."

Johnny went ahead and completed both tasks.

"When can you start, Johnny?"

"Friday, sir."

"I will hand walk your application through the needed process, and you can start Friday, at four a.m."

"I'll be here. Thank you, sir."

"We are glad to have you, and I go by Terry. Haven't been called *sir* in twenty years."

Johnny knew he took a big risk working here, but felt he needed to get moving up the chain of command in the drug world in Great Falls. He risked memorizing each woman's face, as he passed the tee box a second time. He would need to figure out how to eliminate those not involved.

Johnny finished mowing the greens and smoothing the sand traps a few minutes before seven a.m. He enjoyed this job very much. Terry explained his preferences for completing each task on day one. He liked Terry a lot.

While working at the sand washing machine, Johnny heard someone walking the gravel path between the maintenance building and the cleaning station.

Delvin Klingaman called out, "Johnny. . .how do you like working here? I'm Delvin Klingaman."

"Just fine, Mr. Klingaman. I worked at a course before. I needed something to do. Too much free time."

"You could sell cars at my lot on tenth," interrupted Delvin.

"Sorry, I'm not good at selling stuff. I tried cars once before and had a hard time of it. I ate a lot of hot dogs. What I do like is running machines in work where I can see the results instantly. Thank you for thinking of me, though."

"Well, Johnny, word is you are extra skilled at your tasks here, and we are lucky to have you. You ever need anything, just ask. I'll take care of it." He turned on his heels and walked back to his golf cart."

Bill and Delvin Klingaman are *one and the same* person! Why today? The new trainee is here. That was the reason he guessed.

Johnny knew he should call in to the bureau, but decided to meet the new guy first. He possessed a paper map of the route out of St. Mary's village and pictures of the camp sites and Canadian exchange area. He also put the route on his phone, so he could transfer it to the new guy.

He worked at hitting balls at the range, when he received a call, "Bruisers at nine."

"Don't like to be seen there," he mumbled to himself.

Johnny arrived at Bruisers at eight-thirty. Only two open stools at the bar, so he took the one next to a young man he never seen in the place before.

Chet sauntered over, "The usual, Johnny?" Johnny believed Chet to be more involved in the drug business than he was.

"Perfect, Chet." He brought Johnny the house IPA.

"Tony," he whispered as he took a sip of his beer."

He heard a soft, "Yes?"

"What wheels did they give you?" he asked as softly as he could.

"A broken-down dark gray VW," Tony answered quietly. When Chet answered a call for another round from a booth behind them, Tony passed Johnny a note. He took a long last sip of his beer and left by the front door.

Johnny put the note in his pocket, but took his time finishing his beer. He knew the VW had been Jeff's car before he needed to leave or die. Johnny walked the four blocks to his apartment, read the note once while he hiked along. He planned to stop at the abandoned car and get two burner phones from his stash. He knew his apartment was bugged, standard ops for Klingaman.

He read the note a second time with his back to the window of his apartment, "I start at the car lot tomorrow." He read, "The one-bedroom apartment is at 2352 3rd Avenue North. It is not clean and smells funny. We are to meet in Shelby on Saturday at the Coffee Cup at eleven a.m. All I know.' Johnny burned it. Then smoked a small cigar to cover up any lingering smell.

When Johnny arrived at the Coffee Cup, he saw Bill sitting alone at the back table. Bill nodded to an empty chair. Johnny sat down after ordering his breakfast, selected a clean cup, and poured his coffee from a carafe.

"You met Tony."

"Yes," Johnny answered.

"This place is always safe for us. We take pictures of everyone that comes in here and check new faces."

Tony arrived while Bill talked. Bill waved him over, "Order your breakfast on my tab at the counter."

After Tony ordered his breakfast and returned to the red upholstered booth. Bill started the conversation. "Tony, Johnny will be the trainer. If you'll give me your phone, I'll transfer the maps and pictures to yours."

After they completed the transfer, Bill added, "The first trip will be in four days. I have made the necessary calls. Johnny you will have to walk with Tony, as we don't have a second team member yet."

Johnny didn't show any emotion. He knew Bill was testing him. He would have to get his Country Club shift covered.

He didn't know Tony was FBI, or about his previous experience.

Bill spoke again, "Tony will be on his own after that first trip."

"Bill, I have looked at the maps and pictures and can do the trip myself. Johnny doesn't need to go along unless there are two bags to carry," offered Tony.

"Just one bag. Okay, Tony, you can do it yourself. Do you understand about the drops and parking?"

"Johnny and I could drive over there and let me actually see things, and I will be okay.

"That works for me. Johnny does have other duties," finished Bill.

"Tony, I'll drive us over and show you everything and bring you back to your car," said Johnny.

Bill paid for the meals, left and walked to his truck parked in the back lot.

Tony and Johnny immediately left and drove west in Johnny's car. They followed Highway 2 to Cutbank, then to Browning, then to St. Mary's Village. Johnny showed him everything. While on the road back to Cutbank, Johnny looked at Tony and mouthed, "Your car is bugged. So is mine."

Tony nodded.

Back in Shelby, Johnny left first and drove back to Great Falls. He saw Bill in the train depot window. Tony stayed about ten miles behind Johnny. Bill needs to know things, but isn't really shifty.

Johnny did not hear Bill say aloud in his car. "Perfect, back in business."

CHAPTER 108

Meg and I flew to San Francisco on October third, booking a room at the waterfront Hyatt Hotel. The cab ride to the hotel passed through downtown. Meg commented, "I have never seen the downtown in any big city. Amazing, and this is only my second cab ride."

"I have been lucky to visit many big cities during my military time. I may tell you a story or two. We are going to see everything we can and ride a cable car. We will treat ourselves to a stretch limo ride along the waterfront.

"I called the police department asking about safety on the waterfront. She just cautioned about being out extra late, saying they have many patrols active along the hotel row. I told her where we are staying, and we can walk to the cable car terminal and four very fine restaurants. How does that sound to you?"

"We are to have a wonderful time," she smiled as she said it.

"I suggest we try the hotel restaurant this evening." We walked to the restaurant holding hands, feeling close.

"Del, I'm excited, happy, and nervous."

"I feel all those same things. We should keep our feelings first. I am excited to love you this much. I will not talk of Amy, except to say, one of her last comments, 'Don't be lonely'. It is how I have lived since the day she passed away. I do not feel lonely tonight."

l asked for a waterfront window seat.

"We can watch the sunset from here. I feel like a schoolgirl on her first date."

"This is our first date, Meg."

"Yes, it is. Wow is how I feel. I think I will have a seafood platter. There will be some things that I have never tried."

"That is my choice as well. I enjoy most sea food."

"While we wait for our food, I will tell you a story about being in Hong Kong. Our crew of six hired a guide. He took us many places. One included enjoying a Chinese eight-course dinner, including shark fin soup, seaweed, two types of shrimp, and two types of fish, some noodles and rice. Tasted fine and none of us got sick.

"After we walked down the steps back to the street, we saw a bunch of rickshaws with a single man to give you a ride. We all selected one to ride. I chose one, knowing the man did not know any English. I held up one finger, pointed to the rest of the crew, and said, 'American hotel'. He nodded and smiled. He took off and amazed me to no end. He had few teeth and may have weighed a hundred pounds.

"We were first by a long way. A Hong Kong dollar valued near a dime to me, so I gave him a dozen. He started to give most back. I shook my head no, gave all to him, pointing at the stragglers, I held up my one finger, and smiled at him. I remember his smile exactly. If I were an artist I would draw it. Seeing that big smile was one of my lifetime special moments."

"Yes, Del, I can see you doing that. You help people. I feel lucky."

"Shall we walk around the grounds and get familiar with our home for a week?" I asked.

"Perfect, I would like that."

We walked in silence, holding hands, thinking our own thoughts.

"It's getting cool, Del, let's go back."

At breakfast the next morning, we talked of love and how each felt a person should continue to make an effort every day to make it grow. We filled our week seeing everything San Francisco had to offer. We rode the cable cars every day. Ate once at Bubba Gump's, but did not like the noisy crowded atmosphere.

We rented a car and drove the well-marked scenic tour. Then spent a day in the Japanese Garden. We ate some traditional Japanese food, sitting at a small table. I asked a young man to take our picture. I wanted a picture memory of this trip.

Seals and sea lions occupied all the docks and made lots of barking noises. They ruined much of the peacefulness of the ocean. Not to mention the deposits with their smells they left everywhere.

Walking through the off-road shopping district occupied much of our afternoons. Meg selected a souvenir for each of her three sons and Stacy. Meg purchased expensive items she believed they would really like.

The last afternoon Meg decided to take a nap. I used the time to return to a jewelry store and purchased a single gold chain with a small tear-drop ruby in the center to give to Meg. Then proceeded to a knife store and purchased three medium-sized Old Timer knives and watched an engraver etch Jody, Jimmy and Gary on the bigger blade. He then purchased a gift for both Molly and Trevor.

Three cable car trips up the hill to walk through the downtown area, were marred only by the beggars occupying the same place each day.

Sitting in their room the last evening, Meg started talking of Thanksgiving. "Del, can we have your daughter and grandson come visit? We have room to let them stay."

"Consider it done. I will fly them to Saco from Great Falls. They will be excited. I have spoken of the Cummings family often."

We held hands all the way back to Great Falls and to Saco. Love blossomed.

CHAPTER 109

aqui Dresnia is not a nice man—a Jamaican, the paper says. He is not a U.S. citizen, so is scheduled to be deported during the next two weeks.

l read the newspaper story three times, then asked myself, "Do I dare? Really, shall I risk it?" I continued talking aloud to myself. "If I used the same abandoned building, I am near a thousand yards away. The rifle was already set, and the escape after shooting Bustamante, went smoothly. I could spend all two weeks there and watch every day.

Parking his escape car could be problematic. He could park it a different place every day. I decided to fly to St. Petersburg and check everything first, then decide. I particularly watched for police presence.

I stayed, sometimes parking two blocks away, always arriving during darkness. I did not enjoy those long walks, and prepared to shoot every day the entire first week. The van never came. My worry meter pegged at the max every day. No trembling, just nerves.

l felt anxious, so decided to take a big risk. I called the St. Petersburg Police Headquarters.

"How may I help you?" asked a young-sounding policeman.

"This is Lieutenant Ross. I need to complete my preparation for Jaqui. What day is he to go to his deportation hearing?"

"Sir, it is listed as Wednesday in my log."

"Thank you, I can finish all my tasks now," dial tone.

l watched Monday and Tuesday. No van. Wednesday morning, he parked his car by the alley as he did for the Bustamante shooting. Only twenty seconds of exposure. Only half of a block to safety. I stood ready at five a.m. hoping the young policeman gave me the right information. I waited a long time, getting close to worry level. I hoped the young man had been correct.

The van finally showed at ten-thirty. The spotting scope proved the man to be Jaqui. The trigger was pulled. Jaqui fell hard to the concrete steps smashing into them then slipping down to the sidewalk, '*Number nine Curt.*'

I cleaned up my shooting position, making it look like a homeless person used it. The well-used cardboard came from a dumpster by a housing development construction project. The two old blankets were purchased at a thrift store, then taken out to the countryside and driven over, intentionally torn to the point they looked not quite useless.

If anyone came to my shooting site, the homeless look would prevail. No trash, just a sleeping area. I used the same no tread shoes when spending two weeks in the shooting area.

The escape went as smoothly as the Bustamante *adventure*. Driving away I smiled to myself as no trembling or other scared feelings revealed themselves.

The word is satisfied.

CHAPTER 110

aptain Colton Petersen called a special meeting at noon the day Jaqui met his maker. "I don't believe it! I felt certain he wouldn't come back to our city. We told no one anything, and the press was mad as a wet hen about the no info statement."

The young policeman who told a Lt. Ross about the date, never said a word. He kept his secret to himself.

"This shooter is more than daring, but he is saving us some money. My hat is off to him. If we get a lead, we will work it diligently, and I do mean *if.* Do your usually good job today."

After the meeting, he sat in his office and smiled. Three really bad men gone. Good for us. He mused to himself. (He could have said four if he knew about Raphael Diaz.)

Three days later, a letter to the editor appeared in the Tampa Bay Times. Captain Peterson surely read it.

Thank you to the person who dared to shoot Jaqui Dresnia. That man sold drugs to high school kids, to any kid who could find the money. He ruined our daughter's life. So, another thank you, thank you, thank you. Bless you.

l read it aloud to myself and smiled, remembering a letter to the editor after my first *adventure*, in Tucson. Somebody liked me, now two somebody's liked me.

CHAPTER 111

I retrieved the list from my safe containing the names from the trial held after Curt and his best friend were killed senselessly after a wrestling match at school. I did not have a plan yet except to locate them.

My Billings realtor had recently called, saying she had a buyer for the downtown condo. Arranging things, I flew my plane to Billings, and would use James Colbert's library card to locate everyone on the list.

I located all five teens and the man tried as an adult. Two lived in Billings, and the person tried as an adult, Brock Grinden, occupied a cell in the Montana State Prison System. I would ask my attorney to check on him and when or if a parole might be possible.

The rest I will deal with myself. Finding them proved to be relatively easy, as I know my way around those computer programs. First, I should check their lifestyle. Maybe some of them had family.

Reviewing the list, I checked the addresses in Billings and decided to drive by both residences to determine their current lifestyle. One, Jerome Daugherty, lived on the same street as Tyler

Spivey. I decided to watch his house after driving by the other house located in Billings.

Daniel Smythe lived on the western edge near the Yellowstone River. A very nice home with children's toys littering the yard. I will check for an arrest record, and if clean, I will type a sterile note to eventually mail. I will ask him to create a memorial bronze plaque on a large granite rock and have it placed in front of the gym at school for both boys, including suggesting the use of an attorney to facilitate things.

Maybe the Great Falls residents, who are also on the list, will get that same note, but I needed to check there next. I had addresses, all family names, and phone numbers. I needed the people who were on trial for the senseless killing of my son and his friend to step up and do what I feel is right. I cannot allow them to just ignore their responsibility as I see it. There will not be any threats in the note (but hints that the sender of the letter knows things), just instructions.

While in Billings, I needed to learn more about Tyler Spivey. I looked up his ad in the yellow pages of the library phone book. He specialized in medical malpractice claims. I drove past his residence and on to his office location. The first floor housed a small coffee shop and a four-chair beauty shop. Tyler occupied a one-person office on floor five. Only he rented the office, as the rest of the offices were empty. I hid in an empty office at the top of the stairs, waiting for him to finish buying his coffee. He unlocked his office and made a call before I could confront him.

"*Samantha*, you tell, that lazy, bastard husband of yours to get to Miles City and see the man, and get the goods! They arrived a week ago! Yes, the house on the river. . .I want him back tomorrow night. Jerome is to bring everything to my house using the alley. He needs to follow all the rules, he knows that. This is his last chance, or he gets a beating.

"Don't cry to me, just get him going. Shut up! No more excuses. Tomorrow night *period*." The phone slammed in its cradle.

I descended the stairs and returned to my car. I could not believe it. Maybe Cliff will arrest them both. I still planned to give him a beating, just not today. Before I could drive away, Tyler exited the building and drove to a nearby gym.

I followed him in and asked about a membership. As I watched the few people working out, Tyler appeared. After a regime of stretches he proceeded to process through a series of quality kickboxing moves. He looked very polished. I need to study up on kickboxing for sure, and not just challenge him. I may have suffered greatly, if I had confronted him today.

I watched Jerome's house from a full block away hoping to get a type of vehicle and its plate number. I just finished a small crossword puzzle when he drove up met his wife at the door with some groceries. He and his wife had a heated exchange. He handed the two bags through the door and walked down to Tyler's house, rang the doorbell and entered. '*Odd,*' I thought. Maybe just good friends. I checked Jerome's phone number and called his house.

"Samantha, I'm selling subscriptions to a new TV guide, and am hoping you will be the fiftieth person to sign up, there is a special prize."

"How did you get my name? Not interested—goodbye." Dial tone.

That proved to me that Jerome is the person Tyler referred to during the phone call I overheard.

I wondered if I could get the Bill Davis WIN group involved. Most likely, I will do everything myself. I liked being a detective. That never crossed my mind while I worked most of my life as a financial planner.

I flew to Great Falls. I love everything about flying, especially the freedom to be above everything and sense the total personal feelings of doing something well that most people do not do.

I drove past Ralph Richardson's house in a hillside subdivision overlooking the Missouri River. The yard contained many children's toys. He will get the same note Daniel receives. I need to get some drafts of that letter ready.

Watching, I learned Timothy and Adrian lived together, and after following them I saw how they distributed drugs. Cliff will get them when I have all the ducks in a row.

CHAPTER 112

I wrote five different versions of the letter to send to Daniel and Ralph. I settled on the one that gave each the other person's name and phone number, and the exact wording for the plaque. I insisted on an unmovable granite stone, and where it needed to be placed. I strongly suggested using an attorney.

The letter would infer who sent it, but one of the terms to keep both out of jail meant they would say choosing to make the memorial (though long overdue), was *their idea*. I hinted in the letter about their current criminal involvement.

Both were still in the drug business, in a minor client to distributer relationship. Enough to make me hope they would comply.

I started following Timothy and Adrian, using Spencer and James disguises often to make sure my suspicions about their selling held true. I hoped I could gather enough evidence to put those two away for a long time. I have some poor pictures, but felt they only implicated the buyers. I needed more.

While watching their small single-family house on 8th Avenue North, I saw both come out with Adrian carrying a small gym bag. Timothy used a sweeper to check their car. They turned onto 15th St. and continued to 10th Ave. South. Then they pulled into Wholesale Auto and parked next to a Buick SUV. Using my spotting scope, I took many good pictures including the need to sweep their car.

Tyler Spivey excited the SUV, exchanged a medium sized duffle bag for the small duffel Adrian carried. Then I watched Timothy and Adrian drive away.

After the duo departed, Tyler took two larger duffle bags into the small stand-alone sales office, and returned to his SUV caring a small satchel. This happened on a Tuesday exactly at seven a.m. I had pictures of everything.

The same transaction happened one day later on Wednesday then Thursday and so on at seven a.m. each of the next three weeks. That was enough of a pattern to warrant talking to Cliff. He could work with the DEA, but I needed to stay totally immune. I wanted to see Tyler in jail, but I do hope to find a way to confront him. Watching him do his kickboxing routine definitely altered my plans. Surprise is probably my only tactic; we will see.

My lady realtor in Billings told me about the very low offer for my downtown condo. I asked her to call the potential buyer and tell him the sales price is firm. The buyer is to pay that price or find something else. She called them.

They agreed to it. I made a tidy profit.

CHAPTER 119

"**M**orning Charlene, word is you are putting off retiring to still take care of Cliff."

"Yes Del, I am. He is so pleased about this promotion, that I knew I needed to wait a while. We need each other. Part of the deal is I get to train two new people to do my job. Charlsie and Morgan will learn to take over. He was authorized two staff people. One is a transfer from D.C. and the other is from the Denver office. Promotions for both. Now he has the clout he always wanted. Do you need Cliff?"

"Yes, as I need his advice and maybe some help."

"He's in Great Falls, checking things."

"Charlene, I need to go there and look at a duplex to use as an office. So, I will check in with him and hopefully we can do dinner. I am glad you are staying. We have a date to plan."

"I have everything set up for December 7th at the Purple Iris at twelve o'clock, Del."

"Well, I best show up for lunch then. You are a treasure."

"Yes. I am. It will be a pleasure to hold your hand. I will tell Cliff of your call."

Cliff called at near six p.m. before I could call him. "I have Martha's chicken you have the beer. Be there in twenty."

A Gallatin Gateway pickup arrived, and a disguised Cliff showed up with the chicken.

"Del if you will get the food ready, I'll change." When he came out of the bedroom he started asking questions.

"Del, is your house secure?"

"99.9%. Every day I use that fancy sweeper you gave me. I never leave my electronics plugged in when I am gone. I have not had a hit on my car or boat in at least six months, so believe the Peterson's have stopped following me. The patio is blocked by a signal shield I bought from Brisbane Industries. I never talk about my business here, only at the client's home. Why do you ask?"

I'll get to that, how clean and safe is your cabin by Lincoln?"

"Cliff, I bought a hangar at the Lincoln Airport, and it is now burglar proof and electronically monitored, by phone and computer. I save pictures of trespassers and huntable game at my cabin. If I feel someone is up to no good, I call the sheriff, and someone checks.

"I am glad you have things covered. Charlene told me you may need my help. Before we start with your questions, I wish to bring you up to date about Jim and Professor Lansing. Jim will not completely recover from his serious beating for taking Russian guns. He now has a job as a dishwasher in Salt Lake, and helped us at Bully's trial. He is living at a halfway house.

"Professor Lansing is with the Marshal's office in witness protection, and teaching at a community college near Casa Grande, Arizona. He gave us everything about the gold mining scam and many went to jail. I remember you said you liked him. His new name is Scott Powell. But you should avoid any contact, Del."

"Thanks for the update, I do use tutors from that college at Helping Hands in Casa Grande, but those young men and women can liaison with the school. I am not there much, so will avoid the college. Remember when I asked about CDL drivers in Montana?"

"Yup."

"Well, I have a story for you." I told him about my trip to Miles City to find a place to hunt and enough about Joel and the Billings attorney, to make him raise his eyebrows.

"What's going on there, Del?"

"Cliff you will have to trust me. I cannot tell you all yet. I have to learn a way to keep completely immune. I have a very special friend to protect. That said, I need to lead someone who does not know I am the one leading. I need assistance to make things work like they should.

"A retired friend lives in Glendive a few miles north of there, Edwin Cox. He bought a small farm and is trying to grow vegetables. I will ask him."

Cliff stayed the night, telling only Charlene.

The next morning, Cliff called Edwin. "Do you want to do some easy FBI work, mostly watching and setting up to catch? . . . Great. My friend and I are flying to Miles City tomorrow, to do some studying. We should land about ten a.m. We have a car."

Cliff, I have to go to Miles City for knee therapy tomorrow," offered Edwin.

"Great Edwin, then lunch at the Tilt Würks is on me. We will explain how you can help us." Cliff hung up the phone.

"Del, Edwin is 68 now and doesn't like to be called Ed. He told me he just had a knee replaced, so comes to Miles City for therapy three times a week, that means he can cover whatever you need."

Edwin waited for us, "Cliff, you haven't changed a bit."

Shaking my hand, "I'm Edwin Cox."

"Del Sanderson, Cliff told me some stories about you."

"All true for sure, I can have one beer, how about you two?"

"I would enjoy a good IPA," I answered.

"Same for me," added Cliff.

Cliff told Edwin why we were here to watch Joel Cantelay—to ascertain if he is in the drug business. He related what he could do every day he came for therapy. Del and Edwin exchanged phone numbers, discussing what could be important.

"Sounds like fun, Cliff." All in the same car, they drove past Joel's house. They talked about the process and what to expect.

CHAPTER 114

"Gallatin Land management will rent the vacant house across the street from Joel, and be a source to help with the surveillance work. They possess contracts to rework boundaries for three Bureau of Land Management (BLM) parcels near Ingomar, west of Miles City, and to rework the proposed levee options between Glendive and Miles city. They will tell Edwin when Joel is not on the road," offered Cliff.

"Do you want Joel followed?" posed Edwin.

"It's your call, Edwin. If he leaves town, and you can be safe, the answer is yes," said Cliff. "Report your findings to Del. I have a huge problem in Great Falls that requires my full attention. Del is the source about this possible drug group. He is to do the reports that are necessary."

"Works for me. Something better than prepping dirt. Thanks, Cliff, for thinking of me." Cliff nodded and turned to look at me.

"Del, you know what I need to move on this, so keep me up to date."

"Cliff, Edwin and I will do our best."

Cliff and I took Edwin back to his truck and returned to Bozeman.

I worried more than I needed to. Edwin turned out to be very good help. I drove to Glendive and joined Edwin for breakfast. "Edwin, anything new?"

"Not much. When the Gallatin guys call and tell me he's home, he was either working on his truck, shooting pool, or rafting with a couple of buddies. I had the Bureau check those fellows. Nothing yet. They just play hard, but stay out of trouble.

"I followed Joel one afternoon and he exited I-84 at Forsyth, driving to a collection of buildings at the turn to Ingomar (off Hwy 12). He parked there. I continued past. After three quarters of a mile, I turned into a pasture, and climbed to a vantage point. I attached my camera to the spotting scope and watched him.

"Twenty minutes later, he talked on his phone. Ten minutes after his call, a silver Lexus arrived from the west. The driver and Joel passed four duffel bags from the Subaru to the Lexus. I took a picture of the exchange and the license plate, and sent both to Cliff. I haven't heard back from him."

"You have been busy, Edwin. We should go sit on the bench in front of the Hardware store and call Cliff." I paid for breakfast, then we walked the four blocks to the hardware store and sat on the empty bench.

Edwin made the call. "Morning, Cliff, Del is with me in Glendive. I told him about following Joel to Ingomar, and we are wondering what you have learned."

"Let me check, and I'll call you back in ten," answered Cliff.

Edwin and I talked of fishing for paddle fish, a large leathery prehistoric-looking fish. It is mostly light gray sporting a possibly two-foot paddle as a snout. They live in the Yellowstone and Missouri Rivers. I learned Edwin fished for them often. He had the gear and invited me to come next May to catch one. Good for me and my new friend Edwin.

Cliff called back, "The Lexus, now sold, was part of the inventory in a used car lot in Logan, Utah owned by Devlin Klingaman. We know he also owns a similar lot in Great Falls. We now have surveillance on both lots. We have not seen much activity at either lot and believe that is where each driver gets a different car for their trips.

"The Lexus was sold to a young doctor and his wife. We checked briefly, and have ruled them out. Edwin, we hope you can continue working the Miles City side."

"I can help you for the next two weeks. Then I'm going to my granddaughter's birthday party in Williston, North Dakota. I'll be gone two nights."

"Edwin, let Charlene know when you will be gone. Del and I will know what we need to do."

"Cliff, I'm pretty sure Joel will be on the road the whole time I'm gone. Your boys at the Gallatin Land Company could call me if I'm wrong."

"Great, let them know to call Del as well."

CHAPTER 115

allatin Land Management (GLM) is a company operated by a one-time FBI informant, now with the U.S. Marshals in witness protection. Many of the part-time employes are with the FBI. The company has contracts to remark boundaries for three parcels near Ingomar and potential flood levee work between Glendive and Miles City. Their two trucks will be very noticeable in Miles City.

Agent Allen Braddick loved working part-time at GLM. He took online classes to obtain a degree in land management to have a career after he retires from the FBI. The crew of three will eat most of their meals at Tilt Würks, until Cliff changes the rules. The nightly special always tasted better than their own cooking.

Allen enjoyed beer, preferring IPAs, and he liked to shoot pool. He dined alone tonight as his two partners opted for Mexican. The noisy group shooting pool included Joel.

One of the player's hinted Joel was extra lucky. Joel was rail thin, everything he wore was baggy. His hair long and dirty, his teeth poor, and always sported three days of extra whiskers.

"Ain't luck, all skill," he kept saying.

Allen realized his assignment stood only twenty feet away. Growing up in Grand Junction, Colorado in his dad's pool hall and card room, he learned to play and won a tournament or two. His two-quarter entry fee meant he played next. He narrowly beat a man named Russ, then Sullivan and Walt. Joel stood ready to play the following game.

Joel missed a bank shot, and left Allen three finishing shots, which he easily made.

"Allen, how about we play for $100 bucks a game," smiled Joel.

"Too rich for me, Joel. I made enough money to pay for half my dinner."

Joel acted very drunk, yelling at his friends calling them losers, then looked around and saw he was alone and not part of anything. "Hell with you all," he shouted and walked out the door.

Allen followed Joel home. He parked his truck across the street and entered his rented house. But he didn't turn on the light inside, just the porch light for his friends. He wanted to watch Joel. That meant putting him to bed.

Allen saw Joel drive his old little green Subaru into the garage and stumble into his house. He saw some lights come on, and Joel pass by the living room window. Then he saw a second person sitting in Joel's recliner. He wished he could hear, but decided not to risk crossing the street to stand by the window.

Joel jumped backwards and almost fell, seeing Boris sitting in his recliner. "About time, Joel."

"Whoa, Boris, you scared me. How did you get in here?"

"I broke your bedroom window. You are drinking too much, and missed our nine o'clock meeting," answered Boris.

"I was winning. Only one guy beat me all night. I am not late we were to meet at *eleven* and not nine."

"It's nine not eleven. We both go to Kerney, Nebraska next Saturday and get double load and double money. I am to tell you, and now I have. So, now I leave," a gruff reply.

"Wait a minute. That is a lot of risk for us. Someone will notice we have extra goods," whined Joel, as he began to sober up fast. He didn't like Boris and certainly didn't trust him.

"You live in Bozeman, right?"

"Yes, but I move soon to better house, closer to my other property," answered Boris.

"Well, I like Miles City, and ain't moving, till I save the money from two more years work driving. Then I might move to Mexico, or Canada."

"You be in Kerney Saturday." Boris uttered as he stood to leave. Boris was not tall, but thick and meaty. A man stronger than Joel by a huge margin.

Boris left, walking toward the main street, he destined to pass by the grocery store. He was fond of all fast food, but liked pizza the best, and they sold it by the slice. He first cut through an alley and backtracked to Joel's house, waited for the lights to go out then placed a tracker on Joel's semi.

He intended for Joel to arrive in Kerney first, so he could see if extra risk showed anywhere. He had been running drugs for nine years, and felt something could happen in Kerney.

Allen watched Boris leave, sneak back, and place the locater on Joel's semi. He then saw Joel come out and check his truck. Then, he stood still, deciding what to do. Joel found the tracker. Finally, he went back into his house.

I will put that tag on another rig in the lot in Kerney, and piss Boris off to no end," Joel uttered aloud.

The next morning after fixing his broken window, he drove to Billings and purchased a security system. He made the salesman go over the instructions three times, drove straight home and installed the system. He checked his phone, to see if things worked. He saw the mailman come to his door, "Great."

He didn't know what to do. Finally, he felt he needed to make the trip to Kerney, because if he didn't, he would be dead within a week. He really wanted to retire in Mexico.

He thought about a gun, but he knew nothing about pistols. He decided to rely on reading the signs and act accordingly. He also planned to drive to Bozeman and see where Boris lived. He would borrow a friend's car and not use the Subaru. Maybe he could get Boris arrested.

Joel had no clue the FBI watched him. He didn't like the new neighbors, but they would be gone in a couple of months. Allen told Joel how long they would be staying across the street when he played pool with him.

Joel had permission to hunt antelope at a ranch bordering the cluster of buildings at the Ingomar turn off from Highway 12. He knew of an outcropping of rocks where he could watch from. He also knew the same car picked up drugs from both Boris and Joel, about an hour apart. He knew this because he saw the car return after his last transfer.

He also knew Boris processed and cut his drugs. He didn't know Boris sent a trusted driver to deliver his drugs.

Boris didn't take that extra risk.

Joel completed the Nebraska run, but never saw Boris. He put the tracker on a rig that sported Vermont plates, and returned home. No one anywhere acted differently. That worried him. Two Gallatin Gateway trucks sat parked across the street. He saw his three new neighbors emerge and tried to place where he had seen them before.

After they drove away together, he unhooked his trailer, and drove the cab into the shop. He had automatic doors on both ends of his shop, and the Subaru parked on the river side, allowing him to switch the drugs from the cab into the car, ready for the transfer. He never broke the seal on the bags, so he never knew the contents. He liked it that way and felt safer.

He walked to the Tilt Würks and saw a Gallatin truck in the lot. Entering, he noticed the three men and brazenly marched over and sat in their fourth chair. He looked at Allen and loudly announced, "I played pool with you a week or so ago, right?"

"Yes, I am Allen and my friends are Corkey and Harold."

"You guys staying across from me?"

"Yes, I told you we would be here awhile, when we played pool the other night. We have work both directions from here."

"Guess I'll see you boys a bunch. I travel a lot to South Dakota and Iowa," he added while standing. Nice to meet you all. You ever need anything, I've lived here all my life, just ask old Joel."

He turned and briskly joined his buddies in the pool room.

"He is not pleased we are across the street," offered Harold.

"You're right. That means we must keep our image perfect. No chances ever. If he is hauling drugs, we don't take any risks. I will call Cliff tomorrow and ask him to get written contracts to do both tasks we are here for. We must not be trespassers. If I were one of the ranchers next to the BLM land, I would want to see the contracts.

"Tomorrow, we outfit the house, I will know what cliff will provide and what we need to find on our own. They won't keep paying for us to eat out every meal. They will however cover stops at the grocery store. Let's go get a good night's sleep on our new beds and leave early for breakfast. Then we go look at the roads near Ingomar."

Cliff called Allen, "I'll have the BLM contracts to you tomorrow, before you need to leave. A U-Haul will deliver a new TV and enough furniture to make you comfortable. Work at the survey contracts every day. It will take some diplomacy on my part to set up the levee contracts."

Allen told Cliff about Joel's guest and described him.

Cliff had never seen Boris so didn't know to tie him to Joel.

CHAPTER 116

I tried not to be too excited, but used two days to make sure everything I needed was in my custom rig. I was traveling to the Abercrombie ranch to look for a trophy mule deer and hunt antelope. I called Clark and arranged to arrive on the second of November and be a day early to make sure I would be ready.

I loved driving my newly painted rig now gray and not lilac. I drove just shy of one hundred trips, driving for a Missoula firm. My remodeled trailer had room for a small car and a quad and a very small room to use as an office and sleeping quarters. My 308 with elite optics, would allow me to shoot 500-600 yards

After Clark looked through my quarters he commented, "This is hunting in style, great idea."

"I like the arrangement a lot, Clark."

"We have seen two of our biggest bucks and know where they like to hang out. I will show you where you should park your quad and two good shooting locations."

"I am trying not to get too excited."

"If you shoot one, call me, and we will come help. Two of our ranch hands will be more than happy to get out of regular chores."

The next morning, I followed Clark to the parking area, and to the possible shooting spots. Clark pointed out the routes they felt the big bucks used often. Then he returned to the main ranch.

I watched the first two days, seeing many bucks, but no trophies. The third day near three p.m. a superb specimen sauntered into view, keeping close to cover. I checked my numbers three times, waiting. Finally, an opportunity. One shot, and my hunt was finished.

I sat back on his shooting stool and smiled. "Wow, I am *so* lucky." I called Clark.

"Clark, I have a nice mule deer on the ground. I am going to hike over to him. He is just below the huge Ponderosa pine with the four dead branches."

"Del, I'll round up some help, and be there in twenty or thirty minutes."

"Wonderful. Thank you."

I used fifteen minutes to descend into the ravine and climbed back up to his trophy.

"Wow, he is a monster! I think I just shot a Boone and Crockett deer." I sat on the ground next to the deer, sometimes touching the antlers or the front shoulder. A dream come-true. He barely controlled his emotions, but felt very blessed.

Clark and two ranch hands made their way to the deer riding two quads.

"Del you just shot 'double drop,' one of the three biggest racks we've ever seen. You have a Boone and Crockett animal. We'll finish field dressing, and I'll call Merv. He is one of our local official scorers for B&C. He will take care of things, and get you lined up with a trusted taxidermist.

You have to decide if you want the whole deer mounted or just the head and cape. Let's get some good pictures.

"Dinner at the Abercrombie's tonight. We need to celebrate Del's good fortune. Merv will be out for dinner and give you a preliminary score."

"Del, you are going to be on the non-typical list for sure, maybe in the top twenty-five percent. I am especially happy this trophy came from Clark's ranch. I will speak to my taxidermist friend, and we will get this safely mounted," smiled Merv.

"Merv, I will just ask for a head and cape, if I ever shoot another, I will do the whole deer and display it at a Cabella's. Thank you, my friend."

I did hunt for antelope and shot a nice buck, but not a trophy, my first antelope ever. I drove home a happy man. Merv agreed to take care of the mounting and taxidermist. Merv knew some people to give the meat to.

I still needed to deal with Joel and Tyler. Lots of ideas, but none I felt I could use.

I also needed to see about the five-by-five whitetail buck I saw in the Bob.

CHAPTER 117

I left my Lincoln cabin at o'dark-thirty, with a very light pack. I successfully dropped two loaded canisters into Curtis Castle yesterday. I planned to hunt for that nice whitetail buck, and during my down time, would drop some of the quartz into the hideaway and break it up in the cave.

The weather lady hinted the higher elevations may get some snow. If it did snow, I couldn't hunt as I would like, thus would need to abandon hunting in the Bob. I cannot leave tracks for others to follow.

I planned to climb a large Red Fir tree and place a camera to watch the Danaher Bridge. I climbed the tree before entering my valley, positioned the camera with its own satellite transmitter, and trimming the minimum amount to affect watching the bridge. Back on the ground, I cleaned up all evidence of my work.

I climbed to the gold and dropped about eighty pounds of quartz into my hideaway, then hauled it into the cave. I worked a couple of hours separating the gold flakes from the quartz, and saved about ten or twelve pounds of mostly separated rocks to carry back to the Lincoln cabin.

I hunted hard the first two days. No snow and no five point. I watched from a natural blind carved out of a manzanita bush.

The third day, I saw my quarry, but never found a shooting opportunity. I felt tired, so I napped for over an hour. Opening my eyes and listening, I heard horses on the main trail. I left my blind and approached the trail. I knew many hunters visited the Bob and hunted elk.

Six man-made ground blinds covered some of the game trails along the Danaher. I watched a trio of hunters set up their camp by the bridge. I hiked back to Curtis Castle, gathered enough items to create a minimum camp a couple of hundred yards upstream from this unwanted company. I pitched my tent, created a very small fire pit, then walked down to meet the hunters.

"Hi, I am Del."

"Bob here. The big guy is my brother, Thornton, and the little guy by the horses is my brother, Jeter. You hunting or hiking?"

"Hunting. But cannot shoot anything unless it is a trophy. I then can hike out with the antlers, hide and a few choice-cuts of meat. The critters will clean the rest up nicely. How about you guys?"

"We are only shooting elk and we come here every year. The slope where the Young and Danaher Rivers meet is our favorite spot. We could show you a place where you could sit a while. You might get lucky," answered Bob.

"Thank you. That would be great. I will shoot a six-by-six, if I get a decent shot. I did a scouting trip a month ago and saw a nice five-by-five whitetail. I hope to see it during this hunt. Just hope it does not snow."

"We'll leave about five and show you your spot. The three us have hunted here nine years and have a system that usually gets us our three elk. When we get one, we will cut you a steak, so you can join us for steak and beans."

"I will be ready at five, Bob. You three hunt all day?"

"Yup, we stay after huntin', 'til we get our tags filled."

I made my way back to my meager camp. Thorton and Jeter never talked to me. My worry meter buzzed big time. I trust those feeling always. I knew I could be trapped, but just maybe I could shoot a nice elk.

Jeter showed me where I should sit and hope an elk came by. "Thank you, Jeter. Hope you get your elk." My sitting spot was seventy feet above my escape by floating down the river cache. That big old gray log hid the cache. A few yellow flowers struggled by the log trying to last a few more days.

Just a nod, and he started briskly hiking west. About an hour later, I heard two shots. "Elk steak, tonight I said to myself." No elk came by my blind. At near dark, I left the blind and hiked to my camp.

I sat by my small fire, sitting on a log watching the three brothers' camp. Jeter appeared suddenly fifteen feet from my fire. "Bob says your steak is ready," he turned and ghosted away as silently as he came.

Jeter scared me, as I did not believe anyone could sneak up on me. I walked down to their camp, accepted a beautiful piece of meat, on a tin plate with a hefty helping of beans and two slices of white bread.

"You get one already?"

"We got two," said Bob. "But decided to eat first then go get the other one."

"You need any help?" I asked.

"Nah, it's all skinned and ready, Thorton and our big mule will fetch it. How's the steak?"

"Perfect. I just would just have eaten a trail meal."

"You going to the blind tomorrow or chasing that white tail?" asked Bob.

"I should see to that deer, Bob. He has a possible trophy rack. Thanks for letting me hunt with you today."

"We enjoyed your company today. Hope you get your trophy. You going to come back here next year?"

"I do not have any plans about next year, yet. I like the Bob a lot, just not sure." I answered.

No snow greeted me in the morning, allowing me to sneak into Curtic Castle to winterize everything. Then, I took hike into

Willow Creek valley and hid my quartz and gold rocks close to the main trail.

I watched all day. No trophy. Within an hour I heard two shots. I felt sure they did not want me around, while they completed their hunt. An hour later, I heard another shot. Seconds later a fourth shot.

I knew I could not hunt here next year when Bob and brothers are in camp. Returning to my small spot, it became apparent they were finished hunting as their camp was on their packhorses, and on the way back to Monture Creek trail head. I knew beyond a doubt they harvested more than three elk. I am not stupid. But I am not a game warden. Those three brothers will never be my friends. And they knew I couldn't turn them in.

I hunted one more day, but did not see my quarry. Maybe next year. I woke up to two inches of snow on the ground. I packed up my camp items and started home, gathering my rocks on the way. I would drop my extra camping stuff back at the hideaway next spring. I expected snow, but did not wish to hike in mud all day.

Most of the snow melted before I reached the turn to my cabin, but it took some time to make sure no one could see my main trail exit. I faked three trips to the Danaher River to fish, then walked twenty steps in the creek before hiking up to the trail.

Could be other hunters coming by.

I winterized my Lincoln cabin and drove home to Bozeman. I enjoyed a wonderful night's sleep in my own bed. Sleeping on the ground was old after an hour. Four nights proved to me I should not do that again.

CHAPTER 118

Entering my regular bus, I noticed the twins were not on board. I rode solo to the library, chatting with Sanford. He likes to talk about college football.

I went to the Daily Coffee first. Mable waved me to her table. "You have been gone for a while, Del."

"Three weddings, a lot of fishing, and a hunting trip. I like to have things to do. You ready for our walk, Mable?"

"Yes, I am. We can share some coffee when we return." We crossed the street and passed by the library, as we strolled along through a neighborhood devoid of children's items. Peaceful. Mable offered, "This neighborhood we are walking through used to have children's toys everywhere. Now there are extra cars in every driveway. Those children have grown up."

I changed the subject, "Mable, I haven't seen Zella around lately."

"Del, she came to my table two weeks ago and thanked me for letting her work here for four years. Then, said she planned to move on to other things. She didn't tell where or what that meant. I enjoyed her. She always treated me as special. No one here will tell me where she went, if they know. She seemed extra friendly with Michelle. You know, Michelle and her two young friends haven't been around either.

Del, did not answer immediately, then added, "She treated me nicely, too, Mable. Younger people like to keep moving, I guess." No reason to tell Mable what he suspected happened to Zella.

They returned to her table, sipped a fresh cup of coffee, and talked of many things. Mable added the whole story about the bakery called *Mable's Marvels* that she and her husband managed.

Del's last comment to Mable, "If you ever wish to sell the Daily Coffee, I hope you would give me first chance at it."

"I have already decided to sell early next January, and I will give you my price next week on Tuesday, if you come here and share breakfast with me," Mable smiled mischievously.

"Date Mable. I am excited. When we have agreed on things, I will not have to pay and neither will you." She did give me her price, and agreed to let me obtain her records from her accountant.

CHAPTER 119

stopped at the library. Nothing new about any adventures I followed. I rode the bus back to the stop about six blocks from home.

Meg and I talked every day since I got home. I missed her, the more I talked to her. So, we decided I'd fly up and see her.

"I can't wait to see you Del, Phone calls leave too much out."

"Yes, they do Meg. I will fly up tomorrow morning." (My Cash *adventure* would have to wait.)

Meg met me as I taxied up to the trees, "Del, may we go for a short flight?"

"Absolutely, Meg, I would enjoy that."

After they were airborne ten minutes or so, Meg started talking while looking out the side window. "Gary talked to me a long time yesterday. I told the boys you were coming today. He said the three of them talked about you and me. They agreed to have Gary to speak for them. You have impacted our lives immensely. Gary offered, and I quote, 'If you and Del want to get married, we three sons will be very happy to have Del as part of our family.' You and I are as close as two people can be, but I can't be married yet. Frank still has a place in my heart. It may take a while for me to say yes. I am not completely sure why."

"Meg, I have had those thoughts as you have. I know you and I will one day be husband and wife. Being without a companion is a difficult way to pass through life. I will be extra happy when you tell me it is time. You tell me when you are ready. Right now, we should buzz stinky hollow and see if the whooper buck is still around."

"What do you mean by buzz?"

"Meg, trust me, you'll see." I made a wide circle and dropped to tree-top level.

As we reached the top of the hollow Meg exclaimed, "Wow, that was exciting! A lot of deer ran out in every direction. You're a very skilled flyer. Did you see the big buck you hoped to see?"

"Yes, he is still here. Might have to hunt for him yet this season." When we landed, we walked together to the veranda. I selected a Lagunitas, and Meg—a plastic bottle of tea.

"Meg, I apply now in most western states for elk, and deer tags, and do wish to continue those pursuits. I still have 22 clients including the Boltons, that rely on me to cover their money management needs. Maybe I could restrict some of both, but I really like the remaining clients and do still want to continue the hunting."

"I've much to learn about ranching since we developed our financial plan, and my boys come first before my own wishes. I have always been that way. When we are married, you can and should still help those clients, and enjoy hunting.

"Gary and Toby need you to separate the two ranches. Both hope to have free and clear titles after the new ranch is paid for. They will share everything now, until the loan is paid in full."

"I will have Gallatin Land Management complete a survey of both sets of meets and bounds. That will be my wedding present to both of them. Jody will find his lady one day soon."

"That will be wonderful, Del. You continue to surprise me often."

"Meg, would you ever consider a backpacking trip?"

"I have never done that. How much would I have to carry?"

"Nothing, Meg. Everything we would need will be in my pack, or dropped at our destination from my plane."

"Then I would very much wish to try at least one backpack trip."

"Wonderful, we will do at least one. Being in the wilderness is my most precious time, and I get to share it with you."

Allen Braddick with the help of Corky and Harold completed the work necessary to separate the Cummings and Sutherland acreages. Del paid the bill and showed the whole family the actual boundaries

They talked about Shep dragging his feet about selling the marina at Fort Peck. "Jimmy and at least I, should drive to the marina and see what his hang up is. Jimmy would like you to come as well."

"Yes, we should all go tomorrow," I answered.

We three drove to Fort Peck and learned Shep had been ill. We were directed to his home address in Glasgow. His daughter, Clara, met the three of us at the door.

"Come in, please. The marina called us, and we called the accountant. He is on his way here to ask two questions. Our attorney approved things if the accountant's questions are okayed." I know I should have called you. I just had too much to do to get Shep well."

"Thank you, Clara. His health does come first," answered Meg. "Do you need our help?"

"He is improving nicely now, Meg. He has signed everything, hoping the questions can be resolved. He is sleeping right now. Did Jimmy tell you I agreed to work at the Marina for at least next summer?"

"That will help Jimmy a lot, thank you," answered Meg.

The accountant arrived and both questions were answered to his satisfaction. Jimmy and Del now owned a marina. Jimmy and Meg learned I would advance the cash portion of the purchase price, and my company would provide the financial expertise.

Jimmy had a letter pre-prepared to send to the current client list. During the past summer, he camped often, remotely, and fished hard. Jimmy knew things the other two guides didn't. he prepared a new fish locator map to use on each guide boat. He planned to enter his new information as soon as he owned the marina.

A month ago, Jimmy traveled to a fishing expo in Billings. While talking to an American-based international guiding service rep, he was asked to go along with an excursion to Argentina. He agreed to go on the late February trip. His new friend listed the gear he would need. Jimmy purchased everything at the expo. He already had his passport, as he hoped to travel at least into Canada to fish as well.

Jimmy knew he would have a major learning experience owning the Fort Peck marina. He made the most of his guiding trips as he believed it would help him get more clients. I would work at the transfer. He also knew I would be available to help. Maybe I would learn to be a guide.

"Your work is just starting, Jimmy. We will all help wherever we can," I offered.

CHAPTER 120

Last Thanksgiving, I hosted dinner for all my family and his close friends.

This year, the Cummings family, Meg and sons, hosted for me, Molly, Trevor, Cliff, and the Boltons.

Madeline and Jack hosted for Jason and Jacob, Dave and Sally, Cindy, and Dutch.

After everyone stuffed themselves to the max, using Cindy's I-pad and Gary's I-pad a zoom call allowed everyone to get their two-cents worth in. Lots of laughter and soft teasing ensued.

Molly and Meg sat together three different times, and laughed often. I visited with Trevor about his teaching and future plans. We also talked about him hoping to haul out some gold from Curtis Castle. Trevor and Jody were almost the same age. Jody showed him everything he could about ranching, offering a ride on a horse. So, Trevor rode a horse.

Cindy called me privately. "I graduate next June and looked at all the openings in the state of Montana for next fall. Del, I already found an opening in Malta, and intend to apply for it and two in Havre. I will be only ninety miles from my grandmother in Malta, and real close if I get a Havre job. She is over seventy-five and could use some help. I owe her so much and really would like to be close by."

"That is a super idea. You will like the highline as they call it around here. My new friends in the Cummings family are going to show me how to operate some machines and let me help do some planting and haying. Something new for me, farm chores."

"Del, I can tell you are happy, and that makes me happy. You are a most special person. "

"Cindy, we have shared much. I am very happy, and you are too. We will always be special friends. I know you will find a perfect young man to share your life with."

"When I do, will you give me away?"

"That would be a very special day, Cindy. Absolutely."

"Deal. I better get back to the party as dessert is ready. I felt the hug. Thank you, Del."

"I felt it as well. See you one day soon."

"See you," Del hung up and smiled. Cindy could be teaching close by.

CHAPTER 121

ecember 7th was a special day in American history, also, my birthday. I have a date at the Purple Iris with Charlene.

I arrived early with a vase of flowers. When Charlene approached the table, I stood, and greeted her with a soft hug.

"Flowers again, nice touch. I will take them home to remember you."

"Charlene this will always be a special date. Did you know today is my birthday?"

"No, I didn't. Cliff rarely mentions such things, since Mavis passed."

The lunch eaten, and many topics covered, with vase in hand, Charlene asked, "Del do you have time for me to give you a ride to my house and meet someone?"

"Yes, I do."

"Good, we'll use my car and bring you back for yours. You'll be in for a surprise."

"Charlene, I am already surprised."

"Del, I live less than a mile from here. I'll bring you back when you're ready."

Charlene parked in a driveway next to a small brick home with dark brown trim on the wooden portions. Manicured described everything. I followed her into her home. Everything looked to be in a special place. Each room showed its own very soft color. A middle-aged woman, about five foot four, neatly attired in sweater and slacks opened the door. Charlene greeted her and said, "Enid, meet a special friend, Del Sanderson."

"Nice to meet you, sir."

"Enid, I am Del, and it is my pleasure."

"Del, Enid takes care of me and Caroline. She makes everything in my life easier."

"We have arranged coffee in the solarium. May I take your coat?" asked Enid.

"Thank you, I enjoy being spoiled."

They moved to a glassed-in room at the rear of the house, "Your home and yard look very nice, and the setting is special. I like to know about plants and this solarium Is over the top. I need to build one of these at my house."

"Thank you so much, Del. Enid is Caroline ready?"

"Yes, she is, I will find her."

A Charlene look-alike followed Enid into the solarium, which had been set for three.

"Caroline, please meet a very special friend, Del Sanderson."

Caroline performed a slight curtsy, held out her hand, and shyly smiled, "Nice to meet you, Mr. Sanderson," as she selected her place between Charlene and Del.

"Just call me Del, Caroline."

Caroline just smiled.

Charlene explained, "Caroline suffered a bad fall from a swing when she turned eleven. She does most things beautifully, but the brain damage could not be completely repaired. She and I do everything together when I am not at work, so Enid can have time for herself. Caroline is eighteen now and reads everything we can find for her. The learning growth is still ongoing, and she does improve. I am very proud of her."

Del reached out his hand palm up to Caroline.

She accepted his gesture and placed her hand in his.

Del softly closed his hand then offered, "Caroline you are a beautiful woman. You and I will become friends. What else do you like to do when you are not reading?"

She withdrew her hand saying, "I like to play games, especially checkers. They are fun."

"When we finish our coffee, you and I can play checkers together, if you like. My son and I often played together."

"I will go find my checkers, Del. We can play here." She stood and left the room, returning with the checkers box and board.

"Enid, I will help you with these few dishes," said Charlene.

"Of course." Enid knew to accept.

Caroline and I played checkers for nearly two hours. Both winning several games. Caroline took a long time to decide her moves. I just maintained a softness few people ever see.

After they concluded playing, Caroline asked, "Del, will you come back and play other games?"

"Of course, Caroline, I would love to do that."

Charlene drove me back to my car, "Caroline has never taken to anyone as she did with you today. She can take care of most of her personal things, but cannot be left alone. Enid is a treasure. She lives in my house and does everything. Even the yard service operates under her direction. I pay her very well, but I know she earns every cent.

"Charlene, I am sure Caroline senses people better than she lets on. She knew my son is no longer living. I believe I felt her compassion."

"Oh yes, she does, she surprises me often. She already loves you, that is just the way she is. She does not take to everyone. I brought two gentleman friends here and she did not warm to either. Neither lasted with me either after that.

"Next year Del, we will have our date at my home. Caroline will not really notice the time lag."

"Deal Charlene. But I can visit here when I drive through Salt Lake City on my way to Arizona. Then Caroline and I could learn a new game."

Charlene paused a long time before saying, "May I reflect on that option, as I don't want Caroline to ever feel hurt. If she asks about you, we will definitely try. Cliff and Caroline are good buddies, but she never asks about him. Yet, Caroline loves every minute when he's here. I promise I will let you know."

"Perfect, Charlene, that means extra time on our dates."

"Del, Cliff worries about you."

"Yes, I suspect he does. Amy has been gone over a year and it feels like yesterday. He's been through the same loss, and I know you helped him immensely. He has helped me more than he thinks by including me. I know who my friends are and I love them all."

Tears began running down her cheeks as she held my hand. She held it a long time, then said, "Thank you Del, so much. This lady loves you, you see," she got in her car and drove slowly home.

Cliff knew I needed to meet Caroline.

CHAPTER 122

"ash" needed my attention. My research of the minimum-security prison where Cash was housed, showed trees bordering the perimeter of the open spaces. The biggest problem will be where to park the car, so I can safely escape.

I must have a plan B and C escape routes. I needed to escape safely, and undetected.

There was an element of security, and a tower, but all prisoners could just walk away. I did not hear the conversation between Cash and his attorney.

"Mr. Cashman," said Attorney, Joseph Bedford, "I will continue to monitor your three on-line businesses, to ensure they follow all laws, and file everything needed to keep them operating. But there is one absolute requirement. You must serve your time. I will work to reduce your sentence, and petition for either parole or early release. Discrediting all the women at your trial is the only reason you were not sent to a regular prison.

"If you escape, or even try, I am done helping you. Never a chance of me changing my mind. You need to work at a *good behavior release*. You have my word. I will do everything possible to reduce your sentence. I am sure you remember the judge's comments about escaping. If you leave before your term is up, you will be caught and transferred to a full security prison, and your sentence will probably double."

"Joe, I know you got a special plea for me. I will follow whatever you say. I can't thank you enough. I just hope you are able to come here and keep me posted."

"Cash, you keep your three businesses up to date, make some friends. Play some cards. I will visit as often as I need to."

"Joe, I'll behave, but I'll miss the freedom of regular life."

"I will be out to see you next week."

A firm handshake and Joe left to drive back to Little Rock.

alDON JASPERS

CHAPTER 129

Being a tourist in a prison town is a bit restrictive, but so little security at the prison does allow me many freedoms. I learned the general basics of the security system, then watched the local police procedures, following a cruiser as he drove around the prison perimeter, I turned into a Safeway grocery store to avoid scrutiny. I could not see security cameras anywhere. I studied every building every light post and every tree. Something else to worry about. They had to be somewhere.

So far, I couldn't feel comfortable with either escape plan. I tested both escape plans three times, then developed a third. I rented a very small storage unit so my rifle would not be in the trunk if I ever encountered a police inquiry. I purchased a fishing license and visited two local lakes. I asked for tips at a bait shop, but my lack of a southern drawl prevented any real help. However, I would not have any fish to clean.

I changed my plan B escape, to driving to my regular fishing spot and putting a line in the water, hoping to hide in plain sight, then sneak away.

I still did not have a suitable place to park my car. I finally decided to park it in the Safeway lot and walk from my shooting spot to the lot. I practiced doing that four times, using the crosswalk to get to my car. Carrying my backpack with the rifle worried me, but no one seemed to care. The sidewalk did border the edge of the oak trees, so I would be exposed ten to twelve minutes.

I went into the Safeway twice. Each time, three or four policemen sat in the small café drinking coffee.

The only possible time to shoot Cash seemed to be after dinner hour. He usually sat alone then working on his computer. Otherwise, he did things with others.

This Friday evening, I will do a dry run without the rifle. If it's one hundred percent safe, I will shoot him Saturday around seven p.m. If it's not safe, I will regroup. The dry run included walking all the way back to the car. Good enough I thought, so I will risk it tomorrow evening.

Cash sat alone at the back table near the trees. I stood behind an old thick oak tree less than two hundred yards away, an easy shot. I pulled the trigger and the silencer muffled much of the shot. Cash slumped over, resting his head on the table. *"Number ten, Curt."*

The walk back to my car proved to be uneventful. I started the car, excited the lot on to Dale Bumpers Drive, turned north on to State Highway 1. Following the route to I-40, I turned southwest toward Little Rock, and to my plane, parked at Hot Springs Airport. Most of my stress feelings resurfaced, knowing this preparation reached the level I should not accept. Never this much stress again, I vowed.

After settling my bill in Hot Springs, I flew to Grand Island, Nebraska, refueled, and continued on to Cheyenne, Wyoming. Spencer completed all the preliminary work to complete the shot, so he needed to reward himself by eating a meal at the Buster's Brew Pub. Quill worked behind the bar, so he stopped and asked about antelope hunting.

"I have a hunt set up for next year, Quill, near Medicine Bow. The young man I talked to hinted about many quality trophy chances. I will leave my plane here, and they will pick me up, at the Best Western. I am already excited. I need to thank you again."

"My pleasure Spencer. Hope you have luck," as he moved back down the bar to fill another order.

A Reuban was enjoyed with tots and a local IPA. I noticed my hands shaking slightly. I hoped Quill did not see that.

A fellow inmate noticed Cash not moving. He slowly walked over to him and called the guards. Cash was pronounced dead at the scene by EMTs.

The prison and the local police processed the scene, but really didn't seem do a lot. Every felon had enemies. Cash died alone. The seating area he used, closed for a short time while things were processed. They never really worked to locate where Spencer stood to shoot.

Since there were no heirs, Joe took over the three online businesses, as he knew all the codes. His income would triple without many new clients. Cash may have made a lot of bad choices, but he knew how to make money.

CHAPTER 124

Rick and I left Manhattan early on December twelfth to stay at the Lincoln cabin and do some hunting.

"Rick, after you said you were going to hunt with me, I watched my two game trails and two in the Forest Service property. I also constructed some mostly natural blinds for us to use. The animals should be used to the changes. We will hike to all the blinds today, and you can select the one you wish to use."

"Let's go do that hike."

They walked in silence to all the blinds. Rick made his selections and laughed when they crossed Del's tamarack log bridge, "Why don't you just wade the creek?"

"My boots are waterproof Rick, but too often the creek is too deep, and I do not want wet feet."

We hunted four days. Both of us took pictures of animals, but neither of us shot one. My biggest buck, a three-by-three whitetail never knew I sat so close to him. Rick saw two whitetail bucks, but let them live, and took a picture of a five-by-five beautiful bull elk. That big elk bugled right in front of Rick maybe twenty feet away. That sound so close to Rick unnerved him a little. But he snapped a picture of it.

Driving back to Rick's range, "Del, I enjoyed every second of our hunt and will gladly go again next year. You are even a decent cook, but I will bring some of my culinary delights next time. It has been over thirty years since I last hunted. I missed being in the woods, more than I expected."

"Well Rick, by next season, I will have many more choices for us. Locating those spots will be fun for me. We will wait for snow next year. That will make tracking easier"

I dropped Rick at his home, drove to my house, and prepared for a trip to Seattle. A local detective trapped a *Bundy* copycat serial killer, Borden Schrom found guilty. I needed to find a suitable shooting location and set up an exit strategy. Seattle will prove to be a difficult city to escape from. Might prove to be too stressful. I decided to wait. I did not have a satisfactory escape route.

CHAPTER 125

I flew to Saco. The Cummings brothers were going to try to reduce the mule deer population.

All three were at the Sutherland ranch, working on the old equipment, trying to make them usable. Interestingly, Jimmy proved to be the best mechanic.

Meg greeted me with an *I have missed you.* "Del, we have much to talk about."

"Meg, let me go get a couple of things from the plane." Returning, he gave Meg two jars of huckleberry preserves.

"My favorite, thank you," followed by a second hug.

"Del, I'm ready to be married to you. I hope to celebrate a very small wedding with family and friends. Just Molly, Trevor and my big boys, the Bolton's and a few of your friends."

"My heart is extra full. When shall we plan to do this?" I asked as I reached into my pocket, hiding an engagement ring in my hand. "We must make this official," as he knelt on one knee and offered the ring in its box to Meg.

"I should have known you would be ready. I am wholly pleased. Let's set the date for the middle of January, on a day when everyone could come."

"I will ask Cliff, Dutch, Madeline and Jack, and Dave and Sally, and Cindy. I will bring Molly, Trevor and Cindy in my plane. The others I will set up at a motel in Havre. Wow. A big, exciting change for us."

"Del, you go hunting with my sons, and I will start working on a date and start putting things together. We are to have some very special days to share."

I drove the new shortcut to Toby's home. All three were getting the quads ready and had their rifles mounted.

"Let's do stinky hollow first, and see if we can fill a tag or two," said Jimmy.

Toby and Del drew the shooting spots near the top of the hollow. Gary and Jimmy would get to make their way through the tangle of juniper and brush.

Two buck deer came out near Toby, so he shot a nice four-by-four buck. We heard one shot from the hollow, and Jimmy bagged a three-by-three buck. The really big buck bolted at full speed out the top after Toby's shot. No opportunity for anyone to shoot him.

"The big guy won't come back, I'm guessing," offered Gary.

"You are right, Gary. He didn't get that big taking any risks. We should do the field dressing and load them on the quads. Do you plan to hang them in the machine shed?" I asked.

"Yes," answered Gary. "We have a system worked out."

The brothers did all the work, skinning and butchering and wrapping. Two deer done in two hours. "You three have a great system," I noticed. "I can get a single deer done in three hours."

"What is the hunt for tomorrow? Do you have two five gallon buckets I can use to pick chokecherries?" I asked.

"We do and will take them along tomorrow. Then we'll help you pick all you want. Everyone liked your jelly and syrup," answered Gary.

"We will shoot two does, and add the meat to the deer from today, then haul most to the Malta food bank. We always give them the lion's share. Then all of the scraps called straps will be

411

barbequed tomorrow night, and we'll have a feast. We're going to spoil you again. Best venison you will ever eat," a smiling Gary predicted.

Two does were added to the meat supply, then Toby and I delivered most all to the food bank.

"Thank you, so much. I will call my list of families to come and get a share," said the manager.

"You're welcome," as Toby shook her offered hand. They left the food bank, and Toby stopped at the local market. They gathered items from two lists. He talked about his flying lessons and asked, "Should I continue and get an instrument rating? I now have my single engine land rating for propellers."

"Yes Toby. You will be surprised how much better of a pilot you become," I answered.

"I thought so. I'll enroll next Monday."

The barbequed venison with corn and salad hit the spot. The boys cleaned up everything and left to do the chores. I saved enough venison to make four or five meals for me. Eight gallons of chokecherries will also ride with me back to Bozeman. Then I went inside to find Meg.

"Meg, are we going to tell your boys of our decision?"

"I believe we should, as soon as they complete the chores, if that's okay with you."

"Yes, Meg I agree we should tell them together."

All three young men approached the porch, laughing about something.

Meg reached for my hand, then said. "Boys, Del and I plan to be married in January."

Gary spoke first, "We will be super happy to welcome you into our family, Del."

All three hugged their mom and said congratulations as they shook Del's hand.

"Looks like I win the money, brothers," smiled Jimmy.

"Yes, you're a lucky devil," chimed in Toby.

Meg immediately asked, "You boys had a bet going about us?"

"Sure," interjected Toby, "we suspected you two were in love before you two did. We certainly expected that marriage was on the horizon."

"All three of us are very happy for you."

CHAPTER 126

I knew I needed a hike to my hideaway in the Bob starting tomorrow. I wanted to think about things. I made that trip and fished every day, testing the junction of the Danaher and Young Rivers. Two three-pound cutthroats proved the deep hole formed there harbored some exceptional trout.

I hiked into the second canyon on the southern edge of Willow Creek Valley. I found a possibly repairable cabin. The entire box canyon showed very old evidence of mining efforts. I decided to work on those cabin repairs, see if there was any way out of the southern edge of the canyon, and study if the miners ever located any gold. Maybe I will bring some of my climbing gear. A new project. Wonderful.

I intend this location to be mine and only mine, never for anyone else. The lone beaver pond looked very small. I tested it with a few casts and caught and released five super-nice Brookies. I needed to set up camp here. I decided to stay an extra day and at least do a preliminary check for an exit from the canyon. I enjoyed two brook trout and a tinfoil fire baked potato for my dinner.

I used most of my second day hiking to the back of my new hideaway. There was evidence of a steep trail, but I needed more time to do a thorough study of a possible climb. Lots of deer droppings in the canyon. Maybe this was where my five-by-five hung out.

I moved enough items to camp in my canyon. I pitched my camo tent and inflated the mattress under and behind a large Douglas Fir to be sure nothing was visible from the air. Then completed all the measurements and drawings necessary to allow me to repair the old cabin and make it usable, rain or shine. I had a source for weathered wood to make everything look old like it should. The old stove will need to be replaced, and the bunk bed would not handle my six-foot one frame. I needed this cabin to withstand whatever Mother Nature would throw at it. Another fun project.

I studied exactly where I needed to make my air drops to have them land close enough to the new cabin for ease. I need things to do.

Trevor wanted to try breaking down the quartz to separate the gold. I needed to remind to not reveal where it came from.

So much to do. Good for me.

CHAPTER 127

I have so much still on my plate. Tyler, and Joel and Boris. And to finish my project about the young men from Curt's trial.

Not to mention the backpacking trip with Meg.

I will never divulge the amount of the funds the FBI advanced me for my role in the Michelle terrorist caper and the previous help I provided Cliff. I plan to buy a barely used Bonanza 36-6 passenger plane, but will keep the Cessna 182. Two planes for different purposes. I checked and could secure both planes in the Lincoln hangar.

One to drop supplies in the Bob and to land at the Cummings ranch. The other to fly all over America.

I had a reasonably priced used Bonanza located, including delivery to Bozeman. Then Sparky can check me out on it as soon as it is mine. He uses a similar plane for all his personal charters. The learning curve will be substantial. The avionics will be a challenge.

I have places to go and things to do. Especially, take Molly and Trevor to Alaska.

I needed to marry Meg. She has become more than special to me. I love all three of her grown sons that she still calls boys.

I have a compulsion to learn to use the machinery, so I can help Gary and Toby plant their crops and help with the haying and the harvest.

I must hire a *person* to manage my two corporations and assist with my remaining clients. Then complete setting up my new Great Falls office, so my clients can come to me where I have everything, should I need to help them. I plan to stay mostly retired.

My full plate includes four or five new *adventures*. One in Albany, New York, Seattle, Topeka, and Bismark, and las Cruces, New Mexico. Maybe two others.

I will help Peter Sullivan complete his degree.

I hoped to help Cindy obtain the teaching position in Malta. Not sure how yet, but it needed to work somehow. We needed to repair her scar.

I needed to create a way for Jerry and Lyle to catch Simon Castleman in Lincoln, Nebraska.

Chief Johnson needed to get his three-state group up and running.

Bryan needed to learn why Benito hopes to talk to him.

Dutch needed to ride a swamp buggy and fish for big bass.

Rick needed me to run the shooting range for a few days when he was out of town.

I needed to complete the repair on my new hideaway in the Bob.

Jimmy will need all the help he can get, and I must learn to become an extra guide for him.

Cliff has to solve his UC problem in Great Falls.

I absolutely must become one hundred percent competent flying the Bonanza 36. The electronics are so extensive and cover so much new to me.

I wished to learn to make my own clam chowder soup.

I hoped everything worked out, so I could buy the Daily Coffee.

Toby needed a new modular or log kit home at the Sutherland property.

Chief Johnson will need Bryan's help concerning Rose.

Rick and I hoped to start a bowling team and join a league.

Bryan needed to go to Idaho and pick huckleberries, and to visit with Austin after talking to his Tucson detective friend.

I must figure out about float planes, and if drugs are involved.

And, I'll soon have a wife who will expect me to do things with and for her, as well.

I looked over the list. *"So much to do, wonderful."* I said aloud sitting in my recliner, while watching Martha doing the daily watering of her front yard plants.

COMING SOON:

PRECISION OPTICS

A DEL SANDERSON ADVENTURE

CHAPTER 1

I completed all the requirements to test for my black belt and passed the physical test. I felt ready to confront Tyler Spivey. I was keenly aware of Tyler's skill as a kickboxer.

I planned to surprise him. Thus, I waited in the small entry leading to the stairs that Tyler would climb to his fifth-floor office.

I ambushed Tyler and made short work of his beating.

"Listen up, you scumbag! You assaulted a defenseless woman. Today is your turn. I will never tell Cindy. If you ever cause her harm again, you are dead," I warned, as I left him to administer to his many bruises. I would always watch out for Tyler, as I could not trust him.

That task completed, it was now time to send the letter to the men chosen to complete the Memorial for my son Curtis, his wrestling friend Nick, and the two others killed needlessly in front of the school gymnasium. My letter directed them to complete all arrangements for the placement of the granite rock next to the gym, and the exact wording for the attached bronze plaque.

www.ingramcontent.com/pod-product-compliance
Lightning Source LLC
Chambersburg PA
CBHW060809030726
47503CB00002B/406